About the Authors

Lynne Graham lives in Northern Ireland and has been a keen romance reader since her teens. Happily married, Lynne has five children. Her eldest is her only natural child. Her other children, who are every bit as dear to her heart, are adopted. The family has a variety of pets, and Lynne loves gardening, cooking, collecting all sorts and is crazy about every aspect of Christmas.

Judy Lynn Hubbard is a native of Dallas, Texas and has always been an avid reader – particularly of romance. She loves well-written, engaging stories with characters she can identify with, empathize with and root for. She loves to write and when writing, she honestly can't wait to see what happens next; she knows if she feels that way, she's created characters and a story that readers will thoroughly enjoy and that's her goal.

When **Jacqueline Baird** is not busy writing she likes to spend her time travelling, reading and playing cards. She enjoys swimming in the sea when the weather allows. With a more sedentary lifestyle, she does visit a gym three times a week and has made the surprising discovery that she gets some of her best ideas while doing mind-numbingly boring exercises on the weight machines and air-walker. Jacqueline lives with her husband Jim in Northumberland.

D1078786

Dangerous Liaisons

Dangerous Liaisons:
Innocence

LYNNE GRAHAM

JUDY LYNN HUBBARD

JACQUELINE BAIRD

MILLS & BOON

First Published in Great Britain 2021
by Mills & Boon, an imprint of HarperCollins*Publishers* Ltd,
1 London Bridge Street, London, SE1 9GF

www.harpercollins.co.uk

HarperCollins*Publishers*
1st Floor, Watermarque Building,
Ringsend Road, Dublin 4, Ireland

DANGEROUS LIAISONS: INNOCENCE
© 2021 Harlequin Books S.A.

A Vow of Obligation © 2012 Lynne Graham
These Arms of Mine © 2012 Judy Lynn Hubbard
The Cost of Her Innocence © 2013 Jacqueline Baird

ISBN: 978-0-263-29943-4

Printed and bound in Spain
by CPI, Barcelona

A VOW OF OBLIGATION

LYNNE GRAHAM

CHAPTER ONE

'Were you seen coming up to my suite?' Navarre Cazier prompted in the Italian that came as naturally to him as the French of his homeland.

Tia pouted her famously sultry lips and in spite of her sophistication contrived to look remarkably young and naive as befitted one of the world's most acclaimed film stars. 'I slipped in through the side entrance—'

Navarre ditched his frown and smiled, for when she looked at him like that with her big blue eyes telegraphing embarrassed vulnerability he couldn't help it. 'It's you I'm concerned about. The paparazzi follow you everywhere—'

'Not here...' Tia Castelli declared, tossing her head so that a silken skein of honey-blonde hair rippled across her slim shoulders, her flawless face full of regret. 'We haven't got long though. Luke will be back at our hotel by three and I have to be there.'

At that reference to her notoriously volatile rock star husband, Navarre's lean, darkly handsome features hardened and his emerald-green eyes darkened.

Tia ran a manicured fingertip reprovingly below the implacable line of his shapely masculine mouth. 'Don't be like that, *caro mio*. This is my life, take me or leave me... and I couldn't bear it if you chose the second option!' she warned him in a sudden rush, her confident drawl splintering to betray the insecurity she hid from the world. 'I'm sorry, so sorry that it has to be like this between us!'

'It's OK,' Navarre told her soothingly although he was lying through his even white teeth as he said it. He loathed being a dirty little secret in her life but the alternative was to end their relationship and although he was remarkably strong-willed and stubborn, he had found himself quite unable to do that.

'And you're still bringing a partner with you for the awards ceremony, aren't you?' Tia checked anxiously. 'Luke is so incredibly suspicious of you.'

'Angelique Simonet, currently the toast of the Paris catwalk,' Navarre answered wryly.

'And she doesn't know about us?' the movie actress pressed worriedly.

'Of course not.'

'I know, I know…I'm sorry, I just have so much at stake!' Tia gasped strickenly. 'I couldn't stand to lose Luke!'

'You can trust me.' Navarre closed his arms round her slim body to comfort her. Her blue eyes glistened with the tears that came so easily to her and she was trembling with nerves. Navarre tried not to wonder what Luke Convery had been doing or saying to get her into such a state. Time and experience had taught him that it was better not to go there, better neither to know nor to enquire. He did not interfere in her marriage any more than she questioned his choice of lovers.

'I hate going so long without seeing you. It feels wrong,' she muttered heavily. 'But I've told so many lies I don't think that I could ever tell the truth.'

'It's not important,' Navarre told her with a gentleness

that would have astounded some of the women he had had in his life.

Navarre Cazier, the legendary French industrialist and billionaire, had the reputation of being a generous but distant lover to the beautiful women who passed through his bed. Yet even though he made no secret of his love of the single life, women remained infuriatingly keen to tell him that they loved him and to cling. Tia, however, occupied a category all of her own and he played by different rules with her. Accustomed as he was to independence from an early age, he was tough, self-reliant and unapologetically selfish but he always restrained that side of his nature with Tia and at least tried to accommodate her needs.

Later that afternoon when she had gone, Navarre was heading for the shower when his mobile buzzed beside the bed. Tia's distinctive perfume still hung in the air like a shamefaced marker of her recent presence. He would see her again soon but their next encounter would be in public and they would have to be circumspect for Luke Convery was a hothead, all too well aware of his gorgeous wife's chequered history of previous marriages and clandestine affairs. Tia's husband was always on the watch for signs that his wife's attention might be straying.

The call was from Angelique and Navarre's mood dive-bombed when he learned that his current lover was not, after all, coming to London to join him. Angelique had just been offered a television campaign by a famous cosmetics company and even Navarre could not fault her desire to make the most of such an opportunity.

Even so, it seemed to Navarre that life was cruelly conspiring to frustrate him. He *needed* Angelique this week and not only as a screen to protect Tia from the malicious rumours that had linked his name with hers on past occasions. He also had a difficult deal to close with the husband of a former lover, who had recently attempted to reanimate their affair. A woman on his arm and a supposedly serious relationship had been a non-negotiable necessity for Tia's peace of mind as well as good business practice in a difficult situation. *Merde alors,* what the hell was he going to do without a partner at this late stage in the game? Who could he possibly trust to play the game of a fake engagement and not attempt to take it further?

'Urgent—need 2 talk 2 you,' ran the text message that beeped on Tawny's mobile phone and she hurried downstairs to take her break, wondering what on earth was going on with her friend, Julie.

Julie worked as a receptionist in the same exclusive London hotel and, although the two young women had not known each other long, she had already proved herself to be a staunch and supportive friend. Her approachability had eased Tawny's first awkward days as a new employee when she had quickly discovered that as a chambermaid she was regarded as the lowest of the low by most of the other staff. She was grateful for Julie's company when their breaks coincided, but their friendship had gone well beyond that level, Tawny acknowledged with an appreciative smile. When, at short notice, Tawny had had to move out of her mother's home, Julie had helped her to find an affordable bedsit and had even offered her car to facilitate the move.

'I'm in trouble,' Julie, a very pretty brown-eyed blonde, said with a strong air of drama as Tawny joined her at a table in the corner of the dingy, almost empty staff room.

'What sort of trouble?'

Julie leant forwards to whisper conspiratorially, 'I slept with one of the guests.'

'But you'll be sacked if you've been caught out!' Tawny

exclaimed in dismay, brushing back the Titian red spiral curls clinging to her damp brow. Changing several beds in swift succession was tiring work and even though she was already halfway through a glass of cooling water she still felt overheated.

Julie rolled her eyes, unimpressed by the reminder. 'I haven't been caught out.'

Her porcelain-pale skin reddening, Tawny wished she had been more tactful, for she did not want Julie to think that she was judging her for her behaviour.

'Who was the guy?' she asked then, riven with curiosity for the blonde had not mentioned anyone, which could only mean that the relationship had been of sudden or short duration.

'It was Navarre Cazier.' Wearing a coy look of expectancy, Julie let the name hang there.

'Navarre Cazier?' Tawny was shocked by that familiar name.

She knew exactly who Julie was talking about because it was Tawny's responsibility to keep the penthouse suites on the top floor of the hotel in pristine order. The fabulously wealthy French industrialist stayed there at least twice a month and he always left her a massive tip. He didn't make unreasonable demands or leave his rooms in a mess either, which placed him head and shoulders above the other rich and invariably spoilt occupants of the most select accommodation offered by the hotel. She had only seen him once in the flesh, though, and at a distance, the giving of invisible service being one of the demands of her job. But after Julie had mentioned him several times in glowing terms Tawny had become curious enough to make the effort to catch a glimpse of him and had immediately understood why her friend was captivated. Navarre

Cazier was very tall, black-haired and even to her critical gaze, quite shockingly good-looking.

He also walked, talked and behaved like a god who ruled the world, Tawny recalled abstractedly. He had emerged from the lift at the head of a phalanx of awe-inspired minions clutching phones and struggling to follow reams of instructions hurled at them in two different languages. His sheer power of personality, volcanic energy and presence had had the brilliance of a searchlight in darkness. He had outshone everyone around him while administering a stinging rebuke to a cringing unfortunate who didn't react fast enough to an order. She had got the impression of a ferociously demanding male with a mind that functioned at the speed of a computer, a male, moreover, whose intrinsically high expectations were rarely satisfied by reality.

'As you know I've had my eye on Navarre for a while. He's absolutely gorgeous.' Julie sighed.

Navarre and Julie…*lovers?* A little pang of distaste assailed Tawny as she pulled free of her memories and returned to the present. It struck her as an incongruous pairing between two people who could have nothing in common, but Julie was extremely pretty and Tawny had seen enough of life to know that that was quite sufficient inducement for most men. Evidently the sophisticated French billionaire was not averse to the temptation of casual sex.

'So what's the problem?' Tawny asked in the strained silence that now stretched, resisting a tasteless urge to ask how the encounter had come about. 'Have you fallen pregnant or something?'

'Oh, don't be daft!' Julie fielded as if the very suggestion was a bad joke. 'But I did do something very stupid with him…'

Tawny was frowning. *'What?'* she pressed, unaccustomed to the other young woman being hesitant to talk about anything.

'I got so carried away I let him take a load of pictures of me posing in the nude. They're on his laptop!'

Tawny was aghast at the revelation and embarrassment sent hot colour winging into her cheeks. So, the French businessman liked to take photographs in the bedroom, Tawny thought with a helpless shudder of distaste. Navarre Cazier instantly sank below floor level in Tawny's fanciability stakes. *Ew!*

'What on earth made you agree to such a thing?' she questioned.

Julie clamped a tissue to her nose and Tawny was surprised to see tears swimming in her brown eyes, for Julie had always struck her as being rather a tough cookie. 'Julie?' she prompted more gently.

Julie grimaced in evident embarrassment, clearly fighting her distress. 'Surely you can guess why I agreed?' she countered in a voice choked with tears. 'I didn't want to seem like a prude...I wanted to please him. I hoped that if I was exciting enough he'd want to see me again. Rich guys get bored easily: you have to be willing to experiment to keep their interest. But I never heard from him again and now I feel sick at the idea of him still having those photos of me.'

Even though such reasoning made Tawny's heart sink she understood it perfectly. Once upon a time her mother, Susan, had been equally keen to impress a rich man. In Susan's case the man had been her boss and their subsequent secret affair had continued on and off for years before finally running aground over the pregnancy that produced Tawny and her mother's lowering discovery that she was far from being her lover's only extra-marital interest.

'Ask him to delete the photographs,' Tawny suggested stiffly, feeling more than a little out of her depth with the subject but naturally sympathetic towards her friend's disillusionment. She knew how deeply hurt her mother had been to ultimately discover that her long-term lover didn't consider her worthy of a more permanent or public relationship. But after only one night of intimacy, she felt that Julie would recover rather more easily from the betrayal than Tawny's mother had.

'I asked him to delete them soon after he arrived yesterday. He flatly refused.'

Tawny was stumped by that frank admission. 'Well er...'

'But all I would need is five minutes with his laptop to take care of it for myself,' Julie told her in an urgent undertone.

Tawny was unsurprised by the claim for she had heard that Julie was skilled in IT and often the first port of call when the office staff got into a snit with a computer. 'He's hardly going to give you access to his laptop,' she pointed out wryly.

'No, but if I could get hold of his laptop, what harm would it do for me to deal with the problem right there and then?'

Tawny studied the other woman fixedly. 'Are you seriously planning to try and steal the guy's laptop?'

'I just want to borrow it for five minutes and, as I don't have access to his suite and you *do,* I was hoping that you would do it for me.'

Tawny fell back in her seat, pale blue eyes wide with disbelief as she stared back at the other woman in dismay. 'You've got to be joking...'

'There would be no risk. I'd tell you when he was out, you could go in and I could rush upstairs and wait next door in the storage room for you to bring the laptop out to me. Five minutes, that's all it would take for me to delete those photos. You'll replace it in his room and he'll never know what happened to them!' Julie argued forcefully. '*Please,* Tawny…it would mean so much to me. Haven't you ever done something you regret?'

'I'd like to help you but I can't do something illegal,' Tawny protested, pulling a face in the tense silence. 'That laptop is his personal property and interfering with it would be a criminal offence—'

'He's never going to know that anyone's even touched it! That possibility won't even occur to him,' Julie argued vehemently. 'Please, Tawny. You're the only person who can help me.'

'I couldn't— There's just no way I could do something like that,' Tawny muttered uneasily. 'I'm sorry.'

Julie touched her hand to regain her attention. 'We haven't got much time—he'll be checking out again the day after tomorrow. I'll talk to you again at lunch time before you finish your shift.'

'I won't change my mind,' Tawny warned, compressing her soft full mouth in discomfiture.

'Think it over—it's a foolproof plan,' Julie insisted as she stood up, lowering her voice even more to add huskily, 'And if it would make a difference, I'm willing to pay you to take that risk for me—'

'*Pay* me?' Tawny was very much taken aback by that offer.

'What else can I do? You're my only hope in this situation,' Julie reasoned plaintively. 'If a bit of money would make you feel better about doing this, of course I'm going to suggest it. I know how desperate you are to help your grandmother out.'

'Look, money's got nothing to do with the way I feel. Just leave it out of this,' Tawny urged in considerable embarrassment. 'If I was in a position to help out, it wouldn't cost you a penny.'

Tawny returned to work with her thoughts in turmoil. Navarre Cazier, handsome, rich and privileged though he was, had cruelly used and abused Julie's trust. Another rich four-letter word of a man was grinding an ordinary woman down. But that unfortunately was life, wasn't it? The rich lived by different rules and enjoyed enormous power and influence. Hadn't her own father taught her that? He had dumped her mother when she refused to have a termination and had paid her a legal pittance to raise his unwanted child to adulthood. There had been no extras in Tawny's childhood and not much love on offer either from a mother who had bitterly regretted her decision to have her baby and a father who did not even pretend an interest in his illegitimate daughter. To be fair, her mother *had* paid a high price for choosing to bring her child into the world. Not only had her lover ditched her, but she had also found it impossible to continue her career.

Tawny suppressed those unproductive reflections and thought worriedly about Julie instead. She felt really bad about having refused to help her friend. Julie had been very good to her and had never asked her for anything in return. But why the heck had Julie offered her a financial bribe to get hold of that laptop? She was deeply embarrassed that Julie should be so aware of her financial constraints and regretted her honesty on that topic.

In truth, Tawny only worked at the hotel to earn enough money to ensure that her grandmother could continue to pay the rent on her tiny apartment in a private retirement village. Celestine, devastated by the combined death of her beloved husband and, with him, the loss of her marital home, had, against all the odds, contrived to make a happy new life and friends in the village, and there was little that Tawny would not do to safeguard the old lady's tenure there. Unfortunately rising costs had quickly outstripped her grandmother's ability to pay her bills. Tawny, having taken charge of Celestine's financial affairs, had chosen to quietly supplement her grandmother's income without her knowledge, which was why she was currently working as a chambermaid. Prior to the crisis in the old lady's finances, Tawny had made her living by illustrating children's books and designing greeting cards, but sadly there was insufficient work in that field during an economic crisis to stretch to shoring up Celestine's income as well as covering Tawny's own living costs. Now Tawny's artistic projects took up evenings and weekends instead.

But, regardless of that situation, wasn't it rather insulting that a friend should offer to *pay* you to do something for them? Tawny reasoned uneasily. On the other hand, wasn't that inappropriate suggestion merely proof of Julie's desperate need for her assistance?

Would it be so very bad of her to do what she could to help Julie delete those distasteful photos? While Tawny could not even imagine trusting a man enough to take pictures of her naked body, she could understand Julie's cringing reluctance to continue featuring in some sort of X-rated scalp gallery on the guy's laptop. That was a downright demeaning and extremely offensive prospect to have to live with. Would he let other men access those pictures? Tawny grimaced in disgust, incensed that a guy she had believed was attractive could turn out to be such a creep.

'All right, I'll have a go at getting hold of it for you,' she told Julie at lunchtime.

Her friend's face lit up immediately and a wide smile of satisfaction formed on her lips. 'I'll make sure you don't regret it!'

Tawny was unconvinced by that assurance but concealed her fear of the consequences, feeling that she ought to be more courageous. She wore colourful vintage clothing, held strong opinions and her ultimate ambition was to become a cartoonist with a strip of her own in a magazine or newspaper. In short she liked to think of herself as an individual rather than a follower. But sometimes, she suspected that deep down inside she was more of a conventional person than she liked to admit because she longed for a supportive family and had never broken the law by even the smallest margin.

'We'll do it this afternoon. As soon as his room is empty, if there's no sign of him having the laptop with him I'll ring up and you can go straight in and get it. Just leave it in the storage room. I'll be there within two minutes,' Julie told her eagerly.

'You're absolutely sure that you want to do this?' Tawny pressed worriedly. 'Perhaps you should speak to him again. If we get caught—'

'We're not going to get caught!' Julie declared with cutting conviction. 'Stop making such a fuss.'

Tawny went pink, assumed that Julie's outburst was the result of nervous tension and fell silent, but that tart response had set her own fiery temper on edge.

'Just go back to work and act normally,' Julie advised, shooting Tawny an apologetic look. 'I'll call you.'

Tawny returned with relief to changing beds, vacuuming and scrubbing bathrooms. She kept so busy she didn't allow herself to think about that call coming and yet on some level she was on hyper alert for when she heard the faint ping of the lift doors opening down the corridor she jumped almost a foot in the air. Julie's call telling her that his assistant had just left and the room was empty came barely a minute after that. Her heart beating very fast, Tawny sped down the passage with her trolley. Arming herself with a change of bedding as an excuse she used her pass key to let herself into Navarre Cazier's spacious suite. She set the fresh sheets down on the arm of a sofa as her eyes did a frantic sweep of the reception room and zoomed in on the laptop sitting conveniently on the table by the window. Although it was the work of a moment to cross the room, unplug the computer from its charger and tuck it below her arm, her skin dampened with perspiration and her stomach churned. Turning on her heel, she literally raced back to the exit door, eager to hand over the laptop to Julie and refusing to even think about having to sneak back in again to return it.

Without the slightest warning, however, there was a click and the door of the suite snapped open. Eyes huge with fright, Tawny clutched the laptop and froze into stillness. Navarre Cazier appeared and it was not a good time for her to realise that he was much bigger than he had seemed at a distance. He towered over her five and a half feet by well over six inches, his shoulders wide as axe handles in his formal dark suit. He was much more of an athlete in build than the average businessman. She clashed in dismay with frowning chartreuse-green eyes, startlingly bright and unexpected in that olive-skinned face. Close up he was quite breathtakingly handsome.

'Is that my laptop?' he asked immediately, his attention flying beyond her to the empty table. 'Has there been an accident? What are you doing with it?'

'I…I er…' Her heart was beating so fast it felt as if it

were thumping at the foot of her throat and her mind was a punishing blank.

There was a burst of French from behind him and he moved deeper into the room to make way for the bodyguards that accompanied him virtually everywhere he went.

'I will call the police, Navarre,' his security chief, Jacques, a well-built older man, said decisively in French.

'No, no…no need to bring the police in!' Tawny exclaimed, now ready to kick herself for not having grabbed at the excuse that she had accidentally knocked the laptop off the table while cleaning.

'You speak French?' Navarre studied her with growing disquiet, taking in the uniform of blue tunic and trousers she wore with flat heels. Evidently she worked for the hotel in a menial capacity: there was an unattended cleaning trolley parked directly outside the suite. Of medium height and slender build, she had a delicate pointed face dominated by pale blue eyes the colour of an Alpine glacier set in porcelain-perfect skin, the combination enlivened by a mop of vivid auburn curls escaping from a ponytail. Navarre had always liked redheads and her hair was as bright as a tropical sunset.

'My grandmother is French,' Tawny muttered, deciding that honesty might now be her only hope of escaping a criminal charge.

If she spoke fluent French the potential for damage was even greater, Navarre reckoned furiously. How long had she had his laptop for? He had been out for an hour. Unfortunately it would only take minutes for her to copy the hard drive, gaining access not only to highly confidential business negotiations but also to even more personal and theoretically damaging emails. How many indiscreet emails of Tia's might she have seen? He was appalled by the breach in his security. 'What are you doing with my laptop?'

Tawny lifted her chin. 'I'm willing to explain but I don't think you'll want an audience while we have that conversation,' she dared.

His strong jawline clenched at that impertinent challenge as he read the name on her badge. Tawny Baxter, an apt label for a woman with such spectacular hair. 'There is no reason why you should not speak in front of my security staff,' he replied impatiently.

'Julie—the receptionist you spent the night with on your last visit,' Tawny specified curtly, surrendering the laptop as one of his security team put out his hands to reclaim the item. 'Julie just wants the photos you took of her posing wiped from your laptop.'

His ebony brows drawing together, Navarre subjected her to an incredulous scrutiny while absently noting the full pouting curve of her pink lips. She was in possession of what had to be the most temptingly sultry mouth he had ever seen on a woman. Exasperated by that abstracted thought, he straightened his broad shoulders and declared, 'I have never spent the night with a receptionist in this hotel. What kind of a scam are you trying to pull?'

'Don't waste your breath on this dialogue, Navarre. Let me contact the police,' the older man urged impatiently.

'Her name is Julie Chivers, she works on reception and right now she's waiting in the storage room next door for the laptop,' Tawny extended in a feverish rush. 'All she wants is to delete the photos you took of her!'

With an almost imperceptible movement of his arrogant dark head, Navarre directed Jacques to check out that location and the older man ducked back out of the room. Tawny sucked in a lungful of air and tilted her chin. 'Why wouldn't you wipe the photos when Julie asked you to?'

'I have no idea what you're talking about,' he countered with a chilly gravity that sank like an icicle deep into her tender flesh. 'There was no night with a receptionist, no photos. Ditch the silly story. What have you done with my laptop?'

'Absolutely nothing. I'd only just lifted it when you appeared,' Tawny replied tightly, wondering why he was still lying and eagerly watching the door for Julie's appearance. She was sure that once he recognised her friend as a former lover there would be no more talk of calling the police. But didn't he even recognise Julie's name? It occurred to her that she never wanted to become intimate with a man who didn't care enough even to take note of her name.

'It's unfortunate for you that I came back unexpectedly,' Navarre shot back at her, wholly unconvinced by her plea.

Of course she would try to tell him that she had not had enough time to do any real damage. But he was too conscious that she could have copied his hard drive within minutes and might even be concealing a flash drive beneath her clothing. He was in the act of doubting that the police would agree to have her strip-searched for the sake of his security and peace of mind so his attention quite naturally rested on her slender coltish shape.

She had a gloriously tiny waist. He could not help wondering if the skin of her body was as pearly and perfect as that of her face. When almost every woman he knew practically bathed in fake tan it was a novelty to see a woman so pale he could see the faint tracery of blue veins beneath her skin. Indeed the more he studied her, the more aware he became of her unusual delicate beauty and the tightening fullness at his groin was his natural masculine reaction to her allure. She had that leggy pure-bred look but those big pale eyes and that wickedly suggestive mouth etched buckets of raw sex appeal into her fragile features. That she could look that good even without make-up was unparalleled in his experience of her sex. In the right clothes with that amazing hair loose she would probably be a complete knockout. What a shame she was a humble chambermaid about to be charged with petty theft, he reflected impatiently, returning his thoughts to reality while marvelling at the detour into fantasy that they had briefly and bizarrely taken.

Jacques reappeared and shook his head in response to his employer's enquiring glance. Something akin to panic gripped Tawny. Evidently Julie wasn't still in the storage room ready and able to make an explanation. Until that instant Tawny had not appreciated just how much she had been depending on her friend coming through that door and immediately sorting out the misunderstanding.

'Julie must have heard you come back and she's gone back downstairs to Reception,' Tawny reasoned in dismay.

'I'm calling the police,' Navarre breathed, turning to lift the phone.

'No, let me call Reception and ask Julie to come up and explain first,' Tawny urged in a frantic rush. 'Please, Mr Cazier!'

For a split second Navarre scanned her pleading eyes, marvelling at their rare colour, and then he swept up the phone and, while she held her breath in fear and watched, he stabbed the button for Reception and requested her friend by name.

Colour slowly returning to her drawn cheeks, Tawny drew in a tremulous breath. 'I'm not lying to you, I swear I'm not… I didn't even get the chance to open your laptop—'

'Naturally you will say that,' Navarre derided. 'You

could well have been in the act of returning it to the room when I surprised you—'

'But I *wasn't!*' Tawny exclaimed in horror when she registered the depth of his suspicion. 'I had only just lifted it when you returned. I'm telling you the truth!'

'That I had some kinky one-night stand with a camera and a receptionist?' Navarre queried with stinging scorn. 'Do I strike you as that desperate for entertainment in London?'

Suffering her very first moment of doubt as to his guilt in that quarter, Tawny shrugged a slight shoulder in an awkward gesture while her heart sank at the possibility that she could be wrong. 'How would I know? You're a guest here. I know nothing about you aside of what my friend told me.'

'Your friend lied to you,' Navarre declared.

After a tense two minutes of complete silence a soft knock sounded on the door and Julie entered, looking unusually meek. 'How can I help you, Mr Cazier?'

'*Julie...*' Tawny interposed, leaping straight into speech. 'I want you to explain about you asking me to take the laptop so that we can get this all sorted out—'

'What about the laptop? Take *whose* laptop?' Julie enquired sharply, widening her brown eyes in apparent confusion and annoyance. 'What the hell are you trying to accuse me of doing?'

In receipt of that aggressive comeback, Tawny was bewildered. She could feel the blood draining from her cheeks in shock and the sick churning in the pit of her stomach started up afresh. 'Julie, please explain...look, what's going on here? You and Mr Cazier know each other—'

Julie's brow pleated. 'If you mean by that that Mr Cazier is a regular and much respected guest here—'

'You told me that he took photos of you—'

'I have no idea what you're talking about. Photos? I'm sorry about this, Mr Cazier. Possibly this member of staff has been drinking or something because she's talking nonsense. I should call the penthouse manager to deal with this situation.'

'Thank you, Miss Chivers, but that won't be necessary. You may leave,' Navarre cut in with clear impatience. 'I've heard quite enough.'

Navarre motioned his security chief back to his side with the movement of one finger and addressed the older man in an undertone.

In disbelief, Tawny watched her erstwhile friend leave the suite with her head held high. Julie had lied. Julie had actually pretended not to know her on a personal basis. Her friend had *lied,* turned her back on Tawny and let her take the fall for attempted theft. Tawny was not only stunned by that betrayal, but also no longer convinced that Julie had ever spent the night with Navarre Cazier. But if that suspicion was true, why had Julie told her that convoluted story about the nude photography session? Why else would Julie have wanted access to the billionaire's laptop? What had she wanted to find out from it and why?

As Tawny turned white and swayed Navarre thought she might be about to faint. Instead, demonstrating a surprising amount of inner strength for so young a woman, she leant back against the wall for support and breathed in slow and deep to steady herself. Even so, he recognised an attack of gut-deep fear when he saw one but he had not the slightest pity for her. Navarre always hit back hard against those who tried to injure him. At the same time, however, he also reasoned at the speed of light, an ability that had dug him out of some very tight corners while growing up.

If he called the police, what recompense would he receive for the possible crime committed against him? There would be no guarantee that the maid would be punished and even if this was not a first offence she would be released, possibly even to take advantage of selling a copy of his hard drive to either his business competitors or the paparazzi, who had long sought proof of the precise nature of his relationship with Tia. Either prospect promised far reaching repercussions, not just to his extensive business empire, but even more importantly to Tia, her marriage and her reputation. He owed Tia his protection, he reflected grimly. But it might already be too late to prevent revealing private correspondence entering the public domain.

On the other hand, if he were to prevent the maid from contacting anyone to pass on confidential information for at least the next seven days, he could considerably minimise the risks to all concerned. Granted a week's grace the business deal with the Coulter Centax Corporation, CCC, could be tied up and, should his fear with regard to the emails prove correct, Tia's world-class PR advisors would have the chance to practise damage limitation on her behalf. In the event of the worst-case scenario isolating the maid was the most effective action he could currently take.

And, even more to the point, if he was forced to keep the maid around he might well be able to make use of her presence, Navarre decided thoughtfully. She was young and beautiful. And, crucially, he already knew that her loyalty could be bought. Why should he not pay her to fill the role that presently stood empty? With a movement of his hand he dismissed Jacques and his companion. The older man left the suite with clear reluctance.

Tawny gazed back at Navarre, her triangular face taut with strain. 'I really wasn't trying to steal from you—'

'The camera recording in here won't lie,' Navarre murmured without any expression at all, lush black lashes low over intent green eyes.

'There's a camera operating in here?' Tawny exclaimed in horror, immediately recognising that if there was he would have unquestionable proof of her entering the suite and taking his laptop.

'My protection team set up a camera as a standard safeguard wherever I'm staying,' Navarre stated smooth as glass. 'It means that I will have pictorial evidence of your attempt to steal from me.'

Her narrow shoulders slumped and her face fell. Shame gutted her for, whatever her motivation had been, theft was theft and neither the police nor a judge would distinguish between what she had believed she was doing and a crime. She marvelled that she had foolishly got herself into such a predicament. Caught red-handed as she had been, it no longer seemed a good idea to continue to insist that she had not been stealing. 'Yes…'

'Having you sacked and arrested, however, will be of no advantage to me,' Navarre Cazier asserted and she glanced up in surprise. 'But if you were to accept my terms in the proposition I am about to make you, I will not contact the police and in addition I will pay you for your time.'

Genuinely stunned by the content of that speech, Tawny lifted her head and speared him with an ice-blue look of scorn. 'Pay me for my time? I'm not that kind of girl—'

Navarre laughed out loud, grim amusement lightening the gravity on his face as her eyes flashed and her chin came up in challenge. 'My proposition doesn't entail taking your clothes off or, indeed, doing anything of an illegal or sexual nature,' he extended very drily. 'Make your mind up—this is very much your decision. Do I call the police or are you going to be sensible and reach for the lifebelt I'm offering?'

CHAPTER TWO

TAWNY straightened her shoulders. Her mind was in a fog torn between panic and irrational hope while she tried to work out if the exclusion of either illegal or sexual acts would offer her sufficient protection. 'You'll have to tell me first what grabbing the lifebelt would entail.'

'*Rien à faire*…nothing doing. I can't trust you with that information until I know that I have your agreement,' Navarre Cazier fielded without hesitation.

'I can't agree to something when I don't know what it is…you can't expect that.'

His stunning eyes narrowed to biting chips of emerald. '*Merde alors*…I'm the party in the position of power here. I can ask whatever I like. After all, you have the right of refusal.'

'I don't want to be accused of theft. I don't want a police record,' Tawny admitted through gritted teeth of resentment. 'I am not a thief, Mr Cazier—'

Navarre Cazier expelled his breath in a weary sigh that suggested he was not convinced of that claim. Tawny went red and her slender hands closed into fists. She was in a daze of desperation, trapped and fighting a dangerous urge to lose her temper. 'This proposition—would I be able to accept it and keep my job on here?' she pressed.

'Not unless the hotel was prepared to allow you a leave of absence of at least two weeks.'

'I don't have that kind of flexibility,' Tawny said heavily.

'But I did say that I'd pay you for your time,' Navarre reminded her drily.

That salient reminder, when Tawny was worrying about how the loss of her job would impact on her ability to pay her grandmother's mortgage, was timely. 'What's the proposition?'

'Are you agreeing?'

Her even white teeth snapped together. 'Like I have a choice?' she flashed back at him. 'Yes. Assuming there's nothing illegal, sexual or offensive about what you're asking me to do.'

'How would I know what you find offensive? Give me a final answer. Right now you're wasting my valuable time.'

Rigid with resentment, Tawny looked at him, scanning the pure hard lines of his bronzed face. His eyes piercing with the weight of his intelligence, he wore an impenetrable mask of impassivity. He was incredibly handsome and incredibly unemotional. What could the proposition be? She was a lowly chambermaid whom he believed to be a thief. In what possible way could she be of use to such a wealthy, powerful man? Even more to the point, how could she put herself in such a man's power? Logic reminded her that as long as that unseen camera of his held an image of her apparently stealing she was in his power whether she liked it or not.

'How much would you pay me?' Tawny prompted dry-mouthed, her face burning as she tried to weigh up her single option.

Realising that they were finally dealing in business

terms, Navarre's emerald-green gaze glittered with renewed energy. He estimated what she most probably
earned in a year and doubled it in the sum he came back
to her with. Although it went against the grain with him to
reward criminal behaviour, he was aware that if she was
to lose her job in meeting his demands he had to make it
worth her financial while. She went pale, her eyes widening in shock, and in the same moment he knew he had
her exactly where he wanted her. Everyone had their price
and he had, it seemed, accurately assessed hers.

That amount of money would cover any future period of unemployment she might suffer as well as her
grandmother's mortgage for the rest of the year and more,
Tawny registered in wonderment. But the truth that he
had her pinned between a rock and a hard place was still
a bitter pill to swallow. She would accept the money, but
then any alternative was better than being arrested and
charged with theft. She jerked her chin in affirmation.
'I'll do whatever it is as long as you promise to wipe that
camera once it's done.'

'And I will accept that arrangement as long as you sign
a confidentiality agreement, guaranteeing not to discuss
anything you see or hear while you're in my company.'

'No problem. I'm not a chatterbox,' Tawny traded flatly.
'May I return to work now?'

Navarre dealt her an impatient look. 'I'm afraid not.
You can't leave this hotel room without an escort. I want
to be sure that any intel you may have gleaned from my
laptop stays within these four walls.'

It finally dawned on Tawny that he had to have some
highly sensitive information on that laptop when he was
prepared to go to such lengths to protect it from the rest
of the world. A knock sounded on the door and Navarre
strode across the room, his tall, well-built body emanating

aggressive male power, to pull it open. Tawny went pale when she saw the penthouse manager, Lesley Morgan, in the doorway.

'Excuse me, Mr Cazier. Reception mentioned that there might be a problem—'

'There is not a problem.'

'Tawny?' Lesley queried quietly. 'I'm sure you must have work to take care of—'

'Tawny is resigning from her job, effective immediately,' Navarre Cazier slotted in without hesitation.

Across the room Tawny went rigid but she neither confirmed nor protested his declaration. In receipt of a wildly curious glance from the attractive brunette, Tawny flushed uncomfortably. So, she was going to be unemployed while she fulfilled his mysterious mission. It was an obvious first step. Whatever he wanted from her she could hardly continue to work a daily shift at the hotel at the same time. On the other hand, she would be virtually unemployable with a criminal record for theft hanging over her head, and, if she could emerge from the agreement with the French industrialist with her good name still intact, losing her current job would be a worthwhile sacrifice.

'There are certain formalities to be taken care of in the case of termination of employment,' Lesley replied with an apologetic compression of her lips.

'Which my staff will deal with on Tawny's behalf,' Navarre retorted in a tone of finality.

Beneath Tawny's bemused gaze, the penthouse manager took her leave. Navarre left Tawny hovering in the centre of the carpet while he made a brisk phone call to an employee to instruct her to organise appointments for him. A frown divided Tawny's fine brows when she heard him mention her name. He spoke in French too fast for her to follow to a couple of other people and then finally tossed the phone down. A knock sounded on the door.

'Answer that,' Navarre told her.

'Say please,' Tawny specified, bravely challenging him. 'You may be paying me but you can still be polite.'

Navarre stiffened in disbelief. 'I have excellent manners.'

'No, you don't…I've seen you operating with your staff,' Tawny countered with a suggestive wince. 'It's all, *do* this, *do* that…why haven't you done it already? Please and thank you don't figure—'

'Open the damn door!' Navarre raked at her, out of all patience.

'You're not just rude, you're a bully,' Tawny declared, stalking over to the door to tug it open with a twist of a slender hand.

'Don't answer me back like that,' Navarre warned her as his security chief walked in and, having caught that last exchange, directed an astonished look of curiosity at his employer.

'You're far too tempting a target,' Tawny warned him.

Icy green eyes caught her amused gaze and chilled her. 'Control the temptation. If you can't do as you're told you're of no use to me at all.'

'Is that the sound of a whip cracking over my head?' Tawny looked skyward.

'Do you hear anyone laughing?' Navarre derided.

'You've got your staff too scared.'

'Jacques, take Tawny to collect her belongings and bring her back up without giving her the chance to talk to anyone,' Navarre instructed.

'Men aren't allowed in the female locker room,' Tawny told him gently.

'I will ask Elise to join us.' Jacques unfurled his phone.

Navarre studied Tawny, far from impervious to the amusement glimmering in her pale eyes combined with the voluptuous pout of her sexy mouth. Desire, sudden and piercing as a blade, gripped him. All of a sudden as he met those eyes he was picturing her on a bed with rumpled sheets, hair fanned out in a wild colourful torrent of curls, that pale slender body displayed for his pleasure. His teeth clenched on the shot of stark hunger that evocative image released. He was consoled by the near certainty that she would give him that pleasure before their association ended, for no woman had ever denied him.

Gazing back at Navarre Cazier, Tawny momentarily felt as though someone had, without the smallest warning, dropped her off the side of a cliff. Her body felt as if it had gone into panic mode, her heartbeat thundering far too fast, her mouth suddenly dry, her nipples tight and swollen, an excited fluttering low in her belly. And just as quickly Tawny realised what was *really* happening to her and she tore her attention guiltily from him, colour burning over her cheekbones at her uncontrollable reaction to all that male testosterone in the air. It was desire he had awakened, not fear. Yes, he was gorgeous, but under no circumstances was she going to go there.

Rich, handsome men didn't attract her. Her mother and her sisters' experiences had taught Tawny not to crave wealth and status for the sake of it, for neither brought lasting happiness. Her father, a noted hotelier, was rich and miserable and, according to her older half-sisters, Bee and Zara, he was always pleading dissatisfaction with his life or latest business deal. Nothing was ever enough for Monty Blake. Bee and Zara might also be married to wealthy men, but they were both very much in love with their husbands. At the end of the day love was all that really mattered, Tawny reflected thoughtfully, and substituting sex for love and hoping it would bridge the gap didn't work.

That was why Tawny didn't sleep around. She had grown up with her mother's bitterness over a sexual affair that had never amounted to anything more. She had also seen too many friends hurt by their efforts to found a lasting relationship on a basis of casual sex. She wanted more commitment before she risked her heart; she had always wanted and demanded *more.* That was the main reason why she had avoided the advances of the wealthy men introduced to her by her matchmaking sisters, both of whom had married 'well' in her mother's parlance. What could she possibly have in common with such men with their flash lives in which only materialistic success truly mattered? She had no wish to end up with a vain, shallow and selfish man like her father, who was solely interested in her for her looks.

'Are you going to tell me what this proposition entails?' Tawny prompted in the simmering silence.

'I want you to pretend to be my fiancée,' Navarre spelt out grimly.

Her eyes widened to their fullest, for that had to be almost the very last thing she might have expected. 'But why?' she exclaimed.

'You have no need of that information,' Navarre fielded drily.

'But you must know loads of women who would—'

'Perhaps I prefer to pay. Think of yourself as a professional escort. I'll be buying you a new wardrobe to wear while you're with me. When this is over you get to keep the clothes, but not the jewellery,' he specified.

No expense spared, she thought in growing bewilderment. She had read about him in the newspapers, for he made regular appearances in the gossip columns. He had a penchant for incredibly beautiful supermodels and the reputation of being a legendary lover, but none of the ladies in his life seemed to last very long. 'Nobody's going to believe you're engaged to someone as ordinary as me,' she told him baldly.

'*Ce fut le coup de foudre...*' It was love at first sight French-style, he was telling her with sardonic cool. 'And nobody will be surprised when the relationship quickly bites the dust again.'

Well, she could certainly agree with that final forecast, but she reckoned that he had to be desperate to be considering her for such a role. How on earth would she ever be able to compare to the glamorous model types he usually had on his arm? Jacques ushered a statuesque blonde in a dark trouser suit into the room. 'Elise will escort you down to the locker room,' he explained.

'So you're a bodyguard,' Tawny remarked in French as the two women waited in the lift.

'I'm usually the driver,' Elise admitted.

'What's Mr Cazier like to work for?'

'Tough but fair and I get to travel,' Elise told her with satisfaction.

Elise hovered nearby while Tawny changed out of her uniform into her own clothes and cleared her locker. The Frenchwoman's mobile phone rang and she dug it out, glancing awkwardly at Tawny, who was busily packing a carrier bag full of belongings before moving to the other side of the room to talk in a low-pitched voice. That it was a man Elise cared about at the other end of the line was obvious, and Tawny reckoned that at that instant she could have smuggled an elephant past the Frenchwoman without attracting her attention.

'What's going on?' another voice enquired tautly of Tawny.

Tawny glanced up and focused on Julie, who stood only a couple of feet away from her. 'I'm quitting my job.'

'I heard that but why didn't he report you?'

Tawny shrugged non-committally. 'You didn't spent the night with him, did you? What's the real story?'

'A journalist offered me a lot of money to dig out some personal information for him. Accessing Cazier's laptop was worth a try. I've got credit cards to clear,' Julie admitted calmly, shockingly unembarrassed at having her lies exposed.

'Mademoiselle Baxter?' Elise queried anxiously, her attention suddenly closely trained on the two women.

Tawny lifted her laden bags and walked away without another word or look. So much for friendship! She was furious but also very hurt by her former friend's treachery. She had liked Julie, she had automatically trusted her, but she could now see her whole relationship with the other woman in quite a different light. It was likely that Julie had deliberately targeted her once she realised that Tawny would be the new maid in charge of Navarre Cazier's usual suite. Having befriended Tawny and put her under obligation by helping her to move into her bedsit, Julie had then conned the younger woman into trying to take Navarre's laptop. What a stupid, trusting fool Tawny now felt like! How could she have been dumb enough to swallow that improbable tale of sex and compromising photos? Julie had known exactly which buttons to press to engage Tawny's sympathies and it would have worked a treat had Navarre Cazier not returned unexpectedly to catch her in the act.

'You have an appointment with a stylist,' Navarre informed Tawny when she reappeared in his suite and set down her bags.

'Where?'

He named a famous department store. He scanned the jeans and checked shirt she wore with faded blue plimsolls and his wide sensual mouth twisted, for in such casual clothing she looked little older than a teenager. 'What age are you?'

'Twenty-three...you?'

'Thirty.'

'Speak French,' he urged.

'I'm a little rusty. I only get to see my grandmother about once a month now,' Tawny told him.

'Give me your mobile phone,' he instructed.

'My phone?' Tawny exclaimed in dismay.

'I can't trust you with access to a phone when I need to ensure that you don't pass information to anyone,' he retorted levelly and extended a slim brown hand. 'Your phone, please...'

The silence simmered. Tawny worried at her lower lip, reckoned that she could not fault his reasoning and reluctantly dug her phone out of her pocket. 'You're not allowed to go through it. There's private stuff on there.'

'Just like my laptop,' Navarre quipped with a hard look, watching her redden and marvelling that she could still blush so easily.

He ushered her out of the suite and into the lift. She leant back against the wall.

'Don't slouch,' he told her immediately.

With an exaggerated sigh, Tawny straightened. 'We mix like oil and water.'

'We only have to impress as a couple in company. Practise looking adoring,' Navarre advised witheringly.

Tawny wrinkled her nose. 'That's not really my style—'

'*Try,*' he told her.

She preceded him out into the foyer, striving not to notice the heads craning at the reception desk to follow their progress out of the hotel. A limousine was waiting by the kerb and she climbed in, noting Elise's neat blonde head behind the steering wheel.

'Tell me about yourself…a potted history,' Navarre instructed.

'I'm an only child although I have two half-sisters through my father's two marriages. He didn't marry my mother, though, and he has never been involved in my life. I got my degree at art college and for a couple of years managed to make a living designing greeting cards. Unfortunately that wasn't lucrative enough to pay the bills and I signed up as a maid so that I would have a regular wage coming in,' she told him grudgingly. 'I want to be a cartoonist but so far I haven't managed to sell a single cartoon.'

'A cartoonist,' Navarre repeated, his interest caught by that unexpected ambition.

'What about you? Were you born rich?'

'No. I grew up in the back streets of Paris but I acquired a first-class degree at the Sorbonne. I was an investment banker until I became interested in telecommunications and set up my first business.'

'Parents?' she pressed.

His face tensed. 'I was a foster child and lived in many homes. I have no relatives that I acknowledge.'

'I know how we can tell people we met,' Tawny said with a playful light in her eyes. 'I was changing your bed *when—*'

Navarre was not amused by the suggestion but his attention lingered on her astonishingly vivid little face in which every expression was easily read. 'I don't think we need to admit that you were working as a hotel maid.'

'Honesty is always the best policy.'

'Says the woman whom I caught thieving.'

Her face froze as though he had slapped her, reality biting again. 'I wasn't thieving,' she muttered tightly.

'It really doesn't matter as long as you keep your light fingers strictly to your own belongings while you're with me,' Navarre responded drily. 'I hope the desire to steal is an impulse that you can resist as we will be mingling with some very wealthy people.'

Mortified by the comment, Tawny bent her bright head. 'Yes, you don't have to worry on that score.'

While Navarre took a comfortable seat in a private room in the store, Tawny was ushered off to try on evening gowns, and each one seemed more elaborate than the last. When the selection had been reduced to two she was propelled out to the waiting area, where Navarre was perusing the financial papers, for a second opinion.

'That's too old for her,' he commented of the purple ball gown that she felt would not have looked out of place on Marie Antoinette.

When she walked out in the grey lace that fitted like a glove to below hip line before flaring out in a romantic arc of fullness round her knees, he actually set his newspaper down, the better to view her slender, shapely figure. *'Sensationnel,'* he declared with crowd-pleasing enthusiasm while his shrewd green eyes scanned her with as much emotion as a wooden clothes horse might have inspired.

Yet for all that lack of feeling they were such unexpectedly beautiful eyes, she reflected helplessly, as cool and mysterious as the depths of the sea, set in that strong handsome face. Bemused by the unusually fanciful thought, Tawny was whisked back into the spacious changing room where two assistants were hanging up outfits for the stylist to choose from. There were trousers, skirts, dresses, tops and jackets as well as lingerie and a large selection of shoes and accessories. Every item was designer and classic and nothing was colourful enough or edgy enough to appeal to her personal taste. She would only be in the role of fake fiancée for a maximum of two weeks, she reminded herself with relief. Could such a vast number of garments really be necessary or was the stylist taking advantage of a buyer with famously deep pockets? She wondered what event the French industrialist was taking her to that required the over-the-top evening gown. She was not required to model any other clothing for his inspection. That was a relief for, stripped of her usual image and denied her streetwise fashion, she felt strangely naked and vulnerable clad in items that did not belong to her.

Navarre was on the phone talking in English when she returned to his side. As they walked back through the store he continued the conversation, his deep drawl a low-pitched sexy purr, and she guessed that he was chatting to a woman. They returned to the hotel in silence. She wanted to go home and collect some of her own things but was trying to pick the right moment in which to make that request. Navarre vanished into the bedroom, reappearing in a light grey suit ten minutes later and walking past her.

'I'm going out. I'll see you tomorrow,' he told her silkily.

Her smooth brow furrowed. 'Do I have to stay here?'

'That's the deal,' he confirmed with a dismissive lack of interest that set her teeth on edge.

It was after midnight when Navarre came back to his suite with Jacques still at his heels. He had forgotten about Tawny so it was a surprise to walk in and see the lounge softly lit. Three heads turned from the table between them to glance at him, three of the individuals, members of his security team, instantly rising upright to greet him with an air of discomfiture beneath Jacques's censorious appraisal.

From the debris it was clear there had been takeout food eaten, and from the cards and small heaps of coins visible several games of poker. Tawny didn't stand up. She stayed where she was curled up barefoot on the sofa.

Navarre shifted a hand in dismissal of his guards. Tawny had yet to break into her new wardrobe, for she wore faded skinny jeans with slits over the knee and a tee with a skeleton motif. Her hair fell in a torrent of spiralling curls halfway down her back, much longer than he had appreciated and providing a frame for her youthful piquant face that gave her an almost fey quality.

'Where did you get those clothes from?' he asked bluntly.

'I gave Elise a list of things that I needed along with my keys and she was kind enough to go and pack a bag for me. I didn't think that what I wore behind closed doors would matter.' Tawny gazed back at him in silent challenge, striving not to react in any way to the fact that he was drop-dead gorgeous, particularly with that dark shadow of stubble roughening his masculine jawline and accentuating the sensual curve of his beautifully shaped mouth.

Navarre bent to lift the open sketch pad resting on the arm of the sofa. It was an amusing caricature of Elise and instantly recognisable as such. He flicked it back and found another, registering that she had drawn each of her companions. 'You did these? They're good.'

Tawny shifted a narrow shoulder in dismissal. 'Not good enough to pay the bills,' she said wryly, thinking of how often her mother had criticised her for choosing to study art rather than a subject that the older woman had deemed to be of more practical use.

'A talent nonetheless.'

'Where am I supposed to sleep tonight?' Tawny asked flatly, in no mood to debate the topic.

'You can sleep on the sofa,' Navarre told her without hesitation, irritated that he had not thought of her requirements soon enough to ask for a suite with an extra bedroom. 'It will only be for two nights and then we'll be leaving London.'

'To go where?'

'Further north.' With that guarded reply, he walked into the bedroom and a couple of minutes later he reappeared with a bedspread and a pillow in his arms. He deposited them on a chair nearby and then with a nod departed again. He moved with the fluid grace of a dancer and he emanated sex appeal like a force field, she acknowledged tautly, her eyes veiling as she struggled to suppress a tiny little twisting flicker of response to him.

'You know…a real gentleman would offer a lady the bed,' Tawny called in his wake.

Navarre shot her a sardonic glance, green eyes bright as jewels between the thick luxuriance of his black lashes as he drawled, 'I've never been a gentleman and I very much doubt that you're a lady in the original sense of the word.'

CHAPTER THREE

THE next morning, Navarre watched Tawny sleep, curls that melded from bright red to copper tipped with strawberry-blonde ends spilling out across the pale smooth skin of her narrow shoulders, dark lashes low over delicate cheekbones, her plump pink pouting mouth incredibly sexy. He brushed a colourful strand of hair away from her face. 'Wake up,' he urged.

Tawny woke with a start, eyes shooting wide as she half sat up. 'What?'

Navarre had retreated several feet to give her space. 'Time to rise. You have a busy day ahead of you.'

Tawny rubbed her eyes like a child and hugged her pyjama-clad knees before muttering, 'Doing what?'

'A beautician and a hairstylist will be here this afternoon to help you to prepare for this evening's event. A jeweller will be here in an hour. The bathroom's free,' he informed her coolly. 'What do you want for breakfast?'

'The full works—I'm always starving first thing,' she told him, scrambling off the sofa and folding the spread with efficient hands, a lithe figure clad in cotton pyjama pants and a camisole top. 'Where are you taking me this evening?'

'A movie awards ceremony.'

Her eyes widened. 'Wow…fancy, so that's what the boring grey dress is for—'

'It isn't boring—'

'Take it from me, it was boring enough that my mother would have admired it,' she declared unimpressed, heading off to the bathroom, pert buttocks swaying above long slim legs.

'Wear one of your new outfits,' he told her before she vanished from view.

'But if we're not going out until this evening—'

'You need a practice run. Get into role for the jeweller's benefit,' Navarre advised.

Tawny rummaged through the huge pile of garment bags, carriers and boxes that had been delivered to the suite the night before. She had hung the bags on the door of the wardrobe but had felt uneasy about the prospect of stowing away the clothing in a room that he was using. She set out a narrow check skirt and a silk top. It was a dull conventional outfit but, for what he had promised to pay her for her services as a fake fiancée, she was willing to make an effort. She took the undies into the bathroom and went for a shower, using his shower gel but keeping her hair out of the water because she did not want the hassle of drying it.

Navarre watched her walk back across the carpet to join him at the breakfast table, her heart-shaped face composed, her bright curls bouncing like tongues of flame across her silk-clad shoulders. His masculine gaze took in the pouting curve of her breasts, her tiny waist and the long tight line of the skirt, below which her shapely legs were very much in evidence. *'Tu es belle…you are beautiful, mignonne.'*

Tawny rolled her eyes, unconvinced, recognising the

sophisticated and highly experienced charm of a woman-iser in his coolly measuring appraisal. 'I clean up well.'

Navarre liked her deprecating manner and admired the more telling fact that she had walked right past a mirror without even pausing to admire her own reflection. The waiter arrived with a breakfast trolley. Although Tawny knew him the young man studiously avoided looking at her even while she was making her selections from the hot food on offer. Her cheeks burned as she realised that the staff would naturally have assumed that she was sleeping with Navarre.

Navarre had never seen a woman put away that much food at one sitting. Tawny ate daintily but she had a very healthy appetite. After her second cup of coffee and final slice of toast she pushed away her plate, relaxed back in her chair and smiled. 'Now I can face the day.'

'Do you think you've eaten enough to keep you going until lunchtime?' Navarre could not resist that teasing comment.

Her eyes widened in suggestive dismay. 'Are you saying that I can't have a snack before then?'

The biter bit, Navarre laughed out loud, very much amused. In that instant, eyes glittering with brilliance between dense black lashes that reminded her very much of lace, he was so charismatic he just took her breath away and left her staring at his handsome face. It was impossible to look away and as his gaze narrowed in intensity her tummy flipped as if she had gone down in a lift too fast.

Navarre thrust back his chair and sprang upright to extend a hand down to her. Breathless and bemused, Tawny took his hand without thought and stood up as well. Long fingers framed her cheekbone and he lowered his arrogant dark head to allow the tip of his tongue to barely

skim along the fullness of her lower lip. She opened her
mouth instinctively, her entire body tingling with an electric awareness that raised every tiny hair on her skin. His
tongue darted into the moist interior of her mouth in a light
teasing flicker that skimmed the inner surface of her lip.
It was so *incredibly* sexy it made her shiver as if she were
standing in a force-ten gale. Desire rose in her in an uncontrollable wave, screaming through her, spreading heat
and hunger into every erotic part of her body. Helplessly
she leant forwards, longing to be closer to him, insanely
conscious of the tight fullness of her breasts and the hot,
damp sting of awareness pulsing between her thighs. With
a masculine growl vibrating deep in his throat, he finally
kissed her with sweet sensual force, giving her the exact
level of strength and urgency that her entire being craved
from him.

When in the midst of that passionate embrace Navarre
suddenly stopped kissing her and angled his head back,
Tawny was utterly bewildered.

'*C'est parfait!* You're really good at this.' Navarre
gazed down at her with eyes as ice-cold as running water.
'Anyone seeing such a kiss would believe we were lovers.
That pretence of intimacy is all that is required to make
us convincing.'

Tawny turned white and then suddenly red as a tide
of mortification gripped her but she contrived to veil her
eyes and stand her ground. 'Thank you,' she replied as if
she had known all along what he was doing and had responded accordingly.

She was mentally kicking herself hard for having responded to his advances as if she were his newest girlfriend. How could she have done that? How could she have
lost all control and forgotten who he was and who she
was and exactly why they were together? He was paying

her, for goodness sake! There was nothing else between them, no intimate relationship of any kind, she reminded herself brutally. On his terms she was something between an employee and a paid escort and not at all the sort of woman he would normally spend time with. Yet she had found that kiss more exciting than any she had ever experienced and would probably have still been in his arms had he not chosen to end that embarrassing little experiment. He had given his fake fiancée a fake kiss and she had fallen for it as though it were real.

Why on earth did she find Navarre Cazier so attractive? He might be extraordinarily good-looking but surely it took more than cheap physical chemistry to break down her barriers? As a rule she was standoffish with men and a man had to work at engaging her interest. All Navarre had done was insult her, so how could she possibly be attracted to him? Infuriated by her weakness, she took a seat as far away from him as she could get.

A warning knock sounded on the door before it opened to show Jacques shepherding in two men, one carrying a large case. It was the jeweller, complete with his own bodyguard. Navarre brought her forwards to sit beside him. Stiff as a doll and wearing a fixed smile, she sat down and looked on in silence as the older man displayed a range of fabulous rings featuring different stones.

'What do you like?' Navarre prompted.

'Aren't diamonds supposed to be a girl's best friend?' Tawny quipped and the diamond tray immediately rose uppermost.

Navarre took her small hand in his. 'Choose the one you like best.'

His hand was so much larger than hers, darker, stronger, and all she could think about for an horrific few moments was how that hand would feel if it were to touch her body, stroking…*caressing.* What the heck was the matter with her brain? Hungry hormones and heated embarrassment mushrooming inside her, Tawny bent her head over the diamond display and pointed blindly. 'May I try that one?'

'A pink diamond…a superb choice,' the jeweller remarked, passing the ring to Navarre, who eased the ring onto Tawny's finger. It was a surprisingly good fit.

'I like it,' Navarre declared.

'It is just *unbelievably* gorgeous!' Tawny gushed, batting her lashes like fly swats in response to the squeeze hold he had on her wrist.

Navarre shot her a quelling look in punishment for that vocal eruption while the purchase was being made. Several shallow jewel cases were removed from the case and opened to display an array of matching diamond pieces. Without recourse to her, Navarre selected a pair of drop earrings, a slender bracelet and a brooch, which she gathered were being offered on loan for her to wear that evening.

'Try not to behave like an airhead,' Navarre advised when they were alone again. 'It irritates me.'

Tawny resisted the urge to admit even to herself that awakening his irritation was preferable to receiving no reaction from him at all, for that made her sound childish. Had he not been hovering, however, she would have reached for her sketch pad, for his unmistakeably French character traits amused her. Regardless of the apparent passion of that kiss, she was convinced that Navarre Cazier rarely lost control or focus. He was arrogant, cool, reserved and extremely sure of himself.

'My English lawyer will be calling in shortly with the confidentiality agreement which you have to sign,' Navarre informed her, shrugging back a pristine shirt cuff to check the time. 'I have business to take care of this afternoon. I will see you later.'

'Can I go out? I'm going stir crazy in here,' she confided.

'If you go out or contact anyone our agreement will be null and void,' Navarre spelt out coldly. 'Elise will be keeping you company while I'm out.'

Elise arrived and he had barely left the room before Tawny's sketch pad was in her hand and she was drawing. Capturing Navarre on paper with strong dark lines, she drew him as she had seen him while she modelled evening gowns for him at the department store the day before. *'Sensationnel,'* he had purred with his charismatic smile, but she had known meeting his detached gaze that the compliment was essentially meaningless for she meant nothing to him beyond being a means to an end. In the cartoon she depicted the stylist as a curvaceous man killer, standing behind her and the true focus of his masculine admiration. It was artistic licence but it expressed Tawny's growing distrust of Navarre Cazier's astute intelligence, for she would have given much to understand why he felt the need to *hire* a woman to pretend to be his fiancée. What was he hiding from her or from the rest of the world? What were the secrets that he was so determined to keep from public view on that laptop? Secrets of such importance that he was willing to hold Tawny incommunicado and a virtual prisoner within his hotel suite to ensure that she could not share them…

'May I see what you have drawn?' Elise asked.

Tawny grimaced.

'If it's the boss I won't tell anyone,' she promised, and Tawny extended her pad.

Elise laughed. 'You have caught him well but he is not a lech.'

'A cartoon is a joke, Elise, not a character reference,' Tawny explained. 'You're very loyal to him.'

'I was in lust with him for the first year I worked for him.' Elise wrinkled her nose in an expression of chagrin. 'It hurts my pride to remember how I was. He seemed so beautiful I couldn't take my eyes off him.'

'And then he *speaks,*' Tawny slotted in flatly.

'No, no!' Elise laughed at that crack. 'No, I realised what a fool I was being once I saw him with his ladies. Only the most beautiful catch his eye and even they cannot hold him longer than a few weeks, particularly if they demand too much of his time and attention. He would never get involved with an employee, but he is very much a single guy, who wants to keep it that way.'

'I can't fault him for that. Who is the current lady in his life?'

Elise winced and suddenly scrambled upright again as if she had just remembered who Tawny was and what she was supposed to be doing with her. 'I'm sorry, I can't tell you. That is confidential information.'

Tawny went pink. 'No problem. I understand.'

A suave well-dressed lawyer arrived with the confidentiality agreement soon afterwards. He explained the basics of the document and gave it to her to read. When she had finished reading what seemed to be a fairly standard contract she borrowed his pen to sign it and, satisfied, he departed. Elise ordered a room-service lunch for them and when it was delivered Tawny noticed the waiter flicking his eyes repeatedly to the napkin on her lap. She ran her fingers through the folds and felt the stiffness of paper. As she withdrew what she assumed to be a note she pushed it into the pocket of her jeans for reading when she was alone and then shook out the napkin, her heart thumping. A note? But from whom? And about what? Julie was the only member of staff she had got close to and why would Julie be trying to communicate with her again?

As if to apologise for her caginess about her employer's private life, Elise told Tawny about her boyfriend, Michel, who was a chef in Paris and how difficult the couple found it to see each other with Michel usually working nights when Elise was most often free. After a light meal, Tawny went off to the bathroom to unfurl the note and felt terribly guilty about doing so, knowing that her companion was supposed to be ensuring that no such communications were taking place. Unfortunately for Navarre, Elise just wasn't observant enough to be an effective guard.

'If you call…' the note ran and a London phone number followed. 'Information about Navarre Cazier is worth a lot of money.'

It was typed and unsigned. Tawny thrust the note back into her pocket with a frown of discomfiture. Was this a direct approach from the journalist who had tried to bribe Julie into doing his dirty work for him by stealing Navarre's laptop? If it was the same journalist he was certainly persistent in his underhand methods. Was he hoping that Tawny would make use of her current seemingly privileged position to spy for him and gather information about Navarre Cazier?

Distaste filled her. She felt slightly soiled at having even read the note. Navarre Cazier might think she had no standards because she had agreed to let him pay her to act as his fiancée, but Tawny had only agreed to that role because she was determined to ensure her grandmother Celestine's continuing security in her retirement home. If it had only been a matter of personal enrichment, if Navarre had not had the power to force Tawny to give up her employment, she would have refused his offer outright, she reflected unhappily. She would never forget the lesson of how her own mother's financial greed had badly hurt Celestine. Even family affection had proved insufficient to avert that tragedy and Tawny did not think she would ever find it possible to fully forgive her mother for what she had done to the old lady.

When she returned to the lounge Elise was taking delivery of a substantial set of designer luggage. 'For your new clothes,' she explained. 'You'll be travelling tomorrow.'

Feeling uncomfortable with the other woman after secretly reading that forbidden note, Tawny used the delivery as an excuse to return to the bedroom and pack the contents of all the bags, boxes and garment carriers into the cases instead. By the time she had finished doing that the beautician and her assistant had arrived with a case of tools and cosmetics and Tawny had to wrap herself in a towel to let them start work. What followed was a whirlwind of activity in the bedroom, which was taken over, and the afternoon wore on while she was waxed and plucked and massaged and moisturised and painted. By the time it was over she was convinced that there was not an inch of her body that had not been treated and enhanced in some way. As a woman who devoted very little time to her looks she found it something of a revelation to appreciate how much stuff she could have been doing to add polish to her appearance.

By the time the hairdresser arrived, Tawny was climbing the walls with boredom, a mood that was not helped by the stylist's visible dismay when confronted by Tawny's tempestuous mane of spiralling ringlets. When her hair was done, she was made up, and only when that was over could she finally don the grey lace evening gown. She was looking at herself in the mirror and grimacing at how old-fashioned she thought she looked when Elise brought in the diamond jewellery and Tawny put on the ring, the drop earrings and the bracelet. Studying the brooch, she suddenly had an idea and she bent down and pulled up the skirt to hold it above the knee, where it cascaded down in ruffles to her ankles. Ignoring Elise's dropped jaw, she anchored the skirt there with the brooch, straightened, pushed up the long tight sleeves of her dress to her elbow and bared her shoulders as well. The dress, magically, acquired a totally different vibe.

Navarre, waiting impatiently in the lounge to shower and change, glanced up as the bedroom door swung open and there she was, framed in the doorway. The classic elegant image he had expected was nowhere to be seen. There she stood, her magnificent hair tumbling in a rather wild torrent round her shoulders, her face glowing with subtle make-up, dominated by eyes bright as stars and a soft ripe mouth tinted the colour of raspberries. She looked so beautiful that he was stunned. That the dress he had chosen had been mysteriously transformed into sexy saloon girl-style went right past him because he was much too busy appreciating her satin smooth white shoulders and the slender, shapely perfection of her knees and ankles.

The silence filled the room and stretched as Tawny studied him expectantly.

'Is the shower free?' Navarre enquired smoothly, compressing his stubborn mouth on any comment relating to her appearance. She was working for him. He was paying for the entire display. Any remark, after all, would be both superfluous and inappropriate.

CHAPTER FOUR

TAWNY knew she had never looked so good and while she waited for Navarre to get ready she tried not to feel offended by his silence on that score. What was the matter with her? He was not a date, he was not required to pay her compliments and at least he hadn't complained about the liberties she had taken with the grey lace shroud he had picked for her to wear. Shouldn't she be grateful that he was maintaining a polite distance? Did she want the boundary lines between them to blur again? She certainly didn't want another kiss that made her feel as if she were burning up like a flame inside her own skin. Well, actually she *did* want one but that was not a prompting powered by her brain, it was more of a deeply mortifying craving. She told herself that there was no way that she would be stupid enough to succumb to his magnetic sexual allure a second time. Forewarned was forearmed.

'Let's go,' Navarre urged, joining her in an exquisitely tailored dinner jacket, the smooth planes of his freshly shaven features as beautiful as a dark angel's.

In the lift she found it a challenge to drag her eyes from the flawless perfection of his visage. 'Don't you think you should finally tell me where we're going?' she pressed.

'The Golden Awards and the showbiz party afterwards,' he revealed.

Her eyes widened in shock. She struggled to be cool and not reveal the fact that she was impressed to death. A huge number of well-known international celebrities would be attending the opulent Golden Movie Awards ceremony. The GMAs were a famous annual event, beloved of the glitterati. 'All the press will be there,' she said weakly, suddenly grasping why she was wearing a very expensive designer dress and a striking array of diamonds.

Acutely aware of the abnormal number of staff at Reception waiting to watch their departure, Tawny had to struggle to keep her head held high, but there was nothing that she could do to stop her face burning. Everybody would think she was sleeping with him; of course they would think that! People always went for the sleaziest explanation of the seemingly incomprehensible and why else would a chambermaid be dolled up in a designer frock and walking with a billionaire? Navarre escorted her out to the limousine.

'You've got some nerve taking someone like me with you to the Golden Awards,' Tawny dared to comment as the luxury car pulled away from the kerb.

Navarre studied her with amusement gleaming in his eyes. '*Mais non.* No man who looks at you will wonder why I am with you.'

'You mean they'll all think that I have to be absolutely amazing in bed!' Tawny retorted unimpressed.

Navarre shifted a broad shoulder in a tiny shrug that was very Gallic, understated and somehow deeply cool. 'I have no objection to inspiring envy.'

Tawny swallowed the angry words brimming on her tongue and breathed in slow and deep, while staunchly reminding herself of Celestine's need for her financial assistance.

'You're wearing an engagement ring,' Navarre reminded her drily. 'That puts you into a very different category, *ma petite.*'

'Don't call me that— I'm not *that* small!' Tawny censured.

A grin as unexpected as it was charismatic momentarily slashed his wide sensual mouth. 'You are considerably smaller than I am and very slim—'

'Skinny,' Tawny traded argumentatively. 'Don't dress it up. I eat like a horse but I've always been skinny.'

'We met at an art gallery…our fake first meeting,' Navarre extended when she frowned at him in bewilderment. 'If you are asked you will say that we met at an art showing here in London.'

'If I must.'

'You must. I refuse to say that I met the woman I intend to marry while she was changing my bed,' Navarre told her unapologetically.

'Snob,' Tawny told him roundly, crossing her legs and suddenly aware of the sweep of his gaze finally resting on the long length of thigh she had unintentionally exposed as the skirt of her gown slid back from her legs. As she lifted her head and encountered those spectacular eyes of his there was a knot of tension at the tender heart of her where she was unaccustomed to feeling anything.

Hard as a rock as he scrutinised that silken expanse of thigh, Navarre was exasperated enough by his body's indiscipline and her false impression of him to give a sardonic laugh of disagreement. 'I am not a snob. I worked in hotel kitchens to pay my way as a schoolboy. Survival was never a walk in the park when I was growing up and I have never forgotten how hard I had to work for low pay.'

Filled with all the embarrassment of someone labelled a thief and the new knowledge that he did have experience of working long hours for a small wage, Tawny evaded his gaze and smoothed down her skirt. She thought of the very generous tips he had left for her on his previous stays at the hotel and shame washed over her in a choking wave of regret. She wished she had never met Julie and never listened to her clever lies, for she had betrayed Navarre's trust. His generosity should have been rewarded by the attention of honest, dependable staff.

The car was slowing down in the heavy flow of traffic, gliding past crowded pavements to come to a halt outside the brightly lit theatre where the Goldens were to be held. As Tawny glimpsed the crush of sightseers behind the crash barriers, the stand of journalists, a presenter standing talking beside men with television cameras and the red carpet stretching to the entrance, something akin to panic closed her throat over.

'Don't stop to answer questions. Let me do the talking if there are any. Just smile,' Navarre instructed.

Tawny found it a challenge to breathe as she climbed out of the car. As cameras flashed she saw spots in front of her eyes and Navarre's steadying hand at her elbow was appreciated. He exchanged a light word with the attractive presenter who appeared to know him and steered her on smoothly into the building. An usher showed them to their seats inside the theatre. No sooner had they sat down than people began to stop in the aisle to greet Navarre and he made a point of introducing her as his fiancée. Time after time she saw surprise blossom in faces that Navarre should apparently be on the brink of settling down with one woman. That sceptical reaction told her all she needed to know about his reputation as a womaniser, she reflected sourly. Furthermore it seemed to her as though it might take more than diamonds and a designer gown to persuade his friends that she was the genuine article.

She watched as renowned actors and directors walked

up to the stage to collect awards and give speeches. Her hands ached from clapping and her mouth from smiling. It was a strain to feel so much on show and something of a relief when he indicated that it was time to leave.

As they crossed the foyer on their way out of the theatre a musical female voice called breathily, 'Navarre!' and he came to a dead halt.

Tia Castelli, exquisite as a china doll in a stunning blue chiffon dress teamed with a fabulous sapphire pendant, was hurrying down the staircase that led up to the private theatre boxes. Tawny couldn't take her eyes off the beauty, who was very much the screen goddess of her day. Earlier she had watched Tia collect a trophy for her outstanding performance in her most recent film in which she had played a woman being terrorised by a former boyfriend, and she had marvelled that she could be even seated that close to a living legend.

'And you must be Tawny!' Tia exclaimed, bending down with a brilliant smile to kiss Tawny lightly on both cheeks while cameras went crazy all around them as every newshound in their vicinity rushed to capture photos of the celebrated actress. Tawny was knocked sideways by that unexpectedly friendly greeting. Tia was extraordinarily beautiful in the flesh and, confronted by such a very famous figure, Tawny felt tongue-tied.

'Congratulations—I was so happy to hear your news and Navarre's,' Tia continued. 'Join Luke and I in our limo. We're heading to the same party.'

'How on earth did you get so friendly with Tia Castelli?' Tawny hissed as security guards escorted them back out via the red carpet.

'My first boss in private banking took care of her investments. I've known her a long time,' Navarre responded calmly.

Tia paused to greet fans and pose for the TV cameras while her tall, skinny, unshaven husband, clad in tight jeans, a crumpled blue velvet jacket and a black trilby as befitted the image of a hard-living rock star, ignored every attempt to slow down his progress and headed straight for the waiting limousine. With a rueful sigh, Navarre urged Tawny in the same direction and wished, not for the first time, that Tia were less impulsive and more cautious.

'So you're going to marry Navarre,' Luke Convery commented, his Irish accent unexpectedly melodic and soft as he introduced himself carelessly and studied Tawny with assessing brown eyes. 'What have you got that the rest of them haven't?'

'This...' Tawny showed off the opulent pink diamond while finding it impossible not to wonder just how much younger Luke was than his wife. They didn't even look like a couple, for in comparison to her polished Hollywood glamour he dressed like a tramp. She doubted that the musician was out of his twenties while Tia had to be well into her thirties, for her incredibly successful career had spanned Tawny's lifetime. She thought it was good that just for once it was an older woman with a younger man rather than the other way round, and she was warmed by the way Luke immediately reached for his wife's hand when she got into the car and the couple exchanged a mutually affectionate smile.

By all accounts, Tia Castelli deserved a little happiness, for she had led an impossibly eventful life from the moment she was spotted by a film director as a naive schoolgirl in a Florentine street and starred in her first blockbuster movie as the child of a broken marriage. She was a mesmerising actress, whom the camera truly loved. Admittedly Tia was no stranger to emotion or tragedy, for violent and unfaithful husbands, jealous lovers and nervous breakdowns with all the attendant publicity had all featured at one point or another in the star's life. She had suffered divorce, widowhood and a miscarriage during her only pregnancy.

'Let me see the ring,' Tia urged, stretching out a be-jewelled hand weighted with diamonds. 'Oh, I *love* it.'

'You haven't got a finger free for another diamond,' Luke told his wife drily. 'How long do we have to stay at this party?'

'A couple of hours?' Tia gave him a pleading look of appeal.

'It'll be really boring,' Luke forecast moodily, his lower lip coming out in a petulant pout.

Beside her Navarre stiffened and Tia looked as though she might be about to burst into tears. Navarre asked Tia's husband about his upcoming European tour with his rock group, the moment of tension ebbed and shortly afterwards they arrived at the glitzy hotel where the party was being held. Tia was mobbed by paparazzi outside the hotel and lingered to give an impromptu interview to a TV pre-senter. Tawny was startled when Navarre stepped slightly behind her to pose for a photo, mentioning her name and their supposed engagement with the relaxed assurance of a man who might have known her for years rather than mere days. It occurred to her that he was quite an actor in his own right, able to conceal his essential indifference to her behind a convincing façade as though she were in-deed precious to him. While he spoke the warmth of his tall, strong physique burned down her slender spine like a taunting lick of flame and the faint scent of some ex-pensive cologne underscored by clean, husky masculin-ity filled her nostrils and suddenly her body was going haywire with awareness, breasts swelling, legs trembling as she remembered that earth-shattering kiss.

One freakin' kiss, Tawny thought with furious resentment, and she had fallen apart at the seams. He hadn't even made a pass at her. She had to be fair, he wasn't the pawing type, indeed he never laid a finger on her without good reason, but even so, when he got close, every skin cell in her body leapt and dived as if she were a dizzy teenager in the grip of her first crush.

'Are you always this tense?' Navarre enquired.

'Only around you,' she told him, knowing that there was more than one way to read that reply.

Trailing adoring hangers-on like a vibrant kite followed by fluttering ribbons, Tia surged up to them as soon as they entered the function room and complained that Luke had already taken off and abandoned her.

'He hates these things,' she complained ruefully as Navarre immediately took on the task of ushering her to her prominently placed table.

Tia was very much what Tawny would have expected of a beautiful international star. She had to have constant attention and wasn't too fussy about how she went about getting it. She was very familiar with Navarre, touching his arm continually as she talked, smiling sexily up at him, employing every weapon in the considerable armoury of her beauty to keep him by her side and hold his interest. A proper fiancée, Tawny reflected wryly, would have wanted to shoot Tia and bury her deep.

'You should tell him you don't like it,' Luke whispered mockingly in Tawny's ear, making her jump because she had not realised he had come to stand beside her.

'I've got no complaints. Your wife is the life and soul of the party,' Tawny answered lightly, as if she were quite unconcerned when in fact she had felt invisible in Tia's radius.

'No, she likes handsome men around her,' Luke Convery

contradicted, watching the Italian blonde hold court at her table surrounded by attentive males, his demeanour a resentful combination of admiration and annoyance. As if he was determined to defy that view he draped an arm round Tawny's taut shoulders and she stiffened in surprise.

Across the room, Navarre's glittering green gaze narrowed to rest on Tawny, watching her lift her face to look up into Luke Convery's eyes and suddenly laugh. They looked remarkably intimate, he noted in surprise. How had that happened between virtual strangers? Or was the luscious redhead a quick study when it came to impressing rich and famous men? Anger broke like a river bursting its banks through Navarre's usual rock-solid self-discipline and he vaulted upright to take immediate action.

'You should try staying by Tia's side,' Tawny was saying warily to Luke Convery.

'Been there, done that. It doesn't work but you might have more luck with that angle.' The musician shot her a challenging appraisal from brooding dark eyes. 'If you're engaged to the guy, why are you letting Tia take over?'

Reminded of her role, Tawny flushed and headed off to the cloakroom to escape the awkward exchange. How was she supposed to react when a household name with a face that could have given Helen of Troy a run for her money was flirting like mad with her supposed fiancé? When she returned to the party, she was taken aback to see Navarre poised near the doors, evidently awaiting her reappearance. When he saw her, he immediately frowned and jerked his arrogant head to urge her over to him.

'What have you been doing? Where have you been?' he demanded curtly.

Resenting his attitude, Tawny rolled her eyes. 'I was in the cloakroom, trying to discreetly avoid coming between you and the object of your affections.'

He followed her meaningful sidewise glance in the direction of Tia Castelli's table and his strong jawline clenched as though Tawny had insulted him. His eyes narrowed to rake over her with scorn. '*Drôle d'excuse…* what an excuse! Tia and I are old friends, nothing more. But I saw you giggling with Convery—'

'What do you mean by you "*saw*" me with Luke?' Tawny pressed hotly, hostile to both his intonation and his attitude. 'And I'm not the giggly type.'

Navarre flattened his wide sensual mouth into a forbidding line. 'We are supposed to be newly engaged. You are not here to amuse yourself. *Stay by my side.*'

'As long as you appreciate that I'm only doing it for the money,' Tawny shot back at him in an angry hiss, her face stiff with chagrin at his criticism of her behaviour.

'I'm unlikely to forget the fact that I'm paying for the pleasure of your company,' he retorted crushingly. 'That's a first for me!'

'You do surprise me.' Hot pink adorning her cheeks at that cutting retaliation, Tawny stuck to him like glue for the rest of the party. He circulated, one arm attached to Tawny as he made a point of introducing her as his future wife.

Tawny played up to the label, clinging to his arm, smiling up at him, laughing slavishly at the mildest joke or story and generally behaving as if he were the centre of her world. And for what he was paying for the show, she told herself ruefully, he deserved to be.

'Did you have to behave like a bimbo?' Navarre growled as she climbed back into the limousine at the end of the evening, shoulders drooping as exhaustion threatened to claim her.

'In this scenario it works. As you said yourself, if we seem unsuited, nobody will be surprised when the engagement only lasts for five minutes,' Tawny retorted, thoroughly irritated at receiving yet more vilification from his corner. Could she do nothing right in his eyes? What exactly did he want from her? 'Personally, I think I put in a pretty good performance.'

A silence that implied he had been less than impressed stretched between them all the way back to the hotel. In the lift he stabbed the button for a lower floor. 'Elise has offered to share her room with you tonight so that you don't have to use the sofa again,' he informed her glacially. 'I believe she already has had your belongings moved for your convenience.'

Relief filled Tawny as she stepped out of the lift and found the tall blonde bodyguard waiting to greet her. With Elise, she could take off her fancy glad rags, climb into her pjs and relax, which was exactly what she was most longing to do at that instant.

Navarre absorbed the alacrity of Tawny's departure from the lift, frowning at the strangely appealing sound of the giggling she had said she didn't do trilling down the corridor just before the lift doors closed again. He had never had a woman walk away from him before without a word or a glance and his eyes momentarily flashed as though someone had lit a fire behind them. He could not accuse Tawny Baxter of attempting to ensnare him, but he recalled the manner in which she had melted into that kiss and smiled, ego soothed. It was not a very nice smile.

CHAPTER FIVE

'OH…my…goodness!' Tawny squealed in Navarre's ear
as she squashed her face up against the window of the
helicopter to get a better view of the medieval fortress
they were flying over, a sixteenth-century tower house
complete with a Victorian gothic extension. It was late
afternoon. 'It's a castle, a *real* castle! Are we really going
to be staying there?'

'*Oui,*' Navarre confirmed drily.

'You are *so* spoilt!' Tawny exclaimed loudly, winning
Jacques's startled scrutiny from the front seat as she
turned briefly to shoot his employer a reproachful look.
'You're going to be staying in a genuine castle and you're
not even excited! Not even a little bit excited?'

'You're excited enough for both of us,' Navarre countered. His attention was commanded against his will by
the vibrant glow of her heart-shaped face and the anticipation writ large there, eyes starry, lush peachy mouth
showing a glimpse of small white teeth. Adults rarely
demonstrated that much enthusiasm for anything and, to a
man who kept all emotion under strict lock and key, there
was something ridiculously appealing about her complete
lack of inhibition.

The helicopter, which had carried them north from their
private flight to Edinburgh and lunch at a smart hotel

there, landed in a paddock within full view of the castle. Navarre sprang out in advance of Tawny and then swung round to lift her out. 'I could've managed!' she told him pointedly, smoothing down her clothing as though he had rumpled her.

'Not without a step in that skirt,' Navarre traded with all the superiority of a male accustomed to disembarking from such craft with a woman in tow.

Tawny had slept like a log the night before in the room she had shared with Elise. Similar in age, the two young women had chattered over a late supper, exchanging innocuous facts about friends and families.

'The boss warned me that I had to be sure to feed you!' Elise had teased, watching, impressed, as Tawny demolished a plate of sandwiches.

Now she was in the Scottish Highlands for the weekend but Navarre had only divulged their destination after he had invited her to join him for breakfast in his suite that morning, when he had also filled her in on a few useful facts about their hosts.

Tawny was rather nervous at the prospect of meeting Sam and Catrina Coulter. Sam was the extremely wealthy owner of the Coulter Centax Corporation. Catrina, whom Navarre had admitted was an ex, was Sam's second, much younger wife and formerly a very successful English model. The couple had no children but Sam had had a son by his first marriage, who had died prematurely in an accident.

'So is this where Sam and Catrina live all the year round?' Tawny asked curiously as they walked towards the Range Rover awaiting them. 'It must be pretty desolate in winter.'

'They don't own Strathmore Castle, they're renting it

for the season,' Navarre told her wryly. 'Sam's very into shooting and fishing.'

Sam Coulter was in his sixties, a trim bespectacled man with grey hair and a keen gaze. Catrina, a beautiful brunette with big brown eyes and an aggressively bright smile, towered over her empire building husband, who made up for what he lacked in height with his large personality. Refreshments were served before the fire in the atmospheric Great Hall that had walls studded with a display of medieval weaponry, fabulous early oak furniture and a tartan carpet. Catrina made a big thing out of cooing over Tawny's engagement ring and tucked a friendly hand into the younger woman's arm to lead her upstairs, but there was neither true warmth nor sincerity in her manner. Only when Catrina left Navarre and Tawny in the same room did it occur to Tawny that they were expected to occupy the same bed.

'We're supposed to share?' she whispered within seconds of the door closing behind their hostess.

'What else would you expect?'

Unfortunately Tawny had not thought about the possibility. Now she scanned the room. There was no sofa, nothing other than the four-poster bed for the two of them to sleep on, and something akin to panic gripped her. 'You could say you snore and keep me awake *and*—'

'You're not that naive. We must share the bed. It is only for two nights,' Navarre drawled.

'I'm shy about sharing beds,' Tawny warned him.

Navarre studied her, intently. 'I'm *not*,' he told her without hesitation, flashing her a wickedly amused smile.

A painful flush lit Tawny's complexion. But the mesmerising charm of his smile at that instant knocked her sideways and her susceptible heart went boom-boom-

boom inside her ribcage. 'I really don't want to share a room with you.'

'You must have expected this set-up,' Navarre said very drily. 'Engaged couples rarely sleep in separate beds these days.'

It was a fair point and Tawny winced in acknowledgement. 'I didn't think about it.'

'We're stuck with the arrangement,' Navarre countered in a tone of finality. 'Or is this a ploy aimed at demanding more money from me? Is that what lies behind these antiquated protests?'

Tawny froze in astonishment, affronted by the suggestion. 'No, it darned well is not! How dare you suggest that? I just haven't shared a bed with a guy before—'

Navarre quirked a sardonic black brow. 'What? *Never?* I don't believe you.'

'Well, I don't care what you believe. You may sleep around but I never have!' Tawny slung back at him in furious self-defence.

'I didn't accuse you of sleeping around,' Navarre pointed out, his innate reserve and censure never more evident than in his hard gaze and the tough stubborn set of his strong jawline. 'Nor will I accept you throwing such impertinent remarks at me.'

'Point taken but I've always believed in calling a spade a spade and exclusive you're not!' Tawny responded, her temper still raw from the idea that he could think she was using the need to share a bed as an excuse to demand more money from him.

'Tonight we're sharing that bed, *ma petite.*' Navarre dealt her an intimidating appraisal, inviting her disagreement.

Tawny opened the case sited on the trunk at the foot of the bed to extract the outfit she had decided to wear for dinner. She loathed his conviction that she was unscrupulous and mercenary but she saw no point in getting into an argument with him. Navarre would probably fight tooth and claw to the death just to come out the winner. A row might be overheard and he would have reason to complain if anything happened to mar their pretence of being a happy couple.

'And by the way, I am exclusive with a woman for the duration of our time together.'

Bending over the case, Tawny reckoned that that would impose no great sacrifice on a man famous for never staying long with one woman and she murmured flatly, 'None of my business.'

Navarre breathed in slow and deep while on another level he drank in the intoxicating glimpses of slim, shapely thigh visible through the split in the back of her skirt. She straightened to shed her cardigan. Hunger uncoiled inside him. Every time she awakened his libido the effects got stronger, he acknowledged grimly, noting the way her bright rippling curls snaked down her slender spine, somehow drawing his attention to the fact that the top she wore was gossamer thin and revealed the pale delicate bra that encased her dainty breasts. *Merde alors,* he was behaving like a schoolboy salivating for his first glimpse of naked female flesh!

The chosen outfit draped over her arm, Tawny moved towards the wardrobe to hang the garment and as she did so she collided with Navarre's intent gaze. It was as if all the oxygen in her lungs were sucked out at once. Her heart went *thud* and she stilled in surprise as she recognised the sexual heat of that brutally masculine appraisal. 'Don't look at me like that,' she told him gruffly.

Navarre reached for her. 'I can't help it,' he purred.

'Yes, you can,' she countered shakily, longing with

every fibre of her rebellious being to be drawn closer to him while her brain screamed at her to slap him down and go into retreat. But there was something incredibly flattering about such a look of desire on a handsome man's face. Navarre had the ability to make her feel impossibly feminine and seductive, two qualities that she had never thought she possessed.

One hand resting on her hip, Navarre skimmed the knuckles of the other gently down the side of her face. 'You're beautiful, *ma petite.*'

Tawny had never seen herself as beautiful before and that single word had a hypnotic effect on her so that she looked up at him with shining ice-blue eyes. Teased for having red hair at school, she had grown into a sporty tomboy who lacked the curves required to attract the opposite sex. Boys had become her mates rather than her boyfriends, many of them using her as a step closer to her then best friend, a curvy little blonde. Curvy and blonde had become Tawny's yardstick of beauty and what Navarre Cazier could see in her was invisible to her own eyes.

Indecent warmth shimmied through Tawny from the caressing touch of his fingers and she wanted to lean into his hand, get closer on every level while that tightening sensation low in her body filled her with a sharp, deep craving. Struggling to control that dangerous sense of weakness, Tawny froze, torn between stepping closer and stepping back. While she was in the midst of that mental fight, Navarre bent his arrogant dark head and kissed her.

And it wasn't like that first teasing, tender kiss in London, it was a kiss full of an unashamed passion that shot through her bloodstream like an adrenalin rush. One kiss was nowhere near enough either. As his hungry, demanding mouth moved urgently on hers her fingers delved into his luxuriant black hair to hold him to her and she felt light-headed. His tongue delved and unleashed such acute hunger inside her that she gasped and instinctively pushed her taut, aching breasts into the inflexible wall of his broad chest. Gathering her closer, his hand splayed across her hips and she was instantly aware of the hard thrust of his erection. Her knees went weak as a dark tingling heat spread through her lower body in urgent response to his arousal.

He lifted her up and brought her down on the bed, still exchanging kiss for feverish kiss and suddenly she was on fire with longing, knowing exactly what she wanted and shocked by it. She wanted his weight on top of her to sate the ache at the core of her. She wanted to open her legs to cradle him but, ridiculously, her skirt was too tight.

In a sudden movement driven by that last idiotic thought, Tawny tore her lips from his. 'No, I don't want this!' she gasped, planting her hands on his wide shoulders to impose space between them.

Navarre immediately lifted back, face rigid with self-discipline. He vaulted back off the bed to stare down at her with scorching green eyes. 'Yes, you do want me as much as I want you. Together we're like a fire raging out of control and I don't know why you're imposing limits, unless it's because—'

'No, don't say it!' Tawny cut in, sitting up in a hurry and raking her tumbled hair off her brow with an impatient hand. 'Don't you dare say it!'

Navarre frowned in bewilderment. 'Say what?'

'Offer me more money to sleep with you…*don't you dare!*' she launched at him warningly.

Navarre elevated a sardonic black brow and stood straight and tall to gaze broodingly down at her. *'Mais c'est insensé*…that's crazy. I have not the slightest intention of offering you money for sex. I don't pay for it, never have, never will. Perhaps you're angling for me to make you that kind of an offer before you deliver between the sheets. But I'm afraid you've picked the wrong guy to work that ploy on.'

As that derisive little speech sank in Tawny went white with rage and sprang off the bed, the wild flare of her hot temper giving her a strong urge to slap him. But Navarre snapped hands like bands of steel round her wrists to hold her arms still by her side and prevent any other contact. *'No,'* he said succinctly. 'I won't tolerate that from any woman.'

High spots of colour bloomed in Tawny's cheeks as she jerked back from him, his icy intervention having doused her anger like a bucket of cold water. It didn't prevent her from still wanting to kill him though. 'I wasn't trying to put the idea in your head...OK? It's just I know what guys like you are like—'

'Like you know so many guys like me,' Navarre fielded witheringly.

'You're used to getting exactly what you want when you want and not taking no for an answer.'

'Not my problem,' Navarre countered glacially.

Tawny got changed in the bathroom. Her mouth was still swollen from his kisses, her body still all of a shiver and on edge from the sexual charge he put out. She mouthed a rude word at herself in the mirror, furious that she had lost control in his arms. She had genuinely feared that he might offer her money to include sex in their masquerade and she had tried to avert the risk of him uttering those fatal humiliating words, which would have reduced her to the level of a call girl. Unfortunately for her Navarre had actually suspected that she was sneakily making it clear to him that the offer of more money might make her amenable to sex.

Rage at that recollection threatening to engulf her in a rising red mist, Tawny anchored her towel tighter round her slim body and wrenched open the bathroom door in a sudden movement. 'I'm a virgin!' she launched across the room at him in stark condemnation. 'How many virgins do you know who sell themselves for money?'

I am not having this crazy argument, Navarre's clever brain told him soothingly as he cast down the remote control he had used to switch on the business news. She's a lunatic. I've hired a thief and a lunatic…

'I don't know any virgins,' Navarre told her truthfully. 'But that's probably because most of them keep quiet about their inexperience.'

'I don't see why I should keep quiet!' Tawny snapped, tilting her chin in challenge. 'You seem to be convinced that I would do anything for money…but I'm not like that.'

'We're not having this conversation,' Navarre informed her resolutely, stonily centring his attention back on the television screen.

But a flickering image of her entrancing slender profile in a towel with damp ringlets rioting round her small face still stayed inside his head. He didn't pay for sex. That was true. But there had definitely been a moment on that bed when, if he was equally honest, he would have given her just about anything to stay there warm and willing to fulfil his every fantasy. The ache of frustrated desire was with him still. Taking the moral high ground had never felt less satisfying. Even so his naturally suspicious mind kept on ticking. Why was she telling him that she was a virgin? Hadn't he read about some woman selling her virginity on the Internet to the highest bidder? Could Tawny believe that virgins had more sex appeal and value to the average male? Surely she didn't think that he would actually believe that a woman of twenty-three years of age was a total innocent? Did he look that naive and trusting?

Clad in a modestly styled green cocktail dress and impossibly high heels, Tawny descended the stairs by Navarre's side. They pretty much weren't speaking, which felt weird when he insisted on holding her hand. She was looking eagerly around her when Sam came to greet them, ushering them to the fire and the drinks waiting in the Great Hall. Having answered her questions about the old property, he offered them a tour.

The tower house was not as large as it had looked from the air and many of the rooms were rather pokey or awkwardly shaped. But Tawny adored the atmosphere created by the ancient stone walls and fireplaces and she looked at Catrina in surprise when she complained about the difficulty of heating the rooms and the remote location while her husband talked with single-minded enthusiasm about the outdoor pursuits available on the estate. The Victorian extension to the rear of the castle had been recently restored and contained a fabulous ballroom used for parties, modern utilities and staff quarters.

'You haven't been with Navarre long, have you?' Catrina remarked while the men were talking business over by the tall windows. The sun was going down for the day over the views of rolling heathland banded by distant mountains that had a purple hue in the fast-fading light.

Tawny smiled. 'I suppose it shows.'

Catrina sat down beside her. 'It does rather. He's obsessed with his work.'

'Successful men tend to be,' Tawny answered lightly, recalling that her half-sisters often complained about how preoccupied their husbands were with their business interests.

'Navarre will always be more excited about his latest deal than about you,' Catrina opined cattily.

'Oh, I don't think so.' Quite deliberately, Tawny flexed the fingers of the hand that bore the opulent diamond ring and glanced across the room at Navarre, admiring that bold bronzed masculine profile silhouetted against the window. As she turned back to Catrina she caught the other woman treating Navarre to a voracious look of longing. Navarre, she registered belatedly, had lit a fire in the other woman that even her marriage had yet to put out.

'Navarre won't change,' the beautiful brunette forecast thinly. 'He gets bored very easily. No woman ever lasts more than a few weeks in his bed.'

Tawny dealt her companion a calm appraisal. 'I don't begrudge Navarre his years of freedom. Most men eventually settle down with one woman just as he has,' she murmured sweetly. 'What we have together is special.'

'In what way?' Catrina enquired baldly and then she laughed and raised her voice, 'Navarre…what do you find most special about Tawny?'

Sam Coulter frowned, not best pleased to have his discussion interrupted by his wife's facetious question.

'Tawny's joie de vivre is without compare, and her face?' Navarre moved his shapely hands with an elegant eloquence that was unmistakeably French. *'Ca suffit…* enough said. How can one quantify such an elusive quality?'

Unexpectedly, Sam gave his wife a fond smile that softened his craggy features. 'I couldn't have said it better myself. The secret of attraction is that it's impossible to put into words.'

Tawny was hardened to her hostess's little gibes by the end of the evening and grateful that other people would be joining them the following day. Catrina might have been married to Sam Coulter for two years but the brunette was very dissatisfied with her life.

Clad in a silk nightdress rather than her usual pjs, for she was making an effort to stay in her role, Tawny climbed into the wide four-poster bed. 'I used to dream of having a bed like this when I was a child,' she said to combat her discomfiture at Navarre's emergence from the bathroom, his tall, well-built physique bare but for a pair of trendy cotton pyjama bottoms.

He looked absolutely spectacular with his black hair spiky with dampness and a faint shadow of stubble highlighting his carved cheekbones and wide, mobile mouth. He also had an amazing set of pecs and obviously worked out regularly. Her attention skimmed over the cluster of dark curls on his torso and the arrowing line of hair bisecting the flat corrugated muscle of his stomach to disappear below his waistband, and her tummy flipped.

'Full marks for all the questions you asked Sam about the history of Strathmore,' Navarre remarked with stunning cynicism. 'He was charmed by your interest.'

Tawny stiffened. 'I wasn't putting on an act. History was my favourite subject next to art and I've always been fascinated by old buildings. Are you always this distrustful of women?'

Brilliant eyes veiled, Navarre shrugged and got into the other side of the bed. 'Let's say that experience has made me wary.'

'Catrina's still keen on you, isn't she? Is that why you wanted a fake fiancée to bring with you?' she asked abruptly.

'One of the reasons,' Navarre conceded evenly. 'And your presence does at least preclude her from making indiscreet remarks.'

Tawny was suffering from an indisputable need to keep on talking to lessen her discomfiture. 'I have to make a phone call some time tomorrow—'

'No,' Navarre responded immediately.

'I'll go behind your back to make the call if you try to prevent me. It's to my grandmother. I always ring her on Saturdays and she'll worry if she doesn't hear from me,' Tawny told him with spirit. 'You can listen to our conversation if you like.'

Navarre punched a pillow and rested his dark head down. 'I'll consider it.'

Tawny flipped round and leant over him. 'See that you do,' she warned combatively.

Navarre reached out and entwined his long brown fingers into the curling spirals of red hair that were brushing his chest. For a timeless moment his eyes held her as fast as manacles. 'Don't tease—'

Her bosom swelled as her temper surged over the rebuke. 'I *wasn't* teasing!'

'You mean that you didn't tell me you were a virgin to whet my appetite for you?' Navarre derided.

'No, I darned well didn't!' Tawny snapped furiously. 'I only told you in the first place because I thought it would make you understand why I was offended by your assumption that my body has a price tag attached to it!'

Navarre was engaged in studying the pulse flickering at the base of the slim column of her throat and the sweet swelling mounds of her breasts visible through the gaping neckline of the nightdress as she bent over him. Hard as a rock, he was still trying to work out what the price tag might encompass so that he could meet the terms and get much better acquainted with that truly exquisite little body of hers.

'I also thought that my inexperience would be more

likely to put you off,' Tawny admitted, her voice trailing away breathily as she connected with his eyes. 'Let go of my hair, Navarre…'

'Non, ma petite. I'm enjoying the view too much.'

Only then did Tawny register where his attention was resting and, hot with embarrassment, she lifted the hand she had braced on the pillow by his head to press the neckline of her nightdress flat against her chest.

Navarre laughed with rich appreciation. 'Spoilsport!'

Off-balanced by the rapidity of her own movement, Tawny struggled to pull back from him but he tipped her down instead and encircled her mouth with his own, claiming her full lips with a harsh masculine groan of satisfaction. That sensual mouth on hers was an unimaginable pleasure and it awakened a hunger she could not control. Without her quite knowing how it had happened, she found herself lying back against the pillows with a long masculine thigh pinning her in place. Her hands smoothed over his wide brown shoulders, revelling in the muscles flexing taut below his skin. His fingers flexed over the swell of her breast and her spine arched as his thumb rubbed over the straining nipple. Her response was so powerful that it scared her and she jerked away from him.

'This is not happening!' she gasped in consternation. 'We can't—'

'What do I have to do to make it happen?' Navarre asked huskily.

Tawny tensed and then rolled back, ice blue eyes shooting uncertainly to his face. 'What's that supposed to mean?'

Navarre shifted against her hip, making no attempt to conceal the extent of his arousal. 'Whatever it needs to mean to bring about the desired result, *ma petite.* I want you.'

Tawny flushed and imposed space between them. 'Let's forget about this and go to sleep. I'm working for you. And this situation is exactly why working for you should not include the two of us sharing a bed half naked.'

Navarre toyed with the idea of offering her all the diamonds. Just at that moment no price seemed too high. But that would be treating her like a hooker ready to trade sex for profit. She had got her feelings on that message home, he conceded in growling frustration. He scanned her taut little face and then noticed that she was trembling: there was an almost imperceptible shake in her slight body as she lay there. He compressed his stubborn mouth, rolled back to his own side of the bed and switched out the light. She played hot and then cold but he was beginning to consider the idea that it might not be a deliberate policy to fan his desire to even greater heights. What if she really was a virgin? *As if...*

In the darkness tears inched a slow stinging trail down Tawny's cheeks. She felt out of control and out of her depth and she hated it. She had never understood why people made such a fuss about sex until Navarre had kissed her and if he had tried he probably could have taken her to bed right there and then. Unhappily for him he had missed the boat when she was at her most vulnerable and now she knew that Navarre Cazier somehow had that magical something that reduced her usual defences to rubble. Her breasts ached, the area between her legs seemed to ache as well and even blinking back tears she was within an ace of turning back to him and just surrendering to the powerful forces tormenting her body. Stupid hormones, that was what the problem was!

Tawny was still a virgin purely because the right man

had failed to come along. She had never had a serious relationship, had never known the wild highs and lows of emotional attachment aside of an unrequited crush in her schooldays. She had had several boyfriends at college. There had been loads of kisses and laughs and fun outings but nobody who had made her heart stop with a smile or a kiss. She tensed as Navarre thrust back the sheet with a stifled curse and headed into the bathroom. She listened to the shower running and felt guilty, knowing she had responded, knowing she had encouraged him, but finally deciding that he was not suffering any more from the anticlimax of their lovemaking than she was herself. Restraint physically *hurt*.

Early the following morning she wakened and opened her eyes in the dim room to centre them on Navarre. He was poised at the foot of the bed looking gorgeous and incredibly masculine in shooting clothes that fitted his tall, broad-shouldered and lean-hipped physique so well they were probably tailor made. 'What time is it?' she whispered sleepily.

'Go back to sleep—unless you've changed your mind and decided to come shooting?' As Tawny grimaced at the prospect he laughed softly. *'Peut-être pas*...perhaps not. What was that about you not wanting to kill little fluffy birds, *ma petite*?'

'Not my thing,' she agreed, recalling Sam Coulter's dismay at grouse being given such an emotive description.

'Are you joining us for the shooting lunch?'

'I have no idea. I'll be at Catrina's disposal. She mentioned something about a local spa,' Tawny told him ruefully.

'You'll enjoy that.'

'I hate all that grooming stuff. It's so boring. If I was

here on my own I'd be out horse riding or hiking, doing something active—'

'You can ride?' Navarre made no attempt to hide his surprise.

Watching him intently, Tawny nodded. She decided it was that fabulous bone structure that moved him beyond handsome to stunning. 'My grandparents used to live next door to a riding school and I spent several summers working as a groom.'

Navarre sank down on her side of the bed, stretching out long powerful legs. 'You can phone your grandmother this evening before the party.'

'Thank you.' Her soft pink mouth folded into a blinding smile and he gazed down at her animated face in brooding silence.

Navarre ran a forefinger across the back of the pale hand lying on top of the sheet. 'I've been thinking. I may be willing to extend our association.'

Her brow furrowed. 'Meaning?'

'When our business arrangement is complete I may still want to see you.'

His expression told her nothing and she suppressed the leap of hope inside her that told her more than she wanted to know about her own feelings. 'There's no future in us seeing each other,' she replied flatly.

'When I find it a challenge to stay away from a woman, there is definitely a future, *ma petite.*'

'But that future doesn't extend further than the nearest bed.'

'Don't all affairs begin the same way?' Navarre traded.

And he was *so* right that once again she was tempted to slap him. She didn't want to want him the way she did because such treacherous feelings offended her pride and her intelligence. Yet here she was already imagining how she might lie back in readiness as he pushed aside the sheet and shed his clothes to join her in the bed. Her mind was out of her control. Desire was like a scream buried deep inside her, longing and frantically searching for an escape. Her brain might want to wonder where the relationship could possibly go after fulfillment, but her body cared only that the fulfilment took place.

'Tonight, *ma petite*…I would like to make you mine and you will have no regrets,' Navarre purred, stroking his fingertips delicately along the taut line of her full lower lip, sending wicked little markers of heat travelling to every secret part of her as she thought helplessly of that mouth on hers, those sure, skilled hands, that strong, hard body. She couldn't breathe for excitement.

The shooting lunch was delivered to the men on the moors while those women who had no taste for the sport joined Catrina and Tawny for a more civilised repast at the castle. During that meal, liberally accompanied by fine wine, celebrity and designer names were dropped repeatedly as well as descriptions of fabulous gifts, insanely expensive shopping trips and impossibly luxurious holidays with each woman clearly determined to outdo the next. It was all highly competitive stuff and Tawny hated it, finding the trip to the spa something of a relief, for at least everyone was in separate cubicles and she no longer had to try to fit in by putting on an act.

'You and Navarre won't last,' Catrina informed Tawny confidently as they were driven back to Strathmore.

'Why do you think that?'

'Navarre will get bored and move on, just as he did with me,' Catrina warned. 'I was once in love with him too. I've seen your eyes follow him round the room. When he ditches you, I warn you…it'll hurt like hell.'

'He's not going to ditch me,' Tawny declared between

clenched teeth, wondering if her eyes did follow Navarre round the room. It was an image that mortified her. It was also unnerving that she could be unconscious of her own behaviour around him.

When she entered the bedroom it was a shock to glance through the open bathroom door and see Navarre already standing there naked as he towelled his hair dry. Her face burning, she averted her eyes from that thought-provoking view and went over to the wardrobe to extract the evening dress she planned to wear—a shimmering gold gown that complimented her auburn hair and fair complexion. Her palms were damp. He was gorgeous, stripped he was even more gorgeous. *Tonight...I would like to make you mine.* She shivered at the memory of the words that had burned at the back of her mind throughout the day, full of seductive promise and threatening her self-discipline. For never before had Tawny wanted a man as she wanted Navarre Cazier—with a deep visceral need as primitive as it was fierce.

The towel looped round his narrow hips Navarre strolled out and tossed her mobile phone down on the bed. 'Ring your grandmother,' he told her.

She switched on her phone but there was no reception and after a fruitless moment or two of pacing in an attempt to pick up a signal at the window, Navarre handed her his phone. 'Use mine.'

Celestine answered the call immediately. 'I tried to ring you yesterday but I couldn't get through. I thought you might be too busy to ring, *ma chérie*. And on a Friday evening that would be good news,' the old lady told her chirpily. 'It would mean you had a date which would please me enormously.'

'I am going to a party tonight,' Tawny told her, knowing how much her grandmother would enjoy that news. 'Why were you trying to ring me?'

'A friend of yours called me, said she was trying desperately to get in touch but that you weren't answering your phone. It was that work friend of yours, Julie.'

'Oh…forget about it, it wouldn't have been important.' Tawny felt her skin turn clammy as she wondered what Julie was after now. How dared she disturb her grandmother's peace by phoning her? And where on earth had she got Celestine's number from? It could only have been from Tawny's personnel file, which also meant that Julie had used her computer skills to go snooping again. Had her calculating former friend hoped that the old lady might have information about where Tawny and Navarre had gone after leaving the hotel?

'What are you wearing to the party?' Celestine asked, eager for a description.

And Tawny really pushed the boat out with the details, for the old lady adored finery. Indeed Tawny would have loved to tell Celestine about the Golden Movie Awards and Tia Castelli and her husband, not to mention the castle she was currently staying in, but she did not dare to breathe a word of what Navarre probably considered to be confidential information. Instead she caught up with her grandmother's small daily doings and she slowly began to relax in the reassuring warmth of the old lady's chatter. Unlike her daughter, Susan, Celestine was a very happy personality, who always looked on the bright side of life.

'You seem very close to your grandmother,' Navarre commented as Tawny returned his phone to him.

'She's a darling,' Tawny said fondly, gathering up stuff to take into the en suite with her, mindful of the fact she had been accused of being a tease and determined not to give him further cause to believe that she was actively encouraging his interest.

'What about your mother?'

Tawny paused with her back still turned to him and tried not to wince. 'Relations are a little cool between us at present,' she admitted, opting for honesty.

Mother and daughter were still speaking but things had been said during that last confrontation that would probably never be forgotten, Tawny reflected painfully. Tawny could not forget being told what a drastic disappointment she was to her mother. But then mother and child had always rubbed each other up the wrong way. Tawny had refused to dye her red hair brown when her mother suggested it and had sulked when a padded bra was helpfully presented to her. She had done well in the wrong subjects at school. She had declined to train for a business career and as a result had failed to attain the salary or status that her mother equated with success. And finally and unforgivably on Susan's terms, Tawny had failed to make the most of her entrée into her half-sisters' wealthy world where with some effort she might have met the sort of man her mother would have viewed as an eligible partner. Her recent work as a chambermaid had been the proverbial last straw in her dissatisfied mother's eyes. No, Tawny would never be a daughter whom Susan felt she could boast about with her cronies.

Supressing those unhappy memories of her continuing inability to measure up to parental expectations, Tawny set about doing her make-up. She had watched the make-up artist who had done her face for the Golden Awards carefully and she used eyeliner and gold sparkly shadow with a heavier hand than usual, outlining her lips with a rich strawberry-coloured gloss. The dress had an inner corset for shape and support and she had to breathe in hard and swivel it round to put it on without help. Toting her cosmetic bag, she emerged from the bathroom.

Navarre fell still to look at her and it was one of those very rare occasions when he spoke without forethought. 'Your skin and hair look amazing in that colour.'

'Thank you.' Suddenly shy of him but with a warm feeling coiled up inside her, Tawny turned to the dressing table to put on the diamond earrings and bracelet. Even while she did so she searched out his reflection in the mirror, savouring the sight of him in a contemporary charcoal-grey designer suit. So tall, dark and sophisticated, so wonderfully handsome, Navarre Cazier was the ultimate fantasy male…at that point her thoughts screeched to a sudden stricken halt.

Why was she thinking of him like that? It was past time that she reminded herself that absolutely everything, from the fancy clothes she wore to her supposed relationship with Navarre Cazier, was a giant sham. She felt her upbeat spirits dive bomb. After all, she was not living the fairy tale in a romantic castle with a rich handsome man, she was *faking* it every step of the way. It was a timely recollection.

CHAPTER SIX

TOWARDS midnight, Navarre strode into the ballroom, his keen gaze skimming through the knots of guests until it came to rest on Tawny.

In the subdued light Tawny shimmered like a golden goddess, red hair vibrant, diamonds sparkling, her lovely face full of animation as she looked up at the tall blond man talking to her with a hand clamped to her waist. Navarre recognised her companion immediately: Tor Henson, a wealthy banker very popular with women. Although Navarre had been absent for most of the evening while he talked business with Sam Coulter and had left Tawny very much to her own devices, he was not pleased to see her looking so well entertained. She had not gone without amusement; she had, it seemed, simply *replaced* him. A rare burst of anger ripped through Navarre's big frame, cutting through his powerful self-discipline with disorientating speed and efficiency. His strong white teeth ground together as he crossed the floor to join them.

'*Je suis désolé...*' Navarre began to apologise to Tawny for his prolonged absence.

At the sound of his voice, Tawny whirled round, her expression telegraphing equal amounts of relief and annoyance. 'Where have you been all this time?'

'I gather you don't read the business papers,' Tor Henson

remarked with a knowing glance in Navarre's direction for recent revealing movements on the stock market had hinted that major change could be in store for Sam Coulter's business empire.

Navarre captured a slender white hand in his and held it fast. He wanted to haul her away from Henson and take her upstairs to spread her across their bed, a primal prompting that he dimly understood was born of a rage unlike anything he had ever experienced. 'Thank you for looking after her for me, Tor,' he murmured with glacial courtesy.

'I'm not a child you left behind in need of care and protection!' Tawny objected, ice-blue eyes stormy as he ignored the comment and virtually dragged her onto the dance floor with him. 'Why are you behaving like this, Navarre? Why are you acting like I've done something wrong?'

'Haven't you? If I leave you alone for five minutes I come back to find you flirting with another man!' he censured with icy derision, splaying long sure fingers to her spine to draw her closer to his hard, powerful body than she wanted to be at that moment.

The scent of him, clean, warm and male, was in her nostrils and she fought the aphrodisiac effect that proximity awakened in her treacherous body. 'You left me alone for *two hours*!'

'Was it too much for me to expect you to be waiting quietly where I left you?' Navarre prompted shortly, in no mood to be reasonable.

'Yes, I'm not an umbrella you overlooked and I *wasn't* flirting with Tor! We were simply talking. He knows I'm engaged,' Tawny snapped up at him, tempestuous in her own self-defence.

'Tor would get a kick out of bedding another man's fiancée, *n'est-ce pas*?'

She saw the genuine anger in his gaze and the hard-edged tension in his superb bone structure. 'You're jealous,' she registered in wide-eyed surprise, astonished that she could have that much power over him.

His beautiful mouth took on a contemptuous curve. 'Of course I'm not jealous. Why would I be jealous? We're not really engaged,' he reminded her very drily.

But Tawny was not so easily deflected from an opinion once she had formed it. 'Maybe you're naturally the possessive type in relationships... You definitely didn't like seeing me enjoy myself in another man's company. But have you any idea how insulting it is for you to insinuate that I might go off and shag some guy I hardly know?'

'I'd have bedded you within five minutes of meeting you, *ma petite*,' Navarre confided with a roughened edge to his voice, holding her so close to his body that she could feel the effect her closeness was having on him and warmth pooled in the pit of her tummy in response to his urgent male sexuality.

'I'm not like you—I would never have agreed to that!' Tawny proclaimed heatedly, stretching up on tiptoe to deliver that news as close to his ear as she could reach.

'*Mais non*...I can be very persuasive.' Navarre laced long deft fingers into her tumbling curls to hold her steady while he bent his mouth to hers, his breath fanning her cheek. He was no fan of public displays but in that instant he was controlled by a driving atavistic need to mark her as his so that no other man would dare to approach her again. He crushed her succulent lips apart and tasted her with uninhibited hunger, not once but over and over again until she shuddered against him, her slight body vibrating like a tuning fork in response to his passion.

With reluctance, Navarre dragged his mouth from hers, scanned her rapt face and urged her towards the exit. 'Let's go.'

Go where? she almost asked, even though she knew where. She could not find the breath or the will to argue. After all, she *wanted* to be alone with him. She wanted him to kiss her again, she had never wanted anything more, and where once the presence of others might have acted as a welcome control exercise, this time around it was an annoyance. Objections lay low in the back of her mind, crushed out of existence by the fierce longing rippling through her in seductive waves.

'This has to be a beginning, not an end,' Navarre declared, thrusting shut the door of the bedroom.

Tawny didn't want him to talk, she only wanted him to kiss her. As long as he was kissing her she didn't have to think and wonder about whether or not she was making a mistake. Even worse, the wanting was so visceral that she could not stand against the force of it.

He unzipped her gown, ran his fingers smoothly down her slender spine and flipped loose her bra. She shivered, electrified with anticipation, knees turning to water as his hands rose to cup the swelling mounds of her breasts and massage the achingly sensitive nipples. He touched her exactly as she wanted to be touched. She had never dreamt that desire might leave her so weak that it was a challenge to stay upright, but now as she leant back against him and struggled simply to get oxygen into her lungs she was learning the lesson. She turned round in the circle of his arms and kissed him, hands closing into his jacket and pushing it off his broad shoulders. For an instant he stepped back, shedding the jacket, freeing his shirt from his waistband to unbutton it.

Just looking at him made her mouth run dry. A muscular bronzed section of hair-roughened torso was visible between the parted edges of his shirt and she wanted to touch, explore, *taste*...it was as though he had got under her skin and changed her from inside out, teaching her to crave what she had never even thought of before. Now she didn't just think, she acted. She raised her hands to that hard flat abdomen and let her palms glide up over the corrugated muscles to discover the warm skin and revel shamelessly in the way that her touch made him tense and roughly snatch his breath in.

Navarre lifted her free of her gown and she stood there, feeling alarmingly naked in only her high heels and a flimsy pair of white silk knickers. He sank down on the side of the bed and drew her down between his spread thighs, nibbling sensuously at her swollen lower lip while he eased his hand beneath the silk and rubbed the most sensitive spot of all with a skill and rhythm that provoked a series of gasps from her throat.

'I want you naked, *ma petite*...' he breathed thickly as he slid down her knickers and removed them, flipping off her shoes with the careless casual skill of a man practised at undressing women. 'And then I want you every way I can have you.'

Navarre bent her back over his arm and brought his mouth down hungrily on the proud pouting tip of an engorged nipple, drawing on the sensitised bud while his hand continued to explore the most sensitive part of her. Her fingers dug into his black cropped hair as he caressed her, a sharp arrow of need slivering through her. 'You're wearing too many clothes,' she told him shakily.

He settled her down on the bed and stood over her stripping. The shirt and the trousers were followed by his boxers. She had never seen a man naked and aroused before and she couldn't take her eyes off the long thick steel of

his bold length. She was both intimidated and aroused by
the size of him. Her face hot with self-consciousness, she
scrabbled below the covers, her entire body tingling with
extra-sensory awareness. He tossed foil-wrapped condoms
down on top of the bedside cabinet and slid in beside her,
so hot and hard and strong that he sent a wave of energis-
ing desire through her the instant she came into contact
with his very male physique.

He detached the diamond earrings still dangling from
her ears and set them aside, brilliant green eyes locked to
her anxious face. 'What's wrong?'

As he leant down to her she closed her arms round his
neck and kissed him, needing the oblivion of passion to
feel secure, trembling as the hot hardness of his muscular
body connected with hers. He lowered his tousled dark
head and kissed her breasts, teasing her straining nipples
with his tongue and pulling on the oversensitive buds until
her hips squirmed in frustration on the mattress. Only then
did he touch her where she most needed to be touched.
He explored the silken warmth between her thighs with
deft fingers and then he subjected that tender flesh to his
mouth. She was unprepared for that ultimate intimacy and
she jerked away in shock and tried to withdraw from it,
but he closed his hands on her hips and held her fast until
sensation spread like wildfire at the heart of her and en-
trapped her as surely as a prison cell. She wanted more
of that wild, intoxicating feeling, she couldn't help wanting *more;* she was a slave to sensation. The hunger rose
like a great white roar inside her, bypassing her every
attempt to control it. Her body was shaking and the constricted knot at her core was notching tighter and tighter
until the pleasure just rose in a huge overwhelming tide
and engulfed her, leaving her shuddering and crying out
in reaction.

'Navarre...' she whispered jaggedly.

'You liked that, *ma petite,*' he husked with all the satisfaction of a man who knew he had given a woman unimaginable pleasure.

Numbly she nodded, every reaction slowed down. It had never occurred to her that her body could feel anything that intensely and in the stunned aftermath of that climax she was only dimly aware that he was reaching for a condom, and then he was reaching for her again. Her body was pliant with obedience, already trained to expect pleasure from him, and as he pushed back her thighs and rose over her she quivered with the awareness of him hard and bold and alien at her tiny entrance, but there was a sense of trust as well.

'You're so tight,' he groaned with pleasure as he sank into her tender channel with controlled care.

A startled sound somewhere between a gasp and a cry was wrenched from her as he broke through the fragile barrier of her inexperience. Her body flinched and he stilled in the act of possession, staring down at her with scorching green eyes fringed by black, recognising in that heightened instant of awareness that he was the only lover she had ever had. 'You were telling me the truth...'

'Women aren't all liars,' Tawny breathed, shuddering as he drove all the way home to the heart of her body.

Immersed in the molten heat of her, Navarre was fighting for control, leaning down to crush her mouth under his again and breathe in the luscious scent of her skin. She felt so good, she smelt even better. He shifted his lean hips and thrust, wanting to take it slow and easy but struggling against his explosive level of arousal with every second that passed. Tawny arched up into him with a whimper of encouragement and he sank deeper, harder and suddenly he couldn't hold back any more against the elemental storm of need riding him. Holding her firmly, he eased back until he had almost withdrawn and then he thrust back into her with seductive force. The pleasure was building inside Tawny again in a wild surge of sensation that scooped her up and left her defenceless. His provocative rhythm heightened every feeling to an unbearable level and then all of a sudden it was as if a blinding white light exploded inside her, heat and hunger coalescing in a fierce fiery orgasm.

In the heady, dizzy aftermath she thought she might never move again, for her limbs felt weighted to the bed. She was incredibly grateful that she had chosen him as her lover, for he had made it extraordinary and she knew that was rare for a first experience. She hugged him tight, pressed her lips to a smooth brown shoulder, able to reason in only the most simplistic of ways, her brain on shutdown. He rolled back from her and headed for the bathroom.

It crossed her mind that barely a week earlier he had been a billionaire businessman and hotel guest to her. Now what was he? A very desirable lover who could also be absolutely infuriating and the guy who was *paying* her to fake being his fiancée. As cruel reality kicked in Tawny flinched from it, alarmed that she could have forgotten the financial nature of their agreement. It was a complication, but not one that couldn't be handled with the right attitude on both sides, she reasoned frantically, determined to stay optimistic rather than lash herself with pointless regrets. What was done was done. He was her lover now.

Navarre reappeared from the bathroom and strolled back to the bed. She had fallen sound asleep, a tangle of rich red curls lying partially across her perfect profile, a hand tucked childishly below her cheek. That fast he wanted her again and the strength of that desire disturbed him. Desire was wonderful as long as it stayed within certain acceptable bounds. Uninhibited hunger that threatened his control was not his style at all, for it was more likely to add complications to a life he preferred to keep smooth and untrammelled, a soothing contrast to his troubled and changeable childhood years. At heart he would always be an unrepentant loner and he thought it unlikely that he would change, for everything from his birth to his challenging adolescence had conspired to make him what he was. He had seduced her, though, he knew he had, and taking her virginity had roused the strangest protective instinct inside him. Even so he was equally aware that he could not afford to forget that she was a thief whose loyalty was for sale to the highest bidder...

Tawny wakened while it was still dark, immediately conscious of the new tenderness between her thighs and the ache of unfamiliar muscles. Instantly memory flooded back and she slid quiet as a wraith from the bed, padding across the carpet to the bathroom. Although it was almost four in the morning she ran a warm bath and settled into the soothing water to hug her knees and regroup. She had slept with Navarre Cazier and it had been amazing.

She didn't want to get all introspective and female about what had happened between them, for common sense told her that such powerful physical attraction as theirs generally only led to one conclusion. She especially didn't want to think about the feelings he was beginning to awaken inside her: the stab of intense satisfaction she had felt once she had registered that he was jealous of that banker's interest in her, the sense of achievement when he listened to her and laughed, the walking-on-air sensation when he admired her appearance, her unreserved delight in discovering that unashamed passion of his, which was so at variance with his cool, unemotional façade.

She knew without being told that she was walking a dangerous line. She had abandoned her defences and taken the kind of risk she had never taken before. Yet wouldn't she do it again given the chance to feel what he had made her feel? It wasn't just physical either. It was more that astonishing sense of feeling insanely alive for the first time ever, that wondrous sense of connection to another human being. Still lost in her thoughts, Tawny patted herself dry with a fleecy towel. She decided that she wasn't going to act the coward and bail on the experience just because it was unlikely to give her a happy ending. She was only twenty-three years old, she reminded herself doggedly, way too young to be worrying about needing a happy ending with a man. She tiptoed back to bed, eased below the cool sheets, and when a long masculine arm stretched out as though to retrieve her and tugged her close she went willingly into that embrace.

She loved the scent of his skin, clean and male laced with an evocative hint of designer cologne. She breathed in that already familiar scent as though it were an addictive drug, her fingers fanning out across his flat stomach as she shifted position. She adored being so close to him because she was very much aware that when he was awake he was not a physically or verbally demonstrative man likely to make her feel secure with displays of affection or appreciation. Her hand smoothed possessively down a hair-roughened thigh and he released a drowsy groan of approval.

In the darkness a cheeky smile curved her generous mouth when she discovered that even asleep he was aroused and ready for action. Wide awake now and unashamedly keen to experiment she became a little more daring and her fingertips carefully traced the steely length of his shaft. With a muffled sound of appreciation Navarre shifted position and began to carry out his own reconnaissance. She was stunned by how fast her body reacted to his sleepy caresses with her nipples stiffening into instant tingling life while heat and moisture surged between her legs. Muttering a driven French imprecation, he pinned her beneath him, his hands suddenly hard with urgency as he pushed between her slender thighs and drove hungrily into her yielding body again. Instinctively she arched up to him to ease the angle of his entrance and he ground his body deeper into hers with a guttural sound of pleasure. He moved slowly and provocatively in a strong sensual rhythm. Her lips parted as she breathed in urgent gasps, clinging to his broad shoulders as the glorious pressure began to build and build within her. She came apart in an explosive climax as his magnificent body shuddered to the same crest with her. A glorious tide of exquisite sensation cascaded through her spent body.

In an abrupt movement, Navarre freed himself of her hands and rolled away from her to switch on the lights. Blinded by the sudden illumination, Tawny blinked in bewilderment.

'*Merde alors!* Was this a planned seduction?' Navarre flung at her furiously, a powerfully intimidating figure against the pale bedding as she peered at him from narrowed eyes. 'To be followed by a meticulously planned conception?'

Utterly bemused by that accusation, Tawny pushed herself up against the tumbled pillows with frantic hands. 'What on earth are you talking about? Seduction, for heaven's sake?'

'We just had sex without a condom!' Navarre fired at her in condemnation.

'Oh…my…goodness,' Tawny framed in sudden comprehension, her skin turning clammy in shock. 'I didn't think of that—'

'Didn't you? You woke me out of a sound sleep to make love to you. A lot of men would overlook precautions in the excitement of the moment!'

'You can't seriously think I deliberately tempted you into sex while you were half asleep in the hope that you would forget to use a condom?' Tawny told him roundly, colour burnishing her cheeks.

'Why wouldn't I think that? I once caught a woman in the act of puncturing a condom in the hope of conceiving a child without my knowledge!' Navarre ground out in contemptuous rebuttal. 'Why should you be any different? Wealthy men are always targets for a fertile woman. When a man fathers a child by a woman he's bound to support her and her offspring for a couple of decades!'

'I feel sorry for you,' Tawny breathed tightly, her small face stony with self-control. 'It must be crippling to be as suspicious of other human beings as you are. Everybody is not out to con you or make money out of you, Navarre!'

'I've already caught you thieving from me,' Navarre reminded her icily. 'So forgive me for not being impressed by your claim to be morally superior.'

In the wake of that exchange, Tawny had lost every scrap of her natural colour. She had not required that final lowering reminder of how she had attempted to make off with his laptop. Lying there naked with her body still damp and aching from his lovemaking, she felt like the worst kind of whore. He had to despise her to be so suspicious of her motives that even an act of lovemaking could be regarded as a potential attempt to rip him off. It was a brutal wake-up call to the reality that, while she had moved on from the humiliation of their first meeting, his opinion of her was still that of a calculating little thief without morals. Sleeping with her had not changed his outlook and what a fool she had been to believe otherwise. Had he really caught a woman damaging contraception in the hope of falling pregnant by him? She was appalled. No wonder he was such a cynic if that was the sort of woman he was accustomed to having in his bed.

'We'll discuss this tomorrow,' Navarre breathed curtly as he doused the lights again.

'Let's not,' she said woodenly, turning on her side so that her back was turned to him. 'My system's very irregular—I'm pretty sure we won't have anything to worry about.'

But in spite of that breezy assurance she was still lying wide awake and worrying long after the deep even sound of his breathing had alerted her to the fact that he had gone back to sleep. Why, oh, why had she chosen to overlook the fact that he was paying her thousands of pounds to pretend to be his fiancée? Money problems always changed the nature of relationships, she thought wretchedly. The cash angle had put a wall between them. It was the single biggest difference between them, that reminder that he was rich and she was poor, never mind the truth that he had found her apparently stealing from him. Why had she believed that she could handle sex in such an unequal relationship? He had just proven how wrong that conviction could be.

By the time that dawn was lightening the darkness behind the curtains, Tawny had had enough of lying in the bed as still as a corpse. She got up again as quietly as she could and decided that she could go out for a walk without disturbing the entire household. The only clothes of her own that she had packed were her skinny jeans and skeleton tee. She put them on, teaming them with a woollen jacket with a velvet collar and a pair of laced boots. She

crept out of the room and downstairs and was soon out in
the fresh air experiencing a deep abiding sense of relief
and a desperate need to reclaim her freedom.

The charade of their engagement would shortly be over,
she told herself soothingly. Soon she would be back home
and out searching for another job. Hopefully the turmoil of
overexcited feelings that she was currently feeling would
vanish along with Navarre Cazier…

CHAPTER SEVEN

'Tawny! I saw you walking up the drive from the window. Navarre will be relieved—he's been looking everywhere for you!' Catrina told her brightly as Tawny mounted the front steps, muddy and windblown and embarrassed by her long absence and untidy appearance. It occurred to her that her hostess had never smiled at her with such welcoming warmth before but she was in too troubled a state of mind to be suspicious.

'I went out for a walk and got a bit lost,' Tawny muttered apologetically. 'Have I missed breakfast?'

'No. Navarre was worried that you had seen that story in the newspapers and been upset by it…it's so embarrassing when these things happen when you're away from home,' Catrina commented with unconvincing sympathy.

Tawny had frozen in the hallway. 'What newspaper story?'

Catrina helpfully passed her the tabloid newspaper she was already clutching in readiness. 'I'll have breakfast sent up to your room if you like.'

Tawny opened the paper and there it was: *Billionaire and Maid?* There was a beaming picture of Julie, her self-elected best friend, who she could only assume had spilled her guts to a reporter for cash. She supposed that in the absence of any more colourful story about Navarre going with an engagement that had to be a fake must have seemed worthwhile. Almost everything she had ever told Julie that could be given the right twist was there in black and white from Tawny's brief time in foster care as a child to the recent mysterious breakdown in family relations. Oh, yes, *and* what Julie described as Tawny's frantic determination to meet and marry a rich man through her work…*yes,* Julie had had to find an angle to make Tawny sound more interesting and that was the angle she had chosen. Tawny was a rampant gold-digger in search of a meal ticket. According to Julie Tawny had used her employment as a chambermaid to sleep with several wealthy guests in a search for one who would offer to take her away from cleaning and spoil her to death with his money for ever. What insane rubbish! Tawny thought furiously, wondering who on earth would believe such nonsense.

'Wouldn't you prefer to have your breakfast in your room?' Catrina Coulter prompted expectantly.

'Have all the guests seen this?' Tawny enquired.

Catrina gave her a sympathetic glance as unconvincing as her earlier smile. 'Probably…'

'I'll be eating downstairs,' Tawny announced, folding the paper and tucking it casually below one arm to march into the lofty-ceilinged dining room with her bright head held high and a martial glint in her gaze. A moment too late she recalled that her hair was in a wild tangle and her jeans spattered with mud, but she had to tough out that knowledge because her fellow guests turned as one to watch her progress down the length of the long table towards the empty chair beside Navarre.

Navarre, sleek and sexy in a striped shirt and a pair of designer chinos, stood up as she approached and spun out the chair for her. Inside, her body hummed as if an engine had been switched on. Her eyes, with an alacrity all their own, darted over him, taking in the cropped black hair, the brilliant green eyes and the dark shadow that told her he hadn't shaved since the night before. And it was no use, in spite of the fact that she was furious with him the fact that he was drop-dead gorgeous triumphed and she blushed with awareness, her heartbeat quickening in time with her pulse as she sank down into the seat.

'I'll get you something to eat,' Navarre offered, vaulting upright to stride across to the side table laden with lidded dishes laid out on hot plates for guests to serve themselves.

Surprised that he was giving her that amount of attention, Tawny watched him heap a dining plate as high as if he were feeding half the table instead of just one skinny redhead and bring it back to her with positive ceremony.

'You must've walked miles…you have to be starving,' he pointed out when she gaped at the amount of food he had put on the plate.

Trying not to laugh at the shocked appraisal of the blonde with a health conscious plate of fresh fruit opposite, Tawny began to butter her first slice of toast. 'I walked miles more than I planned. I'm afraid I found myself on boggy ground and got lost and very muddy. I ended up having to walk along the road to find my way back here. I shouldn't have gone so far without a map,' she confided breathlessly as he poured her coffee for her.

Tawny sugared her coffee while wondering why Navarre, who had hurt her so much just hours earlier, was now being so kind and attentive. Had he not read the same newspaper spread? Didn't he realise that she could only have tried to steal his laptop to grab his attention and then bonk his brains out in the hope that great sex would make him her meal ticket for life? It was obvious that the rest of the guests had read the newspaper. She was painfully conscious that everyone else at the table was watching her and Navarre closely, clearly hoping for some gossipy titbit or some sign that he was going to dump her right there and then. Thanks to her erstwhile friend she had been depicted in print as a mercenary chambermaid who had seduced innocent hotel guests in an effort to entrap a wealthy husband.

Navarre watched Tawny eat a cooked breakfast with the enthusiasm of a woman who had not seen food for a month. He was relieved to see that a scurrilous article in a downmarket newspaper had not detracted from her appetite. Above all things Navarre admired courage and the courage she had displayed in choosing to take her breakfast as normal in front of an inquisitive audience hugely impressed him. Few women would have kept their cool in such an embarrassing situation.

'I have to pack,' she told him prosaically once she had finished her second cup of coffee.

In the mood Tawny was in the packing did not take long. Ten minutes and it was done. Navarre walked into the room just as she lowered the case to the floor. She would have offered to do his packing as well just to keep busy but he had already taken care of the task. She folded her arms defensively.

'We should talk before the helicopter arrives,' Navarre imparted flatly. 'We'll be staying in another hotel for the next couple of days, after which I will let you return to your life. I'll be tied up with business once we return to London.'

Tawny said nothing. Another hotel, mercifully not the one where she had once been employed. It was clear that their arrangement would soon have run its course. So much for his declaration the night before that their intimacy was to be a beginning and not an end! She had fallen for a line, it seemed.

Navarre studied her with sardonic cool. 'I hope you won't prove to be pregnant.'

Tawny stiffened. 'I hope so too, particularly because it would be my life which would be majorly screwed up by that development.'

'It would screw up *both* our lives,' Navarre countered grimly.

Tawny resisted the urge to challenge that statement. She was too well aware as a child born to a single mother that her birth had made little impact on her own father's life. Monty Blake had paid the court-ordered minimum towards Tawny's upkeep and that was all. He had not taken an interest in her. He had not invited her to visit him, his second wife and their family. Indeed he had deliberately excluded Tawny from family occasions. When her mother had chosen to continue her pregnancy against his wishes he had hit back by doing everything he could to ignore Tawny's existence. Had her older half-sisters not chosen to look her up when she was a teenaged schoolgirl, Tawny would never have got to know them either. Certainly she would never have had the confidence to approach either Bee or Zara on her own behalf when their father had made her feel so very unworthy of his affection. And that hurtful feeling of not being good enough to be an acceptable daughter had dogged her all her life.

That evening, Tawny was once again ensconced in a hotel suite with only Elise for company. Navarre had chatted at length in Italian to someone on the phone while the car travelled slowly through the London traffic and as soon as they checked into the hotel he had gone out again. This time around, however, the suite Navarre had taken had *two* bedrooms. She was not expected to sleep on the sofa or share his bed. Their little fling was over. She reminded herself of the unjust accusation he had made before dawn that same day, relived her fury and hurt at that charge and told herself that it was only sensible to avoid further intimacy and misunderstanding. While Elise watched television Tawny worked through her emotions with the help of her sketch pad, drawing little cartoon vignettes of her rocky relationship with Navarre.

Navarre came back just after midnight, exchanging a word or two with Elise as she raised herself sleepily from the sofa, switched off the television and bid him goodnight. Left alone, he lifted Tawny's sketch pad. The Frenchman, it said on the first page, and there he was in all his cartoon glory, leching at the stylist while pretending to admire Tawny in her evening dress. He leafed through page after page of caricatures and laughter shook him, for she had a quirky sense of humour and he could only hope that the one depicting Catrina as a man-eating piranha fish never made it into the public eye, for Sam would be mortally offended at the insult to his wife. His supreme indifference to the newspaper revelations about her background as a maid was immortalised in print as she showed him choosing to fret instead about how much fried food the English ate at breakfast time. Did she really see him as that insensitive? Admittedly he avoided getting up close and personal on an emotional front with women, for time and experience had taught him that that was unwise if he had no long-term intentions.

'Oh, you're back…' Tawny emerged from her bedroom, clad in her pyjamas, which had little monkeys etched all over the trousers and a big monkey on the front of the camisole, none of which detracted in the slightest from his awareness of the firm swell of her breasts and the lush prominence of her nipples pushing against the thin clinging cotton. 'I'm thirsty.'

He watched as she padded drowsily over to the kitchenette in one corner to run the cold tap and extract a glass from a cupboard. He was entranced by the smallness of her waist and the generous fullness of her derriere beneath the cotton: she was *all* woman in the curve department in spite of her slender build. His groin tightened as he remembered the feel of her hips in his hands and the hot tight grip of her beneath him. He crushed that lingering memory, fought to rise above it and concentrate instead on the divisive issues that kept his desire within acceptable boundaries.

'Why did you take my laptop that day?' he demanded without warning.

Tawny almost dropped the moisture-beaded glass she was holding. 'I told you why. I thought you'd taken nude photos of my friend and refused to delete them. She told me that if I got it for her she would wipe them. I believed her—at the time I trusted her as a good friend but I realised afterwards that she was lying to me and hoping to make money out of it. She was working for a journalist who wanted information on you and your activities.'

'I know,' Navarre volunteered, startling her. 'I had Julie checked out—'

'And you didn't think to mention that to me?'

'I have no proof that you weren't in it for a profit with her, *ma petite*.'

'No, obviously I would think that it would be much more profitable to get pregnant with a child you don't want so that I could be lumbered with its sole care for the next twenty years!' Tawny sizzled back.

'I didn't realise that you'd once been in a foster home as well,' Navarre remarked, carefully sidestepping her emotive comeback, believing it to be the wrong time for that conversation. 'You didn't mention it when I admitted my own experiences.'

'Obviously you read every line of that newspaper article,' Tawny snapped defensively. 'But I was only in foster care for a few months and as soon as my grandparents found out where I was they offered to take me. When I was a toddler my mother hit a rough patch when she was drinking too much and I was put into care. But she overcame her problems so that I was able to live with her again.'

'Clearly you respect your mother for that achievement, so why are you at odds with her now?'

At that blunt question, Tawny paled, for the newspaper article had not clarified that situation. 'My grandfather's will,' she explained with a rueful jerk of a slim shoulder that betrayed her eagerness to forget that unpleasant reality. 'My grandparents owned and lived in a cottage in a village where my grandmother was very happy. When my grandfather died he left half of it to his wife and the other half to his only child, my mother. My mother made my grandmother sell her home so that she could collect on her share.'

Navarre was frowning. 'And you disapproved?'

'Of course I did. My grandmother was devastated by the loss of her home so soon after she had lost her husband. It was cruel. I understood that my mother has always had a struggle to survive and had never owned her own home but I still think what she did was wrong. I tried to dissuade her from forcing Gran to sell up but she wouldn't listen. Her boyfriend had more influence over her than I had,' Tawny admitted unhappily. 'As far as Mum was concerned Grandad might have been Gran's husband but he had also been her father and she had rights too. She put her own rights first, so the house was sold and Gran, who had always been so good to us both, moved into a retirement village where—I have to admit—she's quite happy.'

'Your mother gave way to temptation and she has to live with that. At least your grandmother had sufficient funds left after the division of property to move somewhere she liked.'

Tawny said nothing. She had seen no sign that her mother was suffering from an uneasy conscience and, having put all that she possessed into purchasing her new apartment, Celestine's current lifestyle was seriously underfunded. But Tawny believed that subjecting the old lady to the stress of changing to more affordable accommodation would be downright dangerous, for Celestine had already suffered one heart attack. The upheaval of another house move might well kill her.

'I'd better get back to bed.' But instead Tawny hovered, her gaze welded to the stunning eyes above his well-defined cheekbones, the beautiful wilful line of his passionate mouth.

'I want to go there with you, *ma petite*,' Navarre admitted in his dark, distinctively accented drawl.

As if a naked flame had burned her skin, Tawny spun on her heel and went straight back into her bedroom, closing the door with a definitive little snap behind her. She flung herself back below the duvet, tears of frustration stinging her eyes, her body switching onto all systems go at the very thought of him in the same bed again. Stupid, silly woman that she was, she craved the chance to be with him again!

Navarre had just emerged from a long cooling shower when Tia phoned him. She wanted him to bring Tawny to a weekend party she and Luke were staging on a yacht in the Med. He rarely said no to the beautiful actress but he said it this time, knowing that it would be wiser to sever all ties with his pretend fiancée rather than draw her deeper into Tia's glitzy world. Mixing business, pleasure and dark secrets could not work for long. He would pay Tawny for her time and draw a line under the episode: it was the safest option. He refused to consider the possibility that she might fall pregnant. If it happened he would deal with it, but he wouldn't lose sleep worrying about it beforehand.

Navarre had left the hotel by the time Tawny was ready for breakfast the next morning. She was bored silly and not even her sketch pad could prevent her from feeling restless. 'Where's your boss?' she pressed Elise.

'He's in business meetings all day,' the blonde confided. 'We're returning home tomorrow…I can't wait.'

'You'll see your boyfriend,' Tawny gathered, reckoning that it had to be the strongest sign yet of her unimportance on Navarre's scale that even his employees knew he was leaving the UK before she did.

But life would soon return to normal, she told herself firmly. She had had a one-night stand and she wasn't very proud of the fact. The next day, however, she would be out job-hunting again as well as getting in touch with her agent to see if she had picked up any new illustrating commissions. She would also catch the train down to visit Celestine at the weekend. Elise got her the local papers so that she could study the jobs available and she decided to look for a waitressing position rather than applying to become a maid again. A waitress would have more customer contact. It would be livelier, more demanding, and wasn't distraction exactly what her troubled mind needed?

No way did she need to be wondering how she would cope if she had conceived a child by Navarre! There was even less excuse for her to be wondering whether she would prefer a boy or a girl and whether the baby might look like her or take more after Navarre, with his dramatic black hair and green eyes. If she turned out to be pregnant, she had no doubt that she would have much more serious concerns. Her mother had once admitted that she had been thrilled when she first realised that she was carrying Tawny. Back then, of course, Susan Baxter had naively assumed that a child on the way would cement her relationship with her child's father instead of which it had destroyed it. At least, Tawny reflected ruefully, she cherished no such romantic illusions where Navarre Cazier was concerned.

About ten that evening, Tawny ran a bath to soak in and emerged pink and wrinkled from her submersion, engulfed in the folds of a large hotel dressing gown. At that point and quite unexpectedly, for Elise had believed him out for the evening, Navarre strode in, clad in a dark, faultlessly tailored business suit with a heavy growth of stubble darkening his handsome features. He acknowledged Elise with barely a glance, for his attention remained on Tawny with her vibrant curls rioting untidily round her flushed face and her slender body lost in the depths of the oversized robe she wore. Hunger pierced him as sharply as a knife, a hunger he didn't understand because it had not started at the groin. That lingering annoying sense that something was lacking, something lost, infuriated him on a day when he had more reason than most to be in an excellent mood to celebrate. He was the triumphant new owner of CCC. The deal had been agreed at Strathmore after weeks of pre-contract discussions between their lawyers and various consultants and now it was signed, sealed and delivered.

'Goodnight, Navarre,' Tawny said flatly.

Elise slipped out of the door unnoticed by either of them. 'I'm leaving tomorrow,' he told Tawny without any expression at all.

Tawny smiled as brightly as if she had won an Olympic race. 'Elise mentioned it.'

'I'll drop you off at home on the way to the airport. I have your phone number and I'll stay in touch...obviously,' he added curtly.

'It's not going to happen,' Tawny responded soothingly, guessing what he meant. 'My egg and your sperm are more likely to have a fight than get together and throw a party for three!'

His face darkened. 'I hope you're right, *ma petite*. A child should be planned and wanted and cherished.'

Her eyes stung as she thought of how much truth there was in that statement. Her own life might have been very different had her parents respected that example. Struggling to suppress the over emotional tears threatening, she was only capable of nodding agreement, but she was grateful that he wasn't approaching the thorny subject with hypocrisy or polite and empty lies. He didn't want to have a child with her and she appreciated his honesty. She shed the robe and got into bed where the tears simply overflowed. She sniffed and coughed, furious with herself. He might have lousy square taste in women's clothes, but he was fantastic in bed and that was the *sole* source of her regret where Navarre Cazier was concerned. He would have made a great casual lover, she told herself doggedly, refusing to examine her feelings in any greater depth.

About twenty minutes later, a light knock sounded on her door and she called out, 'Come in!' and sat up to put on the light by the bed.

She was stunned when Navarre appeared in the doorway, his only covering a towel loosely knotted round his narrow hips. 'May I stay with you tonight?'

Her mouth ran dry, her throat closed over, but her body

went off on a roller-coaster ride of instant sit-up-and-beg response. 'Er...'

'I've tried but I can't stop wanting you,' Navarre admitted harshly.

And she admired that frankness and the streak of humility it had taken for him to approach her again after he had attempted to close that door and move their relationship into more platonic channels. He was not so different from her, after all, and it was a realisation that softened her resentment when she couldn't stop wanting him either. 'Stay,' she told him gruffly, switching out the light in the hope it would hide her discomfiture.

That she was too weak to send him packing still offended Tawny's pride. He had suspected that she might be in league with Julie to plunder his life for profitable information that could be sold to the press. He even believed she might have deliberately tried to get pregnant by him because he was a wealthy man. He did not see her as a trustworthy woman with moral scruples. He was rich, she was poor and a gulf of suspicion separated them. She ought to hate him, but when the muscle packed heat and power of Navarre eased up against her in the dimness, a healthy dose of blood cooling hatred was nowhere to be found. Instead a snaking coil of heat uncurled and burned hot in her and she quivered, every nerve ending energised by anticipation.

Navarre had spent the day in an ever more painful state of arousal, which had steadily eaten away at his self-discipline. Throughout he had remained hugely aware that this was the last night he could be with Tawny and the temptation of having her so close had finally overpowered every other consideration. He might be violating his principles, but when had he ever pretended that he was perfect? In any case, he reasoned impatiently, sex was just sex and it would be an even worse mistake to get emotional about a wholly physical prompting. She turned him on hard and fast, she had made sex exciting for him again. What was a moral dilemma in comparison to what she could make him feel?

Having divided his attention hungrily between the large pink nipples that adorned her small firm breasts and discovered that she was even more deliciously responsive than he recalled, Navarre slowly worked his way down her slender body, utilising every expert skill he had ever learned in the bedroom. If she could make him want her to such an extent, that power had to cut both ways and he was not content until she was writhing and whimpering in abandon, pleading for that final fix of fulfilment.

He sank deep into her and an aching wave of pleasure engulfed her, the little shivers and shakes of yet another approaching climax overwhelming her until she was sobbing out her satisfaction into a hard brown shoulder and falling back against the pillows again, weak as a kitten, emptied of everything.

Still struggling to recapture his breath after that wild bout of sex, Navarre threw himself back out of the bed before he could succumb to the need to reach for her again. Once was never enough with her, but he was suddenly in the grip of a fierce need to prove to himself that he *could* turn away from the powerful temptation she offered. In the darkness he searched for his towel in the heap of clothing discarded by the bed. He shook a couple of garments with unconcealed impatience and Tawny stretched up to put on the bedside light.

'Where are you going?' Clutching the sheet to her chest, frowning below the tumbled curls on her brow, Tawny studied him, unable to believe that he could already be leaving her again. A quick tumble and that was that? Was that all the consideration he now had for her? Did familiarity breed contempt that fast?

Navarre snatched up the towel and at the same time what he took for a screwed up banknote on the floor, assuming it had fallen out of an item of her clothing when he shook it. As he smoothed the item out to give it to her he caught a glimpse of his own name and he withdrew his hand and stepped back from the bed to read the block printed words on the piece of paper.

'If you call…' the note ran and a London phone number followed. 'Information about Navarre Cazier is worth a lot of money.'

Seeing that scrap of paper in his hand, Tawny almost had a heart attack on the spot and she lunged towards him with a stricken gasp. 'Give me that!'

His face set like a mask, Navarre crumpled the note in a powerful fist and dropped it down on her lap. *Merde alors!* What information about me are you planning to sell?' he enquired silkily.

After their intimacy mere minutes earlier it was like a punch in the stomach for Tawny to be asked that brutal question. He had simply assumed that, in spite of the fact that he had already offered her a very large sum of money to help him out, she would think nothing of going behind his back to the press and selling confidential information about him. It was a blow that Navarre could still think so little of her morals. She lost so much colour that her hair looked unnaturally bright against her pallor.

'News of my successful buyout of CCC was in the evening papers so you've missed the boat on the business front,' Navarre derided, winding the towel round his narrow hips with apparently calm hands. 'What else have you got to sell?'

Tawny breathed in deep and gave him a wide sizzling

smile that hurt lips still swollen from his kisses. 'Basically the story of what you're like in bed. You know, the usual sleaze that makes up a kiss-and-tell, how you treated me like a royal princess and put a ring on my finger for a few days, had the sex and then got bored and dumped me again.'

Still as a bronzed statue, Navarre focused contemptuous green eyes on her and ground out the reminder, 'You signed a confidentiality agreement.'

'I know I did, but somehow I don't think you'll lower yourself to the task of dragging me into a courtroom just because I tell the world that you're a five-times-a night guy!' Tawny slung back with deliberate vulgarity, determined to tough out the confrontation so that he would never, ever suspect how much he had hurt her.

Navarre could barely conceal his distaste.

'You still owe me proof that that camera that recorded my supposed theft of your laptop has been wiped,' Tawny remarked less aggressively as that recollection returned to haunt her.

His sardonic mouth curled. 'There was no camera, no recording. That was a little white lie voiced to guarantee your good behaviour.'

'You're such a ruthless bastard,' Tawny quipped shakily, fighting a red tide of rage at how easily she had been taken in. Why had she not insisted on seeing that recording the instant he'd mentioned it?

'It got you off the theft hook,' he reminded her without hesitation.

'And you'll never forget that, will you?' But it wasn't really a question because she already knew the answer. She would *always* be a thief in Navarre Cazier's eyes and a woman he could buy for a certain price.

'Will you change your mind about the kiss-and-tell?'

Navarre asked harshly, willing her to surrender to his demand.

'Sorry, no…I want my five minutes of fame. Why shouldn't I have it? Have a safe journey home,' Tawny urged breezily.

'*Tu a un bon coup*…you're a good lay,' he breathed with cutting cool, and seconds later the door mercifully shut on his departure.

There was no hiding from the obvious fact that making love with him again had been a serious mistake and she mentally beat herself up for that misjudgement to such an extent that she did not sleep a wink for what remained of the night. Around seven in the morning she heard Jacques arrive to collect his employer's cases and later the sound of Navarre leaving the suite. Only when she was sure that he was gone did she finally emerge, pale and with shadowed eyes, from her room. She was shocked to find a bank draft for the sum of money he had agreed to pay her waiting on the table alongside her mobile phone. Was he making the point that, unlike her, once he had given his word he stuck to his agreements? He had ordered breakfast for eight o'clock as well and it arrived, the full works just as she liked, but the lump in her throat and the nausea in her tummy prevented her from eating anything. In the end she tucked the bank draft into her bag. Well, she couldn't just leave it lying there, could she? In the same way she packed the clothes he had bought her into the designer luggage and departed, acknowledging that in the space of a week he had turned her inside out.

CHAPTER EIGHT

'IF Tawny doesn't tell Cazier soon, I intend to do it for her,' Sergios Demonides decreed, watching his sister-in-law, Tawny, play ball in the sunshine with his older children, Paris, Milo and Eleni. Tawny's naturally slender figure made the swelling of her pregnant stomach blatantly obvious in a swimsuit.

'We can't interfere like that,' his wife, Bee, told him vehemently. 'He hurt her. She needs time to adapt to this new development—'

'How much time? Is she planning to wait until the baby is born and then tell him that he's a father?' Sergios reasoned, unimpressed. 'A man has a right to know that he has a child coming *before* its birth. Surely he cannot be as irresponsible as she is—'

'She's not irresponsible!' Bee argued, lifting their daughter, Angeli, into her arms as the black-haired toddler clasped her mother's knees to steady her still-clumsy toddler steps. 'She's just very independent. Have you any idea of how much persuasion I had to use to get her out here for a holiday?'

Outside Tawny glanced uneasily indoors to where her sister and her brother-in-law stood talking intently. She could tell that their attention was centred on her again and she flushed, wishing that Sergios would mind his own business and stop making her feel like such a nuisance. It was typical of the strong-willed Greek to regard his unmarried sister-in-law's pregnancy as a problem that was his duty to solve.

But that was the only cloud on her horizon in the wake of the wonderful week of luxurious relaxation she had enjoyed on Sergios's private island, Orestos. London had been cold and wintry when she flew out and she was returning there the following day, flying back to bad weather and her very ordinary job as a waitress in a restaurant. She felt well rested and more grounded after the break she had had with her sister and her lively family though. Sergios had become the guardian of his cousin's three orphaned children and with the recent addition of their own first child to the mix—the adorable Angeli—Bee was a very busy wife and mother. She was also very happy with her life, although that was an admission that went against the grain for Tawny, who was convinced that she could never have remained as even tempered and easy going as Bee in the radius of Sergios's domineering nature. Sergios was one of those men who knew the right way to do everything and it was always *his* way. And yet Bee had this magical knack of just looking at him sometimes when he was in full extrovert flood and he would suddenly shut up and smile at her as if she had waved a magic wand across his forbidding countenance.

'I can't bear to think of you going back to work such long hours. You should have rested more while you were here.' Bee sighed after dinner that evening as the two women sat out on the terrace watching the sun go down.

'The way you did?' Tawny teased, recalling how incredibly hectic her half-sister's schedule had been while she was carrying her first child.

'I had Sergios for support…and my mother,' Bee reminded her.

Bee's disabled mother, Emilia, lived in a cottage in the grounds of their Greek home and was very much a member of their family. In comparison, Tawny's mother was living with her divorced boyfriend and his children in the house she had purchased with her inheritance from Tawny's grandfather. She was aghast that her daughter had fallen pregnant outside a relationship and had urged her to have a termination, an attitude that had driven yet another wedge into the already troubled relationship between mother and daughter. No, Tawny could not look for support from that quarter, and while her grandmother, Celestine, was considerably more tolerant when it came to babies, the older woman lived quite a long way from her and with the hours Tawny had to work she only saw the little Frenchwoman about once a month.

'It's a shame that you told Navarre that you *weren't* pregnant when he phoned you a couple of months ago,' Bee said awkwardly.

'I honestly thought it was the truth when I told him that. That first test I did *was* negative!' Tawny reminded the brunette ruefully. 'Do you really think I should have phoned him three weeks later and told him I'd been mistaken?'

'Yes.' Bee stayed firm in the face of the younger woman's look of reproach. 'It's Navarre's baby too. You have to deal with it. The longer you try to ignore the situation, the more complicated it will become.'

Tawny's eyes stung and she blinked furiously, turning her face away to conceal the turbulent emotions that seemed so much closer to the surface since she had fallen pregnant. She was fourteen weeks along now and she was changing shape rapidly with her tummy protruding, her waist thickening and her breasts almost doubling in size. Ever since she had learned that she had conceived she had felt horribly vulnerable and out of control of her body and her life. All too well did she remember her mother's distressing tales of how Tawny's father had humiliated her with his angry scornful attitude to her conception of a child he didn't want. Tawny had cringed at the prospect of putting herself in the same position with a man who was already suspicious of her motives.

'I know that Navarre hurt you,' her half-sister murmured unhappily. 'But you should still tell him.'

'Somehow I fell for him like a ton of bricks,' Tawny admitted abruptly, her voice shaking because it was the very first time she had openly acknowledged that unhappy truth, and Bee immediately covered her hand with hers in a gesture of quiet understanding. 'I never thought I could feel like that about a man and he was back out of my life again before I even realised how much he had got to me. But there was nothing I could do to make things better between us—'

'How about just keeping your temper and talking to him?' Bee suggested. 'That would be a good place to make a start.'

Tawny didn't trust herself to do that either. How could she talk to a man who would almost certainly want her to go for a termination? Why should she have to justify her desire to bring her baby into the world just because it didn't suit him? So, she decided to text him the news late that night, saving them both from the awkwardness of a direct confrontation when it was all too likely that either or both of them might say the wrong things.

The first test I did was wrong. I am now 14 weeks pregnant,' she informed him and added, utilising block capitals lest he cherish any doubts, *'It is YOURS.'*

Pressing the send button before she could lose her nerve, she slept that night soothed by the conviction that she had finally bitten the bullet and done what she had to do. Bee was shocked that her sister had decided to break the news in a text but Sergios believed that even that was preferable to keeping her condition a secret.

Navarre was already at work in his imposing office in Paris when Tawny's text came through and shock and disbelief roared through him like a hurricane-force storm. He wanted to disorder his immaculate cropped hair and shout to the heavens to release the steam building inside him as he read that text. *Merde alors!* She would be the death of him. How could she make such an announcement by text? How could she text 'YOURS' like that as if he were likely to argue the fact when she had been a virgin? He tried to phone her immediately but could not get an answer, for by then Tawny was already on board a flight to London. Within an hour Navarre had cancelled his appointments and organised a trip there as well.

Tawny stopped off at her bedsit only long enough to change for her evening shift at the restaurant and drop off her case. As she had decided that only actual starvation would persuade her to accept money from a man who had called her a good lay to her face, she had not cashed Navarre's bank draft and had had to work extremely hard to keep on top of all her financial obligations. Luckily some weeks back she had had the good fortune to sell a set of greeting card designs, which had ensured that Celestine's rent was covered for the immediate future. Tawny's work as a waitress paid her own expenses and, as her agent had been enthusiastic enough to send a selection of her Frenchman cartoons to several publications, she was even moderately hopeful that her cartoons might soon give her the break she had long dreamt of achieving.

Navarre seated himself in a distant corner of the self-service restaurant where Tawny worked and nursed a cup of the most disgusting black coffee he had ever tasted. Consumed by frustration over the situation she had created by keeping him out of the loop for so long, he watched her emerge from behind the counter to clear tables. And that fast his anger rose. Her streaming torrent of hair was tied back at the nape of her neck, her slender coltish figure lithe in an overall and leggings. At first glance she looked thinner but otherwise unchanged, he decided, subjecting her to a close scrutiny and noting the fined-down line of her jaw. Only when she straightened did he see the rounded swell of her stomach briefly moulded by the fabric of her tunic.

She was expecting his baby and even though she clearly needed to engage in hard menial work to survive, he reflected with brooding resentment and disapproval, she had still not made use of that bank draft he had left in the hotel for her. He had told his bank to inform him the instant the money was drawn and the weeks had passed and he had waited and waited, much as he had waited in vain for some sleazy kiss-and-tell about their affair to be published somewhere. When nothing happened, when his lowest expectations went totally unfulfilled, it had finally dawned on him that this was payback time Tawny-style. In refusing to accept that money from him, in disdaining selling 'their' story as she had threatened to do, she was taking her revenge, making her point that he had got her wrong and that she didn't need him for anything. Navarre understood blunt messages of a challenging nature, although she was the very first woman in his life to try and communicate with him on that aggressive level.

In addition, he had really not needed a shock phone call from her bossy sister Bee to tell him how *not* to handle her fiery half-sister. Bee Demonides had phoned him out of the blue just after his private jet landed in London and had introduced herself with aplomb. Tawny, he now appreciated, had kept secrets that he had never dreamt might exist in her background, secrets that sadly might have helped him to understand her better. Her sibling was married to one of the richest men in the world and Tawny had not breathed a word of that fact, had indeed 'oohed' and 'ahhed' over Sam Coulter's rented castle and the Golden Awards party as if she had no comparable connections or experiences. In fact, from what he had since established from Jacques's more wide-reaching enquiries, Tawny's other half-sister, Zara, was married to an Italian banker, who was also pretty wealthy. So, how likely was it that Tawny had ever planned to enrich herself by stealing Navarre's laptop to sell his secrets to the gutter press? On the other hand why did she feel the need to work in such lowly jobs when she had rich relatives who would surely have been willing to help her find more suitable employment? That was a complete mystery and only the first of several concerning Tawny Baxter, Navarre acknowledged impatiently.

Tawny was unloading a tray into a dishwasher in the kitchen when her boss approached her. 'There's a man waiting over by the far window for you…says he's a friend and he's here to tell you about a family crisis. I said that you could leave early—we're quiet this evening. I hope it's nothing serious.'

Tawny's first thought was that something awful had happened to her mother and that her mother's boyfriend, Rob, had come to tell her. Fear clenching her stomach, she grabbed her coat and bag and hurried back out into the restaurant, only to come to a shaken halt when she looked across the tables and saw Navarre seated in the far corner. His dark hair gleamed blue-black below the down lights that accentuated the stunning angles and hollows of his darkly handsome features. He threw back his head and she collided with brilliant bottle-green eyes and somehow she was moving towards him without ever recalling how she had reached that decision.

'Let's get out of here,' Navarre urged, striding forwards to greet her before she even got halfway to his table.

Still reeling in consternation from his sudden appearance, Tawny let him guide her outside and into the limousine pulling up at the kerb to collect them. Her hand trembled in the sudden firm hold of his, for their three months apart had felt like a lifetime and she could have done with advance warning of his visit. Thrown into his presence again without the opportunity to dress for the occasion and form a defensive shell, she felt horribly naked and unprepared. Once again, though, he had surprised her in a uniform that underlined the yawning gulf in their status.

'I wasn't expecting you—'

'You thought you could chuck a text bombshell at me and I was so thick-skinned that I would simply carry on as normal?' Navarre questioned with sardonic emphasis. 'Even I am not that insensitive.'

Tawny reddened. 'You took me by surprise.'

'Just as your text took me, *ma petite*.'

'Not so *petite* any longer,' she quipped.

'I noticed,' Navarre admitted flatly, his attention dropping briefly to the tummy clearly visible when she was sitting down. 'I'm still in shock.'

'Even after three months I'm still in shock.'

'Why did you tell me you weren't pregnant?'

'I did a test and it was negative. I think I did it too early. A few weeks later when I wasn't feeling well I bought another test and that one was positive. I didn't know how to tell you that I'd got it wrong—'

'*Exactement!* So, instead you took the easy way out and told me nothing.'

His sarcasm cut like the sudden slash of a knife against tender skin. 'Well, actually there was nothing easy about anything I've gone through since then, Navarre!' Tawny fired back at him in a sudden surge of spitfire temper. 'I've had all the worry without having anyone to turn to! I've had to work even though I was feeling as sick as a dog most mornings and the smell of cooking food made me worse, so working in a restaurant was not a pleasant experience. My hormones were all over the place and I've never felt so horribly tired in my life as I did those first weeks!'

'If only you had accepted the bank draft I gave you. We had an agreement and you earned that money by pretending to be my fiancée,' he reminded her grittily. 'But I understand why you refused to touch it.'

Her glacier blue eyes widened in disconcertion. 'You... *do?*'

'That last night we were together I was offensive, inexcusably so,' Navarre framed in a taut undertone, every word roughened by the effort it demanded of his pride to acknowledge such a fault to a woman.

That unexpected admission made it easier for Tawny to unbend in her turn. 'I made things worse. I shouldn't have pretended that I was planning to sell a story about you.'

'I made an incorrect assumption...time has proven me wrong, for no story appeared in the papers.'

'That note was smuggled in to me before we flew up to

Scotland. Julie would've been behind it. She even phoned my gran to try and find out where you and I had gone. I put the note in my pocket and forgot about it. I never intended to use that phone number.'

'Let the matter rest there. We have more important concerns at the moment.'

'How on earth did you find out where I was working?'

'You can thank your sister Bee for that information.'

Her exclamation of surprise was met by his description of the phone call he had received at the airport. Tawny winced and squirmed, loving Bee but deeply embarrassed by her interference. 'Bee hates people being at odds with each other. She's a tremendous peace maker but I do wish she had trusted me to handle this on my own.'

'She meant well. You're lucky to have a sister who cares so much about your welfare.'

'Zara is less pushy but equally opinionated.' At that point Tawny recalled Navarre telling her that he had no family he acknowledged and that memory filled her heart with regret and sympathy on his behalf. She might sometimes disagree with her relatives' opinions but she was still glad to have them in her life. People willing to tell her the truth and look out for her no matter what were a precious gift.

'Where are we heading?'

'Your sister and brother-in-law have kindly offered us the use of their home here in London for our meeting. We need somewhere to talk in private and I am tired of hotels,' he admitted curtly. 'It's time that I bought a property in this city.'

Tawny was pleased that Bee had offered the use of her luxury home in Chelsea and relieved not to have to take him back to her dreary bedsit to chat. Navarre, with his classy custom-made suits and shoes would never relax against such a grungy backdrop and she did want him to relax. If they were going to share a child it was vitally important that they establish a more harmonious relationship, she reasoned ruefully.

Ushered into the elegant drawing room of Bee and Sergios's mansion home by their welcoming housekeeper, Tawny was grateful to just kick off her shoes and curl up on a well-upholstered sofa in comfort. All of a sudden she didn't care any more that she was looking less than her best in a work tunic with a touch of mascara being her only concession to cosmetic enhancement. After all, what did such things matter now? He was no longer interested in her in that way. Three months had passed since he had walked away from her without a backwards glance—she didn't count that single brief phone call made out of duty to ask if she was pregnant—and for such diametrically opposed personalities as they it had probably been a wise move.

Navarre marvelled at the manner in which she instantly shed all formality and made herself comfortable. She made no attempt to pose or impress him, had not even dashed a lipstick across her lush full mouth. He was used to women who employed a great deal more artifice and her casual approach intrigued him. In any case the lipstick would only have come off, he thought hungrily, appreciation snaking through him as he noted the purity of her fine-boned profile, the natural elegance of her slender body in relaxation. And that hint of a bump that had changed her shape was *his* child. It struck Navarre as quite bizarre at that moment that that thought should turn him on hard and fast.

Tawny was now thinking hard about their predicament, trying to be fair to both of them. Their baby was a complication of an affair that was already over and done with, she conceded unhappily, and the more honest she was with him now, the more likely they were to reach an agreement that suited both of them.

'I want to have this baby,' she told Navarre straight off, keen to avoid any exchange with him in regard to the choices she might choose to make for their child. 'My mother thinks I'm being an idiot because she believes that giving birth to me and becoming a single parent ruined her life. I've heard all the arguments on that score since I was old enough to understand what she was talking about but I don't feel the same way. This baby may not be planned but I love it already and we'll manage.'

'I like your positive attitude.'

'Do you?' She was warmed by the comment and a tremulous smile softened the stressful line of her pink mouth.

'But it does seem that we are both approaching this situation with a lot of baggage from our own childhoods.' Navarre compressed his hard sensual mouth as he voiced that comment. 'Neither of us had a father and we suffered from that lack. It is hard for a child to have only one parent.'

'Yes,' she agreed ruefully.

'And it also puts a huge burden on the single parent's shoulders. Your mother struggled to cope and became bitter while my mother could not cope with parenting me at all. Our experiences have taught us how hard it is to raise a child alone and I don't want to stand back and watch you and our child go through that same process.'

The extent of his understanding of the problems she might have took Tawny aback at the same time as his thoughtfulness and willingness to take responsibility impressed her. 'I'm not belittling my mother's efforts as a parent because she did the very best she could, but she was very bitter and I do think I'm more practical in my expectations than she was.'

'I don't think you should have to lower your expectations at your age simply because you will have a child's needs to consider.'

Tawny pulled a wry face. 'But we have to be realistic.'

'It is exactly because I am realistic about what life would be like for you that I've come here to ask you to marry me. Only marriage would allow me to take my full share of the responsibility,' Navarre told her levelly, his strong jawline squaring with resolve. 'Together we will be able to offer our child much more than we could offer as parents living apart.'

Tawny was totally stunned for she had not seen that option hovering on her horizon at all. She stared back at Navarre, noting how grave his face was, grasping by his composed demeanour that he had given the matter a great deal of thought. 'You're not joking, are you?'

'I want to be there for you from the moment this child is born,' Navarre admitted with tough conviction. 'I don't want another man to take my place in my child's life either. The best way forwards for both of us is marriage.'

'But we know so little about each other—'

'Is that important? Is it likely to make our relationship more successful? I think not,' he declared with assurance. 'I believe it is infinitely more important that we are strongly attracted to each other and both willing to make a firm commitment to raise our child together.'

Tawny was mesmerised by his rock solid conviction. She felt slightly guilty that she had not appreciated that he might feel as responsible for her well-being and for that of their child as he evidently did. Too late did she grasp that she had expected him to treat her exactly as her absent father had treated her mother—with disdain and resentment. He was not running away from the burden of childcare, he was moving closer to accept it. Tears of relief stung her eyes and she blinked rapidly, turning her face away in the hope he had not noticed.

But Navarre was too observant to be fooled. 'What's wrong, *chérie*? What did I say?'

Tawny smiled through the tears. 'It's all right, it's not you. It's just I cry over the silliest things at the minute—I think it's the hormones doing it. My father was absolutely horrible to my mum when she told him she was pregnant and I think I sort of subconsciously assumed you would be the same. So, you see, we're both guilty of making wrong assumptions.'

Navarre had tried to move on from his cynical suspicions about her, she reasoned with a feeling of warmth inside her that felt remarkably like hope. She had not cashed the bank draft, she had not talked to the press about him and as a result he was willing to reward her with his trust. He treated her now with respect. He was no longer questioning the manner of their baby's conception or even mentioning a cynical need for DNA testing to check paternity. In short he had cut through all the rubbish that had once littered their relationship and offered her a wedding ring as a pledge of commitment to a new future. And she knew immediately that she would say yes to his proposal, indeed that it would feel like a sin not to at least try to see if they could make a marriage work for the sake of their child.

This was the guy whom against all the odds she had fallen madly in love with. He was the guy who ordered her magnificent breakfasts and admired her appetite and constantly checked that she wasn't hungry, the guy who had batted not a single magnificent eyelash over those embarrassing newspaper revelations about her background in spite of the presence of a bunch of snobbish socialite guests, who had undoubtedly looked down on his bargain basement taste in fiancées. He was also the guy who was endearingly, ridiculously jealous and possessive if another man so much as looked at her, an attitude which had made her feel irresistible for the first time in her life.

'Do you like children?' she asked him abruptly.

Navarre laughed. 'I've never really thought about it, but, yes, I believe that I do.'

When he smiled like that the power of his charisma rocketed, throwing him into the totally gorgeous bracket, and he made her heart hammer and her breath catch in her throat. 'Yes, I'll marry you,' she told him in French.

'You're an artist. I believe you will like living in Paris.'

He made it all seem so simple. That first visit he insisted on meeting her mother and her partner over dinner the following night at a very smart hotel. At first mother and daughter were a little stiff with each other, but at the end of the evening Susan Baxter took Tawny to one side to speak to her in private and said, 'I'm so happy it's all working out for you that I don't really know what to say,' she confided, tears shining in her anxious gaze. 'I know you were annoyed with the solution I suggested but I just didn't want your life to go wrong while you were still so young. I was afraid that you were repeating my mistakes and it felt like that had to be my fault—'

'Navarre's not like my father,' Tawny cut in with perceptible pride.

'No, he seems to be very mature and responsible.'

The word 'responsible' stung, although Tawny knew that no insult had been intended. She was too sensitive, she acknowledged ruefully. Navarre would not walk away from his child because he had grown up without the support of either a father or a mother and only he knew what that handicap had cost him. For that reason he would not abandon the mother of his child to struggle with parenthood alone. Acknowledging that undeniable fact made Tawny feel just a little like a charity case or an exercise in which Navarre would prove to his own satisfaction that he had the commitment gene, which his own parents had sadly lacked. It was an impression that could have been dissolved overnight had Navarre made the smallest attempt to become intimate with his intended bride again… but he did not. The pink diamond was placed on her engagement finger again, for real this time around, but his detached attitude, his concentration on the practical rather than the personal, left Tawny feeling deeply insecure and vulnerable.

Bee and Sergios offered to stage Navarre and Tawny's wedding at their London home and under pressure from Tawny, after initially refusing that offer Navarre agreed to it. He then rented a serviced apartment for Tawny's use and at his request she immediately gave up her job as a waitress and moved into the apartment while he returned to Paris. From there he hired a property firm to find them an ideal home in London and she spent her time doing viewings of the kind of luxury property she had never dreamt she might one day call home.

Only days after Tawny told her other half-sister, Zara, that she was getting married, Zara arrived in London for an unexpected visit, having left her children, Donata and her infant son, Piero, at home with her husband outside Florence.

'Does this visit now mean you aren't able to come to the wedding next week?' Tawny asked, surprised by the timing of her sister's trip to London. 'I know it was short notice but—'

'No, I just wanted the chance to talk to you alone *before* the wedding,' Zara completed with rather tense emphasis.

Drawing back from her half-sibling's hug, Tawny frowned. 'What's up? Oh, my goodness, you and Vitale aren't having trouble, are you?' she prompted in dismay, for the other couple had always seemed blissfully happy together.

Her dainty blonde sister went pink with discomfiture. 'Oh, no…no, nothing like that!' she exclaimed, although her eyes remained evasive.

The two young women settled in the comfortable lounge with coffee and biscuits. Tawny looked at Zara expectantly. 'So, tell me…'

Zara grimaced. 'I truly didn't know whether to come and talk to you or not. Bee said I should mind my own business and keep my mouth shut, so I discussed it with Vitale, but he thought I should be more honest with you.'

Tawny was frowning. 'R-right…I'm sorry, I don't understand.'

'It's something about Navarre, just rumours, but they've been around a long time and I don't know whether you know about them or even *should* know about them.' Her tongue tying her into increasingly tight knots, Zara was openly uncomfortable. 'I wouldn't usually repeat gossip—'

Tawny's spine went rigid with tension. Zara was a gentle kind person, never bitchy or mean. If Zara felt there were rumours about Navarre that Tawny ought to hear, she reckoned that they would very probably be a genuine source of concern for her. 'I'd like to say that I don't listen to gossip, but I'm not sure I could live without knowing now that you've told me there's something you think I should know about my future husband.'

'Now remember that I'm married to an Italian,' Zara reminded her uneasily. 'And for many years in Italy there have been strong rumours to the effect that Navarre Cazier is engaged in a long-running secret affair with Tia Castelli…you know the Italian movie star…?'

CHAPTER NINE

TAWNY who had literally stopped breathing while Zara spoke, relocated her lungs at the sound of that name and started to breathe again.

'My goodness, is there anyone on this planet who hasn't heard of Tia Castelli?' Tawny asked with her easy laugh. 'Are there rumours about Navarre and Tia having an affair? *Truthfully?* When I saw them together—'

Zara leant forwards in astonishment. 'You've already met Tia Castelli? You've actually seen her with Navarre? The word is that they're in constant contact.'

Tawny told her sister about her appearance by Navarre's side at the Golden Awards and her encounter with Tia and her husband, Luke.

'Surprising,' Zara remarked thoughtfully. 'I should think if that there had been anything sneaky going on Navarre would have avoided their company like the plague.'

'Navarre has known Tia for years and years. He worked for the banker that handled Tia's investments—that's how they first met,' Tawny explained frankly. 'Tia is very flirtatious. She expects to be the centre of attention but she's perfectly pleasant otherwise. I think you'd best describe her as being very much a man's woman.'

'So, you didn't notice anything strange between her

and Navarre? Anything that made you uncomfortable?'
Zara checked.

All Tawny felt uncomfortable about at that moment was
that she did not feel she could tell Zara the truth of how
she had met Navarre and become his fiancée, because she
and Navarre had already agreed that now their relationship
had become official nobody else had any need to know
about their previous arrangement. But it did occur to her
just then that the night she had met Tia Castelli, she had
been no more than a hired companion on Navarre's terms
and he had had less reason to hide anything from her. He
had been very attentive towards Tia, almost protective,
she recalled, struggling to think back and recapture what
she had seen. And Tia *was* an extraordinarily beautiful
and appealing woman. Tawny wondered if she was being
ridiculously naive about their relationship and could not
help recalling Luke Convery's annoyance at his wife's
friendship with Navarre. No smoke without fire, she reasoned ruefully. It was perfectly possible that Navarre and
Tia *had* been lovers at some point in the past.

'Now I've got you all worked up and worried! I
should've kept quiet! Why is Bee always right?' Zara exclaimed guiltily as she tracked the fast changing expressions on the younger woman's face. 'She would never ever
have mentioned those stupid rumours to you.'

Ironically, what Tawny was thinking about then was
the number of times she had heard Navarre talking on
the phone in Italian, a language that he seemed to speak
with the fluency of a native. Could he have been speaking to Tia? Surely not every time she had heard him using
Italian, though, she told herself irritably, for that would
have meant that he talked to the gorgeous blonde almost
every day.

At the end of the afternoon, when Zara departed assuring Tawny that she and her husband would attend her wedding, Tawny was conscious that there was now a tiny little seed of doubt planted inside her that was more than ready to sprout into a sturdy sapling of suspicion.

Prior to her pregnancy, Navarre had seemed so hungry for Tawny, but not so hungry that he had made any attempt to get her back into bed in advance of the wedding. Who had been satisfying that hot libido of his during the three months of their separation? And why was she thinking that him having wanted her automatically meant he could not have also wanted Tia Castelli? Was she really that unsophisticated? After all, Tia was married and the sort of catch many men would kill to possess even briefly. Even if Tia and Navarre were having an affair Tia must surely accept that there would also be other women in Navarre's life. Her peace of mind shattered by that depressing conclusion, Tawny went to bed to toss and turn, troubled by her thoughts but determined not to share what she still deemed might be ridiculous suspicions with Navarre. Revealing such concerns when she had no proof would make her look foolish and put her at a disadvantage.

In the middle of the night she got up and performed an Internet search of Tia and Navarre's names together to discover any links that there might be. An hour later she had still not got to the end of the references, but had discovered nothing definitive, nothing that could not be explained by honest friendship. There were several pictures of Tia and Navarre chatting in public places, not a single one of anything more revealing—no holding of hands, no embraces, *nothing*. And if the paparazzi had failed to establish a more intimate link, the likelihood was that there wasn't one, for Tia Castelli's every move was recorded by the paps. But ironically for the first time Tawny was now wondering what had been on Navarre's laptop that he had so feared having exposed. What had Julie's high-paying journalist really hoped to find out from that computer? About the buyout of CCC? Her worst fears assuaged by that idea, for she recalled Navarre's comment about the deal already being in the news, Tawny went back to bed.

It was a wonderful wedding dress, fashioned by a designer to conceal the growing evidence of the bride's pregnancy. Tawny looked at her reflection in the mirror with her sisters standing anxiously by her side and then hugged Zara, who had located the glorious dress, which bared her shoulders and her newly impressive chest in a style that removed attention from her abdomen.

'You've sure got boobs now, babe,' Zara pronounced with a giggle.

Tawny grinned, her lovely face lighting up for it was true: for the first time ever she had the bosom bounty that she had always lacked and no padding was required.

'Are you happy?' Bee prompted worriedly. 'You're sure Navarre is the right man for you?'

Tawny lifted a hand to brush a wondering finger across the magnificent diamond tiara that anchored her veil and added height to her slim figure. 'Well, it's either him or the diamonds he's just given me,' she teased. 'But it all feels incredibly right.'

An offer had been made and accepted on a town house with a garden in the same area in which Bee and Sergios lived. In a few weeks' time it would provide a very comfortable base for her and Navarre when they were in London, ensuring that she need never feel that she was being taken away from absolutely everything she had ever known. She was on a high because everything in her world seemed to be blossoming. After all, she had just sold her first cartoons as well. One of the publications that her agent had sent her work to had shared them with a French sister magazine and the French editor had offered Tawny a contract to create more of her Frenchman drawings. Ecstatic at the news, Tawny had still to share it with Navarre because she wanted to surprise him by putting the magazine in front of him when the first cartoon appeared in print.

'You should've let me twist Dad's arm to give you away,' Zara lamented. 'He would have done it if I'd pushed him.'

'I don't know our father, Zara. I wouldn't have wanted him to do it just to please you and Bee. I much prefer Sergios. At least he genuinely wishes Navarre and I well,' Tawny pointed out.

Her opinion of Sergios had recently warmed up, for it was thanks to Sergios and his managing ways that her grandmother, Celestine, was being whisked to London in a limousine for the wedding and put up that night in Bee's home so that the extended celebration was not too much of a strain for the old lady.

At the church, Tawny breathed in deep, her hand resting lightly on Sergios's arm before she moved down the aisle, her sisters following her clad in black and cream outfits. All her attention locked to Navarre, who had flown back to France within days of his proposal, she moved slowly towards the altar. Devastatingly handsome in a tailored silver-grey suit teamed with a smart waistcoat and cravat, Navarre took her breath away just as he had the very first time she saw him and she hugged the knowledge to herself that he would soon be her husband. As she reached the altar Celestine, a tiny lady with a mop of white curls, turned her head to beam at her granddaughter.

Although Tawny's head told her that she was entering a shotgun marriage of the utmost practicality, it didn't feel like one. She loved the ceremony, the sure way Navarre made his responses, the firm hold of the hand on hers as he slid on the wedding ring. In her heart she felt that he was making a proper commitment to her and their child. Before they left the church Navarre took the time to stop and greet her grandmother, whom he had not had time to meet beforehand.

'Do you like the dress?' she asked him once they were alone in the limo conveying them back to her sister's home.

'I like what's in it even better, *ma petite*,' Navarre confided, his attention ensnared by the luminosity of her beautiful eyes, and momentarily a pang of regret touched him for the parts of his life that he could never share with her. He had always believed that as long as he kept his life simple nothing could go wrong, but from the instant Tawny had walked into his life to try to steal his laptop his every plan had gone awry and things had stopped happening the way he had assumed they would. He didn't like that, he had learned to prefer the predictable and the safe, but he told himself that now that they were married his daily life would return to its normal routine. Why should anything have to change?

Tawny gazed dizzily into beautiful emerald-green eyes framed by black spiky lashes and her heart hammered. Her breasts swelled beneath her bodice, the pointed tips straining into sudden tingling life. His attention was on her mouth. The tip of her tongue slid out to moisten her lower lip and he tensed, his sleek strong face hard and taut. The silence lay heavy, thick like the sensual spell flooding her treacherous body, and she leant closer, propelled by promptings much stronger than she was.

'I'll wreck your make-up,' Navarre growled, but a hard hand closed into the back of her veil to hold her still while his mouth plundered hers with fierce heat and hunger, the delving of his tongue sending every skin cell she possessed mad with excitement.

Tawny wanted to push him flat on the back seat and have her wicked way with him. That fast her body was aching with need and ready for him. Her fingers flexed on a long powerful masculine thigh and then slid upwards to establish that the response was not one-sided. He was hard and thick and as eager as she was and even as he pushed back from her, surprise at her boldness etched in his intent gaze, she was content to have discovered that the exact same desire powered them both. Her face was flushed as she eased away from him, her body quivering with the will power it took to do so.

'Mon Dieu, ma belle...you make me ache like a boy again,' he confessed raggedly.

And the gloss on Tawny's day was complete. Happy at the response she had received, reassured by his desire, she sailed into her wedding reception in the ballroom of her sister's magnificent home. Perhaps he had only restrained himself sexually with her out of some outmoded idea of respecting her as his future wife, she thought buoyantly, for she had noticed that Navarre could sometimes be a shade old-fashioned in his outlook. Whatever, her insecurity was gone, her awareness of her pregnancy as a source of embarrassment banished while she held her head high and stood by his side to welcome the wealthy powerful guests whom Navarre counted as friends and business connections. Only recently she would only have got close to such people by waiting on them in some menial capacity, but now she met with them as an equal. Tia Castelli kissed her cheek with cool courtesy, her previous warmth muted, while her husband, Luke, gave Tawny a lazy smile. Tawny perfectly understood and forgave Tia for that dash of coolness in her manner, for the actress had to be aware that a married man would be far less available to her than a single guy.

Later that afternoon, it did her heart good when Bee drew her attention to the fact that Navarre was sitting with her grandmother, Celestine. 'They've been talking for ages,' her half-sister informed her.

Tawny drifted over to Navarre's side and he laced long fingers with hers to tug her down into a seat beside him. 'You've been holding out on me, *chérie*.'

'And me,' Celestine added. 'All these months I had no idea you were paying my rent.'

Tawny froze. 'What on earth are you talking about?'

'One of the other residents spoke to me about his problems meeting the maintenance costs and when certain sums were mentioned I knew that I did not have enough money to meet such enormous bills either,' the old lady told her quietly. 'I spoke to my solicitor and although he didn't break your confidence, I soon worked out for myself that there was only one way that my costs could be being met. I felt very guilty for not realising what was going on sooner.'

'Don't be daft, Gran...I've managed fine!' Tawny protested, upset that the older woman had finally registered the level to which her expenses had exceeded her means.

'By slaving away as a chambermaid and waiting on tables,' Celestine responded unhappily. 'That was not right and I would never have agreed to it.'

'I've reassured Celestine that as a member of the family I will be taking care of any problems from now on and that I hope she will be a regular visitor to our home.'

Tawny sat down beside him to soothe the old lady's worries and with Navarre's support Celestine's distress gradually faded away. Soon after that her grandmother admitted that she was tired and Tawny saw her up to the room she was to use until her departure the next morning.

'Navarre is…*très sympathique,*' her grandmother pronounced with approval. 'He is kind and understanding. You will be very happy with him.'

Having helped her grandmother unpack her overnight bag and locate all the facilities, Tawny hurried back downstairs to find Navarre waiting for her at the foot. 'Why didn't you tell me what you needed the money for months ago?' he demanded in a driven undertone, his incredulity at her silence on that score unhidden.

'It was nothing to do with you. She's my granny.'

'And now she's mine as well and you will change no more beds on her behalf!' Navarre asserted fierily.

'It's not a problem. I never had a burning desire to be a maid but it was easy work to find and it allowed me to do my illustration projects in the evenings.'

He tilted up her chin. His gaze was stern. 'Couldn't you have trusted me enough to tell me the truth for yourself?' he pressed. 'I assumed your loyalty could be bought—I thought less of you for being willing to take that money from me in payment.'

'Only because you've forgotten what it's like to be poor and in need of cash,' Tawny told him tartly. 'Poverty has no pride. When I was a child, my grandparents were very good to me. I'd do just about anything to keep Celestine safe, secure and happy.'

'And I honour you for it and for all your hard work for her benefit, *ma petite.* You also took on that responsibility without any expectation of ever receiving her gratitude, for you tried to hide your contributions to her income. I'm hugely impressed,' Navarre admitted, his stunning gaze warm with pride and approval on her blushing face. 'But why didn't you approach your sisters for help?'

'Celestine isn't related to them in any way. I wouldn't dream of bothering them for money,' Tawny argued in consternation.

'I suspect Bee would have liked to help—'

'Maybe so, Navarre,' his bride responded. 'But I've always believed in standing on my own two feet.'

An hour later when Tawny was chatting to her mother and her partner, Susan commented on how effective her daughter's dress was at concealing her swelling stomach. Amused, Tawny splayed her hand to her abdomen, momentarily moulding the fabric to the definite bulge of her pregnancy. 'My bump's still there beneath the fancy trappings!' she joked.

A few feet away, she glimpsed Tia Castelli staring at her fixedly, big blue eyes wide, her flawless face oddly frozen and expressionless before, just as quickly, the actress spun round and vanished into the crush of guests. As Tawny frowned in incomprehension Bee signalled her by pointing at her watch: it was time for Tawny to change out of her finery, and she followed her sibling upstairs because she and Navarre were leaving for France in little more than an hour. Twenty minutes later, Tawny descended a rear staircase a couple of steps in Bee's wake. She was wearing a very flattering blue skirt with floral silk tee and a long flirty jacket teamed with impossibly high heels.

Bee stopped dead so suddenly at the foot of the stairs that Tawny almost tripped over her. 'Let's go back up…I forgot something!' she exclaimed in a peculiar whisper.

But Tawny was not that easily distracted and Bee, unfortunately, was not a very good actress when she was surprised and upset by something. Correctly guessing that her sister had seen something she did not want her to see, Tawny ignored Bee's attempt to catch her arm and prevent her from stepping into the corridor at the bottom of the stairs. Tawny moved past and caught a good view of the scene that Bee had sought to protect her from. Tia Castelli was sobbing on Navarre's chest as if her heart were breaking and he was looking down at the tiny blonde with that highly revealing mixture of concern and tenderness that only existed in the most intimate of relationships. Certainly one look at the manner in which her bridegroom was comforting Tia was sufficient to freeze Tawny in her tracks and cut through her heart like a knife. It was a little vignette of her worst nightmares for, while she had from the outset accepted that Navarre did not love her, she had never been prepared for the reality that he might love another woman instead.

Abruptly registering that they had acquired an audience, Navarre stepped back and Tia flipped round to make a whirlwind recovery, eyes damp but enquiring, famous face merely anxious. 'I had a stupid row with Luke, I'm afraid, and Navarre swept me off to save me from making a fool of myself about it in public.'

It was a wry and deft explanation voiced as convincingly as only a skilled actress could make it. It sounded honest and it might even have been true, Tawny reckoned numbly, but she just didn't believe it. What she had seen was something more, something full of stronger, darker emotions on both sides. Tia's distress had been genuine even though it was hidden now, the blonde's perfect face tear-stained but composed in a light apologetic smile.

'I understand,' Tawny said flatly, for she had too much pride and common sense to challenge either of them when she had no evidence of wrongdoing. But in the space of a moment fleeting suspicion had turned into very real apprehension and insecurity.

'You look charming, *chèrie,*' Navarre murmured smoothly, scanning her shuttered face with astute cool.

He would give nothing away for free. No information, no secrets, no apologies. He would not put himself on the defensive. She knew that. She had married a master tactician, a guy to whom manipulation was a challenging game, which his intelligence and courage ensured he would always excel at playing.

Pale though she was, Tawny smiled as if she had not a worry in the world either. She hoped he would not notice that the smile didn't reach her eyes. She suspected that he was probably more relieved that she did not speak Italian and therefore was quite unable to translate the flood of words Tia had been sobbing at the moment they were disturbed. But at that instant Tawny also realised that someone had been present who could speak Tia's native tongue and she glanced at her linguistically talented sister Bee, who was noticeably pale as well, and resolved to question her as to what she had overheard before they parted.

When they returned to the ballroom, there was no sign of Tia or Luke and Tawny was not surprised by that strategic retreat. Promising Navarre she would be back within minutes, Tawny set off to find her sister again. She was even less surprised to find Bee talking to Zara, both their faces tense and troubled.

'OK…I'm the unlucky woman who just married a guy and caught a famous film star hanging round his neck like an albatross!' Tawny mocked. 'Bee, tell me what Tia was saying.'

Her sisters exchanged a conspiratorial glance.

'No, it's not fair to keep it from me. I have a right to know what you heard.'

Bee parted her lips with obvious reluctance. 'Tia was upset about the baby. I don't think she had realised that you were pregnant.'

'She was probably jealous. She's never been able to have a child of her own,' Zara commented.

'But the normal person to share that grief with would be her own husband, not *mine*,' Tawny completed with gentle emphasis. 'Don't worry about me. This isn't a love match. I've always known that. This marriage may not work out…not if that woman owns a slice of Navarre. I couldn't live with that, I couldn't *share* him—'

'I don't think that you have anything to worry about. Now if you'd caught them in a clinch that would've been a different matter,' Bee offered quietly. 'But you *didn't*. Don't let that colourful imagination of yours take over, Tawny. Be sensible about this. I think all you witnessed was a gorgeous drama queen demanding attention from a handsome man. I suspect that Tia is an old hand at that ruse and Navarre looked a little out of his depth. I also think that from now on he will be more careful with his boundaries when he's around Tia Castelli. He's no fool.'

Tawny struggled to take Bee's advice fully on board while she and Navarre were conveyed to the airport. He chatted calmly about their day and she endeavoured to make appropriate responses but she could not deny that the joy of the day had been snuffed out for her the instant she saw Navarre comforting Tia. She felt overwhelmed by the competition. What woman could possibly compete with such a fascinating femme fatale? Tia Castelli was a hugely talented international star with a colossal number of fans, an extraordinary beauty who truly lived a gilded life that belonged only in the glossiest of magazines. And Navarre *cared* about Tia. Tawny had seen the expression on his face as he looked down at the tiny distressed woman and that glimpse had shaken her and wounded her for she would have given ten years of her life to have her bridegroom look at her like that even once. That, she thought painfully, was what really lay at the heart of her suffering. Seeing him with Tia had only underlined what Tawny did not have with him.

But she would still have to man up and handle it, Tawny told herself in an urgent pep talk while they flew to Paris on Navarre's sleek private jet. She could not run away on the very first day of married life. She would only get one chance to make their marriage work so that they could give their son or daughter a proper loving home with a mother *and* a father. It was what she had always longed for and always lacked on her own account, but perhaps she had been naive as well not to face the truth that any relationship between two people would at times hurt her and demand that she compromise her ideals.

By the time they were in a limousine travelling to his home on Ile de France, several miles west of Paris, Navarre had borne the silence long enough. It was not a sulk—a sulk he could have dealt with. No, Tawny spoke when spoken to, even smiled when forced, but her vibrant spirit and quirky sense of fun were nowhere to be seen and it spooked him.

'I don't know you like this...what's wrong?' he asked, although it was a question that on principle he never, ever asked a woman, but now he was asking even though he feared that he already knew the answer.

Tawny shot him another fake smile. 'I'm just a bit tired, that's all. It's been a very long day.'

'D'accord. I constantly forget that you're pregnant and I'm making no allowances for that,' Navarre responded smoothly. 'Of course you're tired.'

It was on the tip of her tongue to tell him that it was their wedding night and she wasn't *that* tired but that would have been like issuing an invitation and she no longer possessed the confidence to do that.

The awkward silence was broken by her gasp as she looked out of the window and saw that the car was travelling through elaborate gardens and heading straight for a multi-turreted chateau of such stupendous splendour that she could only stare. 'Where on earth are we?'

'This is my home in Paris.'

'You're sure it's not a hotel?' Tawny asked stupidly, aghast at the size and magnificence of the property.

'It was for a while but it is now my private home. It's within easy reach of my offices and I like green space around me at the end of the day.'

Yes, it was obvious to her that he liked an enormous amount of green space and even more obvious why he had not been unduly impressed by Strathmore Castle, the entirety of which might well have fitted into the front hall of his spectacular chateau. Tawny was gobsmacked by the dimensions of the place. Although they had flown from London in a private jet it had still not occurred to her that Navarre might live like royalty in France. Nor had not it crossed her mind until that very moment what a simply vast gulf divided them as people.

'I feel like Cinderella,' Tawny whispered weakly. 'You live in a castle.'

He was frowning. 'I thought you'd be pleased.'

They were greeted by a manservant in the echoing vastness of the hall and every surface seemed to be gilded or marbled or mirrored so that she could see far too many confusing reflections of her bewildered face. 'It's not really a castle, it's more like a palace,' she muttered when he informed her that refreshments awaited them upstairs.

She mounted the giant staircase. 'So how long have you lived here?'

'Several years. You know, you shouldn't be wearing heels that high in your condition—'

'Navarre?' Tawny interrupted. 'Don't tell me what to wear. I'm not working for you any more.'

'No, we're married now.'

Tawny did not like the tone Navarre had employed to make that statement. She felt that he ought to be over the moon about being married to her, or at least capable of pretending to be. Instead he sounded like a guy who had got to bring the wrong woman home and that was not an idea that she liked at all, for it came all too close to matching her own worst fears.

'I don't want to have an argument with you on our wedding day,' Navarre informed her without any expression at all.

'Did I say that I wanted an argument?' Tawny demanded a touch stridently as he thrust open a heavy door and she stalked into yet another vast room, a bedroom complete with sofas and tables and several exit doors. 'It's too big…it's *all* too big and fancy for me!'

As her voice began to rise in volume Navarre cut in. 'Then we'll sell it and move—'

'But then you wouldn't be happy. This is what you're used to!'

'I grew up in a variety of slums,' he reminded her levelly and somehow the way he looked at her made her feel like a child throwing a tantrum.

Tawny gritted her teeth on another foolish comment. Her brain was all over the place. It certainly wasn't functioning as it should be. She kept on picturing Tia's flawless face and her even more perfect and always immaculately clothed body. She was thinking of the frivolous, frothy, wedding night negligee she had purchased with such joy in her heart and feeling sick at the prospect of having to put the outfit on and appear in it for his benefit. Who was she kidding? It would not hide her overblown breasts or her even more swollen stomach.

'You know…' Tawny mumbled uneasily, succumbing to her sense of insecurity. 'I'm not really in the right mood for a wedding night.'

'*Je sais ce que tu ressens*…I know how you feel.' Navarre stood there like a statue.

Tawny had expected him to argue with her, not agree with her. She wanted him to kiss her, persuade her, make everything magically all right again, but instead he just stood there, six feet plus of inert and unresponsive masculine toughness.

'You're tired, *ma petite.* I'll sleep elsewhere.'

Tawny recognised the absolute control he was exerting not to let her see what he really thought. She suspected that he was annoyed with her, that he had hoped she would continue as though nothing whatsoever had happened, as though nothing at all had changed between them. But how could she do that? How *could* she pretend she had not seen the way he looked at Tia? He had never looked at her like that, but she so badly needed him to and, denied what she most wanted, she refused to settle for being a substitute for Tia. And, to be frank, a very poor second-best at that.

Wishing her goodnight with infuriating courtesy, Navarre left the room. Her legs weak, Tawny sagged down on the sofa at the end of the bed as though she had gone ten rounds with a champion boxer. He was gone and she was no happier. She was at the mercy of as many doubts as a fishing net had holes. Had she done the wrong thing? What was the right thing in such circumstances when all she was conscious of was the level of her disillusionment? She turned her bright head to look at the big bed that they might have shared that night had she been tougher and more practical and she imagined she heard the sound of a sharp painful crack—it was the sound of her heart breaking...

CHAPTER TEN

TAWNY signed the cartoon and sat back from it with a
sense of accomplishment. She was working in the room
that Navarre had had set up as a studio for her. For the first
time in her creative life she had the latest in light tables
to work at. Her cartoon series now entitled 'The English
Wife' and carried in a fashionable weekly magazine, had
already attracted a favourable wave of comment from the
French press and she had even been interviewed in her
capacity as cartoonist and wife of a powerful French industrialist. A knock on the door announced the arrival
of Gaspard, who was in charge of the household and the
staff, bringing her morning coffee and a snack.

On the surface life was wonderful, Tawny acknowledged, striving to concentrate only on the positive angles. Navarre had been in London the previous night on
a business trip, but Tawny had not accompanied him because she had work to complete. Furthermore just as he
had forecast she adored Paris: the noble architecture of the
buildings, beautiful bridges and cobblestoned streets, the
Seine gleaming below the autumn sunlight, the entertaining parade of chic residents. Settling in for someone who
spoke French and was married to a Frenchman had not
proved much of a challenge. In fact her new life in France
was absolutely brilliant now that her career had finally

taken off. She had no financial worries, a beautiful roof over her head covered with all the turrets a castle-loving girl could ever want and a staff who ensured that she had to do virtually nothing domestic for herself. The food was amazing as well, Tawny conceded, munching hungrily through the kind of dainty little pastry that Navarre's chef excelled at creating.

In fact after six weeks of being married to Navarre, Tawny was willing to admit that she was a very lucky woman. Cradling her coffee in one hand, Tawny studied herself in a wall mirror. Her hair piled on top of her head in a convenient style that her hairdresser had taught her to do, she was wearing her favourite skinny jeans teamed with an artfully draped jersey tunic that skimmed her growing bump and long suede boots. She had signed up with a Parisian obstetrician and her pregnancy was proceeding well. She had no problems on that front at all: she was ridiculously healthy.

Indeed her only problem was her marriage…or, to be more specific, the marriage that had never got off the ground in the first place. With the calmer frame of mind brought on by the passage of several weeks, she knew that wrecking their wedding night and rejecting Navarre had been the wrong thing to do. An outright argument would have been preferable; a demand for an explanation about that scene with Tia would have been understandable. But refusing to ask questions and hiding behind her wounded pride had not been a good idea at all, for it had imposed a distance between them that was impossible to eradicate in such a very large house. My goodness, he was sleeping two corridors away from her! And she had only found that out by tiptoeing round like a cat burglar in the dark of the night and listening to where he went when he came upstairs at the end of the evening.

There were times, many many times, when Tawny just wanted to *scream* at Navarre in frustration. He did not avoid her but he did work fairly long hours. At the same time she could not accuse him of neglecting her either because he had gone to considerable lengths to make time and space for her presence in his life and show her Paris as only a native could. He would phone and arrange to meet her for lunch or dinner or sweep her off shopping with an alacrity that astonished her. Navarre was a very woman-savvy male. When she was in his company he awarded her his full attention and he was extraordinarily charming, but he still continued to maintain a hands-off approach that was driving her crazy.

Sometimes she wondered if Navarre was very cleverly and with great subtlety punishing her for that rejection on the first night. He took her romantic places and left her as untouched as if she were his ninety-year-old maiden aunt. He had introduced her to Ladurée, an opulently designed French café/ gallery where the beautiful people met early evening for coffee and delicious pastel-coloured macaroons that melted in the mouth. He had shown her the delights of La Hune, a trendy bookshop in the bohemian sixth *arrondissement* of St-Germain. He had taken her shopping on the famous designer rue St—Honoré and spent a fortune on her. She had toured the colourful organic market at boulevard Raspail and eaten pumpkin muffins fresh from a basket. They had dined at Laperouse, a dimly lit ornate restaurant beside the Seine, an experience that had cried out for a more intimate connection and she had sat across the table willing him to make a move on her or even voice a flirtatious comment, only to be disappointed.

And then there were the gifts he brought her, featuring everything from an art book that had sent her into ecstasies to a pair of Louboutin shoes that sparkled like pure gold, not to mention the most gorgeous jewels and flowers. He was never done buying her presents, indeed he rarely came home empty-handed. She had got the message: he was generous, he liked to *give.* But how was she supposed to respond? Her teeth gritted. She really didn't understand the guy she had married because she didn't know what he wanted from her. Was he content with their relationship as it was? A platonic front of a marriage for the sake of their child? Were the constant gifts and entertaining outings a reward for not questioning his relationship with Tia Castelli? Could he possibly be that callous and without scruples?

Yet this was the same man who had gripped her hand in genuine joy and appreciation when he attended a sonogram appointment with her and they saw their child together for the first time on a screen. The warmth of his response had been everything she could have hoped for. Their little girl, the daughter whom Tawny already cherished in her heart, would rejoice in a fully committed and ardent father. She knew enough about Navarre to understand how very important it was for him to do everything for his child that had not been done for him. He might hide his emotions, but she knew they ran deep and true when it came to their baby. It hurt not to inspire an atom of that emotion on her own account.

After a light lunch, she walked round the gardens until a light mist of drizzling rain came on and drove her indoors. She was presented with a package that had been delivered and she carried it upstairs, wondering ruefully what the latest treat was that Navarre had bought her. She extracted an elaborate box and, opening it, worked through layers of tissue paper to extract the most exquisite set of silk lingerie she had ever seen in her life. A dreamy smile softened her full mouth and her pale eyes flared with the thought of the possibilities awakened by that more intimate present. Her fingers dallied with the delicate set. An invitation? Or was that wishful thinking? Was it just one more in a long line of wonderfully special gifts? Maybe she should wear it to meet him off his flight this evening and just ask him what he meant by it. That outrageous thought made her laugh out loud.

But that same thought worked on her throughout the afternoon. Maybe a little plain speaking was all that was required to sort out their marriage. And Navarre was far too tricky and suspicious of women to engage in plain speech without a lot of encouragement. Was she willing to show him the way? Put her money where her mouth was? The concept of putting her mouth anywhere near Navarre was so arousing that she blushed.

Toying with the concept, she went off to shower and rub scented cream all over her mostly slender body before applying loads of mascara and lippy. When she saw herself in that exquisite palest green lingerie she almost got cold feet. The tummy was there, there was no concealing or avoiding it, but it was his baby and he was definitely looking forward to its existence, she reminded herself comfortingly. As long as she wore vertiginous boots and looked at herself face on rather than taking in her less sensually appealing profile, she decided she didn't look silly. Donning a black silky raincoat ornamented with lots of zips that had recently caught her eye for being unusual, she left the bedroom.

At the airport, Navarre was stunned when, engaged in commenting on his reorganisation of CCC to a financial journalist, he glanced across the concourse and saw his wife awaiting him. That was definitely an unexpected development. In truth he had been a little edgy about the latest gift he had sent her. He had worried that it was a step too far, which might upset the marital apple cart even more, and so he had waited until he was out of the country to send it. He could never remember being so unsure with a woman before and he had found it an unnerving experience. As he excused himself to approach her a radiant smile lit up her face and she looked so gorgeous with her spectacular hair tumbling round her fragile features that he almost walked into a woman wheeling a luggage trolley.

'Navarre...' Tawny pronounced, hooking a slender pale hand to his arm.

'I like the coat, *ma petite*,' he murmured, although even with his wide experience he had never before seen a raincoat that appeared to lead a double life as a distinctly sexy garment, for it was short, showing the merest glimpse of long pale thigh and knee above the most incredible pair of long, tight, high-heeled boots.

Luminous pale blue eyes lifted to his face. 'I thought you'd like the boots—'

'*Il n'y a pas de mais*...no buts about that,' Navarre breathed a little thickly, wondering what she was wearing below the coat because from his vantage point no garment was visible at the neck. He watched her climb into the limousine and as the split at the back of the coat parted a tantalising couple of inches along with the movement he froze for a split second at the sight of the pale green knickers riding high on her rounded little bottom.

As the car pulled away, Tawny crossed her legs and asked him about London. His attention was welded to her legs, though, his manner distracted, and when he glanced up to find her watching him, a faint line of colour barred his high cheekbones, highlighting eyes of the most wicked green. 'You have to know that you look amazing,' he stressed unevenly. 'I can't take my eyes off you.'

'That's what I like to hear, but it's been so long since you said anything in that line…or looked,' she pointed out gently.

His lush lashes cloaked his gaze protectively. 'Our wedding day should have been perfect but instead everything went wrong and that was my fault. I didn't feel that I was in a position to make demands. I didn't want to risk driving you away.'

In a sudden movement, Tawny reached for his hand. 'I'm not going anywhere!'

'People said stuff like that to me throughout my childhood and then broke their promises,' he admitted with a stark sincerity that shook her.

'Touching me…I mean,' she said awkwardly, 'it wouldn't have needed a demand.'

Navarre rested a light fingertip below the ripe curve of her raspberry-tinted mouth and said, 'How was I to know that?'

As his hand trailed along her cheekbone Tawny pushed her cheek into his palm, lashes sensually low. 'You know now,' she told him.

'You're so different from the other women I've known. I didn't want to get it wrong with you,' he admitted gruffly, a delicious tension stretching out the moment as she angled her mouth up and he took the invitation with a swift, sure hunger that released a moan of approval from her throat.

Navarre straightened again and a gave her a breathtaking smile. 'I dare not touch you until we get back home. I'm like dynamite waiting on a lit match,' he groaned, studying her with hot, hungry intensity. 'It's been too long and I'm too revved up.'

Alight with all the potency of her feminine power, Tawny grinned and whispered curiously, 'How long?'

His brow indented. 'You know how long it's been.'

'You mean…I was your last lover? When we were together that last time in London?' Tawny specified in open amazement. 'There hasn't been anyone else since then?'

Navarre gave a rueful laugh. 'I've always been more into quality than quantity, *chérie*. I'm past the age where I sleep with women purely for kicks.'

Tawny tacitly understood what he was confirming. Even when their short-lived relationship had appeared to be over he had not taken another lover. Obviously he had not met anyone he wanted enough, which with the choices he had to have was a huge compliment to Tawny. Even more obviously, if she accepted his word on that score, it meant that he could not be engaged in even an occasional affair with Tia Castelli. Perhaps he had once loved Tia and, although it was in the past, he retained a fondness for the beautiful film star, she reasoned feverishly, desperate to explain what she had seen between them on her wedding day.

But she *was* seriously surprised by the news that he had been celibate for months on end. Meeting his level scrutiny, she believed him on that score one hundred per cent and it was as if the weight of the world fell off her shoulders in the same moment. Suddenly she was furious with herself for not asking questions about Tia and demanding answers sooner. She had conserved her pride and remained silent but unhappy and she wasn't proud of the reality that she had behaved like a coward, frightened of what the truth might reveal and of how much it might hurt. Loving a man who could be so reserved might never be easy, but she needed to learn how to handle that side of his nature.

In the vast bedroom that she had become accustomed to occupying alone she let him unzip the coat and part the edges to look down at her scantily clad curves with smouldering appreciation.

'I'm going to have to start buying you stuff,' she began shyly as he laid her down on the bed and started to carefully unzip her boots.

'No, this moment is my gift,' Navarre countered huskily, burying his mouth between her breasts and running a skilful hand along the extended length of her thigh to the taut triangle of fabric between her legs.

Her body was supersensitive after all the months of deprivation. The pulse of need she was struggling to control tightened up an almost painful notch. Sadly the lingerie that had brought them together received precious little attention and was cast aside within minutes while Navarre's shirt got ripped in the storm of Tawny's impatience. She ran her hands over the gloriously hard, flat expanse of his abs and then lower to the blatant thrust of his arousal. His breath hitched in his throat as he protested that he was too aroused to bear her touch.

'You mean you're only good for one go…like a Christmas cracker?' Tawny asked him deadpan.

And, startled by that teasing analogy, Navarre laughed long and hard as he studied her with fascination. 'Where have you been all my life?'

He kissed her passionately again and matters quickly became extremely heated. He tried to make her wait because he wanted to make an occasion of what he saw as a long delayed wedding night, but she was in no mood for ceremony and she refused to wait, holding him to her with possessive hands and locking her slim legs round his waist to entrap him. She had expectations and she was unusually bossy. He was trying for slow and gentle,

she was striving for hard and fast, and with a little art-
ful angling of her hips and caressing and whispered en-
couragements she got exactly what she wanted delivered
with an unrivalled hunger that left her body singing and
dancing with excitement. Desire momentarily quenched,
she lay in his arms, peacefully enjoying the fact that he
was still touching her as if he couldn't quite believe that
he had now reclaimed that intimacy. He stroked her arm
and strung a line of kisses round the base of her throat
while still holding her close to his lean, damp body and
at that instant, with all that appreciation coming her way,
she felt like a queen.

In fact when he got out of bed she almost panicked, a
small hand clamping round his wrist as if he were a fleeing prisoner. 'Where are you going?'

Navarre lifted the phone with a flourish. 'I'm ordering
some food, *ma petite*—we both need sustenance to keep
up the pace.'

'And then?' she checked, heat and awareness still rippling through swollen and sensitive places as she looked
at him.

'We share a shower and I stay...all night?' He was looking hopeful and she knew she wouldn't be able to disap-
point him, particularly when she just didn't want him out
of her sight for a minute.

'And if you should feel the need to wake me up and
jump me during the night at any time,' Navarre drawled
silkily over supper, 'you are very welcome.'

'Well, the pregnancy damage is already done.'

'Don't say that even jokingly,' he urged, feeding her
grapes and Parma ham and tiny sweet tomatoes and reminding her all over again why she loved him so much.
'I can't wait to be a father.'

In the secure circle of Navarre's arms for the first time

ever, Tawny slept blissfully well. To his great disappointment she didn't wake him up for anything so that he could prove all over again that he had nothing in common whatsoever with a Christmas cracker. When she wakened it was late morning and she blinked drowsily. Stretching a hand over to the empty space beside her in the bed, she suppressed a sigh even as she stretched luxuriantly while lazily considering their marriage, which she was finally convinced had a real future. He was gone, of course he was long gone, he left for the office at the crack of dawn most weekdays. Only when she had stumbled out of bed to move in the direction of the bathroom did she realise that Navarre had not even left the room—he was actually seated in an armchair in the dimness.

'My word, I didn't see you over there…what a fright you gave me!' She gasped, stooping hurriedly to pick up her robe from the foot of the bed and dig her arms into the sleeves because she was still somewhat shy of displaying her pregnant body to him. 'Why are you still at home?'

'May I open the curtains?' At her nod, he buzzed back the drapes and light flooded in, illuminating the harsh lines etched in his taut features. 'I've been waiting for you to wake up.'

'What's wrong? What's happened?'

'Your cell phone has been ringing on and off for a couple of hours…your sisters, I assume, your family trying to get in touch with you…I didn't answer the calls.' Navarre lifted a shoulder in a very Gallic shrug and surveyed her with brooding regret. 'I switched off your phone because I wanted to be the one to tell you what has happened—'

'I need to use the bathroom first!' Tawny flung wildly at him and sped in there like a mouse pursued by a cat, slamming the door behind her. She didn't want to know; she didn't want to hear anything bad! She had wakened feeling happy, safe and insanely optimistic for the first time in a long time. How could that precious hope be taken away from her so quickly?

CHAPTER ELEVEN

ONCE Tawny had freshened up and mentally prepared herself for some sort of disaster, she emerged again, pale and tense.

'Has someone died? My gran—?'

'*Merde alors*…no, it is nothing of that nature!' Navarre hastened to assure her.

Tawny breathed again, slow and deep, striving to remain calm when all she really wanted to do was scream and be hysterical and childish because she had never wanted bad news less, and now she feared that he was about to tell her something or *confess* something that would destroy her and their marriage. If nobody had died or got hurt, what else was there?

'I saw Tia while I was over in London. She took a hotel room and I visited her there. Yesterday an English tabloid newspaper published an account of the fact that we were in that hotel suite alone together for more than an hour and printed photos of us entering and leaving the hotel separately.'

Tawny drew her body up so stiff with her muscles pulled so tight that she stretched at least an inch above her normal height. 'You went to an hotel with her…you're admitting that?'

'I won't lie to you about it.'

'You know a normal man would be rendezvousing with his secretary or a colleague between five and seven in the evening for clandestine sex before he comes home to his wife. That's the norm for a mistress—you're not supposed to be shagging a world-famous film star!' Tawny condemned shakily, throwing words in a wild staccato burst while nausea pooled in her stomach because she immediately grasped the appalling fact that his confession meant that all her worst fears were actually true. She felt as if she had woken up inside a nightmare and did not know what to say or do. She hovered on the priceless Aubusson rug, swallowed alive by her anguish.

Navarre was watching every flicker cross her highly expressive face and he too had lost colour below his bronzed complexion. 'Tia is not and has never been my mistress. We're friends and we lunched in her suite in private, that's *all*,' Navarre declared, shifting an emphatic hand to stress that point. 'The paparazzi never leave her alone. Her every move is recorded by cameras. She has to be very careful of her reputation because of her marriage and her career, which is the only reason why we usually meet up in secret—'

'Never mind her. What about *your* marriage?' Tawny asked him baldly, wondering if he could seriously be expecting her to swallow such an unlikely story. Lunch and no sex? What sort of an idiot did he think she was?

A hasty rat-a-tat-tat sounded on the bedroom door and, with a bitten-off curse that betrayed just how worked up he was as well, Navarre strode past her to answer it. Hearing Gaspard's voice, Tawny rested a hand on a corner of the bed and slowly, carefully sank her weak body down on the comfortable mattress. Her legs felt like wet noodles and she felt dizzy and sick. It was nerves and fear, of course, she told herself impatiently. She wasn't about to faint or throw up like some silly Victorian maiden. Her husband had slept with Tia Castelli. In fact he obviously slept with the actress on a very regular basis, for by the sound of it their meeting arrangements seemed to be set in quite a cosy little routine. That suggested that their private encounters had been taking place for at least a couple of years.

Navarre closed the door and raked long restive fingers through his short black hair. Momentarily he closed his eyes as he was struggling to muster his resources.

'What did Gaspard want?'

Navarre expelled his breath in a hiss and shot her a veiled glance. 'To tell me that Tia has arrived—'

'Here? She's *here?*' Tawny exclaimed in utter disbelief.

'We'll talk downstairs and settle this for once and all,' Navarre pronounced grimly. 'I'm sorry I've involved you in this mess—'

'Tia will be even sorrier if I get my hands on her,' Tawny slammed back strickenly. 'How on earth could she come here? What sort of a woman would do that?'

'Think about it,' Navarre urged tautly. 'Only a woman who is not my lover would come to the home I share with my wife—'

'That might be true of most women, but not necessarily when the woman concerned is a drama queen like Tia Castelli! I'll get dressed and come down…but don't you dare go near her without me there!' Tawny warned him fierily while she dug frantically through drawers and wardrobes to gather up an outfit to take into the bathroom.

He's having an affair and his lover has got the brass neck to come to the home he shares with his pregnant wife, she thought in shock and horror. Yet last night they had been so close, so happy together. How could she have been prepared for such a development? In a daze she pulled on her jeans and a loose silk geometric print top. She couldn't even *try* to compete with an international star in the looks department.

He had belonged to Tia first, Tawny reasoned wretchedly, only choosing to marry Tawny because she was pregnant and possibly because he had wanted to make his own life away from Tia's. After all, Tia was married as well. And she could have forgiven him for the affair if he had broken off his liaison with the blonde beauty to concentrate on his marriage instead. But he had not done that. Indeed Navarre appeared to believe that he could somehow have both of them in his life. Did he aspire to enjoying both a mistress *and* a wife?

'What is she doing here in France?' Tawny pressed Navarre on the way downstairs.

'We'll find out soon enough,' Navarre forecast flatly.

A very large set of ornate pale blue leather cases sat in the hall and Tawny was aghast at that less than subtle message. Tia had not only come to visit but also, it seemed, to stay. Tia, sheathed in a black form-fitting dress that hugged her curves, broke into a tumbling flood of Italian as soon as Navarre and Tawny entered the drawing room.

'Speak in English, please,' Navarre urged the overwrought woman. 'Let us be calm.'

Tawny dealt him a pained appraisal. 'Only a man would suggest that in this situation.'

'Luke's thrown me out—he won't listen to anything I say!' Tia cried in English and she threw herself at Navarre like a homing pigeon. 'What am I going to do? What the hell am I going to do now?'

Standing there as superfluous as a third wheel on a bicycle and being totally ignored, Tawny ground her teeth together. 'Well, you *can't* stay here,' she told Tia loudly, reckoning that it would take a raised voice to penetrate the blonde's shell of self-interest.

Slowly, Tia lifted her golden head from Navarre's chest and focused incredulous big blue eyes on Tawny. 'Are you speaking to me?'

'You're not welcome under this roof,' Tawny delivered with quiet dignity.

Ironically, in spite of all that had happened, Tia seemed aghast at that assurance. She backed off a step from Navarre, her full attention locking to him. 'Are you going to allow her to speak to me like that?'

'Tawny is my wife and this is her home. If she doesn't want you staying here in the wake of that scandal in London, which affects me as much as you, I'm afraid you will have to listen to her,' he spelt out.

A little of Tawny's rigid tension eased.

'You should be putting me first—what's the matter with you?' Tia yelled at him accusingly, golden hair bouncing on her shoulders, slender arms spread in dramatic emphasis.

'I'm putting my marriage first but I should have done that sooner,' Navarre murmured levelly and, although he spoke quietly, his deep dark drawl carried. 'Allow me to tell Tawny the truth about our relationship, Tia—'

Tia stalked back towards him, her beautiful face flushed with furious disbelief. 'Absolutely not...you can't tell her...not under *any* circumstances!'

'We don't have a choice,' Navarre declared, his impatience patent while strain and something else Tawny couldn't distinguish warred in his set features as he looked expectantly at the older woman.

Tia shot Tawny a fulminating appraisal. 'Don't tell her. I don't trust her—'

'But I do...' Navarre reached out to Tawny and after

a moment of surprise and hesitation she moved closer to accept his hand and let him draw her beneath one arm. 'Tawny is part of my life now. You can't ignore her, you can't treat her as if she is of no account.'

'If you tell her, if you risk my marriage and my career just to please her, I'll never forgive you for it!' Tia sobbed in a growing rage.

'Your marriage is already at risk but that's not an excuse to put mine in jeopardy as well.' Navarre's arm tightened round Tawny's taut shoulders. 'Tawny…Tia is my mother, but that is a very big secret which you can't share with anyone at all outside this room—'

'Your m-mother?' Tawny stammered, completely disconcerted by that shattering claim and twisting her head to stare at him. 'For goodness' sake, she's not old enough to be your mother!'

Navarre was wryly amused. 'Tia is a good deal older than she looks.'

Tia went rigid with resentment at that statement. 'I was only a child when I gave birth to you—'

'She was twenty-one but pretending to be a teenager at the time,' Navarre extended wearily. 'I'll tell you the rest of the story some other time but right now the fact that she is my mother and that we like to stay in regular contact is really all that's relevant.'

'His…mother,' Tawny framed weakly, still studying the glamorous older woman in disbelief, for, according to what Navarre had just told her, Tia had to be into her fifties yet she could still comfortably pass for being a woman in her late thirties. Shock was still gripping Tawny so hard that she could hardly think straight.

'But that can never come out in public,' Tia proclaimed, angrily defensive. 'I've told lies. I've kept secrets. It would destroy my reputation and I don't want Luke to know that his own mother is younger than I am—'

'I bet she's not a beauty like you, though,' Tawny commented thoughtfully and earned an almost appreciative glance from the woman whom she had just discovered to be her mother-in-law.

'I think Luke could adapt,' Navarre interposed soothingly. 'You're still the same woman he loved and married.'

Tia shuddered. 'He would never forgive me for lying to him.'

'Why were you crying on our wedding day?' Tawny enquired to combat the simple fact that she was still dizzily thinking, She can't be his mother, she *can't* be!

'Do I *look* like I want to be a grandmother?' Tia demanded in a tone of horror. 'Do I look that old?'

'I don't think you'll ever be asked to carry out that role,' Tawny responded drily, weary of the woman's enormous vanity and concern about her age while she instinctively continued to study those famous features in search of a likeness between mother and son. And she realised that when she removed their very different colouring from the comparison there was quite a definite similarity in bone structure. He was so good-looking because his mother was gorgeous, she registered numbly.

'Right now I only want to lie down and rest. I'm exhausted,' Tia complained petulantly, treating both her son and his wife to an accusing look as though that were their fault. 'I assume I can stay now that I've shown my credentials.'

'Yes, of course,' Tawny confirmed, marvelling that such a selfish personality had ever contrived to win Navarre's loyalty and tenderness. And yet, without a shadow of a doubt, Tia had. Tawny had not been mistaken over what she had thought she had seen in Navarre when he was with his mother on their wedding day. He cared for the volatile woman.

'If you want to sort this out with Luke you will have to let him into the secret,' Navarre warned his mother levelly.

Tia told him to mind his own business with a tartness that was very maternal, but which would have been more suited to a little boy than an adult male. Gaspard was summoned to show Tia to her room. Tawny had offered but was imperiously waved away, Tia clearly not yet prepared to accept a friendly gesture from her corner. Tawny grasped that she had a possessive mother-in-law to deal with, for Tia undoubtedly resented Navarre's loyalty to his wife.

Tia swept out and the door closed. Navarre looked at Tawny.

Tawny winced and said limply, 'Wow, your mother's quite a character.'

'She's temperamental when she gets upset. I wanted to tell you but a long time ago I swore never to tell anyone that I was her son and she held me to my promise.'

'Your mother...' Tawny shook her head very slowly. 'I never would have guessed that in a million years.'

Over breakfast and only after Tawny had phoned her sisters to tell them that, *no,* she really wasn't concerned about silly stories in the papers, Navarre explained the intricacies of his birth, which had been buried deep and concealed behind a wall of lies to protect Tia's star power. According to Tia's official history she had been discovered as a fifteen year old schoolgirl in the street by a famous director. Her first film had won so many awards it had gone global and shot her to stardom. In fact the pretence that she was much younger had simply been a publicity exercise and her kid sister's birth certificate had been used for proof when Tia was actually twenty-one years old. Soon after her discovery she had fallen pregnant by the famous director. A scandalous affair with a married man threatened to destroy her pristine reputation and her embryo career, so Navarre's birth had taken place in secrecy. Tia had travelled to Paris with her older sister and had pretended to be her so that her baby could be registered as her sister's child. That cover up achieved, Tia had returned to show business while paying her sister and her boyfriend to raise Navarre in a Paris flat.

Tawny was frowning. 'Then how come you ended up in foster care?'

'I have no memory of my aunt at all. She only kept me for a couple of years. The money Tia used to buy her sister's silence was spent on drugs and when my aunt died of an overdose I joined the care system. I had no idea I had a mother alive until I was eighteen and at university,' Navarre extended wryly. 'I was approached by a lawyer first, carefully sworn to silence—'

'And then you met your mother. Must've been a shock,' Tia remarked.

An almost boyish expression briefly crossed his lean taut face as he looked back into the past and his handsome mouth took on a wry cast. 'I was in complete awe of her.'

Tawny could hardly imagine the full effect of Tia Castelli on a teenager who had been totally alone in the world all his life. Naturally his mother had walked straight into his heart when he had never had anyone of his own before. 'She's very beautiful.'

'Tia may not be showing it right now but she does also have tremendous charm. Ever since then we've been meeting up at least once a month and we often talk on the phone and email. That's one of the reasons I was so concerned that someone might have accessed my laptop,' he confided. 'I've seen her through many, many crises and have become her rock in every storm. I'm very fond of her.'

Tawny nodded. 'Even though she won't own up to you in public?'

'What would that mean to me at my age? I know she's far from perfect,' Navarre acknowledged with a dismissive lift of an ebony brow. 'But what else does she know? She was an abused child from a very poor home.'

Tawny was not as understanding of his mother's flaws as he was. 'But what did she ever do for you? You had a miserable childhood.'

'But it made me strong, *chérie*. As for Tia, even after decades of fame she still lives in terror of losing everything she has. She did what she thought best for me at the time. She helped me find my first job, invested in my first company, undoubtedly helped me to become the success that I am today.'

'That's just the power of money you're talking about and I doubt if it meant much to someone as rich as she must be.' Her eyes glittered silver with moisture, the tightening of her throat muscles as she fought back tears lending her voice a hoarse edge. 'I'm thinking of the child you were, growing up without a mother or love or anyone of your own…I can't bear the thought of that.'

In an abrupt movement that lacked his normal measured grace, Navarre vaulted upright and walked round the table to lift Tawny up out of her seat. *'Je vais bien…* I'm OK. But I admit that I didn't know what love was until I met you.'

Assuming that he had guessed how she felt about him, Tawny reddened. 'Am I that obvious?'

A gentle fingertip traced the silvery trail of a tear on her cheek.

'There is nothing obvious about you. In fact you defied my understanding from the first moment we met and, the more I saw of you, the more desperately I wanted to know what it was about you which got to me when other women never had.'

Her lashes flicked up on curious eyes. 'I…got to you? In what way?'

'In every way a woman can appeal to a man. First to my body, then to my brain and finally to my heart,' Navarre specified. 'And you dug in so deep in my heart, I was wretched without you when we were apart but far too proud to come looking for you again.'

Tawny rested a hand on a broad shoulder to steady herself. 'Wretched?' she repeated doubtfully, unable to associate such a word with him.

A rueful smile shadowed Navarre's wide eloquent mouth. 'I was very unhappy and unsettled for weeks on end. I thought I was infatuated with you. I tried so hard to fight it and forget about you but it didn't work.'

'Navarre…' Tawny breathed uncertainly. 'Are you trying to tell me that you love me?'

'Obviously not doing a very good job of it. I think it was love at first sight.' His eyes gazed down into hers full of warmth and tenderness. 'I've been in love with you for months. I knew I loved you long before I married you. Why do you think I was so keen to put that wedding ring on your hand?'

'The b-baby.'

Navarre drew her back against him and splayed a possessive hand across the firm swell of her stomach. 'I have very good intentions towards our baby but I married you because I loved you and wanted to share my life with you, *n'est ce pas?*'

'But you said you were strongly attracted to me and that that was enough.'

'I said what I had to say to get that ring on your finger for real,' Navarre breathed, pressing his mouth to the sensitive nape of her neck and making her shiver with sudden awareness. 'I'm a ruthless man. I would have said whatever it took to achieve that goal because I believed the end result would be worth it. I was determined that you would be mine for ever, *ma petite*.'

Overjoyed by that admission, Tawny twisted round and pressed her hands to his strong cheekbones to align their mouths and kiss him with slow, sweet brevity as more questions that had to be answered bubbled up in her brain. 'What on earth was on that laptop of yours?'

'CCC buyout stuff and some very personal emails from Tia. She tells me everything.'

'No wonder Luke's jealous of you.'

'As long as Tia refuses to tell him the truth I am powerless to alter that situation.'

Tawny treated him to a shrewd appraisal. 'She's part of the reason you wanted a fake fiancée for the Golden Awards, isn't she?'

'I promised Tia that I would bring a girlfriend and I too believed it to be a sensible precaution where Luke was concerned. Unfortunately the lady backed out at the last minute and—'

'And you hired me instead,' Tawny slotted in. 'What happened to the lady who backed out?'

'I told her that I'd met someone else when I got back to Paris.'

'But that wasn't true...you had already left me.'

His eyes glimmered. 'But I still didn't want anyone else. You had me on a chain by then. Don't you remember that last night in London when I came to your door?'

Tawny stiffened. 'I also recall how it ended with you telling me I was a good—'

Navarre pulled her up against him and gazed down at her in reproof. 'Wasn't that in response to you threatening to tell the world what I was like in bed?'

A sensual shimmer of response wafted through Tawny and she pressed closer, tucking her head into his shoulder to breathe in the deliriously addictive scent of his skin. 'Well, now that you mention it, it might have been,' she teased, acknowledging that she had met her match while relishing the claim she had had him on a chain by that stage. A chain of love and commitment he refused to give to a woman who was a failed thief threating to tell all to the newspapers? She didn't blame him for that, she couldn't blame him for walking away at that point, for one thing she did appreciate about the man she loved was his very strong moral compass.

'When I saw you with Tia at the wedding I feared the worst,' she confided as his arms tightened round her.

'I was desperate to tell you the truth and relieved when you didn't force a scene because I didn't want to break my promise to my mother,' he admitted grimly. 'But I should have broken the promise and told you then. Unfortunately it took me a few weeks to appreciate that as my wife you have to have the strongest claim to my loyalty.'

'Sorry about the wedding night that never was,' she mumbled ruefully. 'I felt so insecure after seeing how close you were to her. I could *see* that there was a connection between you and I love you so much...'

Navarre pushed up her chin and stared down at her searchingly. 'Since when?' he demanded and his beautiful mouth quirked. 'Since you saw my beautiful castle in France?'

His wife dealt him a reproving look. 'I shall treat that

suggestion with the contempt it deserves! No, I fell for you long before that. Remember that breakfast in Scotland after that nasty newspaper spread which revealed that I was a maid? When you brought me my food and stood by me in front of everyone as though nothing had happened, I really *loved* you for it…'

'Snap. I loved you for your dignity and cool, *ma petite.*' A tender smile softened the often hard line of his shapely mouth. Long fingers stroked her spine as he crushed her to him and kissed her with a breathless hunger that made her knees weak.

For once, Tawny had a small breakfast because the conversation and what followed were too entertaining to take a rain check on. He urged her upstairs to the bed they had only shared once and they lost themselves in the passion they had both restrained for so long.

In the lazy aftermath of quenching their desire, Tawny stared at her handsome husband and said, 'What on earth game have you been playing with me all these weeks we've been married?'

'It was no game.' Navarre laughed. 'We had no court-ship—we never dated. I was trying to go back to the be-ginning and do everything differently in the hope that you would start feeling for me what I felt for you.'

In dismay at that simple exclamation and touched that he had gone to that amount of idealistic effort without receiving the appreciation he had undoubtedly deserved, Tawny clamped a hand to her lips. 'Oh, my goodness, how stupid am I that I didn't see that?'

Navarre looked a touch superior and stretched luxuriantly against the tumbled sheets while regarding her with intense appreciation. 'Of the two of us, I'm the romantic one. Don't forget that reality when you next draw a cartoon in which I figure merely as a skirt-chasing Frenchman!'

Tawny smoothed a possessive hand over his spectacular abs and smiled down at him with unusual humility. 'I won't,' she promised happily. 'I love you just the way you are.'

EPILOGUE

JOIE, named for the joy she had brought her adoring parents, toddled across the floor and presented Luke Convery with a toy brick.

'She's cute but I wouldn't want one of my own,' the rock musician said with an apologetic grimace as he dropped down on his knees to place the brick where Navarre and Tawny's daughter, with her fantastically curly black hair and pale blue eyes, wanted it placed. 'I grew up the youngest of nine kids and I've never wanted that kind of hassle for myself.'

'Kids aren't for everyone,' Tawny agreed, thinking of how much her mother had resented being a parent, yet Susan Baxter had proved to be a much more interested grandmother than her daughter had expected. In fact mother and daughter had become a good deal closer since Joie's birth in London eighteen months earlier.

Tawny often spent weekends in London to meet up with her sisters and her mother before travelling down to see her grandmother. She had been married to Navarre for two years and had never been happier or more content. She and Navarre seemed to fit like two halves of a whole. Her liveliness had lightened his character and brought out his sense of humour, while his cooler reserve had quietened her down just a tiny bit. Through her cartoons, Tawny had become quite a familiar face in Parisian society, and when 'The English Wife' cartoons had run out of steam she had come up with a cartoon strip based on an average family, which had done even more for her career.

A peal of laughter sounded in the hall of Navarre and Tawny's spacious London home followed by an animated burst of Italian, and Luke grinned and sprang upright. 'Tia's back...'

Tawny's mother-in-law, swathed in a spectacular crimson dress and looking ravishingly beautiful, posed like the Hollywood star she was in the doorway, and her husband grinned and pulled her into his arms with scant concern for their audience. Within the space of thirty seconds they had vanished upstairs. Tia had just finished filming in Croatia and Luke was about to set off on tour round the USA. As they had been apart for weeks and Luke had a stopover in the city Tia had invited herself and her husband to dinner and to spend the night.

From the moment that Tia had finally faced reality and persuaded Navarre to take care of the challenging task of telling Luke who he really was, all unease between the two couples had vanished. Luke had been very shocked, but relieved by the news that he had no reason to feel threatened by Navarre's bond with Tia, and certainly the revelation did not seem to have dented Luke's devotion to his demanding wife. Navarre would be Tia's big dark secret until the day he died but that didn't bother him and if the paparazzi were still chasing around trying to make a scandal out of his encounters with his mother, it no longer worried him or her. The people that mattered knew the truth and Navarre had no further need to keep secrets from Tawny.

Tia was a fairly uninterested grandmother, freezing with dismay if Joie and her not always perfectly clean hands got too close to her finery. Tia's life revolved round her latest movie, her most recent reviews and Luke, whom she uncritically adored. She had initially taken a step back from her son but that hadn't lasted for long, Tawny thought wryly, for Tia rejoiced in a strong manly shoulder to lean on and Navarre was very good at fulfilling that role when Luke was unavailable. Tia's marriage had become rather more stable and fortunately the passionate disputes had died down a little, so Navarre was much less in demand in that field. Tawny, who had nursed certain fears, also had to admit that Tia never interfered as a mother-in-law. She had become friendlier, but at heart Tia Castelli would always be a larger-than-life star and she didn't really 'do' normal family relationships or even understand them.

Navarre, who had flown Tia back from Europe in his private jet, appeared in the doorway.

'Where have our guests gone?' Tawny's tall, darkly handsome husband enquired, bending down to scoop up the toddler shouting with excitement at his appearance.

Tawny watched with amusement as Navarre's immaculate appearance was destroyed by his daughter's enthusiastic welcome. His black hair was ruffled, his tie yanked and he was almost strangled by the little arms tightening round his neck, but he handled his livewire child with loving amusement.

'Our guests are staging their reunion…we just may find ourselves dining alone tonight,' Tawny warned him, her easy smile illuminating her face.

'That would be perfect,' Navarre confided as he set Joie down to run to her nanny, who had appeared in the hall. *'Merci,* Antoinette.'

'I don't really want company either when you've been away for a couple of days,' Navarre admitted bluntly once the door closed on their nanny's exit with their daughter. 'Whose idea was this set-up anyway?'

'You need to ask? Tia's, of course. You're so possessive, Monsieur Cazier,' Tawny teased, but when those intent green eyes looked at her like that she knew she was loved and she adored that sensation of warm acceptance.

'And with you getting more beautiful every day that's not going to change any time soon, *ma petite.*'

'How do I know you haven't simply become less picky since you met me?' Tawny teased.

'Because every month that I have you and Joie in my life I love you even more,' he murmured with roughened sincerity as he drew her into his arms. 'My life would be so empty, so bleak without you both.'

'I missed you,' she admitted in reward.

'So much,' Navarre growled, leaning in for a hungry, demanding kiss. 'What time's dinner?'

'I thought, since our guests have made themselves scarce, we could go out…later,' Tawny whispered encouragingly.

'This is why I love you so much,' Navarre swore with passionate admiration. 'You've worked out what I want before I even speak.'

Tawny knotted his tie in one hand and laughed. 'And sometimes I even give you what you want because I love you…'

'And I love you,' Navarre husked, making no attempt to conceal his appreciation.

* * * * *

THESE ARMS
OF MINE

JUDY LYNN HUBBARD

To my beloved sister, Carol.
I wish you were here to see this day,
but you'll live forever in my heart.

Prologue

Alesha Robinson took a deep breath and held it in for several long seconds before releasing it slowly. She continued the silent argument with herself to combat the foolhardiness of what she was about to do. She should turn around and go home. She started to do it—for the thousandth time, she started to do it—however, she kept walking, almost running toward her destination, as if she were eager for the impending meeting when nothing could be further from the truth.

Would he listen to her? Was there a chance in hell that he would understand and forgive her? Was she just fooling herself by thinking she could appeal to his good side? In the short time they had dated two years earlier, she had often been privy to his charm, wit and good humor. He had been a perfect gentleman, someone she had wanted to get to know better, but circumstances had not worked in their favor. For reasons he still was unaware of, she had abruptly ended their relationship without explanation. Would he hold that against her now?

He had a reputation of being fair and she knew firsthand that he was, or rather had been. But was she remembering a man from a lifetime ago? Did she dare hope that man still existed after the horrible way they had parted?

She mumbled a slight apology after nearly colliding with another pedestrian on the sidewalk, then continued on her way. She was almost there, and still she had no idea what she was going to say to him. She resolved to cross that bridge when she came to it and continued determinedly on her way to an unscheduled yet overdue meeting.

She pulled her light coat tighter around her as a biting blast of October wind forced its unwelcomed way in between the gaps of the coat's loosely tied opening. Absent fingers brushed a stray strand of shoulder-length curly black hair, which had been loosened from its clasp by the teasing gust. What was she going to say? How should she begin? She rehearsed one scenario and then another, and another, yet she still had no idea what would come out of her mouth when she opened it.

Her hesitant feet suddenly stopped outside the forty-story building that was her destination. Craning her head, she glanced up the tall, foreboding black glass frame. She wondered, would the foe she must now face be as formidable and as unyielding? Lowering her eyes to the front door, she took another deep breath and exhaled it before walking through the double doors to face the fire, uncertain she could evade the scorching that was sure to come.

Chapter 1

Derrick Chandler stared in exasperation at the man sitting across from him. Why did campaign managers always have to try to change your life? He listened in annoyance as Cameron Stewart continued to tell him what he must do in order to win the Senate race, which he had recently entered.

He wondered why he hadn't just stuck to corporate law instead of throwing his hat into the political arena. He decided the main reason was the city in which he resided—if you were a successful lawyer and lived in Washington, D.C., it seemed predestined that a foray into the world of politics would occur at some time or another.

Fingers absently tapped his chocolate-colored, clean-shaven chin impatiently and then brushed a piece of lint off the breast pocket of his immaculate navy blue suit. After Cameron talked until he was satisfied, then Derrick would have his say—the other man in the room would not be pleased with what he would hear. He disliked anyone telling him what he should and should not do, and Cam was treading on dangerous ground.

"Derrick, the simple fact is that you need a wife." Cam succinctly summed up his ten-minute tirade.

Derrick bolted upright in his chair, his gray eyes growing hard and cold. His voice matched his angry countenance. "And you need a psychiatrist."

Cam sighed audibly, not in the least put off by his friend's frigid tone. "Just listen to me…"

"No, you listen to me." Derrick held up a hand forestalling his friend's words. "I tried the marriage scene once, and we both know what a fiasco that was."

"Well, I told you before you married her…"

Derrick's darkening eyes stopped Cam cold. "You're treading on dangerous ground, Cameron."

"I know, Derrick, but just hear me out." He quickly continued before his friend could object, "You hired me to increase your chances of being elected and, whether you like it or not, I've got to tell you what I think."

"Well, I don't like it, but if you want to hear yourself talk, be my guest."

He scratched his lightly bearded chin. "We're doing great in all demographics except for women."

Derrick frowned. "I thought our numbers looked pretty good there."

"Pretty good, but if you had a woman in your life, one who could relate with and talk to other women, one on one, about their concerns, I have no doubt our numbers would double."

"Wouldn't a female member of my staff work?"

"Please!" Cam's look of disgust elicited a chuckle. "Man, this is America—the land of opportunity, the home of apple pie and baseball."

Derrick rolled his eyes. "This sure sounds like a commercial."

"With the election a little over a year away, now is the perfect time for you to be seen as someone who has deep ties to the community, someone who has something in common with his constituents, someone who shares their dreams and hopes. The best way to identify with them is to be seen as a family man."

"You're not married."

"I'm not running for public office, either." Cam folded his arms across his chest. "You are and you need someone, and not just any woman—a wife. Just think about it, a built-in hostess for parties and a date ready and willing to go with you whenever and wherever. I know I'm getting through to you." Cam carefully studied Derrick's purposefully unreadable expression.

"Wouldn't a German shepherd accomplish the same thing as a wife?" Derrick smiled slightly.

Cam closed his eyes in frustration before quickly opening them again. "Will you try to see my point of view?"

"No, you try to see mine. I am not going to marry anyone ever again!" He deliberately emphasized each word.

Cam opened his mouth to speak, but closed it again as a buzz sounded from the phone on the desk.

Derrick yanked up the handset impatiently. "Yes, what is it?"

He was more than a little annoyed—he had left instructions not to be disturbed.

"If she won't tell you, then tell her I'm in conference and can't be disturbed!"

He unceremoniously slammed the receiver back into its cradle. He made a mental note to apologize to Dorothy once Cameron left. He was in a foul mood, brought on by the other man's ludicrous suggestion.

Cam was shaking his head disapprovingly. "People skills, Derrick. People skills!"

"What do I pay you for?" In spite of himself, he almost smiled at his friend's dismayed tone.

"To tell you what others dare not."

"Well, you certainly seem to enjoy that part of the job." This time, a genuine smile tilted the corners of his frowning mouth.

"My mother always told me I love a challenge, and you certainly are that." Cam picked up his briefcase and prepared to leave.

"Are we done?"

"Yes, we're done. I'll try to sell you on getting a wife later."

"Oh, joy." Derrick rose to shake his hand.

"Do you have anything else you need to talk to me about?"

"No, please go." Derrick reclaimed his seat behind the desk.

"See you tonight at seven sharp."

As Cam walked toward the door, Derrick grimaced at the thought of another political dinner/debate—he loved the debates, but he detested sitting around with strangers, making senseless small talk over steak or chicken that tasted like rubber and vegetables that had much in common with plastic.

"How could I forget?"

"Just be there, and on time."

"Anything else, Mom?"

"As a matter of fact, yes. But I don't have the strength to discuss it with you right now." He ran a hand over his bald head. "I used to have hair before you and I became friends."

"Later, Cameron." Derrick's sigh turned into a chuckle at

the exasperated look he received before his friend left with a decisive click of the door.

Alone at last, he laughed out loud and ran a hand over his short-cropped hair. He enjoyed needling Cam, almost as much as he enjoyed his newfound career in politics. Best friends since law school, Derrick and Cam looked like brothers—each sharing the same dark coloring, height and build. They had been friendly rivals who had quickly developed a deep, lasting friendship.

Another chuckle escaped from his lips. Cam was right—Derrick could always count on him to say what others dared not to. He supposed that was one of the reasons he liked him so much. That and the fact that he had always been intensely loyal and dependable—two attributes Derrick valued greatly.

Picking up from his desktop a manila folder containing information on his running mate, he reclined in his plush black-leather chair as he began to leaf through the pages carefully, familiarizing himself with every detail—it was always best to know one's opponent better than oneself.

Curious as raised voices wafted through the closed door to his assistant's office, Derrick wondered what had prompted the argument. Seconds later, the door abruptly swung open to admit a woman he thought he would never see again—Alesha Robinson. Automatically, he stood and his icy eyes locked with her uneasy ones.

"It's all right, Dorothy. I'll see Miss Robinson."

He broke eye contact and nodded curtly in his assistant's direction. The woman glanced angrily at Alesha before firmly closing the door as she left.

He felt as if he had been punched hard in the gut, and it wasn't a pleasant feeling. Alesha Robinson was here, standing a few feet away from him, looking as beautiful as he remembered. Damn her! Damn himself for wanting to quickly close the distance between them, crush her in his arms and fuse his starving mouth with hers.

"What brings you to my door, Alesha?" He silently blessed his voice for sounding coolly controlled, when he felt anything but.

She looked lovelier than he remembered, dressed in a plain white sweater and black slacks. That silky light brown skin of hers begged to be caressed. His fingers itched to oblige. Her thick black hair was pulled back from her face, held in a clasp at her nape. He knew from experience that her hair was soft—softer than anything else this world had to offer. To keep from walking over to her he sat back down in his chair. His eyes then went to her left hand and he wasn't sure whether he was relieved or angered that no engagement or wedding ring rested there.

He continued to survey her hungrily. His eyes drank in every aspect of her face, afraid she was a mirage he had to memorize before she quickly disappeared. He had sometimes wondered if the predicament her brother had gotten himself into would force them to see each other again. He couldn't decide if he was glad or angry that outside pressure had precipitated her return to his life, instead of her own desire.

Her steps faltered as her eyes refamiliarized themselves with Derrick's extremely handsome face—she had almost forgotten the effect the mere sight of him had on her. Since their first chance meeting when they had both stopped to help out at the scene of a multicar accident, he had done strange things to her equilibrium. Although currently his face was hard and foreboding, she remembered how his infectious smile could send her heart racing frantically. He sat before her after all this time like a statue—a beautiful bronze statue, she amended. She recalled how unbending his body had been against the yielding softness of hers—they had been the perfect complement for each other in so many ways. That is, until everything had fallen apart by her own hands.

Her stomach churned queasily and her heart began beating faster and louder in her ears as she stopped just in front of the mahogany desk behind which he sat. Her heart leaped in her chest, but was it from anxiety or happiness at seeing him again? Anxiety, definitely. She was here for business—to ask him for a monumental favor—and for no other reason.

"Mr. Chandler, I need to speak with you." She was pleased with the steadiness of her precise and crisply articulated sentence.

"Why so formal, Alesha?"

"I'm here to discuss business, Mr. Chandler."

She made her voice curt, hoping the tone would end his unnerving inspection of her, which was causing every nerve ending in her body to silently cry out for what she knew from experience was his masterful touch.

He had an almost irrepressible desire to trace his fingers down that silky skin of hers—it couldn't possibly be as soft as he remembered. Yet, instinctively, he knew it was. And her full, faintly tinted brown lips—would kissing her still feel like exquisite torture? Pure heaven, that was how he remembered feeling with her in his arms, and he was sure that observation was still accurate.

She waited uneasily for him to say something, anything. He seemed content to just stare at her. Piercing eyes traveled leisurely over her. What was he thinking? Instinctively, she knew she didn't want to know. Was he as disconcerted by seeing her again as she was at seeing him? She couldn't tell—he seemed cold, almost frigid. She felt like fleeing. Why didn't he say or do something?

"Mr. Chandler?"

"I'm busy."

He was annoyed at himself for behaving like a moon-struck idiot. With great effort, he tore his eyes away from her lovely face and angrily picked up a piece of paper from his desk. It took all his self-restraint to totally ignore her.

She bit back the angry retort that sprang to her lips at his callous actions. One thing she didn't need was to put him on the defensive. She had come to him for help, after all—help that she really didn't deserve.

"Surely you can spare me a few moments." Her tone indicated she would accept nothing less.

He returned the paper to his desk and reluctantly looked at her once again. He mentally scolded himself as he felt his pulse rate increase as she ran her tongue over her upper lip.

"What do you want?"

She silently cursed him for asking a question he obviously knew the answer to. *You might offer me a seat first,* she silently fumed.

"I'm here about Robert."

At the mention of her brother's name, he closed the folder in front of him and motioned for her to be seated in the chair Cam had just vacated. She was painfully aware of the intense focus of his eyes and an emotion she dared not name hidden in their now-frigid depths.

"I was wondering when he would send you in to plead his case." In fact, he had been counting on it.

Her spine stiffened in the soft leather chair and quickly contradicted him. "He didn't. I came on my own to ask you not to press charges against him."

He smiled slightly at that. "You must be as mad as your brother is if you think I'm going to allow him to embezzle $100,000 from my campaign fund and just walk away, free as a bird."

"If you will just let me explain..." She squared her shoulders for a fight she had known was inevitable.

"There's no explanation you have that I am interested in hearing. He took the money—that's all I need to know."

"Regardless, I'm going to tell you the reason my brother *borrowed* the money from you."

His eyes narrowed at the slight edge evident in her tone. What did she have to be bent out of shape about? He was the one who had been wronged by her brother—and by her. What right did she have to treat him as the villain or even to be here asking anything of him?

"*Borrowed?* That's an interesting choice of words. Go on. Tell me, why did your brother *borrow* the money?" He crossed his arms across his broad chest, drawing attention to his muscular physique.

She had the feeling she was wasting her time, but she had to try, for her family's sake. Maybe he would be sympathetic once he learned why Robert had stolen from him. At least she prayed he would.

"Well?" he prompted. "Let me guess. He used it to bet on the ponies." At her blank stare he tried again. "The slots? Sports? Cards?"

"I don't approve of my brother's actions."

"Neither do I and I intend to make my disapproval a matter of public record by filing charges against him." When she remained silent, he continued, "I don't know what you hoped to accomplish by coming here." *Except to remind me of what you needlessly snatched away from me—from both of us—two years ago.*

At this moment neither did she. "I thought I could make you understand."

"Did your brother take my money?"

"Yes." The single word was spoken through gritted teeth.

"Was it his money to take?" He continued in the same no-nonsense courtroom tone.

"You know it wasn't!" She felt like a petulant child he was taking great pleasure in chastising.

Yes, Robert had been wrong to take Derrick's money, but couldn't he show a little compassion? She wondered how much of his unbending attitude had more to do with her past actions than with Robert's thievery.

He had been dreaming of and dreading this moment for two long years. Against his will, he noticed those heavenly eyes of hers sparkle as her temper rose, making her even more beautiful, more desirable. His inappropriate observations annoyed him, making his next words clipped and terse.

"By your own admission, and your brother's, he committed a crime—a felony. What more do I need to understand?" He opened the folder on his desk again, dismissing her.

"Robert's sorry."

He laughed without humor. "I'm sure he is, now that he's been caught."

She was favored with another of his piercing gazes. And somehow resisted the almost irrepressible urge to run as fast and as far from him as her legs could carry her. Even after two years, he still unnerved her completely while he seemed completely unaffected by seeing her again. No, that wasn't true. He was angry, but not at her brother.

"He knows what he did was wrong."

"Well, that's very touching, but it doesn't replace my $100,000, does it?"

He was tired of talking about her brother and would much rather talk about her. What had she done in the two years they had been apart? Had she missed him? Had she second-guessed and third-guessed her fateful decision that had ruined both of their lives? Had she spent sleepless nights wondering where he was and whom he was with? He hoped so. Because against his better judgment, he had thought about her often—about the satisfying relationship they could and should have been enjoying during that time, if only she hadn't destroyed things between them.

He was disheartened to learn that despite her betrayal, she still had the power to move him and make him want to rewrite their story to his satisfaction. Why couldn't they turn back the clock and be meeting coincidentally for the first time? Why did they have to be enemies by virtue of their past relationship?

She remembered him as caring, compassionate and passionate. He had made her feel as if she were the most important person in the world to him. He had made her want to lose herself in him. He had both thrilled and frightened her. Where had that Derrick Chandler gone? Had she somehow destroyed him? If she had, why did that thought disturb her so much?

"I have a lot of work to do."

He needed to get her out of here before he made a complete fool of himself. He didn't like where his memories were leading him or how hard he had to fight to keep himself from touching her. She had nearly ruined his life, and he shouldn't want anything to do with her, should he?

"We'll pay you back."

He sighed fully before giving her his full attention again. "When?"

"As soon as we can." At his dubious look she nearly shouted, "You don't need the money. You don't even miss it!"

"That's not the point."

The coldest eyes she had ever encountered locked on hers. She forced herself not to retreat from his frigid gaze—she knew from past experience he could utterly melt a woman's heart and resistance without even trying. After all this time, he still unnerved her. He made her feel completely raw and vulnerable.

"So, what is the point?"

"Your brother took something that belonged to me. No one does that without suffering the consequences—no one."

The darkening of her eyes let him know that his reference to their relationship was not lost on her.

"How can you be so heartless?"

"Look, I didn't ask your brother to embezzle funds from me, and I didn't ask you to come here today, pleading with me to show mercy to someone who should be—no, who will be—prosecuted."

Why didn't she leave and stop torturing him with her very presence? Lord, what had he done in his life to deserve this?

"I don't know what else to say." She closed her eyes as if seeking divine intervention.

Unable to bear staring at her beauty another second, he swiveled his chair to look out the huge wall-to-wall windows. "You can show yourself out."

She quickly weighed telling him the real reason Robert had embezzled from him. It had nothing to do with gambling, as he had suggested. If he knew Robert's actions were motivated out of love, not greed, would it change his attitude? Would the truth soften his hard heart? She didn't want to bare her soul to him, but if it would save her brother, she didn't have a choice in the matter.

"Won't you please just listen to me?" She faced the back of his head. "Robert's not what you think. He took the money because…"

He swiveled in his chair and held up a hand to forestall the remainder of her explanation. He'd had enough and needed her to leave.

"Alesha, I don't care why Robert took the money—all that matters is that he's an embezzler! Nothing you have to say will change that or make me change my mind about pressing charges against him. I've heard you out, now goodbye."

She quickly stood, realizing she was wasting her time. There was no use in trying to appeal to his better nature. His words made that perfectly clear and she had no intention of giving him the satisfaction of watching her beg.

She snatched up her purse. "What happened to you? How did you become so cold?"

"I am what people like you have made me."

God, she was torturing him. Her very presence tormented him; yet she also made him feel like he hadn't felt in a long, long time, and he was angry and unsettled by that.

"You are what you want to be." She was angry with herself and with her absurd reaction to seeing him again. "I'm sorry I wasted your time." She turned and walked toward the door.

"Alesha?"

He spoke her name softly, almost caressingly. She felt it run down her spine like soothing, exciting fingers of desire—the sensation stopped her in her tracks. She prayed he would stop being so informal with her because the way he said her name—intimately, for her alone—was destroying her. How could a man's voice stroke her in forbidden places so forcefully that she wanted nothing more than to be utterly immersed in him?

She was about to walk out. However, despite his better judgment, he didn't want her to go. What was it about Alesha Robinson that had always sent his blood simmering and then, just as quickly, boiling out of control?

She turned turbulent eyes on him. "We don't have anything else to say to each other."

"You started this, Alesha." He arrogantly lifted an eyebrow before deliberately adding, "And I'm going to finish it."

"We're done."

She turned to leave again, not just because he annoyed

and angered her, but because there was something about Derrick Chandler that was setting off small explosions of awareness within her entire body. Her legs felt wobbly and her heart ached for something that had once been within her grasp and now seemed light-years away. She needed some air; she had to get out of here before she made a complete fool of herself.

"What if I told you that I wouldn't press charges against your brother?" His unexpected words halted her departure.

Had she heard him correctly? She turned and her puzzled gaze encountered his.

"What did you say?"

"I think you heard me."

"Don't toy with me."

An arrogant half smile turned up the corners of his mouth at her chastising tone.

"I never play, unless I choose the game and am assured of victory."

She believed him. He was a man used to getting his way—always, except once with her. She slowly walked back until she was standing in front of his desk again.

"So you're serious about letting Robert off the hook?"

"Yes."

Something in his tone worried her, yet she stood her ground. She had the feeling she would regret her next question, but she had to ask it.

"What do you want in return?"

He stood and slowly walked until he was standing in front of her, so close that their bodies were almost touching. She resisted a strong impulse to turn and run or take the few steps necessary to bring them breast to breast. She faced him unwaveringly as she waited apprehensively for his response.

His eyes roamed over her from head to toe. His blatant

inspection made her feel as if she were a piece of prime meat he was preparing to devour with that wicked mouth of his. Her heart began to beat erratically, not from fear, but from another emotion just as strong.

"Something only you can give me."

"Which is what?" She tilted her head up his tall frame, staring at him uneasily.

He continued to subject her to his slow scrutiny, his eyes lingering long on her moist, slightly parted lips, before lifting to meet her eyes once again. His thorough examination was more disquieting than anything she could have imagined he would say. However, his next words proved her wrong.

"I want you," he answered truthfully.

Chapter 2

He was unblinking and serious as he continued staring into her huge, horrified eyes. After a few seconds of silence, he laughed out loud at her apparent shock. He knew his declaration was the last thing she had expected to hear—it was honestly the last thing he had expected to utter.

She didn't make a move as his brief laughter reverberated in the quiet office before silence returned. He said nothing further and she was unable to respond. Instead, she stared at him unblinkingly, a hand slowly going to her suddenly constricted throat while her heart thudded loudly.

When she finally found her voice it was hushed and strained. "You can't be serious!"

"Can't I?"

She searched his face for signs that he was being facetious, yet found none. Still, he had to be joking. Her other hand moved to her throbbing temple and she tried to laugh dismissively—she couldn't have heard him correctly.

"I must have misunderstood you."

"Did you?" His piercing eyes studied her face carefully.

"Did you say that you want...me?" She forced herself to repeat his ridiculous statement.

"You understand me correctly."

"What do you mean by *want?*" As she articulated the question, she was petrified of his response.

"Want. A transitive verb meaning to desire, to have need for, to crave."

Every word he used to describe his meaning brought vivid pictures to her mind. She swallowed hard to dispel the lump that had rapidly risen in her throat, but to no avail. She stared at the man in front of her, amusement still twinkling in his eyes. Yet, underneath the levity lurked something else—a seriousness that terrified her.

"Are you saying you expect me to...you expect us to... that you want..."

She couldn't force herself to finish that sentence.

"I want you to marry me."

"Marry you?" She sank into the chair she had vacated earlier.

"What did you think I meant?" He studied her distraught face carefully. "Alesha, you didn't think I wanted us to live together in sin, did you?"

"Why do you want to marry me?" She needed a cold compress for her head.

"Because I need a wife." He reclined against his desk.

"You *need* a wife?" She paused before continuing. "Why?"

"According to my campaign manager, it would be good for me to be seen as a family man, and having a wife would equip me with a full-time hostess and date."

He took no pleasure in reiterating Cam's earlier words. Although seeing the woman who had single-handedly ruined his life two years ago in acute distress was very gratifying, indeed.

"How romantic."

Her dry tones made his eyebrow rise slightly—he had no clue how she managed to be sarcastic at a time like this.

"You once made it clear that you didn't want romance from me. Has that changed?"

"Do you always do what others tell you?" She deliberately sidestepped his previous question.

"Never." He firmly shook his head.

"Then why start now?"

She couldn't marry him—or anyone else—under these circumstances. The very idea was absurd!

"I've already answered that question." His face was unreadable.

"Have you?"

Of course, he didn't tell her that until she had walked through his office door, he had no intention of agreeing to Cam's suggestion. Even having put the proposal on the table, he couldn't believe he had done so. Yet, there had always been something about her—something that sparked a chord inside him. He was dismayed to learn his reaction to her hadn't dissipated with the time they had spent apart—time she had forced them to spend apart, he angrily went over in his mind. Despite his better judgment, he still wanted her, and this time he was determined to have her—all of her.

"You don't even like me."

She waited for him to respond but he remained silent. Slowly, he smiled without humor and neither denied nor confirmed her observation. Lord, she wished she had never come here today! She had thought, prayed, that time would have healed old wounds. However, it was painfully apparent it had not. He obviously wanted nothing to do with her, but if that was true, why was he suggesting that they get married?

"'Like' is irrelevant, Alesha."

"How can you say that? How can you suggest that we get married?"

"I told you why already."

He sighed, his tone implying he had no desire to explain his reasons to her again or to justify them to himself.

She lowered her aching head into her hands and willed herself to wake up from this nightmare. However, when she raised her head again, the man in front of her had not vanished, as she had hoped. Rather, his presence was undeniable as he watched her closely.

"You're serious."

"I am." He nodded affirmatively.

"Is this about revenge?" She articulated the only possibility that made any sense to her.

"It's about fate, Alesha."

"Fate?"

Her disdainful, soft echoing of his single prophetic word caused a slight clinching of his jaw—or did she imagine that?

"Yes."

There was uncomfortable silence as each tried to guess what the other was thinking. Each one of them would have been surprised to realize their feelings were more in sync than not. Since parting, they had been destined to come to this point and now they were here. Where their lives ended up from here was a mystery to them both.

"If I agree to your proposal, what do you expect?"

She couldn't believe she was actually contemplating his unorthodox proposition. However, she didn't have a viable alternative—not if she wanted to save her brother.

"Model behavior, public affection. There'll be a great deal

of publicity and we will have to appear happily married and very much in love."

Intense dread spread throughout her entire soul as he rattled off his requirements for a wife as if he were reading from a shopping list. He seemed so hard—had she done that to him? Somehow she knew she had and that hurt more than anything.

"And privately?" She stared into those cool gray eyes of his.

"You'll have to be more specific."

His mocking smile showed that he knew exactly what she referred to. He was getting immense pleasure in needling her.

Taking a deep breath and releasing it on a sigh she elaborated, "This will be a marriage in name only?"

"No, it will not."

She stood up at that, her chest heaving rapidly. "You can't expect me to…for us to…" Her voice trailed off, unable to finish that sentence.

"I can, and I do." His eyes swept appreciatively over her slender, shapely body.

"This is ridiculous, and I'm a fool for even considering your absurd proposition!" She turned and walked rapidly toward the door.

She had a right to be angry at his suggestion. He would have been disappointed if she weren't. He could have picked up the phone and had ten women in his office within a matter of minutes, willing to do whatever he wanted. But he didn't want any other woman. He wanted Alesha. Damn her, he always had. He didn't want to desire her, but he couldn't help it any more than he could help breathing. She intrigued him and he wanted the chance she had denied them both two years ago—to get to know each other better, intellectually and intimately. And, God help him, he didn't care that he was literally blackmailing her to get that opportunity.

He knew he was treading on dangerous ground—he also knew there was absolutely nothing he could do to stop himself. He craved Alesha, and this time he was going to do whatever it took to get her and to make her admit that she wanted him, as well. He wouldn't allow himself to dwell on why her desiring him was of the utmost importance to him.

"You're a smart woman, Alesha." His words halted her progress toward the door. "I think you know this is the only way to save your brother from a sure conviction and a lengthy prison term."

She slowly retraced her steps to stand several feet away from him and tried one last time to reason with him. "Mr. Chandler…"

"Derrick."

"Mr. Chandler." At her refusal to use his first name, she received another one of his mocking smiles, which she had quickly grown to hate. "We're virtually strangers. How can you expect me to marry you and become your wife in every sense of the word?"

"First of all, we are hardly strangers, Alesha. Secondly, when you grow a little older and a little wiser, you'll realize a lot of people do things that they don't want to do every day because their survival or the survival of those closest to them requires it."

"Is that supposed to make your ridiculous offer easier to accept?"

"You might surprise yourself and actually enjoy being married to me." He silently promised himself that would be the case.

She glared at him. "Never!"

"Never say never, Alesha."

He pushed away from the desk and walked over to stand

inches from her. Reaching out his hand, he trailed a finger lightly down her soft cheek, and he nearly groaned at the contact he had longed for since she had first entered his office.

She shuddered at his touch. He merely smiled before his finger moved to trace the outline of her lower lip, causing her flesh to tingle uncontrollably—and not from revulsion. His intense gaze mesmerized her and she was unable to step away, even when he removed his finger from her face. Ravenous eyes slowly, carefully studied every inch of her from the top of her head to the tip of her toes.

It was difficult to take in enough air to properly expand her lungs. Where his fingers had lightly touched, she burned and yearned for something forbidden. The spicy scent of his aftershave wafted up to her nostrils, causing her mouth to water. Despite her qualms, she wanted to be pressed close to his hard body and feel his strong arms around her.

She remembered how those lips had felt against hers and longed to see if her memories were accurate. She swayed toward him slightly, and he smiled even more, yet he made no further attempt to touch her, much to her dismay.

His inaction and her bizarre reaction to him cautioned her to get as far away from him as possible, but her limbs refused to obey the silent command. What was the matter with her? Was he hypnotizing her? Why didn't she turn and run away?

As his eyes admired her beauty, he knew exactly how she felt—he felt the same way, too. It didn't make any sense. This strong attraction between them was the last thing he needed, yet here it was, and he was absolutely helpless to do anything about it, except try to assuage it in hopes of finally purging it forever.

He continued his perusal, eyes moving to the soft curls of her hair, which was pulled away from her face by a clasp. He longed to free the soft tresses he knew would be smooth and silky. Her face showed the barest traces of makeup, yet her type of beauty didn't require any artificial enhancements. Her brown eyes were distraught, her smooth brown skin begged to be touched, her lightly tinted full lips were made for kissing—an invitation he had accepted often in the past and almost consented to now. The bulky sweater she wore hid her attributes from his piercing gaze, yet he knew from experience that beneath it was a curvaceous, beautiful body that he was certain would give him the most intense pleasure.

She could barely breathe. His eyes thoroughly destroyed her equilibrium as they sensuously appraised her. She didn't allow herself to speculate on his thoughts—knowing instinctively that they would disturb her more than his blatant perusal did. She felt hot, uncomfortable and something else she refused to put a name to.

"You're a beautiful woman, Alesha, but then you've always known that, haven't you?" His voice hardened perceptibly as his hand moved up to cup the side of her face, his lips mere inches from hers.

"How dare you!"

His condescending tone propelled her into action. She pushed his hand away from her face and moved several steps back, placing much-needed distance between them. She silently willed her wayward pulse to return to normal—impossible until she was no longer in his presence.

"You'll find that I dare quite a lot."

Silently, he promised himself he would taste those lips again soon enough. For, try as she might to find another way, his was the only course of action she could take to save her brother. He knew that and so did she. He was certain she would agree to his terms.

"What makes you so sure I will be around you long enough to realize anything about you?"

"Because your brother's life is in your hands. I think you'll do anything to save him—even marry me."

She was tempted to tell him to go to hell and take his demented proposal with him. Unfortunately, she knew it wasn't a question of whether she could live with his unreasonable proposal, but rather whether she could live with herself if she didn't even try. This was the only way to save the two people she loved most in this world.

He walked back behind his desk and sat down in his chair. He knew she loved her brother and would do anything to get him out of this horrible situation—her presence here was evidence of that. However, maybe this was too high a price for her to pay. But could she live with herself if she didn't try to help him? Could she live with herself if she did?

"If I agree to marry you, why can't it be a marriage in name only?" To her horror, Alesha blurted out a question that made it obvious she was considering his offer.

All she had to do was take one look at him to answer her own question. Derrick Chandler was a handsome, virile man. He wouldn't go without a woman for days, let alone months—he would never have to. Besides, their past relationship wouldn't allow him to marry her only for show. He wanted what she had denied him—of that, she was certain.

"Alesha, I expect our marriage to be real, because that's the way it has to be."

"Why?" She grudgingly admitted, "You're a handsome man. You can have any woman you want. Why me?"

"Thank you for the compliment." He smiled. "I'm running for public office. I can't be married to you and then be seen around town with other women." He felt compelled to add, "And I have no intention of living the life of a monk."

"But why me?"

"I think you already know the answer to that question."

He reclined in his chair, studying her distraught countenance.

"But…"

"I've got a lot of work to do."

His statement was true. However, more to the point, he needed to get her out of his sight so that his pulse could return to normal. This reunion was more upsetting than he had anticipated. Why, after the hell she had put him through, did she make him feel like a damn schoolboy asking a girl out for a first date?

"I'll give you twenty-four hours to decide. If I haven't heard from you by this time tomorrow, I'll take that as a no and contact the police."

He was proud his voice remained steady, when he felt anything but. He lowered his head and began to study the papers on his desk once again, totally ignoring her.

She opened her mouth to try to convince him to give up this ridiculous idea, but closed it again, realizing the futility of that gambit. He had set his terms and the next move was up to her. Without another word, she turned and left, slamming the door forcefully behind her.

He leaned back in his chair and let out his breath on a loud sigh. Tense fingers loosened his tie a bit. She hadn't left a moment too soon. Why had seeing her again affected him so profoundly? It was because he hadn't been with a woman in a while—that was it. That had to be it.

He shook his head in satisfaction and returned his eyes to the manila folder on his desk. After a few seconds, he gave up trying to concentrate on anything other than anxiously awaiting Alesha's return tomorrow, even though he already knew what her answer would be.

Alesha entered her mother's home and forced herself to appear happy and carefree, even though her heart was heavy, laden with the ultimatum Derrick Chandler had just issued to her a few hours earlier. Despite the dark cloud of gloom that hung over her, she could not risk letting her mother know she was upset—her mom had already had one heart attack a year and a half ago. Alesha would make sure she didn't find out about the events currently transpiring in her children's lives.

"Mom?" She searched for her mother as she walked through the house, throwing her coat onto a chair in the hallway.

"I'm in here, darling."

Following her mother's voice, Alesha made her way toward the bedroom. Once there, she was extremely glad to see that, for once, her mother was taking her doctor's advice, reclining in bed, though she was fully dressed.

Alesha walked over and kissed her mother's cheek warmly before perching lightly on the side of the bed. "How are you feeling?"

"I'm fine, darling." Barbara Robinson smiled as her daughter eyed her carefully.

Alesha marveled at what a beautiful lady her mother was. At age fifty-six, her black hair was sprinkled with gray and was cut short, attractively framing her oval face. Alesha smiled lovingly at her and silently vowed she would do everything in her power to make sure her mother stayed healthy and happy.

"What have you been up to today, dear?"

"Just the usual." She smiled. "Have you been following doctors' orders?"

"Yes, dear. I've been behaving." Barbara rolled her brown eyes heavenward. "Honestly, I don't know how much more rest and relaxation I can stand."

"Mother…"

"I know. I know." Barbara sighed heavily and then smiled slightly.

"You just continue to be a good girl, and Bobby and I will be around to make sure that you do." Alesha grasped her hand and surreptitiously took her pulse.

Before her mother could respond, the front door opened and closed and Robert's voice called out, "Mom? Alesha?"

"We're in here, Bobby." Alesha walked over to the bedroom door.

Seconds later her brother found them. He was about two inches taller than Alesha, though they both possessed the same café-au-lait coloring. Entering the bedroom, he bent down and placed an affectionate kiss on his mother's forehead, brought out a beautiful bouquet of colorful flowers from behind his back and handed them to her. Alesha noted and engraved in her memory the happy look on her mother's face. She would do anything to keep her that way forever.

"For the most beautiful lady in the world." He smiled as he straightened to stand beside the bed.

"They're lovely. Thank you." Barbara brought the bouquet to her nose and sniffed appreciatively.

"Let me get you a vase for them." Alesha took the flowers from her mother's hands and glanced pointedly at Robert, silently communicating that he should follow her.

"Is there anything sinful to eat in the kitchen?" Robert's brown eyes twinkled mischievously.

"Well, you know I'm not allowed," Barbara complained, "but, there is some chocolate cake."

"Perfect!" Robert smacked his lips in anticipation.

"Mother, what are you doing with a cholesterol-filled chocolate cake?" Alesha quickly returned from the doorway to glance at her mother disapprovingly.

"Relax, darling. I didn't eat any. Antonia came by today and left it. I couldn't turn her down, now could I?"

"I suppose not." Alesha sighed before adding, "I'll be sure to take it with me when I leave—just to remove the temptation."

"Sorry, Mom, but you know how she is." Robert smiled sympathetically.

"I do, indeed."

"Don't you two start ganging up on me." She wagged her finger at them good-naturedly. "Come on and get your cake." Alesha pushed her brother ahead of her out of the room.

Robert's eyes focused on the cake sitting on the counter. "Mmm, this looks great!"

When the door was safely shut behind them, Alesha spoke slowly and calmly, "I went to see Derrick Chandler today."

"What?" He whirled to face her.

"Shh! I don't want Mom to hear you." Her voice was barely above a whisper, but firm.

"Why did you go see him? I thought you were going to stay out of this." He'd lowered his voice, yet his tone remained angry.

"You decided that, not me." She filled a vase with water. "I had to see if I could make him listen to reason."

"Did you?" He knew the answer before she replied.

Turning her back on him to cut a slice of cake, she replied cryptically, "In a way."

Robert walked around to stand in front of her, placing a finger under her chin and lifting her eyes level with his own. "What exactly does that mean?"

"He agreed not to press charges against you." She hoped he would leave it at that for now.

"If…" He knew there had to be an *if*.

She gave him his cake, took a deep breath and released it slowly before replying, "If I agree to marry him."

Robert nearly dropped the plate onto the countertop. He stared at his sister, horrified.

When he spoke, his voice was barely controlled. "Please, tell me you're joking."

She walked away from him to stare out the kitchen window. "I wish I was, but you know I wouldn't joke about this."

"Damn him!"

Alesha quickly walked to his side and placed a restraining hand on his arm. "Be quiet! Remember, Mom is just down the hall. We can't let her know what's going on."

When he spoke next, his tone was lower, but just as enraged. "I hope you told him what he could do with his idiotic proposal!"

She remained silent, lowering her gaze from his. Robert's heart skipped a beat at her demeanor.

"Alesha, you didn't agree to this insanity, did you?" He watched her closely.

She raised her eyes and responded truthfully, "He's given me until tomorrow to decide."

"There's nothing to decide. There's no way I'm going to allow you to sell yourself to him to save me! I knew what I was doing when I took that money. I'll suffer the consequences for it."

"Bobby, even though you were wrong to embezzle from him, I won't let you go to jail if there's anything I can do to stop it."

"I won't let you do this." He was equally unyielding.

"You can't stop me." She shook her head. "If Mother finds out what you did and you're sent to prison, the shock would kill her—you know that."

"But, Alesha…"

"No buts." She placed silencing fingers on his lips. "I can't risk losing either of you. If that means I have to marry Derrick Chandler, then I'll marry him." She wished she felt as calm as she sounded.

"You're a wonderful sister, but I will not allow you to marry someone you don't love to save me."

He turned and left the kitchen. She ran after him, but reached the front door only in time to see his car pulling away.

She closed the door and sighed. Her decision was already made—it had been the very second Derrick had made her the offer. She would do whatever it took to save her loved ones, even if it meant sacrificing herself in the process.

Cam's mouth was wide open in shock. "What did you say?"

Derrick laughed heartily before reiterating, "I'm getting married."

"To whom? When? How?" Cam shook his head vigorously as he fought to comprehend his friend's unexpected announcement.

"To Alesha Robinson and very soon." He chuckled at Cam's understandable confusion.

"Who?" He frowned as he racked his brain to put a face to the name he instinctively knew he should recognize.

"Robert Robinson's sister." Derrick played with the slender stem of his wineglass.

"Robert Robinson?" Then leaning closer to Derrick and lowering his voice so as not to be overheard, he asked, "The dude who embezzled from your campaign?"

"The one and only." Derrick nodded before bringing the glass of wine to his lips.

"Have you lost your mind?"

Cam's question was relayed so earnestly that Derrick couldn't refrain from laughing out loud again. He had laughed more today than he had in a very long time.

"You're the one who said I needed a wife." His gray eyes twinkled with merriment.

"I know, but…"

"Cam, this is perfect." His countenance was that of a kid set loose and given free rein in a candy shop. "It's a business arrangement, no emotional entanglements—just a plain, simple agreement that I will end once it's served its purpose."

It was also an opportunity he had waited two years for, a chance to exorcise the demons Alesha's abrupt departure had left in her wake. He was certain once he had some answers, and maybe even a measure of retribution, he would be able to permanently purge the tenacious memories of their past association from his mind and heart once and for all.

"Which is what?"

"To help me get elected, of course." Derrick sighed loudly. Boy, was Cam being dense tonight!

Cam's eyes took on a seriousness that was relayed by his next words. "Sometimes when we think we have something figured out, it takes on a life of its own and goes in directions we never expected."

"What am I going to do with you?" Derrick raised his eyes heavenward in exasperation at his friend's prophetic statement. "If I don't do what you suggest, I never hear the end of it, and if I take your advice, I get prophecies of doom and gloom."

"When I suggested marriage, I wasn't referring to the farce you're contemplating." Cam took a much-needed gulp of his wine.

"Never again." Derrick adamantly shook his head.

"Derrick, you're my best friend. I'd like to see you happy." He lowered his glass to the table.

"I appreciate that, buddy, and I am happy. I'm also going to marry Alesha—on my terms."

"She's agreed to this?"

"Not yet, but she will tomorrow." His voice was confident as he fingered the slender stem of his wineglass.

"How can you be so sure?" He couldn't shake the nagging feeling that there was more to his friend's inane proposal than met the eye.

"She doesn't have a choice. It's the only way to save her brother."

"She might surprise you. Maybe she'll decide the price is too high to pay." Cam played devil's advocate.

"She won't." His short response was delivered confidently.

"Why won't she?"

"As I said before, she doesn't have a choice." Derrick hadn't noticed his tone turn somewhat cold.

"I get the feeling you know this lady—very well. Have you met her before?"

"Two years ago." Derrick silently cursed himself for slipping up in front of Cam, of all people.

"Wait a minute." His eyes reflected understanding. "Is this the same Alesha you dated briefly?"

"She is." He didn't see any reason in denying it.

"The one you abruptly stopped seeing, which sent you into one of the longest and foulest depressed moods of your life?"

"You're exaggerating." Derrick took a suddenly much-needed swig of his drink. Cam wasn't exaggerating. If anything, he was being kind.

"No, I'm not." Intense eyes bore into his. "You wouldn't talk about her—not even to me."

"There was nothing to say."

"Really? I didn't believe you then and I don't now."

"Cam, we dated once or twice, it didn't work out and we ended it." He silently cursed the nerve in his jaw that was pulsing erratically.

"We both know there's more to it than that." He refused to be silenced. "I was there, remember? I know what happened to you shortly after the breakup." At Derrick's continued silence, Cam asked, "Are you out for revenge?"

"Don't be ridiculous." Cam's astute observations and Derrick's own contradictory feelings as far as Alesha was concerned made him uneasy, although his words appeared confident.

"I think you should reconsider this."

"There's nothing to reconsider. I'm going to marry Alesha and that's that." Derrick's tone was firm and final.

"Derrick, are you sure…"

"Yes, absolutely."

"How do you plan to pull this off?" He knew when it was useless to try to reason with his friend, and this, unfortunately, was one of those times. "Alesha will be in the limelight *all* the time. I assume you realize the public must perceive your marriage as real."

"Of course." Derrick shook his head in agreement. "In public, we'll appear as a couple very much in love. You, Alesha, Robert and I are the only ones who will know about our arrangement."

"And what about privately?" Cam leaned forward, studying his friend closely. "What do you expect, and—more importantly—want from Alesha privately?"

"Mr. Chandler, it's time for you to take your place onstage." Both men turned in the direction of the man who interrupted them.

"Certainly."

Derrick smiled and stood, grateful to escape his friend's last probing question.

Chapter 3

The following morning Derrick was engrossed in work when the intercom buzzed. Without being told, he knew who was here to see him and his heartbeat quickened.

"Yes?"

"Sir, Ms. Robinson is here to see you."

"Please send her in."

Standing, he walked over to the door seconds before it opened, admitting Alesha. She opened her mouth to speak and then closed it again. He remained silent. This was her show.

She took a deep breath, released it and, before she lost her nerve, said, "I'll marry you."

"I see."

"You don't seem very surprised." She raised an arched eyebrow.

He ushered her over to a chair in front of his desk and then perched on the edge. "I'm not. You didn't have much of a choice."

"No, I didn't."

She didn't try to hide the resentment in her voice before angrily lowering her gaze from his. She was uncomfortable with him so close and wished he would move away. Yet, even as the thought entered her mind, she realized she would have to get used to being in much closer proximity than this to him—after all, they would soon be husband and wife. At that thought, she shuddered visibly.

"Are you cold?" His hand rose toward her.

"No."

Sensing her discomfort, he dropped his hand to his side, stood up, walked behind his desk and sat down. He smiled slightly as she breathed a silent sigh of relief.

"Do you have any questions?" He leaned back in his chair and studied her somber expression.

"Such as?"

"In case you've forgotten in the time we've been apart, my age, religion, likes, dislikes, etc."

"Tell me whatever you want."

He smiled slightly at her tone, which infuriated her. Why did he always act as if she amused him? He was so frustrating!

"To refresh your memory, I'm thirty-six, born and raised in Washington. I was an only child. My parents are deceased. My favorite food is Italian." He rambled off facts she was mortified to realize she still remembered.

"I'll make a mental note of all that."

"You do that." He leaned forward. "Let's discuss specifics, shall we?"

What he really wanted to do was touch her—to experience the softness of her skin for a much longer duration than yesterday's brief contact. He wanted to release her bountiful mane from its clasp, bury his face in the feathery soft tresses and see firsthand if they were as silky and soft as he remembered. He wanted to devour those pouting, luscious lips…

"All right, but I have one condition."

He raised an eyebrow. "You're in no position to make any demands."

His arrogance was born out of desperation rather than disdain. He didn't want to be cold with her, but it was either that or make a complete fool of himself by acting on his longings.

The hair on her neck stood on end at his insufferable tone. However, her voice was measured when she responded. "I realize that, but I really must insist on this one."

"What is it?"

"My mother must believe our marriage is real. I don't want to upset her."

Did she imagine the softening of his features at her sincere confession? That was ridiculous. He hated her and marriage to him would be his ultimate revenge.

Much to her surprise, he agreed. "Fair enough. Everyone has to believe our marriage is real—that includes your mother." At her continued silence, he said, "Anything else?"

"Yes." She paused, trying to find the best way to phrase her next request.

"Well…" He drummed his fingers on the desktop, not out of frustration or impatience, but to keep them from trying to touch her.

"I'd like us to be engaged for a few months so that my mother will buy our relationship."

His fingers immediately stilled. "Impossible."

"Why not?"

"I have a little over a year until the election. We must be married as soon as possible." He paused, considering a compromise. "I can give you a month at the most."

What he didn't tell her was that he doubted he could wait longer than that to quench his burning desire for her—he prayed he wouldn't go mad trying. Damn her and him! Why, after all that had transpired between them in the past, did she still have the power to unnerve him the way no other woman ever had?

"This will never work, you know." She shook her head.

"It will work." He smiled confidently. "Wait and see."

"If you say so." Her tone belied her skepticism.

"Do I need to remind you what I expect from this marriage?" His gray eyes bore into hers.

Nervously wringing her hands in her lap, she warily met his gaze. "No."

"You're positive?" He stood and walked slowly toward her until he reached her side.

"I'm positive." She also stood to be on a more level plane with him.

"Don't say you didn't know what to expect."

"Is there anything else?" She unflinchingly met his determined gaze.

"Just three things."

He motioned for her to resume her seat, which she did reluctantly. He perched on the desk in front of her. He wished she would stop looking so sad, as if she were being handed a death sentence.

"What are they?"

"First of all, I don't know whether you're on birth control or not, but if not, you will need to start immediately."

She felt her cheeks grow warm at his intimate demands. How could he expect her to discuss such things with him! His words made her fully aware of what their relationship would be, and all she could do was stare at him in embarrassment.

"Since this is only a business arrangement, neither of us needs or wants any unnecessary complications."

She found her voice and whispered resentfully, "Why is it always the woman's responsibility?"

"Well, I can't speak for other men, but as for me, I dislike the feel of a condom. I don't want anything to come between me and…"

"I'll take care of it."

She blushed hotly at his blatant admission, wanting to get off this subject as soon as possible. She reached up to touch her suddenly constricted throat.

He smiled at her as his eyes moved down her face to rest on her slightly quivering, espresso-colored lips, before traveling slowly back up to encounter her distraught eyes, and his smile deepened. However, there was something else present in her eyes—a deep longing, an expectation, a need. He saw it there, silently admitting that it echoed similar smoldering feelings within him.

She really was delicious. He had a feeling he was going to enjoy being married to her very much—while it lasted. He forced himself to mentally add the last observation and forcefully reminded himself that theirs would only be a brief alliance to purge her from his life once and for all. He didn't want or need anything more permanent.

"What's number two?" Her voice was breathless as she brought a hand up to her suddenly burning cheeks.

"It concerns your job." His tones took on an ominous ring.

"What about it?"

"You'll have to give it up."

Her eyes changed from wary to disbelieving to angry as she glared at him. He felt an absurd desire to pull her in his arms and tell her everything was going to be all right.

"Give up nursing? Why?"

"The main reason for this marriage is so that I will have a ready-made hostess. You'll have to be available at a moment's notice. That's hardly possible for someone in your profession."

"I love my work. I don't suppose that matters to you."

"I understand, and I know that you're very good at it." The sympathy in his voice was overshadowed by the sacrifice he was asking her to make.

"How do you know that?"

"Have you forgotten that I saw you in action when we first met at the accident scene?"

She remembered everything about their intense first meeting. It had been a multivehicle accident that both had stopped to help at. He had been strong, unshakable at the sight of blood and torn flesh and had been very receptive to taking orders from a woman.

"No, I haven't forgotten."

He had watched the play of emotions flit across her beautiful face. He wanted to ask if she remembered every detail of their breakup, too, but that was unnecessary. Finally having her in his presence again, he wanted to know why she had shut him out of her life. To this day, her rejection still rankled him, and that was one thing he was fighting tooth and nail to keep from her.

"What else do I have to give up?"

"Are you agreeing to my second condition, or do we end this right here?" His hooded eyes watched her carefully.

"Yes, what's your third condition?"

Her words should have thrilled him, yet instead they cut through him like a hot knife. He didn't know why he had the urge to apologize to her or why her understandable unhappiness made him so unhappy. He reminded himself that this was only a business arrangement, not an emotional entanglement. Either she agreed to his terms, or he would call the deal off and have her brother prosecuted. He wasn't forcing her to marry him. She had a choice—one he knew she wouldn't take—but a choice nonetheless.

"My third condition is this."

Unable to hold himself in check another second, he stood and slid one strong arm beneath her coat around her slender waist, pulling her closer as his other hand moved to the back of her head, pulling her lips toward his.

"What do you think you're doing?" She pressed her hands against his solid chest, trying unsuccessfully to break free from his unwelcomed embrace.

"You'll have to do better than this, or you won't convince anyone that you're madly in love with me." He lowered his head toward hers.

She continued to struggle in vain. However, when his lips were mere inches from hers, one hand released her silky tresses from their confining clasp, allowing the shoulder-length tendrils to slide over his fingers as he pulled her mouth toward his. As he had known it would, her hair felt like silk against his fingers. His appreciative eyes swept her distraught face thoroughly.

"I prefer your hair loose, remember?"

"Mr. Chandler, I don't care what you prefer."

"Oh, but you will care." His softly voiced promise caught in her throat as he once again instructed her to use his first name.

"No." She strained against his ironclad embrace.

"You'll say my name on moans of passion in just a few seconds."

"Never."

She knew her denial lacked believability because her voice was breathless, and a strange feeling began forming in her stomach at his nearness.

"We'll see."

Before she could respond, determined lips closed over hers in a strong kiss. His mouth was warm and inviting, not cold and repulsive as she had hoped it would be. She had known from past experience that his lips would feel like this—wonderful and vital. Days, months and years were swept away by his sensual mouth as it thoroughly refamiliarized itself with hers.

Her heart began to beat rapidly—not in fear, but in arousal. She moaned in protest to her thoughts and his actions, and her mouth parted slightly in shock and surrender.

That was all the encouragement he needed. He took full advantage of her surprise, sliding his tongue between her lips to slip into the honeyed recesses beyond. He continued to masterfully taste every centimeter, every tantalizing crevice of the bounty he had uncovered.

Her hands moved to his shoulders to push him away, yet stopped there, resting instead. Did she really want to escape? That simple yet complex question rolled around in her dazed mind. A hundred confusing sensations bombarded her entire being as Derrick continued his mind-shattering caresses. She hadn't expected to be blown away by a simple kiss after two years. However, there was nothing remotely simple about Derrick's kiss, or her disheartening responses to the masterful, sensual onslaught he was unleashing on her.

One of his hands slid languidly down her back to rest on her hip, pressing her closer against his hard length as his mouth continued to plunder hers. Her eyes were half closed, as sensation after sensation—each an awakening, each frightening and intensely pleasurable—began to overpower her self-proclaimed resentment of the man whose arms she was nearly melting into. The hands resting on his shoulders flexed and then tightened their grip as she resisted an almost irrepressible urge to entwine them around his neck and press herself even closer against his hard length.

Never in a million years would she have dreamed she would be in Derrick's arms again, enjoying his kisses and caresses. Yet, here she was, wanting, almost reveling, in this intimate contact with a man she should hate for blackmailing her into marriage. She hadn't bargained for this. She hadn't expected to still be attracted to him physically. How could this be? Even as the question arose in her mind, she admitted that he was the only man who had ever elicited such thorough, satisfying, mind-boggling passion from her and, to her dismay, he had lost none of his skills when it came to arousing her hidden desires.

His lips slowly drew apart from hers, despite a slight moan of protest from her, and he huskily commanded, "Say my name."

"No."

Her voice was soft and tortured. For the life of her she didn't know where the strength to articulate came from.

Her refusal made him pull her closer, until she felt every hard inch of his wonderful body pressed intimately, maddeningly against her own. Unapologetic hands slipped beneath her sweater to touch the satiny heated flesh of her back, and she thought she would die from something very close to rapture when he pulled her yet closer.

Playful lips nipped at hers before sliding down her jaw to burrow into her softly scented throat. She gasped as he raked his strong teeth across her skin, and then his tongue traced the outline of her collarbone before he raised his head to stare into her confused, dazed, passion-glazed eyes.

"Say my name." As he softly repeated his previous command, one of his hands moved to her hair, his fingers entangling there.

He was as surprised as she looked at the shock of pleasure

holding and kissing her elicited within him. It was as if the damnable time they had spent apart had never occurred. He pulled her mouth to within centimeters of his. His tongue skimmed her lips lightly before retreating again, refusing to give her what she wanted until she yielded to his demands.

"Say it."

His warm breath intermingled with hers as the hand at her back moved to rest between her shoulder blades before sliding back down her satiny flesh. He needed to hear his name on her lips, whispered with passion before he muffled the sound with his ravenous, hungry mouth.

She closed her eyes briefly before acquiescing. She spoke so softly he thought he had imagined it.

"Derrick."

"Again." He softly kissed her quivering lips—lips that were as addictive as anything he had ever known.

"Derrick," she reiterated on a sigh, and then on a moan, as he had foretold, as his lips and hands continued to lightly caress her. "Derrick."

The last thing she saw was his smile—not of triumph, but of understanding—before her eyes closed once her mouth was finally, ravenously recaptured. He kissed her again and again and she prayed he would stop soon before she begged him never to. His lips were like a magnet, attracting her against her will, holding her mesmerized, unable to break away.

The last thing she wanted was to escape from this intensely pleasurable embrace. Her mind screamed out for her to put as much distance between them as possible, yet her body craved closer contact with his—much closer. How could she remotely tolerate kisses from a man who was single-handedly ruining her career and stealing her freedom? What in the name of God was wrong with her? She couldn't begin to formulate an answer anymore than she could deny that she craved and enjoyed his kisses, almost to the point of self-destruction.

After endless, sweet minutes of torture, his firm, strong, warm lips dragged themselves from hers. She fought the urge to pull his mouth back to hers and gradually opened her confused, embarrassed eyes to find him staring at her with an unreadable expression. Her cheeks were warm, her lips were trembling, and she could just die from the embarrassment.

He smiled slightly, one of his fingers trailing over her quivering, moist lips as he huskily said, "I think our arrangement will be very profitable and pleasurable—for the both of us."

She pushed away from him at his words, partly in anger and partly just needing to escape from his overpowering presence and from her own desires. She needed to get out of there! This time he let her go, and this time she nearly ran out the door, not stopping to look back—certain she would find him following her.

Had she turned to stare at him, she would have seen echoing arousal, disbelief and dismay etched on his handsome features. Her retreating pace accelerated until she was safely out of his maddening reach—for the moment.

A few days later, she sat beside Derrick in one of the most upscale jewelry shops in Washington. Even though she had insisted she didn't want an expensive ring, he had been adamant that she would wear a ring to be marveled at, for appearances' sake.

She hadn't seen him since the devastating kisses in his office, yet the time apart had done nothing to ease her mind, nor squelch her anticipation of their next encounter. She didn't know what was the matter with her or who she was becoming. Even more unnerving, when she was with him, she wasn't sure she even cared.

"What about this one?" He held up a three-carat brilliant-cut diamond solitaire, set in a split band of platinum.

"It's beautiful but…" She carefully took the exquisite ring from his fingers.

"But what?" He eyed her closely.

"It's too expensive—all these rings are."

She placed the exquisite ring back onto the black velvet cover on the table next to the matching wedding band, which was inset with a carat of diamonds halfway around it, and the man's wedding band, which was a thick circle of brightly polished platinum with scrollwork over its surface.

"Nonsense." He smiled at her assertion. "Besides, when this is all over, you'll have something to sell that will bring you a nice piece of change."

She turned hurt and angry eyes on him. When she spoke, her voice trembled slightly, "Why did you say that to me? You know I'm not marrying you for your money."

The somewhat mocking smile on his face slowly faded as he realized he had hurt her. Part of him had meant to, but he derived no pleasure from the fact that he had succeeded. Instead he felt miserable about it. He wasn't a cruel person and there was no reason for him to act like one.

"Alesha, I'm sorry."

He cupped her sad face between his hands tenderly—more tenderly than he would have imagined himself capable of.

"Are you?"

Her whispered words implied she didn't believe him. She was, however, oddly moved by his unexpected and uncharacteristic apology.

"Yes, I am. Very." Soothing fingers lightly rubbed over her cheekbones.

"You wanted to hurt me." Her voice was barely audible.

"Maybe I did," he admitted softly, eyes never breaking contact with hers.

Despite knowing the reason, she would have asked him why. However, his lips lowered toward and captured hers. He kissed her softly, soothingly at first, but as if the barest contact with her mouth inflamed him, the kiss soon became passionate, and the hands on her face pulled her closer to his ravaging mouth.

Her own hands slid up to rest on his chest as she allowed herself to enjoy the wondrous sensations washing over her body as Derrick's expert lips and tongue continued to mate hotly with her own. He had to be the best kisser in the world, she dazedly thought as, against her will, his mouth slowly lifted from hers.

"Why are you always kissing me?" Her question was formed breathlessly against his lips, which still rested lightly against hers.

"Because I enjoy it and so do you." He earnestly traced the outline of her moist lower lip with his tongue, feeling her quiver. "You always did, remember?"

She did, but she wouldn't tell him that. She realized she didn't have to articulate it. He knew—just as he knew she wanted him to kiss her again and again.

"Derrick, I…"

"What?"

"Nothing." She shook her head, not knowing what to say—or to confess.

His eyes bore into hers as he continued, "Your mouth is made for kissing—soft, moist, sweet and tempting—like a ripe, juicy, luscious strawberry. It begs to be stroked, caressed…consumed." He ended his erotic assertion on a ravenous whisper before his lips slowly tasted hers again.

His sensuous, hypnotic words stole her breath. Her heart

began to beat erratically at his nearness and the vivid imagery he had created within her head. She couldn't have responded if she wanted to, and it was just as well because, as if to prove his point, his lips pulled at hers, tasting them, before closing over hers again. Of its own volition, her right hand moved up his chest to his shoulder, to rest at the nape of his neck as he continued his exploration of her quivering mouth.

His hands moved to her back as his lips continued to kiss hers. She sighed in pleasure and her mouth opened wider as he continued to taste the sweet nectar he found within.

She had forgotten where they were and so had he, until a loud cough interrupted what had become a heated, passionate embrace. To her disappointment, Derrick's lips reluctantly slid from hers as they both turned toward the sound.

"Excuse me." The salesman's embarrassed countenance greeted them as they simultaneously turned passion-glazed eyes in his direction.

Alesha quickly lowered her gaze from his, so embarrassed she would have moved away, yet Derrick's hands on her back wouldn't allow her to. As always, he seemed completely in control of the situation.

"Forgive us—we're very much in love." He smiled at the salesman, who nodded in understanding.

"Of course, it's such a joy to see." The man beamed at the two of them. "Have you decided on rings?"

"Yes, we'll take these." Derrick handed the man the most expensive set in the case, the one with the trillion-cut solitaire. Then, turning loving eyes to her, he said, "Right, darling?"

"Yes." She was surprised anything audible passed from her passion-constricted throat.

"Excellent choice, sir, madam." The man barely contained his enthusiasm. "Shall I wrap them for you?"

"The wedding rings, but she'll wear the engagement ring." Derrick lifted the solitaire off its black-velvet base and placed it onto Alesha's finger before lifting her hand to his lips and kissing it as his eyes bore deeply into hers. If she didn't know better, she would think he loved her dearly.

"The perfect ring for the perfect fiancée." He lowered her hand from his lips, but continued to stare into her bewildered eyes.

"Let's just see how that fits." The salesman took Alesha's hand from Derrick's to inspect the ring. "It looks like an excellent fit. How does it feel?"

"It—it's fine." Alesha's eyes were still mesmerized by Derrick's.

He reclaimed her hand, kissing it again before he abruptly stood. "Darling, I'll be right back." Then he followed the ecstatic salesman over to the register.

Once alone, she placed sweaty palms against her burning cheeks. Uneasily, she contemplated what had just transpired between her and the enigma who was her fiancé. Trembling fingers lightly touched her moist, thoroughly kissed lips.

God, what was happening to her? With confused, forlorn eyes, she stared furtively across the room at Derrick, and she felt a twinge of longing in the pit of her stomach. Unashamedly, she wished he were still seated beside her, kissing and caressing her. She glanced down at the twinkling diamond on her left hand and, for a moment, wished her engagement to Derrick was real instead of simply a business arrangement. She shook her head to dispel the vivid longing that suddenly invaded her soul for something forbidden and terribly exciting, which she feared only Derrick could give her.

She was treading on very dangerous ground and must take extreme care not to think of Derrick as anything other than a means to an end. Marrying him would ensure her brother's freedom and her mother's continued ignorance of what Robert had done—nothing else good would come from their union. She had to keep repeating the suddenly distasteful truth that he was using her, as she was him. There were no emotional entanglements or involvements as far as they were concerned and she didn't want any. If only she could believe her silent assertions.

Why couldn't she hate him? She wanted to—things would be so much simpler if she did. But she didn't. Perhaps it was the realization that her still-unexplained actions were the basis for his angry feelings toward her. She understood his anger toward her better than he did.

In her mind, two years ago she had done what was necessary when she had ended things between them. Yet the decision still plagued her, even after all this time. Therefore, how could it not affect Derrick the same way? Besides, Robert had stolen an enormous amount of money from him, and he had a legitimate right to want to extract retribution from both of them, didn't he?

She knew he didn't love her. At times, she was certain his feelings for her leaned more toward hatred. However, there was no denying that he wanted her physically, and she instinctively knew he wasn't happy about that. She knew Derrick wanted nothing to do with her on a permanent basis, just as she wanted nothing to do with him. However, she was forced to admit to herself that she came to life in his arms as she did at no other time.

After two years, he still had a power over her body and sometimes her mind, but she silently vowed that she would not let that power extend to her heart. She couldn't afford to lower her guard with him because their relationship—although once very real—was now only a sham, a farce, an emotionless business arrangement. She must never let herself forget that, because if she did, she would truly be in danger of losing her soul.

Chapter 4

"Is your sweet young man coming for dinner tonight?"

Barbara Robinson smiled at her daughter as they sat in the living room of her house. Robert glanced up from his magazine with a scowl, but made no comment.

"Yes, Mom." Alesha grimaced slightly at her mother's choice of words.

Of all the adjectives she would use to describe Derrick Chandler, *sweet* was certainly not one of them. She would have chosen words like *gorgeous, enigmatic* and *arousing*. She grudgingly admitted she would also add the word *kind* to the list of adjectives. For he had been unbelievably kind to her mother in the past two weeks since she had been told about their imminent marriage and, if she were completely honest, kind to her, as well. Her mother had taken to Derrick remarkably well—too well for Alesha's taste.

"I'm so happy for you, darling." Barbara's sincere words broke into her disturbing thoughts. "I like Derrick. He's a good man—strong, dependable—and very handsome." She tagged on the last comment with a laugh.

Yes, he was devilishly handsome and sexy, Alesha admitted. Yet, there was also a hardness to him that hadn't been present years earlier. She knew she was the one responsible for its creation—a source of guilt to her. Now she wondered if she could also possibly be the one to eradicate it.

"Thanks, Mom. I'm glad you like him." She forced a lightness in her voice she was far from feeling.

"How could I not like him after seeing how he dotes on you?" Barbara beamed proudly.

Alesha smiled at her, but remained silent. Yes, Derrick certainly played the role of the doting fiancé very well—too well for her taste. The memory of the many kisses they had shared over the past few weeks made her cheeks burn with embarrassment. Kisses? That was a tame word to describe their passionate, near-consummated encounters since they'd become engaged. She blushed hotly at the memories.

He was *always* touching and kissing her, always raising her to a fever pitch, yet refusing to go any further. Though she should have been happy about that, she was disturbed to admit she was not. Irrationally, she wanted to know the fulfilling promise his smoldering kisses hinted at and truthfully believed he was trying to drive her insane with unfulfilled longing. Much to her dismay, she couldn't wait to experience the conclusion of Derrick's devastating caresses and kisses. Instinctively, she knew it would surpass anything she had experienced in her life.

Dear Lord, she couldn't believe her thoughts! What was the matter with her? What had he done to her in so short a time and what would he do to her sense of self once they were married? Married! Her mind slowly repeated that word. Soon, very soon, she would be Mrs. Derrick Chandler. Her life would definitely change then, but for better or for worse?

Alesha stood as the doorbell chimed. "I'll get it."

She reached and opened the front door to Derrick.

"Hello, sweetheart." He smiled lovingly at her.

His easy use of the endearment caused her heart to somersault. He handed her one of the bouquets of flowers he held in his hands. With his free arm, he encircled her waist and placed a firm, passionate kiss on her soft, moist, waiting lips.

When he released her, she was breathing erratically. He whispered in her ear before escorting her into the living room with his arm still around her waist.

"Try to look happy."

She nearly told him she didn't have to try to look happy—she *was* happy to see him. Of course, that was only because he had presented a reason to escape from her disquieting thoughts, wasn't it?

"Derrick, how lovely to see you again."

"Thank you, Barbara. It's nice to see you, too." He released Alesha and bent to kiss her mother's cheek while handing her the other bouquet of flowers. "Hello, Robert."

"Derrick." Robert's voice was clipped. "Excuse me. I need to make a call." He shook Derrick's hand before walking out of the room.

Alesha sighed as she sat down in a chair near her mother. She could see why her mother liked Derrick—he was absolutely charming. He did know how to make a person feel special.

"Thank you. These are lovely." Barbara sniffed the flowers appreciatively.

"I'm glad you like them." Derrick straightened and sat on the arm of Alesha's chair, his arm draped along the back.

She tried to listen to the small talk going on around her, but Derrick's nearness was making that impossible. His arm moved from the back of the chair to rest on the nape of her neck, absently massaging her tense flesh. Instead of sooth-ing her, it had the opposite effect. He lightly caressed her soft skin, driving her to distraction. She wouldn't give him the satisfaction of knowing how much his actions unnerved her. She didn't have to because he already knew—a fact that was confirmed when she glanced up into his eyes.

"Darling, you're wearing your hair down, just the way I like it."

"You like her hair long?" Her mother's query thankfully saved her from responding.

"Oh, yes." Derrick's voice was a potent caress as he con-tinued to lightly finger her silky tresses.

"I tried to get her to cut it, but she said it would be too much bother."

They continued to discuss her as if she weren't present, which suited her just fine. She didn't think she could for-mulate a coherent sentence if her life depended on it.

"I'm glad she didn't—I love it the way it is."

He bent down and brought a handful to his nostrils, in-haling its fresh scent. Then he let it trail through his fingers back against her warm cheek, his fingers still absently play-ing with a handful of strands.

She stopped paying attention to the conversation alto-gether at that point. Derrick's nearness and actions banished any logical thoughts from her mind, replaced by desires only for him. She wanted to reach up and bring his satisfying lips down to hers, and once again feel the burning ecstasy of his kiss.

"Isn't that right, darling?"

She glanced up at Derrick, who was smiling down at her lovingly and if she didn't know better, she would honestly believed he cared for her.

"I'm sorry, what?" She shook her head slightly as she forced herself to refocus on the conversation around her.

"Baby, were you daydreaming about our wedding again?" His finger lightly trailed down her burning cheek.

She swallowed the lump in her throat and forced a smile to her lips. "I'm afraid I'm guilty as charged, darling."

"Your mother was asking where we were going to spend our honeymoon, and I told her we had decided to go to my house in the country for a week and take a *real* honeymoon later on." His eyes laughed at her once again.

"Yes, Mom, that's right." She didn't know how she managed to make her voice sound cheerful when she felt anything but. "Excuse me—I think I need to check on dinner."

"Sweetheart, you just checked." Her mother frowned.

"I—I know, Mom, but it was almost ready. I'll be right back." She stood and hurriedly left the room, but not before she caught a glimpse of Derrick's mocking eyes as he followed her. No doubt, he knew exactly what she had been thinking and feeling. Damn him and herself!

A short time later, they were all seated around the dining room table. Alesha, of course, sat next to Derrick. Her mother and Robert sat on the other side.

"Sweetheart, tell me the full story of how the two of you met."

Her mother's question took her completely by surprise. She had assumed her brief response weeks ago had satisfied her mother's curiosity. She nearly choked on the piece of food she had just placed in her mouth and hurriedly took a sip of water before turning to Derrick.

"Why don't you tell her, darling?"

"All right, baby." He lightly kissed her lips before turning to her mother. "Well, Barbara, Robert sent Alesha to my office to pick up a check for a television spot." He glanced at Robert who was silently fuming. "I was floored by her visit, but more so by her beauty." He paused, this time to stare appreciatively at Alesha, and she grew warm under his burning gaze.

After he knew he had made her thoroughly uncomfortable, he said, "I was surprised when she wanted to discuss my campaign strategy. I had taken one look at her and my brains flew right out of the window. I asked her out to lunch, and she accepted." He kissed her cheek before continuing, "One meal with her wasn't nearly enough. I knew I had to see more of her, and we began to date. It became apparent that we were both swept away. The rest, as they say, is history." Derrick finished his tale and, much to her mother's delight, picked up Alesha's left hand and brought it to his lips.

"That's so romantic!" Her mother eyed them both with pure happiness.

"Yes, Mom, so much so that I almost can't stand it."

Thankfully, her sarcasm was lost on her mother. Derrick merely smiled and gave her hand a little warning squeeze. God, how she amused him! His eyes strayed to her tantalizing mouth and he resisted an almost irrepressible urge to capture those tasty lips with his own and spend untold minutes feasting on every sweet curve. He couldn't wait until they were married, until she was legally his wife and intimately his woman.

"Why did you wait so long to tell me you were seeing Derrick?" Her mother directed the question toward her.

"Tell her what you told me, darling." Derrick's eyes danced with mischief.

"Well, Mom, it was because…because everything happened so fast and we wanted to be sure about how we felt before we said anything." Alesha rattled off what she hoped sounded like a plausible answer.

"I understand." Barbara sighed as she glanced approvingly at the loving couple before her.

I'm glad you do, Alesha silently thought. Would this dinner never be over with? All she wanted was to get away from Derrick's disturbing presence, her alarming reactions to him, Robert's understandably sulky mood and her mother's glowing countenance as she bought into every shameful lie and half truth they fed her.

"It's partly my fault, too, Barbara. I was just getting to know Alesha, and I wanted her all to myself. I hope you can forgive me." He placed a lingering kiss on the corner of Alesha's mouth.

"Of course I can, Derrick."

Robert couldn't take another second of this nauseating display and quickly stood. "I hope everyone will excuse me, but I have to leave."

"So soon?" His mother frowned.

"I'm sorry, Mom. I thought we'd be through with dinner by now, and I have other plans." If he stayed here another second, he would surely throw up.

Derrick took everyone by surprise as he stood up, too, and said, "Robert, I was going to ask you this later, but since you're leaving, I'll just do it now."

"What is it, Derrick?" Robert tried to hide his dislike of the man for his mother's sake.

"Alesha and I have thought a lot about this, and we want you to be the best man at our wedding."

"What?"

Derrick thoroughly surprised everyone present. Robert and Alesha stared at Derrick in absolute shock.

"Oh, Derrick, how wonderful," Barbara said with great enthusiasm. "Isn't it, Robert?" She prompted him to respond to Derrick's offer.

"Are you sure, Derrick? Don't you have someone else you'd rather have stand up for you?" Robert tried to gracefully decline.

"Of course I'm sure. After all, you were instrumental in us getting together." Derrick smiled as he took Alesha's hand, causing her to stand before pulling her close to his side. "If it wasn't for you, we never would have become engaged."

"What about Cam?" Robert searched for a way out.

"He'll understand why I want you." Derrick refused to relent. "What do you say?"

"Sure." Robert glanced helplessly at Alesha who shook her head in resignation. "I really have to go now." He bent down to kiss his mother's cheek, and then dashed out the door.

"Derrick, that was so nice of you." Barbara continued to sing his praises, much to Alesha's dismay.

"It was nothing, Barbara. As I said to Robert, he's the reason Alesha and I are getting married. I can't think of anyone who deserves to be my best man more than he does."

Alesha stared at him, trying as hard as she could to hide the anger consuming her. He brought out such a range of emotions in her—one moment he could make her feel intense longing and desire. In a millisecond he could elicit a feeling of understanding and deep friendship. Just as quickly as he did now, he could spark a flame of anger, burning so brightly that she thought it would consume her. Her eyes blazed fury into the smiling, mocking depths of his.

At this moment, she was convinced that his sole purpose on earth was to bring chaos and disorder into her family's lives. His smile intensified, as if reading her mind, and somehow she resisted an urge to pick up her fork and use it as a weapon against him.

After dinner, Derrick sat on the sofa as Alesha paced angrily back and forth in front of him. Obviously, she was angry and he knew why.

She spoke to him in hushed, incensed tones. "You really enjoyed yourself tonight, didn't you?"

"Very much." His eyes followed her tense body as she walked away from him.

"How could you ask Robert to be your best man? You deliberately placed him in an untenable position." Her voice was angry, yet deliberately low enough so as not to disturb her mother.

"He could have said no."

"How? Momma would have become suspicious if he had."

"I hardly think Robert is the injured party in any of this."

"You're right about that." She stepped away and took several deep breaths. "Derrick, please reconsider. You don't want to marry me."

He stood at her words and walked over to face her. "On the contrary, I do."

"Why?" She was both flabbergasted and pleased to hear sincerity in his voice.

"Because you amuse me." He intentionally left unspoken the fact that she also inflamed, excited and captivated him.

"How flattering!"

"What do you want me to say? That I'm madly in love with you?" She remained silent and he continued, "You know why I'm marrying you, Alesha—it's purely business."

Even as he spoke the carefully chosen, cold words, he knew he was lying to both of them.

"How can I forget?" she hissed angrily. "You remind me every time I see you."

"You sound upset." He placed a hand under her chin and forced her turbulent eyes to meet the piercing depth of his own.

"Don't be ridiculous." She snatched her chin away, disturbed by his nearness and his insightful statements.

Despite her vehement denial, she knew he was right—she hated hearing him refer to their marriage as nothing more than a business arrangement, even though she knew that was exactly what it was. She tried to walk around him, but he grabbed her upper arm, stopping her.

"Maybe this is what you want to hear." He paused for what seemed like an eternity. "I want you, Alesha, very much. I've wanted you for a very long time, and this time I'm going to have you—all of you."

Her breath caught in her throat at his blatant, unexpected admission and arrogant assertion. She tried unsuccessfully to quash the vivid erotic images that sprang to mind as a result of his confession.

He moved closer until he was standing mere inches from her, causing her breathing to increase. Her heart thundered loudly in her ears as she continued to meet his scorching gaze. His hands reached out and grabbed her shoulders, pulling her body closer to his own.

"There's no one around to impress." She silently cursed her voice for sounding expectant and aroused instead of angry.

"I know that." He shook his head in agreement. "I'm doing this simply for my own pleasure—and yours."

He made her wait for an eternity until his burning mouth finally covered hers. She promised herself she would not respond. However, she soon found that her traitorous body had its own agenda. His hands moved to her lower back, pressing her intimately against the rock hardness of his own body. His tongue barely touched her lips and they parted, allowing him unlimited access to the hidden, inviting caverns of her sweet mouth. His hot tongue scalded hers.

Despite herself, she heard a moan of pleasure escape from her mouth and her arms slowly moved up his chest until they were entwined around his neck. He smiled slightly before pulling her up until she was standing on her tiptoes as he sucked her lips against his and massaged her tongue urgently with his own. Never in her life had she been kissed so thoroughly or devastatingly. Each kiss was different, yet achingly similar. When it came to arousing and satisfying a woman, Derrick Chandler was no novice, but then she already knew that. Without even trying, he could ignite her desire for him.

The hands at her back moved to trail lightly up her sides, resting at her breasts before sliding between her shoulder blades, pressing her closer as he continued his devastating assault on her mouth. She felt a similar sensation to one she hadn't known of until he had first kissed her, as the way he was now, building in pit of her stomach. It was a type of hunger, not for food, but for something entirely forbidden.

Her fingers fastened behind his head, holding him close. Her lips opened wider beneath the insistent, maddening pressure of his. Their kisses deepened. God, she wanted… What? What did she want? Something she was afraid to name, something she knew only he could give her.

Reluctantly, his lips slid from hers, and he stared deeply into her half-opened eyes. He studied the play of emotions dancing in their brown depths, and knew she was disturbed by her strong attraction to him. He himself was a little surprised and even troubled that, after all that had transpired between them, she still had the power to make him lose control.

The reason he kept reminding her about why they were marrying was that he needed to be constantly cognizant of that. Still, regardless of how they had come into each other's lives again, he couldn't wait for her to become his in every sense of the word. And though she would never admit it, he knew she was also anticipating the day when they would be husband and wife, but, more important, lovers.

His lips claimed hers again in another scorching kiss. Her eyes closed against the blinding passion mirrored in his, and she sighed in rapture against his bruising lips as they continued to devour hers. His fingers entangled in her hair, pulling her mouth closer still as he continued to savor her enticing lips. One of his hands moved to pull the hemline of the burgundy blouse she wore from the waistband of the matching skirt, sliding beneath to caress the warm, satiny skin of her lower back. She gasped against his mouth at the intrusion, but instead of moving away, she wantonly pressed closer, suddenly wishing their clothes would disappear, leaving only their bare bodies. She didn't know what was happening to her common sense, and at this moment, she didn't really care.

He felt her total surrender. He knew he could take her now and she wouldn't resist. For that reason, he also knew he couldn't, regardless of how much he longed to do so. He had silently promised himself not to consummate their relationship until they were married. He had convinced himself it was because he wanted to give her time to get to know him again, but the truth was that he was afraid that once he made her his, he would risk losing himself. He wanted... What did he want from her? Revenge, retribution or something simpler yet much more complicated and disturbing?

"I can't wait until we're married."

His admission was whispered against her moist lips. His mouth was so close to hers, she could still feel its imprint. There was no mistaking his meaning, and that prompted her eyes to flutter open as she stared at him, embarrassed by her actions and the fact that she hadn't wanted him to stop kissing or caressing her. Even now, her skin tingled from the light trails his fingers had blazed across it.

Unexpectedly, she pushed out of his arms and hotly responded, "Well, we're not married yet!"

She was angrier with herself for responding as eagerly as she had than she was with him for initiating the kiss. Turning her back on him, she prepared to leave him standing there alone. However, his hands prevented her from moving. He pulled her back and turned her around until she faced him again.

"But soon."

He placed a quick, hard kiss on her moist lips before he left her standing there alone, staring after him longingly, with nothing but her disturbing thoughts to torment her already tortured soul.

Chapter 5

Alesha sat in the hospital lounge, dressed in pale pink scrubs, checking the surgery schedule for the day. She tried unsuccessfully to ignore the envious banter of the four friends and colleagues who shared the lounge with her.

"Alesha, you're so lucky!" one of her friends cooed as she passed around a copy of *Time* magazine with Derrick's handsome face on the cover. She had to admit the eight-by-ten glossy photo from which the cover image was taken didn't begin to do him justice.

"How did you ever land such a marvelous catch?" the woman continued.

Returning her eyes to the schedule on her lap, she responded, "Just fortunate, I guess."

"I'll say you were!"

She sighed at the response. The slight sarcasm in her voice had been lost on her friends, who continued to salivate over Derrick's picture.

"Angie, you're on with Dr. Ryan at 3:00 p.m. in O.R. 12." She tried to redirect everyone's attention from her private life and back to work.

"Fine." The slender brunette with the short-cut hair nodded before returning to the subject that was on everyone's minds. "Come on, Alesha. Out with the dirt."

She looked up at her best friend, her exasperation evident. "What dirt, Angie?"

"How is he in the romance department? I'll bet he knows exactly what to do and does it expertly."

Alesha blushed at the explicit question, especially as she remembered the many ardent kisses she and Derrick had exchanged. What would Angela say if she told her she had never slept with Derrick—or with any man? She wanted to confide in her best friend. She could use some guidance in the romance department.

"Angie, leave Alesha alone. Can't you see you're embarrassing her?" said Linda, another one of her friends.

"I'll bet she could tell us all stories that would have our hair standing on end!" Angela picked up the magazine to take a closer look at the gorgeous man on the cover. "You'd better hold on tight—he's one sexy guy!"

"Why, thank you."

All heads turned in the direction of the door, to find the object of their conversation and desire lounging against the door frame, dressed impeccably in a charcoal suit, crisp white shirt and red tie.

"Derrick, what are you doing here?"

Alesha automatically stood and walked over to him. Dear Lord, how long had he been standing there and how much had he heard?

"I couldn't wait until tonight to see you, darling."

To the delight of her friends, he placed his hands around her slender waist, pulled her close and lowered his head purposefully toward hers. As always, they shared a breathtaking kiss. She clung to the lapels of his suit as she once again experienced the passion in his embrace. She didn't know how long he kissed her—time was suspended—however, when he finally lifted his head, she was more embarrassed than ever. She was sure that the blatant desire on his face, and hers, must be obvious to everyone in the room.

"Ahem!" Someone coughed loudly, making both of their heads turn in the direction of the other occupants of the room.

"Mr. Chandler, it's a pleasure to meet you." Never one to be accused of being shy, Angela walked up to shake his hand.

"Derrick." He smiled at them all in turn as they introduced themselves. "Please forgive me for interrupting your break."

His hand resumed its possessive position on Alesha's waist. He kissed her on the cheek.

She leaned against his chest and looked at him adoringly before plastering a stupid grin on her face, something she had gotten very good at in the last month. She hoped no one would ask her anything, because she didn't think she could trust herself to speak.

"It's no intrusion at all."

Alesha glanced at all of her friends as they nearly swooned at Derrick's feet. He could ask any of them all to jump out the fifth-floor window and they would do so gladly.

"I hope to see all of you at the wedding." At their gleeful promises, he added like a true politician, "And I hope I can count on your votes."

"Thank you. We wouldn't miss it for the world. And you definitely have my vote," Angela said, and the others promised to support him at the ballot box, as well.

"We can hardly wait for the big day ourselves." Derrick pulled Alesha closer. "Right, darling?"

All she could do was nod because, as always, his nearness was affecting her ability to think clearly. She wished he would let her go so she could breathe again. As if sensing her unspoken desire, and doing just the opposite, he pulled her even closer.

Everyone else reluctantly returned to work. Alesha would have gone with them, but Derrick refused to release her. Once they were alone, she turned to stare at him angrily.

"Was that really necessary?" She suddenly found her elusive voice.

"What?" He feigned innocence.

"You know what—that nauseating scene you just played."

"Weren't there a few parts you enjoyed?" His voice was slightly husky as he traced the outline of her trembling lower lip with the fingers of his free hand.

Despite herself, she felt a shudder pass down her spine to the tips of her toes at his touch and was certain he felt it, too. She longed for his lips to recapture hers once again.

His eyes shifted from hers to her slightly parted lips and back to her eyes again, yet he made no move to kiss her. Why was he toying with her? More importantly, why was she quivering in anticipation, craving another of his devastating kisses?

"Do you know what I want right now?" His voice was a whisper—his lips were a hair away from hers.

"What?" She fought to keep herself from swaying toward him.

Without answering her, his lips brushed against hers before he released her waist. Taking her hand instead, he led her out of the lounge into the busy hallway.

"Where are we going?"

They got onto the elevator. She glanced out to find all her friends watching enviously.

"To lunch."

"I can't leave the hospital. I have surgery in an hour and a half." She tugged against his hand.

"You'll make it. We're going to the hospital cafeteria." His smile widened as the doors closed.

After a brief stop at her office, which Derrick insisted on seeing, they boarded the elevator again. When it stopped on the twelfth floor, Derrick grabbed her hand and pulled her out.

"Where are we going? The cafeteria's on the first floor."

"You'll see."

He smiled and led her toward the doctors' conference room. A sign reading "In Use" was posted, but he disregarded it and began to open the door.

"Derrick, what are you doing?" Her hand covered his to stop him. "We can't go in there!"

"Of course we can." He swung the door open and ushered her inside.

She was still trying to reason with him when suddenly all her friends and colleagues ran toward them, yelling, "Surprise!"

They all beamed at her shocked face as she looked around the room, seeing for the first time that it was decorated with streamers, balloons and signs wishing her well. She quickly returned her astonished gaze to Derrick.

"You knew about this?" she gasped.

"Knew about it?" Angela walked over and hugged her tightly before continuing. "He's been a doll! We invited him, and he assured us he would be here, whenever, wherever."

"I—I don't know what to say." She stared at him in disbelief before quickly turning and adding to everyone, "Thank you all so much."

She was bombarded with hugs, well wishes and gifts. Someone shoved a glass of punch into her hands. Derrick was by her side constantly as she spoke with everyone. However, someone ushered him away to talk politics, and she was alone in the midst of another group of friends. Despite their good intentions, their words began to make her feel uncomfortable. She felt like a hypocrite, allowing people she had worked with for years to believe she was blissfully happy about her impending marriage, when nothing was further from the truth.

"Alesha, what's wrong?" Angela grabbed her hand in concern as she noticed the pained expression on her friend's face.

"Nothing, nothing." She forced a tearful smile.

"This is your best friend you're talking to. Tell me." She squeezed her fingers comfortingly.

"Oh, Angie, it's just…" She paused.

Even though Angela was her best friend, she had never spoken to her or anyone about Derrick—not two years ago, and certainly not now. How could she explain her inner turmoil to her friend, or to anyone here? No one could begin to understand what she was going through except…Derrick.

She searched for him, longing to be with anyone with whom she didn't have to pretend to be happy about leaving a job she loved in only two days. Her eyes encountered his as he stood across the room speaking with the head of surgery. He smiled at her reassuringly, and she automatically returned his smile. As odd as it sounded, she suddenly was very glad he was here. Her feelings were so complicated as far as he was concerned. Even though a part of her vowed to dislike him—a promise she had, thus far, been unable to keep—more times than not she enjoyed his company. That was a scary admission.

"What is it?" Angela's persistent tugging on her hand forced Alesha to refocus her attention.

"I'm just going to miss everyone so much." She hoped that would appease her friend.

"It's not as if you're never going to see us again. Besides, you'll be so busy with your handsome new husband and your exciting life that you won't give us a second thought."

"You may be right." She forced herself to assume a teasing demeanor.

She turned to respond to a question from another friend and, seconds later, felt a strong arm around her waist. She knew the arm belonged to Derrick. Her friends tactfully excused themselves, and she turned to face her soon-to-be husband.

He lowered his head and kissed her softly on the lips. "You looked like you needed rescuing," he whispered, his sympathetic eyes staring into her pained ones.

"I'm fond of all of these people—this is really hard."

"I know." He pulled her slightly closer.

Her hands automatically rested on his broad chest as she gazed into the compassionate depths of his eyes. In that instant, she felt that everything was going to be all right. To everyone present, they looked totally in love with each other.

"Why did you agree to come to this party?" She felt and heard him sigh as he studied her face.

"It was a good opportunity to test how others react to us as a couple." He deliberately chose his words to see how she would respond.

"I should have known," she hissed softly.

"If I had refused after being invited, it would have looked suspicious."

His words enraged and saddened her. She should have known he had only been thinking about his career! Anger darkened her eyes and she tried to free herself from his suddenly unwanted embrace.

"We certainly wouldn't want that." She tried in vain to free herself. "Will you let go of me?"

"Alesha, stop struggling before someone notices." His voice was low, but firm, commanding obedience. Yet she refused to comply.

"Let go!" She brought her free hand up to his chest and pushed. He moved his hand from her waist to her back, effectively sandwiching the hand on his chest between their bodies.

"There is another reason I came." He placed his free hand underneath her defiant chin and lifted her angry eyes to meet his.

"I don't care to hear it." She tried unsuccessfully to free her chin from his grasp.

She couldn't stand to hear any more of his heartless comments. She needed kindness from him, not taunting.

"I'm going to tell you anyway." He brushed a brief hard kiss on her lips, his hand moving from her chin to cup her jaw.

"Please stop, Derrick."

"I know it's hard for you to give up your career, even if just for a little while." His fingers softly caressed her cheek. "I thought today, of all days, having at least one person here with whom you didn't have to pretend to be happy about that choice—even if it was me—would make this farewell somewhat more bearable for you."

She immediately stopped struggling to free herself, but remained silent, unable to believe her ears. She searched his face for signs of teasing or deceit, and instead found only sincerity. He had articulated her feelings perfectly. How could he be so in tune to her feelings? How could he be both the cause of her pain and the only means to alleviate it? He never ceased to amaze or confuse her.

"What?"

"Contrary to your belief, I really don't want to make this any more difficult than it has to be." Fingers absently brushed stray strands of hair away from her eyes before he ruefully added, "I don't suppose I could expect you to believe that."

She stared at him, speechless, for a few moments before finding her voice. "I do believe you."

"Well, that's progress, isn't it?" He softly kissed her and she automatically responded to the warm, comforting pressure.

"I guess it is." She couldn't remove her gaze from the genuine tenderness reflected in his eyes, directed toward her.

"Did I tell you how beautiful you look tonight?"

"No." Her eyes registered surprise at his question.

"Well, let me remedy that." He took her hand and brought it to his lips. "You look gorgeous."

"Thank you." Her voice was wispy soft. "You don't look too bad yourself."

"Thanks."

He treated her to one of his devastating smiles before turning his attention to the traffic he was expertly weaving in and out of. They drove on in silence for a while. She had easily slipped into the role of Derrick's fiancée.

He pulled his sports car up to the restaurant and turned to face her. "Now remember, I told Cam that we met again…"

Alesha's fingers on his lips halted his words. "Derrick, you've told me a hundred times. I won't forget."

"I'm being a pain, huh?" He captured her hand with his own, refusing to release it.

"A little bit." She was breathless. Suddenly the close confines of the car became suffocating.

"I'm sorry." His eyes darkened.

"Um, I guess we should go in." Instead of moving away, an invisible magnet drew her closer to him.

"I guess."

Though he agreed with her, neither of them made any move to leave. Inevitably, they kissed. Lightly, at first, but then the unexpected passion consumed them. Her hands rested on his chest and he cupped her face, tilting his head one way and then another, bringing her sweet mouth closer.

A cool blast of air forced them slightly apart. "I beg your pardon sir, madam," A red-faced doorman apologized.

As always, it was Derrick who regained his composure first, glancing over her shoulder. "It's no problem. We were just getting out." Then, returning his attention to her, he asked, "Ready?"

She ran her tongue over her slightly damp lips, tasting him and nodded slightly. She didn't trust herself to speak. He released her face and opened his door before walking around to help her out. He continued to hold her hand as they entered the restaurant, where they were to meet his best friend.

As their coats were checked, Alesha used her fingers to wipe off traces of her lipstick staining his lips. Their eyes met and held for several suspended seconds before they were shown to a table. At their approach, a tall man who closely resembled her fiancé in build and height stood. He was dressed like Derrick in a dark navy suit with a red tie. He smiled easily, and Alesha instantly liked him.

"Well, well, I don't believe it. You're on time." The man chuckled at Derrick and then turned to Alesha. "It must be due to your good influence."

"Very funny." Derrick smiled. "Cameron Stewart, Alesha Robinson."

"Alesha, it's a pleasure." Cam shook her hand warmly. "Derrick said you were beautiful, but not exquisite."

"Thank you. I'm glad to finally meet you, Cameron." She smiled as he brought her hand to his lips briefly before releasing it.

"Cam. No one calls me Cameron except my mother—and Derrick when he's mad at me." He winked at his friend.

"Which you take deep pleasure in making sure is often," Derrick said as they were seated in the booth.

"Untrue." Cam shook his head. "I'm the easiest person to get along with you will ever meet."

"Hah!" Derrick snorted good-naturedly.

That was the way their dinner progressed. It was quickly apparent that Derrick and Cam were the best of friends, and could talk to each other only as best friends could and get away with it. Alesha enjoyed herself very much. She saw a side of Derrick that was completely relaxed—one she hadn't seen in a long time and one she liked very much.

Cam was a gem. He had a natural talent for making people feel at ease. Alesha took to him like a bee to honey. She felt a bit uneasy about deceiving him, but as Derrick had continually drilled into her head, everyone—including their friends and family—had to believe they were very much in love.

"Alesha, may I have this dance?" Cam stood and extended his hand in her direction after giving a chivalrous bow.

"I'd love to." She kissed Derrick's cheek. "You don't mind, do you, darling?"

"No, but you will once you experience his two left feet."

"He's just jealous because I'm a much better dancer than he is."

He *was* jealous, but not of Cam's dancing skills. Rather,

that Cam would be holding Alesha in his arms—something he himself longed to do.

"In your dreams." Derrick's words trailed after them as they walked away.

"Well, what do you think?" Cam glanced expectantly at Alesha as he twirled her around the dance floor.

"Very nice." Alesha smiled.

"You be sure and tell Derrick that." He winked at her and she laughed.

"I will." She returned his smile.

"You know, Alesha, I was blown away when Derrick told me he was getting married—and to whom."

"Were you? Why?" She feigned innocence, reminding herself to keep her answers short—there was less chance of slipping up that way.

"It was so sudden." Cam's words were an understatement. "Also, given your past relationship, it was the last thing I expected to happen."

"Our decision to get married is anything but sudden." Cam's dubious stare forced her to elaborate. "It took us two long years to realize we were destined to be together."

"Is that how you feel? As if you and Derrick were destined to be together?" Cam watched her with the attention of a hawk, studying its prey.

"Yes." She smiled at him and prayed for a change in topic.

"Really?" He twirled her out of the way of an approaching couple.

"Yes." She faced his piercing stare that was very similar to Derrick's. "I realize you don't know me very well, Cam, but believe me, I'm marrying Derrick because I want to."

"What's changed between now and two years ago?" He had skillfully maneuvered them into a relatively secluded part of the dance floor so that their conversation wouldn't be overheard.

She almost laughed out loud at his question. She wanted to ask how much time he had for her to list the monumental changes that had occurred in her life over the past two years.

"A lot." She silently cursed herself because even to her ears her voice sounded strained.

"I'm not prying just to stick my nose into yours and Derrick's business, Alesha." His voice was a little defensive.

"I realize that." And it made her feel all the worse for lying to him. "You're Derrick's best friend, and I know you have his best interest at heart."

"I do."

"For reasons I don't want to get into, Derrick and I weren't ready for each other two years ago. Now we are and we know what we want." Her words held shades of the truth and thus were spoken confidently.

"And that would be each other?" She felt as if she was on the witness stand and the case would be made or broken by her next words.

"Yes. Nothing else will satisfy either of us. We've finally realized that, thank God." She prayed for the music to end, because she didn't know how much more of this grilling she could take.

"Well, I suppose it's the romantic beginning and ending to a relationship any woman would love to have." Cam suddenly smiled and she heaved a sigh of relief.

"Yes."

"So it would seem that this time true love triumphed in the end."

He studied her closely—too closely. She realized this was the moment she would either sell the lie or destroy it.

"It has. I finally realized that Derrick is everything I want in a man and in a husband."

Her expression was appropriately dreamy as her eyes

sought out Derrick's from across the room. She sighed happily before returning slightly watery eyes to meet Cam's.

"I'm happy for you both." Cam smiled.

"Thank you." She gave a silent prayer. Apparently, he was buying her nauseating performance.

"No, thank you for returning to Derrick's life."

His words made her feel like a first-class heel. He was a nice man and a loyal friend, and she truly hated deceiving him. Even reminding herself that it was necessary didn't help salve her heavy heart.

"I like you very much, Cam."

"I like you, too." He smiled. "I see why Derrick jumped at the chance to marry you."

No, you really don't.

"Thanks." She smiled.

The song ended a few moments later, and they made their way back to Derrick.

"What were you two talking about so earnestly?"

"I was trying to steal her away from you." Cam winked at Alesha.

"Never happen," Derrick said.

Derrick placed a possessive arm around her shoulders and pulled her close. Absently, his fingers played with the strands of her hair.

"Sure of himself, isn't he?"

Cam smiled. He wondered if Derrick realized that he was always touching Alesha, or how his expression softened when he looked at her. His friend was in for a big surprise if he thought his marriage to Alesha was going to be a cold, antiseptic business arrangement.

"Very. But he's right, I'm afraid." Alesha joined in their infectious banter, placing a possessive hand on Derrick's chest.

"Man, have you done a job on her." Cam feigned disgust.

"It's called love," Derrick corrected, placing a brief kiss on her lips. "Right, baby?"

"Right." She willed her fluttering heart to be still.

"Now that you see how devoted she is to me, will you stop trying to steal my fiancée?"

"No promises." Cam displayed a devilish grin.

"Will you two excuse me?" Alesha said.

She rose, as did her dinner companions, and walked in the direction of the ladies' room. She definitely needed a moment to compose herself.

"You and Alesha are very good actors."

"Why do I feel a judgment coming?" Derrick took a sip of his coffee.

"No judgment, just an observation," Cam said with a smile.

"I know I'll regret this, but let's hear it."

"I don't think either of you is completely acting about your feelings."

"That's ridiculous." Derrick took a much-needed swig of his drink.

"Is it?"

Cam's razorlike eyes homed in on Derrick's. Derrick suddenly felt like an insect under a microscope.

"Yes, very. You know why we're getting married."

"Yes, I think *I* know." He leaned closer and added, "But I don't think either of you has a clue."

"Cameron…" Derrick's voice held a warning.

"Shh, here comes your fiancée." Cam laughed at his friend's scowling features.

"Did I miss something?"

Alesha sat beside Derrick once again. The atmosphere was noticeably thicker than when she had left.

"No, I've just made Derrick angry with me again, but

he'll get over it." Cam laughed and received a dark glare from his friend.

"Oh, I see." Alesha carefully glanced from one to the other.

"Alesha, it was a pleasure to finally meet you, but I have to go now." Cam took her hand and brought it to his lips.

"Thank you, Cam. I enjoyed meeting you, too." She smiled genuinely.

"See you tomorrow, Derrick." He continued to grin broadly.

"Goodbye, Cameron."

Derrick's stilted response made his friend laugh.

"See, I told you he was mad at me." He winked at Alesha, who chuckled as he departed.

"What was that all about?" She turned to face her still-scowling fiancé.

"Nothing. Just Cam being Cam." Derrick quickly dismissed a topic of conversation he didn't want to pursue.

"Are you angry with him?"

"Always." Derrick laughed, and she relaxed as his black mood seemed to suddenly dissipate. "You did a wonderful job tonight." He placed his arm alongside the back of the booth, bringing her that much closer.

"Thanks. I was nervous," she admitted with a slight laugh.

"You needn't have been. I told Cam you could do it." He impulsively hugged her shoulders.

"You what?"

She frowned at his words, and pulled slightly out of his embrace. She had been led to believe that Cam didn't know anything about their arrangement.

Chapter 6

"Cam knows." As her frown grew into a glare, he said, "Remember, we're still in public."

She forced a slight smile, though her eyes still shot daggers at him. "You lied to me."

"No. I never said Cam didn't know."

She was annoyed by his truthful reminder. She would have moved farther away, but his arm held her captive.

"But you insinuated as much." Her words were quietly hissed through gritted teeth. "What did you two do? Have a great laugh at my expense?"

"I didn't bring you here tonight to make fun of you."

"Then why?" She resisted an urge to empty the contents of her water glass onto his head.

"Because I needed to know if you could really pull this off with someone who wasn't a friend, a colleague or related to you—someone whose questions you couldn't anticipate, someone who would take you completely off guard. *You* needed to know."

"You still could have told me." Her voice had lost some of its edge as his words sank in.

"It would have undermined the purpose if I had." His logic was inescapable. He studied her closely. "You believe that I wasn't trying to make a fool of you, don't you?"

She studied his earnest expression, and the remainder of her anger dissipated. She might be an idiot, but she did believe him.

"Yes, I believe you." Her body relaxed noticeably.

"Good." He released his breath on a sigh.

"You sound as if you actually care what I think." She fingered the white linen dinner napkin, though her eyes never left his.

"I do."

"Why?" She stopped fiddling with the napkin.

"Do you know what I want to do?"

He didn't answer her question on purpose. It wasn't that he couldn't have, but rather, he wasn't sure she would like his response, or if he cared to hear the truth himself.

"No, what do you want?"

"I want to kiss you." He glanced around the room before returning his full attention to her. "But, unfortunately, we do have quite an audience."

"That's never stopped you before." Her whispered invitation surprised them both.

"No, no, it hasn't." He smiled slightly before his lips captured hers.

It was an earth-shattering kiss. One of his hands cupped her jaw, tilting her head until it lay over his arm as his mouth plundered. Her hand slid up his chest to rest at his nape as she kissed him back. She didn't know how long their mouths feasted, but when he lifted his head, she wished he hadn't stopped. As if reading her thoughts, his mouth settled against hers again and she sighed in pleasure. Her fingers fastened on the back of his head as she held his mouth closer. Long minutes later when he lifted his head again, they were both breathing heavily.

"I'd better get you home." His voice was thick with passion, his eyes dark with longing. She felt the same way.

"Yes." Her voice was barely audible.

His head lowered toward hers again and she waited for another kiss, yet it never came. Instead, he pulled back and summoned the waiter, to pay for their bill.

Neither spoke as they left the restaurant or once they were seated inside the car. Alesha silently contemplated their supposedly purely business alliance, which had quickly evolved into something completely different than she believed either of them had anticipated, yet it seemed that neither was unable or unwilling to arrest its unexpected evolution.

November 29 dawned cold and clear as Alesha and Derrick exchanged their wedding vows. She wore a white, sequined designer gown made especially for her, and her hair was covered by a headpiece and a cathedral veil that trailed behind her when she walked down the aisle. It was a beautiful formal evening affair that rivaled some of the most elegant weddings of celebrities and royalty.

They posed for what must be the thousandth picture of the day, facing each other, bodies pressing close, arms encircling each other as they smiled into the camera. She had to admit that all day they had presented the picture of a deliriously happy couple, very much in love. If she didn't know any better, she herself would swear they were crazy about each other.

Suddenly, the lights dimmed and a space miraculously appeared as people moved to one side in preparation for their private dance. Derrick took her hand and led her slowly onto the dance floor. She gathered the white lace veil closer to her as she went into her husband's waiting arms.

She gratefully buried her face in Derrick's shoulder and dropped the fake smile from her aching countenance. She was able to escape from the peering eyes and cameras for a few blissful minutes. As she moved closer to Derrick, her hand moved from his shoulder to the back of his neck.

"You're doing remarkably well. Don't stop now."

His whispered reminder in her ear annoyed her no end. Why couldn't he be quiet and let her fantasize about this being real?

"Raise your head and give me a kiss for the people like a good wife."

She almost refused—not because she didn't want to, but because she didn't like being ordered to play a part when everything that had transpired today had held special meaning for her. However, she complied and his lips slowly neared hers before closing warmly, firmly over them as they continued to sway slowly to the music. Through her closed eyes, the bright light of camera flashes was evident as more pictures were taken and she heard the hushed sighs of delight as people witnessed the touching scene before them.

Dear Lord, how long did he intend to kiss her? His lips continued to caress and take her breath away, which further delighted the crowd, who whistled and cheered the loving couple before them.

After what seemed like an eternity—and, if she were honest with herself, not an unpleasant one—he lifted his head, yet maintained eye contact with her. She was mesmerized by his gaze, unable to look away.

To onlookers, it must have seemed as if they were totally enamored of each other, impatiently waiting for this elongated celebration to end so they could escape and privately express their love. Of their own accord, her thoughts drifted to the time in the near future when she and Derrick would be completely alone together.

She was at war with herself—part of her wanted more than anything to finally culminate the desire that had been building within her and had gone unquenched since his first touch years ago. Another part of her wished that the reception would go on forever, even though she secretly hated every moment of it. Shamefully, she couldn't decide which part she wanted to win out, and oh, how that bothered her.

The song finally ended, and he led her off the dance floor with his arm still around her waist. She plastered the happy smile on her face once again as they approached her mother and brother.

"I'm so happy for you, dear." Her mother embraced her warmly.

"Thanks, Momma." Alesha smiled as her mother released her. She possessively placed her arm through Derrick's, who covered her hand with his own.

"Derrick, I'm so glad you're a member of our family." Barbara warmly kissed her son-in-law's cheek.

"Thank you, Barbara. You'll never know how much that means to me." He held Alesha close as he smiled at her mother.

Alesha resisted the urge to slap his face. It was one thing lying to all these strangers, but it was another thing doing it to her mother. But was he lying? He seemed genuine enough. She believed he liked her mother and she knew her mother adored him.

Derrick didn't like deceiving this nice lady. She had been nothing but kind to him since they had met, and he genuinely liked her. When she found out the truth, he hoped she would understand. Suddenly, he realized he would hate to lose the special friendship he had developed with Alesha's mother.

That surprised and worried him. He hadn't meant to become attached to Alesha again or anyone in her family. However, that's just what had happened—and in a very short time. What was it about his new wife that captivated him so? He had to be careful not to let himself become any more involved with his wife or her family. Yet, he feared it was already much too late to stop that from occurring.

"How about a glass of punch, Barbara?" Derrick spoke more to quiet his unwanted thoughts than anything else.

"I'd love one, Derrick." Barbara linked her arm through his.

"Excuse us, darling?" He kissed Alesha's lips lightly.

"Of course, sweetheart. I'll be right here." She smiled lovingly at him as he led her mother off.

She was alone with Robert, and she dreaded it. "Robert, don't start," she warned before he could utter a word.

"I don't have anything to say, except I can't believe this is happening." His response was somber.

"It's done. We'll all have to make the best of it."

"Can you do that?" He eyed her closely.

"I have to."

Truthfully, she feared that being Mrs. Derrick Chandler wouldn't be nearly as hard as having to stop being Derrick's wife.

"I'm so sorry."

"I know." She squeezed his hand. "I want you to know that I don't blame you—you know that I understand why you did what you did."

"I know you do." He suddenly grabbed and hugged her close, as if he would never let her go. "If he hurts you…"

"He won't."

She knew without a doubt that Derrick wouldn't harm her physically. However, she was afraid there had already been irreparable damage done to her emotionally. How much more there would be after months of living with him as his wife, she couldn't begin to guess.

"He'd better not."

"Smile." She forced herself to follow her own advice.

He tried, but the smile didn't quite reach his eyes. Her own eyes grew distant as she contemplated her immediate future. Soon, very soon she would have to leave here with her husband—with Derrick. She would have to be alone with him, and she would be expected to give herself to him totally, a prospect that didn't repulse her, but rather unnerved and, dare she think it, excited her.

Today marked the start of new life as Mrs. Derrick Chandler and in a few short hours, she would truly begin her life as his lover. She shivered at the thought. There was no longer any denying to him, and certainly not to herself, that she wanted him physically. In a matter of hours, she would have him and he would, in turn, have all of her with all that implied.

Derrick and Cam stood together watching as Angela, Alesha's maid of honor, and her bridesmaids surrounded Alesha on the other side of the room. Derrick watched his bride with mixed emotions—he had felt strange all day. He had been mesmerized as she had made her stunning entrance at the church. As they had recited their vows, an emotion he dared not name had assailed him. Of course, he knew their marriage was a carefully orchestrated arrangement, but he *really felt married* to her. It was unnerving and exciting. He wondered if she felt the same way.

"Well, you two did it—and very well, I might add." Cam slapped him on the back.

"Did you ever doubt it?" Derrick smiled, grateful for the intrusion on his disturbing thoughts. "Thanks for understanding why I had Robert as my best man."

"No problem. It looked good for the photographers."

"Spoken like a true campaign manager." Derrick chuckled.

"Alesha is a beautiful bride."

"Yes, she is."

Derrick's eyes easily found his wife across the room. She was smiling at something one of her bridesmaids had whispered to her—a beautiful smile, a smile he was sure could light up the world as it lit up his heart.

Cam studied his friend closely as he watched his bride. There was something in his expression that Cam couldn't put a finger on. He had watched the two of them all day, and as he had informed his friend weeks ago, he didn't think either of them was as aloof toward this marriage or each other as they insisted they were.

Derrick, aware of Cam's thoughtful scrutiny turned cool eyes toward his friend. "Don't start."

Cam smiled. "I wasn't going to say a word."

"Oh, yes, you were. But don't."

Derrick's eyes gravitated back to stare at his beautiful bride. Cam's eyes followed Derrick's and his smile widened; though, as his friend had suggested, he remained silent.

All too soon, Alesha sat alone in her dressing room. She gazed at her frightened expression in the mirror. Now that she was alone, she was finally able to let her happy facade fade. Her heart was beating frantically, and she knew if she didn't gain control of herself very soon, she would faint.

She stood and smoothed nervous hands down the front of the pale blue suit she wore. The long jacket almost reached the hem of her just-above-the-knee matching skirt, which had a half-inch slit up the right front side. She brushed her hair until some of the curls had disappeared, but left it loose, though it was brushed away from her face. She slowly sat down again, her wobbly legs unable to support her.

She knew the reason for her apprehension—soon she would be alone with her husband, and would, therefore, put an end to all the imaginings her mind had conjured up about the night that was rapidly approaching. She shuddered visibly as she thought of Derrick and her alone in the most intimate of situations and positions. Despite herself, her heart skipped several beats in…anticipation?

A knock at the door made her jump. Taking a last look at her nervous reflection, she stood, walked over to open the door and found Derrick there.

"Are you ready to go?" His piercing eyes took note of her pale cheeks and troubled eyes.

"Ready as I'll ever be." She placed her arms through the coat he held up for her.

"You look excited."

"What do I have to be excited about?" She pulled away from him, angry that he could read her so easily.

"Nothing yet," he paused suggestively. "But soon."

She gasped. "Are you ready?"

He smiled. "More than ready."

He placed an arm around her slender waist as they walked down the hall. When they reached the top of the spiral staircase, she saw that the single women had gathered at the bottom of the staircase. Alesha turned her back to them and threw the bouquet down. Laughter and shouts of glee reached her as Angela came up with the bouquet, minus a few flowers that had been snatched out along the way as many hands had tried to grab it. Alesha threw a kiss to her best friend, who smiled and held up the bouquet as if she didn't know what to do with it.

She turned toward Derrick, who was smiling wickedly. He slowly slid his hand under the hem of her skirt, raising it slightly to reveal her upper thigh and the pale blue garter that rested there. She braced herself so as not to melt as his hand splayed warmly against her sensitive skin before his fingers began to remove the garter from her thigh. Ever so slowly he pulled the elastic down before finally straightening, eyes gleaming with merriment as he stared into her flushed, embarrassed face. He placed a kiss on her luscious lips before turning and throwing the garter down into the howling men below, right into Cam's outstretched fingers.

"Way to go, Cam!" Derrick's shout caused everyone to burst out in laughter.

"Thanks, bro." Cam's dry tone prompted more laughter from the gathered crowd.

Cam and Angela turned to stare at each other, smiling slightly. He walked over to her slowly, and amid more laughter and wolf calls, placed the garter on her thigh.

"I guess we're next." He smiled into Angela's good-natured eyes.

"That is the tradition." She returned his smile. They both turned to stare as Derrick and Alesha made their way down the stairs.

"I've never been one for traditions, but I think I could make an exception in this case," Cam whispered in her ear.

"Maybe I could, too," she softly responded with her back still toward him, not daring to turn around to face him.

All too quickly, Derrick and Alesha were off amid flying birdseed and well wishes. She caught a glimpse of her mother and brother and blew them both a kiss. Her mother looked ecstatic, while her brother's expression was a mask of melancholy.

They exited the door and ran hand in hand to Derrick's black Jaguar. Once tucked inside, Alesha tried unsuccessfully to quell the nervousness mounting within her. Derrick started the car and it moved smoothly and speedily down the road. She stared out the window until the reception hall was a tiny blur in the distance. Lord help her, she had done it. She was on her way to her new life—a life that, if she was honest with herself, didn't terrify her nearly as much as she had thought it would.

They had been driving for a little over an hour, saying little, each engrossed in their own thoughts. She placed a hand on her nervously churning stomach and closed her eyes, resting her head on the soft leather headrest. She tried to calm her nerves. She wouldn't think about anything for a few minutes. She would just relax and listen to the soft music wafting from the speakers.

Derrick glanced at Alesha's silent profile. Her eyes were closed and she looked tenser than he had ever seen her. He knew she was nervous, but he didn't know what he could do to alleviate that. He had tried to talk and she had been unresponsive. Maybe once they arrived at the house, she would relax, although he silently admitted she would probably get even more tense. He knew she was worried about being alone with him.

He reminded himself again that she had known exactly what she was letting herself in for. He hadn't lied to her or tried to deceive her in any way. He had told her what he had expected, and she had agreed to his terms. Now she would just have to learn to live with her decision.

"Well, here we are."

She jumped nervously at his voice. Opening her eyes, she glanced out the frosty window at the lovely two-story house (which he had called a cottage) as he stopped the car. She remained inside until he walked around and opened the door for her. Taking her hand, he helped her out before leading her inside.

"It's beautiful." She glanced around her apprehensively.

"Thanks." He took her coat and hat, placing them onto a chair in the hallway.

He went back out into the cold night air and returned moments later with their bags, which he sat down in front of the stairs. "Would you like to go to our bedroom and change for dinner?"

Our bedroom, she silently echoed. Oh, the visions those little words fired off in her head. "Yes, thank you."

He nodded and, picking up their bags, started up the stairs. "Follow me."

He ushered her into a spacious room with a huge cherry-oak, king-size bed covered with a black-satin comforter and shams. Much to her relief and dismay, he quickly excused himself after showing her where the bathroom was.

She walked over to the bed and sat down nervously. She fingered the soft comforter, her eyes lingering on the huge bed she and Derrick would be sharing shortly. Visions of the two of them lying there naked, entangled in the soft sheets, tortured and teased her mind. What would his skin feel like against hers? What would it be like to...? She refused to complete that thought, quickly jumped up and almost ran into the bathroom, hoping a hot shower would ease the confusion and maddening sense of anticipation coursing through her veins.

Chapter 7

Approximately forty minutes later, she descended the stairs, wearing an emerald-green, long-sleeved silk dress. Her hair was swept away from her face, though she had left it loose.

Following soft strands of romantic music, she entered the study. Derrick was standing in front of a floor-to-ceiling window, but turned to stare appreciatively at her as she entered.

He was dressed in tan slacks and a burgundy sweater. He had shaven, and seeing his slightly damp hair, she realized that he had showered, too. At least he had not barged in on her. She conceded he was trying to be considerate—for that she was grateful.

At her puzzled gaze, he said, "I used the guest bedroom to change." He slightly stressed the word *change,* making her aware that he would not be using it later when it came time for bed.

She forced herself to walk over to where he stood, stopping inches in front of him. She would have spoken to break the uneasy silence, but she didn't know what to say.

"Did you find everything you needed?" With great difficulty, he resisted the need to touch her.

"Yes." She linked her hands together nervously.

"Dinner is ready, if you are."

"I'm ready." She paused before quickly elaborating, "I'm ready for dinner."

He smiled broadly at her words, but made no further response, ushering her into the dining room where a romantic, candlelit table for two was set. A magnum of champagne was beside the table, and a bouquet of red roses lay beside her plate. She almost laughed out loud as her eyes surveyed the romantic scene before her. If things were different, she would have been pleased—a big part of her was pleased, even now.

He held out her chair for her as she sat down before seating himself opposite her at the small table. He only had to reach his hand out to touch her face—that thought made her breath catch in her throat. To remove her eyes from the disturbing depths of his, she looked at the roses, fingering a soft petal lightly.

"These are beautiful."

"I'm glad you like them."

He wondered why he had an absurd impulse to say something corny, like she was the most beautiful woman he had ever known, or that he was glad she was his wife. "Would you like some champagne?"

"I'd love some." She gratefully accepted, raising her glass as he popped the cork before placing some of the foaming liquid into her glass.

She downed the contents in one gulp before the bubbles had subsided and offered her glass for more. Derrick raised an eyebrow at her actions, but refilled her glass nevertheless. She disposed of that in the same fashion and offered her glass for more. But he shook his head.

"Getting drunk is not going to help anything." He replaced the champagne in its holder.

"I'm not trying to get drunk."

She only wanted to relax—something that seemed impossible to do in his presence.

"Alesha, try to calm down. I'm not going to devour you."

Absurdly, she thought it might not be such a bad thing if he did. She wanted to unleash the passion that had been hinted at every time they had touched. She wanted him, but she was afraid—both of him and of herself.

She managed a half smile. "Derrick, I…"

Unexpectedly, he grabbed her hand, his fingers lightly caressing hers. "It's not as if this is your first time."

She blushed hotly and looked away. How did he expect her to discuss such intimate matters with him? If she told him that he was her first, he wouldn't believe her. He wouldn't believe her because she had led him to believe otherwise, she silently amended.

"Alesha." The soft yet firm way he called her name made her look at him. "I won't rush you."

"I know." Her voice was barely audible as tiny shivers of anticipation raced up her arm at his light, teasing touch.

"Do you?" He spoke so softly she thought she had imagined it.

"Yes." She took a deep breath and then released it slowly. "Maybe if I had a few days to…"

"No, Alesha, there will be no days, weeks or months," he quickly yet gently interrupted, fingers stilling their seduction of her wrist. "I mean to make love to you tonight."

She snatched her hand away from his. "Do you have to talk so bluntly?"

He sat back in his chair and poured himself a glass of

champagne. Taking a sip he reminded, "We are husband and wife."

"I know, but it's so…new…" Her voice trailed off. She suddenly longed for some more champagne—a lot more.

"You want me, don't you?"

His question made her eyes grow to twice their normal size. She was glad she didn't have any champagne in her glass to drink. She would have choked on it.

"How can you ask me such a thing?" She brought a hand to her suddenly constricted throat.

"It's obvious." He smiled slightly at her distress. "That bothers you, doesn't it?"

"What do you expect? Ours is not exactly a normal marriage, is it?" She didn't deny or confirm his words. "Can't you try to be more patient?"

"I am, and I have been." His response was calm. "I could have already taken you while we were engaged. However, I gave you time to adjust."

"Don't say that!" She fidgeted uncomfortably in her seat as red stained her cheeks.

"Say what?" He smiled slightly, knowing to what she alluded.

"You know what." She ran her tongue across her dry lips and his eyes watched her every movement. "It sounds so, so…animalistic." He laughed heartily at her words, and that was her undoing. "Damn you. Don't be amused by me!"

"It's hard not to be." He wiped the tears of merriment from his eyes. *"Animalistic?"* he echoed, still smiling. Then, seriously, he said, "You don't know what animalistic is…" He paused for emphasis before adding, "yet."

She stood abruptly, food forgotten. "I'm really not very hungry. I'd like to…" She stopped herself, eyes widening in shock at what she had been about to say.

He also stood. "You'd like to what?" He smiled wickedly.

"Go to bed?" He'd correctly interpreted what she had been about to say.

"No, I wasn't going to say that, I…" Her voice trailed off as her heart leaped in her throat.

"Let's both go to bed." He took her hand and nearly dragged her up the stairs, not stopping until they reached their bedroom.

Once inside, he started to pull her into his arms. "Wait!" She placed hands on his chest to ward him off. Things were moving too fast—much too fast. "I—I have to change."

"Why? You won't wear it for long." He pulled her body closer again.

"Please, please, Derrick." Her hands on his chest warded him off.

He looked at the nervous expression on her face and he knew she needed a little more time. "All right, but don't take too long."

"I won't." She picked up her overnight case before almost running to the bathroom, shutting the door behind her and locking it.

She leaned weakly against the door. She tried to quiet the frantic thudding of her heart as she opened her overnight bag. She should be angry and appalled that in a few minutes she would be expected to make love to Derrick, but she wasn't. If she were honest with herself, she was expectant. She was also nervous, excited and confused.

Damn Derrick's undeniable effect on her and damn Robert, too, for getting her into this mess! With a sigh of resignation, she glanced into her overnight bag and saw a white silky negligee with matching robe, which left nothing to the imagination.

"Oh, Mother!"

How could her mom have done this to her? She must have taken out her flannel gown and replaced it with this one. She couldn't go out there wearing this! She rummaged further into her luggage and saw other negligees, all just as revealing. Carefully inspecting the diaphanous, flimsy creation in her hands, she admitted it was a knockout. The long gown was made of several layers of the sheerest chiffon she had ever seen, and the bodice and waist consisted of lace, which would allow tantalizing glimpses of her skin to peek out. The single-layer chiffon robe might as well be nonexistent for all that it covered. Well, it was either wear this sexy creation or nothing, so she quickly donned the ensemble and almost fainted when she saw how little it actually hid.

After several minutes of deep breathing, which did nothing to calm her nerves, Alesha went to the door and grabbed the doorknob. She willed herself to calm down. She was married now, and on the other side of the door, her husband waited for her. Though their marriage was the result of a distasteful arrangement, she silently admitted that their mutual desire for each other was very real—as real as real could get. Soon she would know the culmination of the scandalous kisses they had shared. At that thought, she trembled visibly and, gathering the folds of the robe closer to her in one hand, she opened the door with the other and slowly exited the bathroom.

The only light in the bedroom came from candles beside the bed, which had been turned down. Derrick stood on the opposite side of the room, though he faced her as she entered. He was dressed in a black robe.

Alesha stopped just outside the bathroom. He couldn't believe the tremendous surge of hunger he felt just staring at her luscious body in that sexy gown. In fact, he couldn't believe she had packed such a piece of lingerie, but he was glad she had.

She was the most beautiful woman he had ever seen. He wanted her as he had wanted no other. He couldn't believe that finally she was going to be completely his. Slowly, purposefully, he walked toward her, expecting her to flee at any moment. Yet she remained rooted to the spot, nervous, expectant eyes making tentative contact with his. The pulse at the base of her neck was beating rapidly and he longed to place his lips there. He stopped mere inches away.

"*Beautiful* is too mild a word to describe how you look."

He reached out his hands and lightly cupped her warm cheeks. A shudder passed through her at his touch. He took her breath away for he was staring at her as if she were the most important person in the world. If she didn't know any better, she would think he was madly in love with her.

"Alesha, we've waited a long time for this."

She shook her head in agreement. "I know, but…" She paused, unable and unwilling to try to verbalize her topsy-turvy feelings as far as he was concerned.

"But what?" His hands dropped to her shoulders, lightly massaging her tense flesh.

"I—I don't know…" Her voice trailed off again.

"You don't have to know anything." His strong hands made soothing circles on her overheated skin. "Except that I want you."

"Do you?" His sincere words helped quiet some of the butterflies intent on making mincemeat out of her stomach lining.

"Yes, I do. Very much." The ease of his confession left little doubt as to its veracity. "Do you believe me?" He had always wanted her, and finally she was going to be his.

"Yes." She sighed the word.

"And you want me."

She gasped lightly as his fingers drew the robe from her shoulders and let it fall in a soft heap at her feet. His eyes mesmerized her.

"I…" She couldn't bring herself to admit that, too.

"It's all right. I know."

That voice of his was turning her bones to mush. His hands slid down her bare, silky arms and back up again several times, causing her breathing to increase expectantly.

"All right."

The arms on her shoulders drew her closer until their bodies were touching lightly. His eyes never left hers. Though she made no effort to move out of his arms, he knew she was still apprehensive. He wanted to replace her anxiety with passion and longing—emotions he knew were smoldering just beneath the surface.

He slowly lowered his lips to hers, and placed a light kiss on her quivering mouth. His lips then trailed down her cheek to her earlobe, where he gently bit into her flesh before moving to the side of her neck, his teeth and tongue lingering there, reverently tasting her silky, delicately perfumed skin.

Something strange was happening to her as he continued his pleasing caresses. She felt a little breathless as overpowering feelings began building within her body. After several long, pleasing minutes, his mouth trailed down her shoulder, his hands sliding the thin straps of her gown out of the way, down her arms, as his lips explored her tremulous skin. She closed her eyes, allowing herself to enjoy the extraordinary sensations engulfing her body at his every touch.

His lips moved to her other shoulder, teeth gently scraping across her skin, sending shivers of delight up and down her spine. The hands that had been resting on his muscled arms tightened slightly as he trailed his hot tongue from her neck to her cheek, slowly outlining her tender lower lip. Her eyes were half closed as wonderful tremors coursed through her.

His hands moved from her shoulders to her lower back, to rest intimately on her buttocks, pulling her closer to his masculine physique. She was suddenly aware of every muscle in his body as she was molded to his hard frame. The ache in the pit of her stomach increased almost unbearably.

His lips played lightly with hers, rubbing, nipping softly and then pulling away again, but refusing to end the sweet torture he was subjecting her to. She unashamedly longed to feel his mouth close warmly and decisively over her own. What was he doing to her? This question ran through her dazed mind while she could still think, before, finally, she received what she wanted when his strong mouth hotly engulfed hers.

Like a starving man feasting, his lips hungrily wandered over hers, his marauding tongue sliding beneath the quickly conquered barrier of her white teeth to find and engage in a slow, thorough dance of rising passion with hers. She felt light-headed, overwhelmed with sensation and completely wanted and desired. They had shared many kisses since their engagement, but this was different because she knew, this time, there would be no stopping, interruptions or turning back, and she was absurdly pleased about that. After an eternity of waiting, she was about to fully experience Derrick's lovemaking, and she wanted that more than she had ever wanted anything.

Her arms on his shoulders encircled his neck of their own will. Her fingers tentatively massaged his nape. At her response, his mouth hardened, crushing her lips beneath the pressure his exerted as he intimately deepened the kiss, voraciously ravaging her sweet mouth.

She moaned in pleasure, on fire and wanting—what, she didn't know. Vaguely, she felt him slide the gown from her overheated body and realized she was standing naked in his arms, but she didn't care. All that mattered was that he not stop kissing her—ever. She clung to him unashamedly as he thirstily drank again and again from her luscious lips.

As he lifted her easily, she then felt the cool, satiny softness of the sheets beneath her back. She vaguely realized they were both lying on the bed. Derrick still wore his robe and the textured material brushed against her overly sensitive flesh.

He reluctantly released her enticing lips and withdrew from her slightly to stare at her face. She was so beautiful, and he wanted her so much, yet he couldn't rush her or himself. After years of waiting, he was determined that she would enjoy this as much as he was going to. She stared at him through half-closed, aroused eyes, a thousand questions in her expression.

He smiled slightly and, propping himself up on one elbow, trailed one hand from her collarbone to the tip of a firm, ripe breast, slowly drawing circles around her chocolate nipple. He smiled as she audibly gasped in pleasure. His smile deepened and his traveling fingers became more ardent as he continued his masterful manipulations of her willing flesh.

When his thumb and forefinger encircled her hard nipple, she moaned aloud, unable and unwilling to stop herself. His mouth slowly lowered to taste the flesh his hand had just caressed. She waited for what seemed like hours until his hot, warm, rough tongue licked across her nipple and she groaned louder, closing her eyes against the sweet pain rapidly invading her body.

His hand trailed down her flat, trembling stomach, his palm rubbing against her skin as his mouth enclosed her breast. He pulled at her skin, softly at first, but then with increasing intensity. She felt as if she would die at any second from the exquisite torture he was inflicting on her.

Her hands drifted to the back of his head, holding him closer to her flesh. When he bit into her skin, she simultaneously bit her lip to hold back the scream that wanted so desperately to escape from her mouth, while her hands held him closer still. After several agonizingly wonderful seconds, his hot roving mouth moved to repeat the process on her other breast. She stopped trying to hide her pleasure at his touch and passionate moans of pleasure escaped from her lips.

Her fingers ran up and down his head, holding him closer still, and the hand on her stomach moved to trail across one of her silky inner thighs, before moving to touch her more intimately than anyone ever had, and she was suddenly lost in a savage, merciless storm.

Raising his head, he watched the play of emotions that crossed her face as he did things to her she had only dreamed of. Her body shuddered uncontrollably and her hoarse screams of pleasure filled the room as he continued his mind-shattering stroking of her pliant body. He wanted her to forget every other man she had ever been with. His would be the face she saw, his the name she uttered. She would cling to his body and give herself to him completely.

He fought the urge to plunge into her. She was so wet, so warm, so inviting. His teeth bit into her nipple again and she arched against him, her hips moving rhythmically against his skillful fingers as he continued to assail her with passion.

Why hadn't someone warned her that she would feel this way as his expert hands stroked her novice body? She had never imagined that anything could feel so marvelous! It couldn't get any better than this, could it? Her question was answered emphatically yes with each subsequent devastating caress Derrick bestowed on her. She clung to him weakly, unabashedly begging for release of the sweet tension coiling inside her. She didn't think she could take much more, but each touch proved her wrong.

Derrick shrugged out of his robe and immediately covered her soft, welcoming body with his own. She gasped at the intimate contact, feeling every hard, masculine inch of him against her. His lips covered hers again and again. Her arms entwined around his neck before moving to slide down his powerful shoulders and his muscled back, enjoying the rough texture of his flesh against the satiny softness of her own. Her body begged him to end the wonderful torment he had stirred up within her.

He tore his mouth away from hers to bury it in the soft hollow of her neck as he rasped her name over and over again before lifting his head to stare at her face—highly aroused, yet somewhat troubled. She opened her eyes slightly within a few seconds and stared at him questioningly. He wanted to bury himself in her, he wanted to lose himself in her, and he was going to do just that and more.

His eyes burned her with their intensity, his body lighting an answering inferno within her own as one of his muscled legs slipped between her satiny thighs. She gasped at the intimacy and her heavy eyelids began to droop.

"Alesha, just enjoy it—enjoy us," he urged. "Just feel," he added as he devastated her in a kiss that seared her to her very being.

His limbs entangled closely with hers. Intent on savoring each second, he slowly, inch by inch, merged their bodies into one. She felt engulfed by heat and slight pain as he slowly filled her—he was hot, hard and throbbing. He then glanced down at her, shock evident in his expression.

"Alesha?"

He couldn't comprehend what his mind and her body was telling him. She was a virgin! How could she be a virgin? He continued to stare into her shimmering eyes. He started to withdraw, but she was so soft, so warm and fluid that he couldn't bring himself to leave her, so he pressed deeper. He lay motionless for a few moments, and when she began to whimper against his hot mouth, and the hands on his back began to caress him, only then did he begin to move—slowly at first, yet urgently.

Her body shuddered beneath his as momentary pain quickly gave way to immense pleasure. Hot molten lava flowing through her veins at his every erotic, pleasurable touch. Sensations she hadn't dared to imagine erupted from the core of her being as Derrick opened her eyes to a wondrous desire whose existence she had never suspected.

His powerful body continued to move frantically against hers. She instinctively arched to get closer to him. He groaned at her actions and his hands moved down her sides to rest on her hips, pressing her closer still, wrapping one of her slender legs around his waist as their passion rose higher and higher still, threatening to consume them both with its ferocious intensity.

Many times, she had dreamed of this moment—what it would feel like to make love to Derrick completely and totally—yet this surpassed all her expectations. Forgotten was the fact that she had once driven him away, as was the fact that she had married him only to save her brother. Now, right now, he was the only person who could give her the release she so desperately craved. He was the only one who could bring her dormant body to glorious, vibrant life.

They floated high, higher still on tenuous waves of life-affirming passion. When the moment of culmination came, she cried out into his mouth and he into hers. Her eyes, filled with wonder, flew open to stare into the blazing depths of his. Their bodies began to shake uncontrollably as the throes of their passion blinded them to everything except the unparalleled bliss they experienced in each other's arms as they drifted slowly into a miraculous abyss of complete and total fulfillment.

Some time later, he marshaled enough energy to remove

his body from hers. They lay breast to breast on their sides, his hand resting on her waist.

"Did I hurt you?" His warm breath vibrated against her ear.

"No." Her single-word response was muffled as she hid her face in his hair-covered chest, inhaling the heady male scent of him, which intoxicated her.

On the contrary, she silently amended. He had made her feel wonderful, vibrant and alive. She had wantonly enjoyed his thorough possession of her, as she had never enjoyed anything else in her life. She had clung to him, whimpering, begging for his kisses and caresses. She had found rapture in his arms beyond belief. Had he known? Of course, he must have. Why didn't that bother her? She had responded shamelessly to him and her body felt completely fulfilled against his, as if this was where she was meant to be.

Out of duty to some absurd unwritten rule, she tried to roll away from him, but was glad when he wouldn't let her go. His strong arms held her close to his masculine form, a body that had moments before given her the greatest gratification she had ever imagined. She stayed where she was, where she wanted to be, close to her husband.

Derrick knew she wanted some time to rationalize what had just happened between them, and he knew that no matter how hard she tried, she wouldn't be able to. She would never be able to discount what they had just shared—neither would he. She felt so good lying in his arms, her soft body yielding against his.

She was so inexperienced, but she had aroused him as no other woman ever had. He was her first lover, the first one to awaken her to the desires of her own sumptuous body. Given what had happened two years ago, he didn't understand how that could be. However, it was undeniably true—Alesha had been a virgin. Why had she lied to him about that?

Slowly, he ran his hands down her slender, silky back, pressing her closer, feeling her shudder against him. He wanted her again and again. Yet he resisted temptation for the moment—they needed to talk. He needed some long-overdue answers. He lowered his head to look at her and she tried to bury her face into his chest. His hand moved under her chin, forcing her to meet his gaze.

"Look at me."

When she complied, he placed a lingering kiss on her tempting lips, but pulled away before things got out of hand. Her beautiful face was marred with uneasiness and he knew she was aware of the questions swirling through his mind.

"Derrick…"

"Alesha, why didn't you tell me you were a virgin?"

He asked the question she dreaded but expected. How in the world should she respond?

"I don't want to talk about it." She lowered her head onto his chest to escape his piercing gaze.

"We have to talk about it." A firm hand under her chin lifted her eyes to meet his darkening ones. "Why did you lie to me two years ago?"

"Derrick, please. I can't talk about this now—not now." Her eyes begged him to understand what he couldn't possibly.

"I don't know what game you're playing…" His voice was understandably upset.

"It's not a game," she quickly contradicted. It hurt her to have him think of her as deceptive when she was merely confused.

"Then, what?" He studied her with simmering anger evident in his expression. "Why the pretense?"

She longed to tell him everything, but what had once seemed so clear and logical now seemed silly and juvenile. She could no longer justify to herself her reasons for hurting him two years ago and for denying them the bliss they had just shared. How could she justify it to him?

All she wanted was to snuggle in his arms, close her eyes and enjoy being with him, but she couldn't. She felt too ashamed and too confused to do that, and she couldn't face any more of his justifiable anger and questions, either.

"Please, just leave me alone."

Avoiding his eyes, she turned away from him again. This time, he allowed her to break free from his embrace. She immediately missed his warm hard body and felt completely bereft.

He looked at her bare back oddly and started to touch her, but stopped himself. Damn her, she owed him an explanation, and he wanted one! He reached out a hand to turn her around to face his righteous anger, but stopped himself. He needed to calm down. If they spoke now, he would say things out of anger he would regret later. Unable to help himself, he swore out loud and she jumped at the sound, though she made no move to face him again. He lay back against the pillows and placed a hand on his head in disbelief. Given the sweet rapture they had just shared, how ludicrous that they were now acting like complete strangers. Damn her, and damn himself for still wanting her with every breath he took!

She pulled the satin sheet closer about her and her body tingled as the soft material brushed against her flesh, made overly sensitive by Derrick's hands, mouth and body. Even now, she unabashedly wanted him. Her body ached for his, but did he still want her?

Chapter 8

Hours later, she was still lying with her back to him as far to her side of the bed as possible—not wanting any incidental contact of their bodies to spark any smoldering flames in either of them. She had never been so uncomfortable in her life, afraid almost to breathe for fear that he would know she was awake and once again ask questions she didn't know how to answer.

She wanted him as desperately as she had hours ago. She longed to feel his strong arms around her, but she couldn't face the anger or the questions that she knew would still be reflected in his eyes when he looked at her. What was she going to do now? How was she going to continue in this marriage and face his inquiries about her past behavior on a daily basis?

What she silently feared and longed for occurred when he shifted suddenly, placing a strong arm around her waist, pulling her back against his warm, hard body. The fingers of one of his hands splayed across her stomach as his lips caressed the side of her neck and shoulder.

The hand on her stomach moved up slowly, massaging her pliant flesh to cup a full breast. He stroked her skin as his warm lips explored the soft skin of her neck, shoulder and back.

She closed her eyes as familiar sensations began to overwhelm her. When one of his legs slid between hers, she moaned with pleasure. His wandering fingers slid languidly back down her quaking body to her stomach and lower, moving to gently explore her pulsing depths, pushing deeply inside her again and again, eliciting ecstasy within her.

"Oh, God," she whispered as he continued his devastating caresses.

She felt him smile against her shoulder and his teeth bit gently into her flesh. She arched back against him and one of her hands covered his as his fingers drove her crazy with longing.

His hands slowly turned her until she was lying on her back and his mouth captured hers in a singeing, greedy kiss, which stole her labored breath away. His body covered hers, his hands entangling themselves in her hair as he pulled her mouth closer to his. Her hands clung weakly to his shoulders before urgently moving down his back to rest on his hips as his mouth continued to ravage hers again and again. She wanted him so much it hurt.

He never said a word, yet his body spoke volumes. She didn't doubt he was still angry at her, but he also still wanted her. Perhaps that would be enough for now.

Her body melted against his. She willingly lifted her hips as he plunged forcefully into her waiting void—filling her completely. She closed her eyes and traveled with him to that wonderful place he had carried her to before, where nothing mattered except the two of them and their passion for each other.

He manipulated her, controlled her, sent her into such a fever pitch, she thought she would literally burst from the mind-bending pleasure she felt. She didn't, though, but rather yearned for more. His lips slid from hers to rest in the hollow of her neck, opening moistly over the pulse beating erratically there, his teeth scraping over her skin. His body continued to masterfully caress hers.

Hoarse moans of pleasure escaped from her lips. Her eyes were tightly shut as her body began to shudder, softly at first, but with increasing intensity, as did his. Her fingers stroked his rippling back as she pressed closer to the man who was now her husband and her lover. His body pressed hers into the soft mattress as they soared higher and higher on waves of desire. Once again, she obtained a glimpse of heaven in her husband's arms.

She slowly awakened the next morning, stretching languidly against the unfamiliar feel of satin on her naked skin. Her hair covered her eyes, and she pushed it away with an impatient hand.

She glanced around the unfamiliar room. Why was her body so sore? Where was she? These and many other questions tumbled through her dazed mind, until she suddenly remembered. Slowly, she turned to look toward the side of the bed on which Derrick had lain last night but, to her relief—and dismay—he was gone.

She slowly brought a trembling hand to her mouth as she remembered him turning to her again in the night. More importantly, she remembered her response to him. She had to admit that he had been a wonderful, considerate and passionate lover. In fact, he had been everything she had ever fantasized about and more.

Sighing, she slid out of bed, taking the sheet with her. She walked by her robe and gown, which Derrick had strewn carelessly on the floor. As she bent to pick them up before placing them on a chair, her mind again drifted toward last night and the wonderful discovery it had held.

She entered the bathroom and dropped the sheet. Her mouth dropped open as she caught a glimpse of herself in the full mirror and stopped in shock. Was this her? Her face looked different, maturer. Her lips were slightly swollen from the numerous ardent kisses Derrick had placed there. Her breasts looked full and tender from his hands and mouth. Hot color flooded her cheeks as she beheld the evidence of Derrick's conquest of her body. She was a woman now—she was Derrick's woman. Derrick, her husband, a man who baffled and inflamed her mind, body and soul.

Turning away from the disturbing picture she presented, she walked over and turned the shower on full blast. Stepping under the steaming spray, she grabbed a bar of soap and slowly foamed her still-tingling body. Where was Derrick? What would she say to him when she saw him? She still had no satisfactory answers to his questions.

Long minutes later, she stepped out of the shower, her skin squeaky-clean. She wrapped a towel, sarong-style, around her wet hair and grabbed a bath sheet to place over her body. Before she could accomplish that task, however, the door burst opened and Derrick appeared casually dressed in jeans and a white sweater—looking very handsome and desirable.

She gasped at his intrusion and tried to pull the towel in front of her. However, his strong hands stopped her. Taking the plush material from her fingers, he slowly proceeded to thoroughly dry every inch of her.

He slid the towel slowly down her shoulders and arms. Then he drew the material across her collarbone and sensuously across her swollen breasts, which hardened at the contact of his toweled hands. A soft sigh escaped from her lips as she waited for him to go further.

His eyes moved from her aroused face to follow the path of his hands as they continued their descent down her satin skin, moving to brush across her flat stomach, shapely hips, thighs and feet before he slowly walked behind her and dried her back, buttocks and legs.

Returning to stand in front her, he dropped to his knees, his toweled hands moving to her inner thighs with increasing urgency, staying there longer than was necessary before he totally discarded the towel and replaced it with his fingers. Her knees went weak, and she swayed until her back gratefully encountered a nearby wall.

Her breathing was ragged and her fingers flexed on his broad shoulders to steady herself as his fingers continued their manipulation of her fevered body. When his mouth replaced his fingers, she cried out at the multitude of new wonderful feelings that assaulted her tremulous body.

His hot tongue delved deeply into her moist, pulsing recesses, darting, twisting, turning, retracting and seeking again and again—first slowly, then faster and faster. He drove her to the brink of ecstasy and back. All the while she longed for more, much more.

Her body shook convulsively. She closed her eyes tightly and her head rolled from side to side as he continued his devastating exploration of her all-too-willing flesh. A thousand tiny, brilliant stars exploded behind her closed eyes as his mouth and lips slowly trailed back up her body to stare at her face, clouded by passion, silently pleading with him for a release only he could give. He removed the towel from her wet hair, fingers sliding through the damp tresses.

She was trembling as he reverently stared at her naked form, his eyes burning her with their intensity. She almost pleaded with him to make love to her. She didn't have to verbalize her desire—he knew what she wanted, and he wanted the same thing.

He reached out and lightly brushed her nipple, which hardened automatically at his now-familiar touch. He smiled slightly as he drew her into his arms and placed a passionate, all-consuming kiss onto her quivering lips. Despite her resolve not to, she welcomed his erotic kisses as much as she had his intimate caresses.

His hands pulled her slightly away from the wall to roam down her bare back, pressing her closer. He suggestively rubbed his hips against hers and she whimpered against his mouth. Her arms encircled his neck and she ardently returned his kisses. Feelings—similar to those that had surfaced last night, yet somehow stronger—began to overwhelm her, nearly crippling her. God help her, she wanted him with every painful breath she took.

His mouth plundered hers for several wonderful minutes. She began to moan against his lips, opening her mouth wider beneath his, wishing he would stop this sweet, sweet torture and satisfy them both.

She was quivering uncontrollably as his lips slid from hers and he slowly took a full breast into his hot mouth. His hands moved to her round buttocks, holding her closer against his intense need as he continued to taste her overheated skin.

He hadn't meant for this to happen. He had wanted to catch her off guard and demand answers to questions she had evaded last night. However, one look at her luscious body and all rational thought had fled—just as it had last night. He didn't know why, despite her obvious deceit, but she excited him and made him feel more alive than he ever had.

Her fingers held his head closer to her and his teeth bit

into her nipple, causing her to gasp out aloud. His hands lightly caressed her sides before moving to her back as he lifted his head to again ravage her mouth, simultaneously sliding his hands up to rest on her lower back. Her fingers held his head fast as their wild, unexpected, intensely satisfying encounter proceeded.

Suddenly, he pulled his mouth away from the intoxicating depths of hers and, disengaging her hands from his head, placed them on his chest instead. She opened passion-glazed eyes to stare longingly at him, not wanting him to stop— ever.

"Undress me."

His soft, urgent command made its way through the foggy recesses of her mind. She gasped audibly, but her fingers moved to obey, sliding beneath the sweater he wore, lightly touching his muscled, hairy chest, making him suck in his breath sharply. Her fingers lightly stroked his chest before she pulled the garment up and over his head, throwing it in a careless heap on the floor. Fascinated eyes watched as her fingers slowly smoothed over his powerful shoulders to his arms, enjoying every nuance of the journey.

"Now my pants." His words were whispered against her mouth, his tongue urgently reaching between her lips to touch hers.

His hands guided her to the snap of his jeans, helping her unfasten it. Her hands would have moved away, and he knew it. So his own hand captured one of hers, slipping it beneath the material to encounter his burning flesh.

She gasped, her eyes staring into his hypnotic gaze. She saw the blatant desire written in his eyes and knew it mirrored her own. At his insistence, she touched him fleetingly before his fingers urged her to engulf him totally.

Her breathing was now ragged, as was his. She wanted to move her hand away, yet wanted to continue her forbidden exploration of his marvelous masculine form. He filled her hand as she longed for him to fill her body. Again his lips closed over hers hotly, eyes blazing bright before hers closed against the intense brilliance.

Somehow, his jeans were discarded and he grabbed her buttocks, lifting her slightly before he entered her easily. Her legs automatically wrapped themselves around his waist as he pressed her against the cool, white-tile wall with his body, frantically.

She clung to him wildly, her mouth mating recklessly with his. As she raked her nails down his rippling back, she vaguely wondered who this ravenous stranger was. It couldn't be her! Just as soon as the thought entered her mind, it left, as Derrick's masterful body continued to bombard hers, driving all rational reasoning from her mind. Agonizing pleasure built inside her until she thought she would explode from the force rapidly mounting to near bursting.

"You're so sweet—so sweet," he murmured against her mouth, his breath erotically intermingling with hers before engulfing her lips once again.

Her hands moved up and down his muscled back, her nails digging into his rippling flesh. The legs around his waist tightened, pulling him closer to her as his writhing body continued to both soothe and excite hers. After several long, agonizing moments, she hoarsely screamed into his mouth as he fulfilled her totally. His mouth took her screams, cries and whimpers as their bodies fiercely gave and took from each other.

She suddenly opened her eyes, staring into the fiery depths of his as their passion reached the wonderful moment of gratification. In that instant, she knew, as she was sure he did also, that her body belonged to him. There was no way she could deny that. However, she must take special care to ensure that her heart didn't follow suit. Yet she silently admitted it was already much too late for that.

Later, about 2:00 p.m., they walked side by side dressed alike in jeans, sweaters and leather jackets. Despite herself, Alesha had to admit she was having a good time with her husband. It was a cloudy, cold November day with the temperature in the forties. She sniffed appreciatively as different pleasant fragrances assailed her overactive senses.

Much to her surprise, Derrick made no attempt to question her about the revelations of last night, but rather showed her particular points of interest, and what she had seen of the grounds on which his house sat was lovely. They stopped to sit on a cobblestone bench in front of a babbling brook.

She unexpectedly asked, "Why have you never married?"

Did she imagine it or did a shadow fall over his face at her query? She didn't know what had made her ask that question, or why she waited with baited breath for his response.

He stood and walked to stare into the water with his back to her. She waited for him to speak.

"I'm sorry if that was too personal."

He threw a rock into the pond and turned to face her. "I was married briefly after we broke up."

Her mouth dropped open in shock. She couldn't help it, nor could she seem to force it to close again. She waited silently for him to continue, his demeanor telling her there was much more to the story.

"Nothing to say?"

His voice was bitter, and though he still had his back to her, she imagined his eyes matched his suddenly dark mood.

"I—I don't know what to say."

He smiled slightly without humor. "No questions?"

She had a thousand, but she didn't dare ask any of them. Who had he married? Had he loved her? How soon after their breakup had he married her? When and why had they divorced? Did they keep in touch? Did she live in Washington?

"Do you want to tell me about it?"

She stood and walked over to him. She watched, intrigued, as a multitude of emotions, none of which she could name, crossed his face. He treated her to a piercing, unnerving stare.

"There's nothing to tell. To make a short story even shorter, after too much liquor, I married her in Vegas on the spur of the moment—it was the worst mistake of my life. We didn't know each other, but it soon became apparent that we wanted different things out of life, so we quickly divorced." He succinctly, coldly summed up the worst period of his life.

"I'm sorry." Even to her own ears, her apology sounded pathetic.

"Why are you sorry, Alesha?" He walked closer to her. "Because you know your actions drove me to it?"

"No." She shook her head and stood abruptly. "I didn't know."

"Oh, but you did." He grabbed her arm and pulled her close. "How does that make you feel? Strong? Elated? Happy?"

"No!" She tried to pull her arm free, but he wouldn't release her.

"Why? Why did you do it?" He grabbed her other arm and pulled her closer.

"I don't know what you mean."

"The hell you don't!" His grip tightened on her.

"I don't want to talk about this." Her heart was pounding frantically—surely he must hear it.

"Well, I do!" His fingers tightened on her flesh to the point of bruising. "Tell me!"

"I don't know." She shook her head slowly, trying unsuccessfully to free herself.

"Don't give me that, Alesha. Dammit, you owe me the truth!"

She had never seen him this angry, and she hoped she never would again.

"I don't…" The pure rage in his eyes halted her words.

"Tell me!" He shook her slightly.

"You frightened me!" she blurted out and almost fell as he suddenly released her.

"Frightened you?" He stood and looked as if she had struck him.

"Yes." She rubbed her throbbing arms.

"How?" That one word was spoken tightly and contained a multitude of anger and pain.

She moistened her lips and met his incredulous gaze. "We had only known each other for a short time, yet what I felt for you, what I sensed you felt for me, was so intense. You consumed my every waking and sleeping thought. I was saturated with you. I—I just couldn't handle it anymore."

"So you let me believe you had just been passing time with me, playing with my emotions while your lover was out of town?" He shook his head disbelievingly.

"I never meant to do that." Her eyes and voice pleaded with him to believe her.

"But that's what you did!"

"I didn't have a choice."

"You didn't have a choice?" He stared at her as he tried to comprehend her statement.

"You wouldn't leave me alone," she said softly, resuming her seat on the bench. "When you came to my apartment that morning and found Kevin there, one look in your eyes and I knew what you were thinking and I let you think we were lovers because it meant I wouldn't see you again." With difficulty, she recounted the event that had sealed their fate.

"And that's what you wanted?"

It wasn't the chilliness of the day that sent a shiver down her spine, but rather his frigid eyes as he tried to comprehend what she was saying. No, it wasn't what she had wanted at all, but at the time she had thought it was the only option available to her—now she wasn't so sure.

"That's what I needed."

"What you did to both our lives is a crime." His voice was angry, tired and sad.

"I didn't have a choice," she miserably whispered.

"Yes, you did. But for whatever reason, you made the wrong one."

His voice was colder than she had ever heard it and, unfortunately, it was directed toward her. Her actions had made perfect sense to her two years ago, but right now she agreed with his assertion.

"I did what I had to do."

Even as she said the words, she didn't believe them. She deliberately didn't tell him the rest of the story. Why, she didn't know—perhaps because she now doubted her fateful choices, as well.

He opened his mouth to ask one of the thousand questions that he still had, yet closed it again. He turned away as if the sight of her disgusted him and lifted his eyes heavenward. She wanted to say something—anything—but there was nothing she could say, so she remained silent. After long minutes, he turned and gazed at her again.

"Do you know what your rejection taught me?" His voice held an eerie aloofness, which his eyes now echoed.

"What?" She was not sure she really wanted to hear his response.

"That love doesn't exist. It's just a pretty word people

use to get others to do what they want." He smiled without humor.

"You don't mean that."

Her heart contracted at his cold assertion. She had seen a soft and passionate side to him only a few hours ago. The man she knew he was didn't at all fit with the callous picture he was painting for her now.

"I assure you I do."

He stared at her as if he didn't know her, and it was the loneliest she had ever felt in his presence. She forced herself to remain expressionless, but his words hurt—more than she would have thought possible. She understood his feelings and agreed with them. Honestly, she didn't understand her actions herself, anymore—how in the world could she expect him to?

She stood up suddenly. "I'm ready to go back now."

He looked at her strangely before following her as she retraced their steps back to the house. Both were silent as they walked side by side, neither looking at the other, but rather glancing straight ahead contemplatively. When they entered the house, the phone was ringing. Derrick answered it angrily and she stood in the hallway, waiting for him to finish. As he hung up the headset, he told her he had to drive into the city to meet with Cam.

"Do you have to go?"

She should be happy for a respite from his anger, but she wasn't. She hated leaving things as they were between them, even though she had no idea how to repair the damage her lies had inflicted.

"Politics never sleeps." He glanced at her oddly before shrugging and promising, "Don't worry, I'll be back tonight."

"Will you?" Her question was spoken so softly, he thought he had imagined hearing it.

Though he was still upset with her, unable to resist, he placed a hand under her chin and lifted her mouth to his. He kissed her and she returned the kiss, her hands tentatively resting on his shoulders. Though their mouths ate voraciously, he purposefully kept their bodies apart, because if they touched intimately, both knew they wouldn't stop with just a kiss. After long, fulfilling moments, his mouth slowly released hers and he walked to the door.

"I'll see you later."

She sighed heavily. He might hate her for what she had done in the past, but clearly he still wanted her. That was something, wasn't it? Perhaps they could rebuild some semblance of a civil relationship on that. She hoped so, just as she prayed one day he wouldn't look at her with veiled anger and disappointment in his eyes.

Chapter 9

After Derrick left, she wandered around the study before choosing a lengthy murder mystery to read. Before she knew it, she had finished the novel and it was after 6:30 p.m.

She fixed herself a snack then returned to the study, turned on the television and found to her delight that *Casablanca* was on. It was one of her favorite movies. Shortly thereafter, a loud clap of thunder rattled overhead. She walked to the window and opened the blinds. To her amazement, ominous clouds loomed in the sky and streaks of lightning could be seen in the horizon.

The out-of-season storm had blown in without warning. She didn't mind, though—there was nothing she liked better than a good movie and a thunderstorm. Walking back to the television, she turned up the volume to drown out the thunder and sat down again with her feet curled under her. Some minutes later, lightning lit up the room, there was a particularly violent clap of thunder and the TV went black, as did the lamp on the table beside her.

"Oh, no," she moaned, getting up and trying the light switch on the wall, which also refused to illuminate the dark room. "Great! So much for television."

It was almost impossible to see, but she felt her way back to the kitchen and, after searching through several drawers, she found some candles and a box of matches. Lighting several, she walked into the hallway and peered out at the ghostly reflections made by the barren tree limbs when the lightning briefly illuminated the dark. After several seconds, she decided she might as well go upstairs.

Once there, she tried the light switch, just in case, but the room remained in darkness. Placing one candle beside the bed, she lit the other candles Derrick had placed there last night, before taking one with her into the bathroom.

She turned on the water and began to draw a hot bath for herself—hoping the soothing water would help alleviate the jitters, which had suddenly crept up on her.

Once the tub was full, she undressed and sank into the sudsy, steaming water. As she slowly ran her hands over her body, she remembered other hands that had explored her flesh the night before and this morning—Derrick's hands—strong, sensual and pleasing.

Try as she might, and Lord knew she had tried, she could not deny that she wanted him with a single-minded passion that overwhelmed, frightened and yet empowered her. Last night and this morning, she had longed for him to somehow defy the laws of physics and merge their bodies into one. At several points, she had felt as if he had done just that.

Vivid memories of crying out in his arms, clinging to him, and the feel of his naked flesh against hers tormented her. Against her will, her eyes were drawn across the room to one of the white-tile walls. Hot color flooded her cheeks as she remembered how she had shamelessly clung to Derrick this morning as they had made love in this very bathroom.

She grudgingly admitted that he was a fantastic lover—better than all the heroes in the romance novels she had read and in all the love stories she had watched on television or at the movies. With one look from those expressive eyes of his, he could inflame her soul. The slightest touch of his fingers turned her into a mass of putty that begged to be shaped by him. Yes, she was inexperienced, but she somehow knew that no one would ever compare to him.

She sighed audibly as she closed her eyes again, trying without success to make sense out of her ambivalent feelings as far as her husband was concerned. Would he still be angry at her when he returned? No doubt, he would. He had every reason to be. She wondered if she should tell him the rest of the story. Would it make her more sympathetic in his eyes, or more pitiful?

She opened her eyes and slowly stood. Her thoughts wouldn't allow her to relax as she had hoped when she had sunk into the tub. All she seemed capable of doing was thinking of Derrick—wondering where he was, what he was thinking and feeling—and both dreading and looking forward to his return.

Her fingers grabbed a huge black bath sheet and began to dry her body. Automatically, memories of this morning rushed to her mind. She dreamily remembered how his mouth had caressed hers and how his body had... Damn! She forcefully ended that train of thought, angrily threw the towel down and picked up another seductive negligee. This one was black satin and clung to her every curve. In spite of herself, she smiled slightly as she mentally pictured her mother shopping for the revealing nightgowns she had placed into Alesha's luggage.

She shivered as she reentered the bedroom and walked

over to switch on the gas-powered heat before climbing beneath the soft satin sheets and comforter, pulling the cover up to her chin. In a few seconds, she felt completely warm. Her limbs relaxed and her mind was quiet.

All that was missing was... No! She would not say his name again. The rain now mixed with something that sounded like sleet and pelted against the window. She snuggled down against the fluffy pillows beneath her head and began to drift off into sleep. Despite herself, the last thought she had was of Derrick as she wished for his safe return.

Derrick listened impatiently as Cam outlined the remainder of his campaign strategy. Although he hated to admit it, his mind was not on this meeting, but rather on his wife. It was a little after 8:30 p.m. He had been gone longer than he had expected. The snow mixed with sleet worried him, and he hoped she was all right. He had tried to phone her about an hour ago, but the phone lines were down.

"Cam, how much longer are we going to be?" He tapped his fingers against the mahogany tabletop.

"Not much longer, why?"

"Because I'm tired and I want to get back home before the roads get too bad." He sprang off the sofa like a caged tiger and went to stare out the frosty window.

Cam walked over to stand by his friend. "It's not the road conditions that are prompting your sudden lack of interest in your campaign."

Derrick turned to face him, wishing Cam couldn't read him so well. "I am not unconcerned—I'm just tired."

"You're worried about Alesha, aren't you?"

He sighed in annoyance. "Come on, man. Don't start speculating on my relationship with Alesha. We have a business arrangement—that's all!" he insisted with more force than was necessary.

Truthfully, after what had transpired between them last night and this morning, he wasn't sure where they stood, or what he wanted to happen between them. Despite her unexplained lies, all he knew for certain was that he couldn't get her out of his mind, out from under his skin or, he grudgingly admitted, out of his heart.

"If that's true, why are you so worried about her?"

"She's alone in an unfamiliar place with no transportation or phone, and a snowstorm is raging outside. Isn't that enough reason for anyone to be concerned?" Derrick's reasoning was flawless, but he knew it wouldn't fool his best friend.

"Yes."

"But?" Derrick knew he was not going to leave it at that.

"But I think there's more to it than that. I think that, despite yourself, you care for Alesha—that you really see her as your wife, not just as a means to an end."

Hearing his feelings articulated so brilliantly by his friend was unnerving and frustrating. Frustration oozed from every pore.

"Look, Cam, we both know that I tried that once, and I'm not going to make that mistake again."

"Please! As for your first wife, if you want to call her that, she was never right for you. I tried to tell you that. Alesha, however, is another story. But then, you know that, don't you?"

"I'm using her—that's where it begins and ends!" His forceful insistence was more for his own benefit than for Cam's.

"If you say so, Derrick." Cam smiled.

Derrick rolled his eyes. "You believe what you want—you will, anyway. I'm going home." He picked up his jacket and walked to the door.

"Derrick?"

"What?" He turned around impatiently.

"Give Alesha a kiss for me."

"Good night, Cameron," he said, sighing heavily before opening the door.

"Good night, bro." Cam smiled. "Drive carefully."

Derrick made his way home as fast as the lousy weather would permit, which was at a slow crawl, giving him too much time to meditate on Cam's words. Was he beginning to care for Alesha, despite his resolve not to? He knew the answer was yes—he had known that from the moment he had seen her again. He had been strongly attracted to her when they had first met two years ago. He had wanted her since their first touch and had burned for her since their first kiss. Now, after finally making love to her, he couldn't deny that he still cared about her very much.

Why had she lied to him two years ago? He could understand her feelings for him scaring her—hell, he had felt the same way—but why had she allowed him to believe she was involved with someone else? Why not just tell him she felt overwhelmed? It didn't make any sense. There had to be more to it than she was admitting, but what?

He sighed loudly. Why did her motivations matter to him one way or another? He was only using her, wasn't he? As he had told Cam, once he had won the Senate seat, he would let her go and he wouldn't think twice about it. He promised himself that he would. However, he knew he was lying, because the thought of life without Alesha left him chilled to the bone.

Alesha was up nervously pacing the floor when she heard a car drive up around 11:00 p.m. She carefully peered out of the bedroom window and was relieved to see Derrick. She absently noted that the ground was covered with a layer of snow. She ran to the door and prepared to open it, but

stopped herself abruptly. What was she doing? She couldn't
let him know she had been waiting up for him!

Changing course, she ran over and jumped into the bed,
pulling the covers over herself before turning onto her side.
Closing her eyes, she began to breathe heavily and evenly as
if in a deep sleep. Seconds later, the bedroom door opened
and Derrick came in. She felt him peer down at her and
forced her breathing to remain even.

He smiled slightly as she pretended to be asleep. He had
seen her silhouette at the window, and knew instinctively she
had been worried about him; that pleased him immensely.
He picked up a candle, humming as he walked into the bathroom, leaving the door partially open. Seconds later, Alesha
heard the shower running and Derrick singing.

"Inconsiderate oaf." She sat up slightly. "What if I really
was asleep? He could wake up the dead with all of that
noise."

When he shut the water off some long minutes later, she
quickly resumed her previous position, once again feigning
sleep. She heard him walk through the door and, seconds
later, the bed shifted beneath his weight as he slid underneath the covers, naked beside her.

She held her breath as he rolled closer to her, placing his
arm around her waist, before turning her on her back. She
continued to feign sleep, hoping he would take the hint that
she didn't want to talk about the past anymore.

"I know you're not asleep. Stop pretending," he said
softly, leaning over her.

Knowing it was useless, she slowly opened her eyes to
stare at him—his face was only inches away from hers. She
resisted the sudden urge to trace the rugged outline of his
face with her fingers, followed by her lips. Thankfully, he
didn't seem angry, just tired. She prayed he wouldn't bombard her with more questions she had no idea how to answer.

"Do you want to talk?" she asked in spite of herself.

"No. No, I don't want to talk."

He lowered his head to hers and she stared at him, mesmerized by his hungry eyes as his lips ever-so-slowly neared hers and touched her mouth. He caressed her lips with butterfly kisses until she was trembling with need. It was all she could do to refrain from begging him to stop this sweet torture and make love to her, and she knew that he knew it, too.

"Cam asked me to give you something."

"What?" Why in the world was he talking about Cam at a time like this?

"This."

His hands threaded themselves into her thick hair and lifted her head slightly off the pillows, forging his lips with hers. He kissed her in a way that should have been illegal and probably was. There was no way she could fail to respond to the sensual assault, and she offered no resistance. Rather, she capitulated without thought or question.

Her lips melted against the incinerating heat of his, her tongue responding to the insistent pressure of his. He laid her head back on the pillows and his body half covered hers as he continued to devastate her with his mouth.

His hands moved to her shoulders, easing the thin straps of her gown down as his fingers explored her creamy, burning flesh. His lips slid from her mouth to her chin, gently biting into her burning skin before moving down her silky throat to rest in the valley between her full breasts.

Her breathing increased rapidly at his touch, and a familiar ache began slowly spreading through her abdomen at his increasingly ardent caresses. He pulled the gown down to reveal her breasts and blew his warm breath onto one of her nipples, which stiffened in response. She moaned as he pulled her swollen flesh into his mouth—his tongue and teeth ravaging her softly scented skin.

His wandering hands moved to pull the gown farther down her quivering body, from her stomach to her hips, as he continued to devour her with increasingly ardent caresses. Her hands moved to his shoulders, pressing closer to his body as he continued to ignite her with his fiery touch.

She began to moan, wantonly craving his total possession. She clung to him openly, her own hands exploring his rippling back, pressing him tightly against her throbbing body. At times his caresses hurt, at others they soothed— yet, always they pleased and inflamed.

He raised his head to lightly touch his lips to hers, and she dazedly realized that she no longer wore her gown. Their bare, heated bodies now touched intimately. She waited for his kiss, and when it didn't materialize, she opened her glowing eyes to encounter the smiling yet darkly excited depths of his as he stared down at her.

"Do you want me to leave you alone?"

His question was whispered against her lips as his mouth touched hers again and again—refusing to satisfy her by thoroughly claiming what she so readily offered. Why did he have to make her verbalize what was so evident by her actions? Her body arched against his convulsively as his hands trailed down her sides to rest on her firm buttocks, pressing her feverish body closer still to his own hard length, making her wholly aware of his need for her.

"Do you?" He persisted when she remained silent, running his tongue along the outline of her lips.

Aching pleasurably all over, she still held back admitting what he already knew. He sought her complete capitulation—mentally and physically—and she didn't have the strength to resist him.

"Why do you have to make me say it?" Her desire-laden voice was barely above a whisper.

"Because I need to hear it, and you need to admit it."

He took her lower lip between his teeth, pulling at her flesh slightly as his strong hands slowly slid up her body to rest at her waist. She moaned aloud, her fingers moving to the back of his head, pressing him closer.

As she pulled his lips to hers, she hissed into his mouth, "No—God help me—I don't want you to leave me alone."

At her admission, his smile deepened before her eyes closed and his lips claimed hers in a scorching kiss. She couldn't think or breathe—all she could do was feel. He sent the blood coursing through her veins boiling out of control with every touch. There wasn't a part of her that didn't belong to him and she was unashamedly glad about that.

She decided then and there to accept their mutual desire and try to make the best of their complicated relationship—while it lasted. She would focus on his being a man, her being a woman and on their sharing the basic needs, even though she reluctantly conceded that she wanted much more than that from him. But did he want more from her?

He rolled onto his back suddenly, taking her with him so that she was lying on top of him. His hands intertwined in her hair, withdrawing her clinging lips from his reluctantly. He smiled at her dazed, questioning expression.

"Touch me." At his soft command, he sensed rather than saw the rush of color that flooded her cheeks as she lowered her eyes demurely. "Alesha." His insistent calling of her name made her to look at him again. "Touch me."

As if spellbound by his tone and his request, she brought her hand up and ran her fingers lightly over his cheek. It was not long before she had memorized every curve, every line of his handsome face. She lowered her head and her lips and tongue slowly followed the path her fingers had left behind. She inhaled deeply at his neck, intoxicated by the clean smell of his flesh. She couldn't believe she was doing this—wanting and needing to do this. It was as if she were outside her body, watching someone else. She was unable to stop her investigation of his body, though, because what she was doing felt too good to end.

Her fingers lightly touched his chest before threading themselves in the short hair she found there, tugging lightly. His quick intake of breath told her she must be doing something right. She raked her long nails down the length of his chest before bringing them back up again. Then she lowered her head, tasting his salty flesh, slowly covering his chest and abdomen with wet kisses—thoroughly enjoying herself. Her tongue licked his lower stomach, sliding in and out of his belly button, but she was still too inhibited to explore any further, and though he longed for her to, he refrained from demanding more than she was able to give.

After several moments longer, she raised her head and lowered her lips toward his. As they touched, he started to take control of the kiss, but resisted the urge. He wanted her to realize she could arouse him and initiate intimacy instead of just responding to his advances. As her eyes stared deeply into his, her mouth continued its descent until their lips touched. Her hair fell over her face and his as she opened her mouth over his, kissing him amorously. His hands cupped her face, holding her closer as she continued to kiss him with mounting passion.

Her hands moved to cover his as they rested on her face, moving them to her breasts before moving her own to frame his face as they continued to kiss. He groaned at her initiative, his hands moving from her breasts to her hips, lifting her slightly before bringing her back down to engulf him totally.

She gasped and straightened to stare at him with passion-glazed eyes. His hands showed her how to please him and herself—for several long wonderful minutes she was in control of their passion and she reveled in it.

Suddenly, unable to bear her sweet torture another second, he reared up and rolled until she was beneath his hard, throbbing body and he took control of their passionate dance.

"You feel so good," he breathed into her mouth as his body bombarded hers.

She wanted to tell him he felt good, too, but coherent words eluded her. So, she just moaned in agreement. Incredible pleasure began to fill and overflow from her burning body once again. Trembling hands moved to his back, holding him tight. She pressed against him and draped one of her legs over his in order to bring him deeper into her as she pulsed around him, intensifying the pleasure with his every thrust. Nothing else mattered except the wonderful wildfire racing through her veins and the sound of Derrick's ragged, hoarse breath intermingling with hers. Nothing was important except the strong beating of his heart next to hers—nothing, except the rapture she experienced once again with him.

The next morning, she awakened with a heavy weight on her chest, which she soon realized was Derrick's head. One of his arms was draped casually across her waist, his eyes were closed and his breathing was even and steady, evidence that he was still asleep.

Her heart skipped several beats at the intimacy of their positions. She was tempted to awaken him, but stopped herself suddenly. Why would she choose a course of action she knew would lead to another passionate bout of lovemaking between them? As she gingerly smoothed a few tendrils of hair away from her eyes, she admitted that, even now, her body craved his. She should be exhausted, but she wasn't. She was becoming an addict, and his body was the drug she now needed more than anything else in the world. And, like all addicts, she didn't think she would be able to give him up until he nearly destroyed her.

Softly, her fingers moved to trace the outline of his sleeping face, remembering the sweet love they had made together last night. There had been a blending, a sharing of emotions that each of them was powerless to stop. Once she would have been troubled by that. Instead, the knowledge now made her happy and hopeful. Her heart somersaulted as she fought the impulse to slide down level with his face, kiss him awake and once again experience a bit of heaven in his arms.

She closed her eyes and sighed contentedly, enjoying the feel of him against her. She could lie here with him this close to her all day and never need to move. Her body had never felt so relaxed or so alive, nor had her soul. As her fingers lightly moved across his lips, she remembered the intense delight they had given her last night. She again fought against waking him so that she could experience the mind-boggling enjoyment she found only when they were pressed close as one. Despite her resolve not to, she silently admitted that she had lost a huge piece of her heart to him last night.

Quickly, she reopened her eyes, fingers stilling their exploration of his handsome outline. God, what was she doing? How had she allowed herself to reach this point? She hadn't meant to become emotionally involved with him again, and yet, against her better judgment, she had. It had been so easy and, what was more terrifying, she wasn't the least bit sorry that she had.

He was a good man and she was tired of fighting the fact that she needed and wanted him in her life. The real question was this: did he feel the same way about her? Once, she had been certain he had, but now, she didn't know how he felt about her. He wanted her, but what did he think about them being together permanently? She finally knew what she wanted without a doubt, but what did Derrick want?

Very slowly, she inched herself away from her husband's warm, inviting body. He stirred several times before rolling away from her onto his side of the bed. She waited a few moments and then carefully got up so as not to awaken him and donned a thin robe over her naked form. Immediately, she missed the heat of his body as the coldness of the room engulfed her.

Tiptoeing over to the thermostat, she adjusted it higher before walking quickly and quietly to the bathroom, softly closing the door behind her. Once there, she leaned against the door and let out a sigh, partly thankful that she had made it without waking him, and partly disappointed because she hadn't. She then flipped the light switch and was glad to see that the power had returned overnight.

Derrick lifted his head from the pillow and sat up in the bed. His fingers slowly retraced the spot on his face that Alesha had just caressed. He tamped down the urge to join her in the bathroom, realizing she needed some space and so did he.

Even as his body longed for hers, he resisted fulfilling the desire that was never far from his mind when he thought of his wife. Even though they had just been married a few days and had some important issues to resolve between them, she felt much more like his wife than the woman who had held the title before her. There were questions he still needed answers to—answers only she could give him—and he would get those answers soon. He had to, because his feelings for her were growing astronomically. He didn't know how to contain them. Did he even want to try?

* * *

An hour later, Alesha placed a glass of orange juice next to the plate of steaming pancakes she had just prepared for herself and Derrick. She shivered as she looked out at the snow-covered terrain beyond the window, and walked out of the kitchen to the foot of the stairs.

"Derrick, breakfast is ready," she yelled.

"I'll be right down."

She turned, went back into the kitchen and sat down. She had just taken a sip of her juice when he came through the door dressed casually in a Washington Redskins sweat suit. He stopped by her chair to kiss her cheek, nearly causing her to spill her juice before sitting down opposite her.

"Good morning." He smiled and looked out at the snowy day. "It's a good thing we don't have to go out today."

"Yes, it is." She watched him as he cut into a pancake and placed a large piece in his mouth—a mouth that had given her the most gratification she had ever known.

"Mmm, this is delicious," he said, breaking into her disturbing thoughts.

"Thank you."

There was welcome silence as he continued to eat and she pretended to do so. She felt so odd, as if they were really a married couple enjoying a leisurely breakfast together. Of course, they were, but this was hardly an ordinary relationship, she firmly reminded herself. However, she wished it was. Suddenly, she wanted to talk to him about little things, to have him smile at her without mockery, to freely touch him and to feel…

"Alesha?"

"I'm sorry, what?" She reluctantly roused herself from her disquieting contemplation.

He smiled then, that smile she hated—the one that said he knew exactly what she was thinking. Why did he seem to know her so well, at times even better than she knew herself?

"I said you're an excellent cook," he slowly reiterated, razor-sharp eyes studying her flushed features.

"Thanks." She smiled slightly, a little embarrassed.

"I missed you when I woke up."

His seemingly innocent sentence caught her off guard, making her drop her fork noisily onto the plate in front of her. She swallowed the lump in her throat and glanced up from her plate.

She stared into his eyes as warm color began to flood her cheeks and stammered, "I—I, um, well, you were out so late and I wanted to let you sleep in."

He smiled that shrewd smile before replying, "I know what you wanted."

Her pupils dilated to twice their normal size. Had he been awake when she had caressed his face? Had he known she had almost awakened him with kisses and an invitation not for food, but for herself? At that thought, her discomfiture increased almost unbearably.

"Would you like some more coffee?" She stood up, seeking an escape from his presence.

"Alesha, don't be afraid of me," he said, grabbing her hand as she prepared to walk past him, halting her progress.

"I'm not," she whispered without looking at him.

"Yes, you are," he softly contradicted, pulling on her hand until she was sitting in the chair next to his, forcing her to meet his intense gaze. "You're also afraid of yourself and of us," he correctly surmised.

"This is all so new to me." She didn't bother to deny his observation.

"It's new to me, too," he assured her.

"You were married before," she reminded him, daring to glance into his understanding face.

"Not like this," he said quickly, surprising himself and pleasing her.

"No?" Why did her heart skip a beat at his admission?

"No," he reiterated, refusing to elaborate. "It doesn't have to be an unpleasant experience."

"It's not," she replied before she could stop herself, waiting for a sarcastic response that never came. Instead, he smiled at her more gently than he ever had. In doing so, he melted her heart.

"And that's what bothers you."

"Yes," she replied truthfully, unable to look away from his irresistible eyes.

His free hand moved to lightly touch her warm cheek as he suggested, "Stop berating yourself for what you feel as far as we're concerned."

"I don't know if I can."

She couldn't believe they were having a serious soul-searching conversation. It was a novel, yet welcome, experience.

"Maybe it will help if you know that I feel the same way, too," he admitted.

"Do you?" Surprised eyes stared deeply into his warm ones.

"Yes, I do." He brought her hand to his lips. "We both know why we married, but what we have together is real—as real as it can get. There's no shame in admitting that."

He was being so kind to her—she didn't know what to say. This was the last thing she had expected when she had bared her soul. It added just one more layer of confusion to her already troubled heart.

"It feels real." She sighed softly.

"It is real." He traced the outline of her lower lip with his fingers. "We're the only two people who will ever know what we feel when we're together. I promise I won't ever use that knowledge against you, or make you sorry for wanting me."

"You're shattering all my evil illusions about you, Derrick Chandler." Her voice was husky with emotion as she fought back tears his compassionate words evoked.

"Good. You should have none when it comes to people. You should make up your own mind."

The smile he gave her was tender and, dare she think it, loving. She felt her heart melt even further at the look he gave her, and knew she was very rapidly losing her battle not to become any more emotionally involved with him.

"You're right."

"Let's take it one day at a time," he suggested.

He continued to smile, not the smile she hated, but one she knew she could definitely learn to love.

"One day at a time." She raised her glass of juice and lightly touched it with his before taking a sip.

Their eyes locked and held. She felt raw and wonderfully alive. She suddenly knew she was fighting a losing battle as far as he was concerned. In such a short time, he had completely insinuated himself into her life and, more importantly, her heart. She doubted she would ever be able to totally extricate herself again and wondered if she even wanted to try.

Chapter 10

They had returned from Derrick's country house a month ago and their life had switched into high gear. Their days were full with campaigning, and their nights were full of unbelievable passion. Derrick smiled as he contemplated being alone with his wife tonight. Thoughts of her caused the days to linger interminably and being with her made the nights go by much too quickly.

His smile was replaced by a frown as he riffled through a ton of mail that had accumulated since yesterday. He was grateful to be interrupted by the buzz of the intercom.

"Yes, Dorothy, what is it?"

"Sir, Mrs. Chandler is here."

He frowned at his assistant's strange tone. "Send her in."

"Yes, sir."

He stood and walked from behind his desk. When the door opened, the smile that had been plastered on his face changed into a shocked frown as a tall, slender woman sauntered into his office.

"Hello, Derrick."

"Diana. This is a…"

She smiled brightly. "Pleasure?"

"Surprise."

She kissed his stiff cheek. "A good one, I hope."

He reclined against his desk. "What are you doing here?"

"You know I've been out of the country."

"No—" he shook his head "—I didn't."

"I just got back to the States and imagine my surprise when I saw my husband's picture plastered all over the news."

He raised an eyebrow. "Ex-husband."

"Anyway—" she walked closer "—I just had to see you."

"Why?"

"To congratulate you on your senatorial run. The polls say your chances are excellent."

"A phone call would have sufficed."

"I know." She placed a hand on his thigh. "But I like the personal touch."

"What's with calling yourself Mrs. Chandler?" He pointedly removed her hand. "You didn't use my name when we were together."

"I wanted to make sure you would see me."

"I would have seen you."

She smiled. "That's good to know."

"There's something else you should know."

She leaned toward him. "What?"

"There is a new Mrs. Chandler in my life."

"Yes." She ran fingers through her short hair. "I've heard you remarried."

"I did." He stood, walked around his desk and sat down.

"So, how's married life treating you the second time around?"

"Great."

"Really?" She sat on the edge of his desk and crossed her long legs.

He smiled. "Really."

"I can't wait to meet her."

"Why?"

She shrugged. "I'm just curious."

"Don't be." He picked up an envelope from his desk. "If you'll excuse me, I have a lot of work to do."

"I thought we could catch up."

He shook his head. "We don't have anything to catch up on."

She smiled at his bent head and stood. "All right. I'll be seeing you around, Derrick."

"I doubt it." He glanced at her briefly. "We run in different circles."

"You never know." She blew him a kiss and left.

Once he was alone, he slammed the folder shut and glared at the closed door. This unexpected, unpleasant turn of events was the last thing he needed.

"Damn!"

Alesha took a glass of champagne from a passing waiter. She made her way onto the covered and heated balcony while Derrick and Cam talked with a donor inside the ballroom. Tonight, they were attending another in a long line of political fundraisers.

"Hello, Alesha."

She turned and smiled at the woman who touched her arm. She was tall with short hair and smooth brown skin, and she wore a red figure-hugging, low-cut sequined gown that made Alesha's long-sleeved black dress seem dowdy by comparison.

"Hello, do I know you?"

"We haven't been formally introduced." The woman smiled. "Nice party, isn't it?"

Alesha returned her smile. "Very."

"I prefer quieter, more intimate settings, myself."

"So do I, but this is the political life," Alesha said, laughing. "Are you here alone?"

"Mmm." She sipped her drink. "Yes, I wanted to hear Derrick speak in person."

Alesha's eyebrow rose at the woman's familiar use of her husband's name. "Do you know Derrick?"

"You could say that," the woman said, smiling secretively. "I'm sorry. Allow me to introduce myself." She paused for maximal effect before revealing, "I'm Diana Chandler."

Alesha choked on her drink. "Who?"

"Diana Chandler." She smiled at her discomfiture. "I guess I should say Diana Davis-Chandler."

Her eyes widened. "You're Derrick's ex-wife?"

"Yes. I'm sorry if I shocked you."

Alesha knew she wasn't sorry at all. Diana had deliberately sought her out to announce herself. The question was, why hadn't Derrick told her?

"Didn't Derrick tell you I was back in town?"

"No." Alesha shook her head. "No, he didn't."

"Well—" she shrugged dismissively "—I'm sure it just slipped his mind."

"It must have."

She placed a hand on her hip. "So you're the new Mrs."

"Yes, I am."

"We must trade stories some time."

"I don't think so." Alesha placed her half-empty glass on a passing waiter's tray. "Excuse me."

"Surely. It was nice to meet you."

She didn't return Diana's sentiments as she walked away quickly. Why hadn't Derrick told her his ex was in town?

Had he been meeting secretly with her? What did she want? As she reentered the ballroom, her arm was grabbed by a familiar hand.

"Alesha, where have you been?"

"On the patio."

Derrick glanced at her distraught face. "What's wrong?"

"Nothing." She shook her head.

"Come on, Alesha. What is it?"

"I just met Diana."

He frowned. "She's here?"

"Yes." She stared at him. "Why didn't you tell me she was in town?"

"There was no reason to."

She glared at him. "No reason to?"

"No." He studied her closely. "What did she say to you?"

"Nothing."

"Alesha…"

"I need to get out of here, Derrick. Now!" She pulled her arm free and ran from the room.

Diana watched the scene from across the room gleefully. Derrick encountered her smiling eyes and shot her an angry glare before following his wife out.

They entered their house and Alesha angrily threw her purse and coat down on the hall table before stalking into the living room. Derrick sighed and followed her slowly.

"How long am I going to get the silent treatment?"

She turned from the window to glare at him. "You want to talk?" At his positive nod, she obliged him. "Fine! Why didn't you tell me Diana was in town?"

He sighed. "Her comings and goings don't have anything to do with me or, more importantly, us."

"Derrick." She walked closer. "I deserved to know!"

"Why?"

"Why?" She spread her hands wide. "Oh, I don't know. Maybe so I would be prepared for a woman accosting me at a fundraiser claiming to be Mrs. Chandler!"

He scowled. "She didn't."

"She did!"

Anger darkened his eyes. "Damn that woman!"

"Damn you both!"

"Alesha." He deliberately kept his voice measured. "I didn't know she was going to be there tonight."

"But you knew she was in town!"

"I only found out today."

"That was long enough to tell me, Derrick!"

"Dammit, I didn't see a reason to tell you!" His frustration was evident. "As far as I was concerned, I didn't expect to see her again."

She eyed him suspiciously. "Of course you didn't."

He frowned. "What is that supposed to mean?"

"I'm sure you can figure it out."

"Will you stop behaving so irrationally?"

"I'm sorry that I'm not cold and sophisticated enough for you."

"What are you talking about? I didn't say that."

"You implied it." She was angry and hurt, and she didn't want to be reasonable. "If my company displeases you so much, why don't you go and find Diana? I'm sure she'll accommodate you any way she can."

She pushed past him, but he grabbed her arm, halting her retreat. Her eyes sparkled furiously.

"Don't be an idiot!" he said.

She gasped. "So now I'm an idiot?"

She tried to pull her arm free. He refused to release her, pulling her closer instead.

"You are if you think I want anything to do with Diana."

"You married her."

He had married Diana voluntarily—it hadn't been an antiseptic arrangement, like their marriage.

"I also divorced her—quickly."

"Do you regret that decision?"

Damn, he thought they were beyond nonsense like this. He had hoped they were building something special and permanent over the past months. They had been before Diana's sudden reappearance in his life.

She held her breath and waited for his response. A response she dreaded yet needed to hear. His prolonged silence sent fingers of fear dancing up her spine.

"Where are these absurd questions coming from?"

"Answer me!"

He squared his shoulders. "No, I don't think I will."

They stubbornly stared at each other for a few pregnant seconds before she pulled her arm from his and stalked from the room. He followed.

"Where are you going?"

"To bed." She paused before pointedly adding, "Alone!"

"Alesha…"

"I don't want to talk to you anymore tonight!"

"That's fine with me!" He grabbed his keys from the table.

She paused on the stairs. "Where are you going?"

"Do you care?"

"No, I don't care at all." She continued up the stairs.

"Good!" He stormed out, slamming the door behind him.

Early the next morning, Alesha was sitting on the sofa in her robe, drinking her second cup of coffee when she heard the front door open. Seconds later, Derrick walked into the room, disheveled, still dressed in his tuxedo from the night before. He looked exhausted. He barely glanced at her as he walked over and poured himself a cup of black coffee.

"Where were you last night?"

"Why?" His voice was terse.

Her lips thinned. "Were you with her?"

He made contact eye contact with her. "With whom?"

"With Diana."

"You sound like you're jealous." He watched her closely. "But that's impossible, isn't it?"

She lowered her eyes. "Of course it is."

"Yeah, it would be since our marriage isn't real, is it?"

His observation cut her to the quick. To her, their marriage was very real—she had thought he felt the same way. With superhuman effort, she turned to him with a frosty expression.

"You know the answer to that."

His eyes burned. "We're just playing house, aren't we?"

"Yes." She picked up her juice and resisted an urge to throw it in his face.

"Then why do you care where I was?" He nearly shouted the question, angered by her response.

"I don't." She smiled coldly. "You can stay with Diana, for all I care."

"I wasn't with Diana!" He slammed his cup down hard, sloshing liquid onto the table.

"Is that right?"

"Yes, that's right!" At her disbelieving stare he swore savagely, "Dammit, nothing is going on between us and if you don't believe me, then that's your problem!"

Before she could respond, she watched Derrick turn and angrily walk up the stairs, two at a time. Was he telling the truth? She wanted to believe him with every breath she took, but could she trust him? She had before Diana's arrival. Should she now?

* * *

Cam watched as Derrick continued pacing angrily in front of his desk.

"What's the matter with you?"

"Nothing!"

"Really?" An eyebrow rose in disbelief. "Is that why you look like you're contemplating murder?"

"Maybe I am."

"Who's the target?"

Derrick leaned against his desk. "Diana."

Cam frowned. "Diana who?"

"Davis."

"What?" Cam stood to face his angry friend. "Is she in town?"

"Unfortunately."

"What has she done?"

"She was at the fundraiser last night and accosted Alesha."

"Oh, no." Cam rolled his eyes. "Tell me all about it."

"She introduced herself to Alesha as Mrs. Chandler!"

"That woman!" Cam shook his head in exasperation.

"Alesha and I had a fight last night. She's angry because I didn't tell her Diana was in town."

"When did you find out?"

"Yesterday afternoon. She came by my office."

"Why didn't you tell Alesha?"

"I had hoped she would just go away."

Cam sighed. "Wishful thinking."

"I should find her and wring her neck!"

"No." Cam placed a hand on Derrick's shoulder. "Just stay away from her. She's nothing but trouble."

He sighed. "You're right."

"Nice to hear you admit it for once."

Derrick continued to frown. His friend's attempt at humor was completely lost on him.

"What does she want, Cam?"

He shrugged. "Running for office is just like winning the lottery—people come out from the woodwork, trying to latch onto your coattails."

"I suppose, but she's not going to ruin my marriage."

"Your marriage of convenience?"

Derrick silently cursed his slip of the tongue. He had enough trouble right now without getting into a philosophical discussion with his friend about the status of his marriage.

"I'm not going to let her screw up my election chances."

Cam smiled. "No, you had it right the first time."

"Cameron..."

He laughed. "Save your protestations for someone else."

Derrick rubbed his tired eyes. "How did everything get so out of control?"

"It's called life, my friend." He patted Derrick's shoulder comfortingly.

Derrick reopened determined eyes. "I'm not going to let Diana demolish what I've worked so hard to build."

"I hope not." He couldn't resist adding, "What you and Alesha have is special, but then, I don't have to tell you that, do I?"

Derrick sighed heavily. "This has nothing to do with Alesha."

"Oh, man, why don't you stop lying to yourself?" Cam shook his head in remonstration. "You care about your wife very much and if you won't admit it to me, at least admit it to yourself."

Derrick made eye contact with his friend, but remained silent. There was no need to say a word because they both knew he was right. The question was, what was he going to do about it?

That afternoon Alesha smiled wistfully as she listened to the antics of her onetime colleague, related as only Angela could. She hadn't seen Angela since the wedding and had missed her terribly, but she wasn't miserable in her new life as she had thought she would be—that is, not until Diana had shown up.

"So, how's married life?"

"Great." She forced a smile.

"I should be so lucky to find a guy like Derrick." Angela took a sip of her water.

"There are other fish in the ocean. What about Cam?"

"Derrick's friend?"

"Yes, the man who took great care placing my garter on your thigh at my wedding."

"Oh, yeah. I remember him." Angela smiled secretively.

"He's very cute."

"I noticed."

"Really? What else did you notice?" Alesha leaned forward.

"Nothing."

"So did you two talk?"

"We exchanged a few words."

"And?"

"And nothing. You've already taken the top prize."

"And I intend to keep him." Her teasing smile faltered slightly when she realized how much she meant the words she had so easily spoken.

"I didn't doubt that for a moment." Angela's smile turned to a frown. "Hey, what's wrong?"

Alesha blinked rapidly. She had been trying with all her might to appear carefree and happy, and had thought she was doing an admirable job until Angela's question.

"Nothing's wrong." She sipped her drink. "Why would you think that?"

"Something's bothering you." She frowned. "What is it?"

"It's…"

"Don't you dare say 'nothing'!" Angela touched her hand. "Tell me."

She remained silent as she contemplated answering her friend's question. The truth was, she needed to talk to someone and Angela was her confidante. She would keep her secret. Besides, she could use some wise advice right about now.

"Derrick and I went to a fundraiser last night."

"And?"

"His ex-wife was there."

Angela's mouth dropped open in shock. "He was married before?"

"Briefly, two years ago."

"Did you know?"

"Of course," she said.

Angela frowned suspiciously. "What did she do to you?"

She sighed. "She introduced herself as Diana Chandler."

Angela gawked. "No, that hussy didn't!"

Alesha chuckled at her choice of words. "She did."

"The nerve of her!"

Alesha sipped her drink. "Oh, she has plenty of that."

"What did Derrick do?"

"He wasn't around when we met."

"Well, you don't have anything to worry about."

"I don't?"

"Of course not. Anyone seeing you and Derrick together can see you're meant to be."

"We are?"

"Definitely. His ex is just jealous that you have what she couldn't hold on to."

"I suppose you're right." Alesha prayed she was right.

"You're not worried about her, are you?"

"No."

"No?"

She sighed. "Maybe a little bit."

"Did you talk to Derrick?" After Alesha nodded, Angela said, "What did he say?"

She left out all the colorful language and shouting and succinctly responded, "That he's not interested in her."

"Of course he's not. I rest my case." She frowned at her friend. "You do believe him, don't you?"

"Of course. It was just unnerving meeting her out of the blue."

"I'm sure it was, but, girl, Derrick is so hung up on you he's not going to let anyone come between you, especially not his ex-wife." She paused. "And *ex* is the operative word."

"I know." She smiled. "You're right."

"Of course I'm right. Diana is just trying to stir up trouble where none exists. Don't give her the satisfaction. You're Mrs. Chandler now—not her."

"Yes, I am," she said, smilingly.

"And don't you forget it," Angela ordered.

"I won't," Alesha promised, and that was one promise she intended to keep.

Alesha returned home a little after 7:00 p.m. after making several appearances at different functions and giving a speech at a women's club—all after her much-needed lunch with Angela. She was exhausted.

She kicked off her black high-heel pumps and walked into the living room. There, she threw her purse and keys onto the tabletop and limply fell onto the plush black-leather sofa, closing her eyes contentedly as she let out her breath on a deep, grateful sigh. Thankfully, Derrick wasn't home—she didn't have the strength to fight with him again.

They needed to talk about Diana, but she promised herself that when they did, they would do it civilly. She grimaced at the thought of the woman who had upset the tenuous balance of their world. What did Diana want? She silently reprimanded herself. It was obvious that she wanted Derrick. The question was, did he want her? A queasy feeling invaded her stomach as she considered the last question. He said he didn't. He gave no indication that he did. She wanted to believe him, but should she?

"Rough day?"

She opened her eyes to stare into Derrick's, not realizing she had briefly dozed off. He was smiling down at her with a bouquet of red roses and thankfully appeared to be in a better mood than he had been that morning. Frankly, so was she after her lunch with Angela. Maybe Cam had calmed him down. She hoped so.

She sat up and tucked her legs beneath her. "Are those for me?"

"Yes." He handed her the flowers. "They're a peace offering.

"Thank you." She smiled. "Derrick, about last night and this morning…"

"Alesha." He sat down on the coffee table in front of her. "I don't want to argue with you again."

"Neither do I." She sighed in relief. "I'm sorry."

"Me, too." He paused before admitting, "I should have told you about Diana."

She watched him closely. "Why didn't you?"

"I honestly didn't think I would see her again, or that you two would ever meet."

"Why is she here, Derrick?"

"I don't know and I don't care, but it has nothing to do with me or us."

She fingered a soft petal. "Doesn't it?"

"Not as far as I'm concerned." He touched her hand and serious eyes bore into hers. "I'm not interested in Diana. Do you believe me?"

She nodded slowly. "Yes, I do."

He smiled in relief. "Good." He kissed her briefly before standing and going to the bar.

"Does it really matter to you what I think?"

"Yes, it does." He turned to stare at her. "For the record, I spent the night in my car, which is why I was in such a foul mood this morning."

His words were like music to her ears. She had suffered last night and today, envisioning him with that witch, Diana.

"Why did you do that?"

He smiled sheepishly. "To teach you a lesson."

She laughed. "I think I got the better end of the stick—I slept in our nice, comfy bed."

His eyes darkened. "I'll join you tonight."

She blushed before changing the subject. "Um, I saw Angela today."

"How is she?" He noisily dropped a few pieces of ice in a glass.

"She's Angela." She chuckled and he joined her.

"Can I get you something?"

"No, thanks." All she wanted to do was to stay where she was and continue their polite conversation.

"We'll have to invite her to dinner soon."

"That would be nice. Maybe we can invite Cam, too."

"Matchmaking?" He sipped his drink and walked back toward her. A whimsical smile tilted the corners of his mouth.

"No, not really."

"No?"

"Well, maybe a little," she confessed.

He sat down beside her on the sofa, placed his drink on the side table and pulled her legs across his lap, forcing her to lean back, and softly began massaging her weary feet and legs. She started to protest, but what he was doing felt so wonderful. She sank into the cushions and watched him through half-closed eyes.

"Oh!" She moaned gratefully, instantly forgetting what they had been talking about. "That feels wonderful."

He smiled at her and continued in silence. His strong fingers kneaded her tired flesh until it was putty in his hands. His fingers slid up and down the soles of her aching feet before moving to her ankles, making soothing little circles on her silky skin.

"How was your day?" She fully opened her eyes to stare at his handsome profile.

"Very profitable."

He glanced at her shortly before returning his eyes to her legs. His magical fingers continued massaging her calves.

"Perhaps you're in the wrong line of business." She sighed dreamily.

He frowned at that and turned to stare at her. "Why do you say that?"

"You should be a masseur."

He laughed out loud, a pleasing sound she never tired of hearing. "You think so?" He ran his hands forcefully up and down her tingling calves.

"Oh, yes." She nearly purred the words.

His hands moved up to her thighs underneath the wool skirt she wore, suddenly causing a different kind of sensation—a familiar pain began growing in the pit of her stomach. His warm, strong hands caressed her inner thighs.

She stared longingly into the darkening intensity of his eyes and knew he was thinking the same thing she was. She realized how this encounter was going to end, and she welcomed it. She silently admitted she had been secretly waiting for this moment all day long.

Suddenly, there was a knock at the door followed by the entrance of their housekeeper. "Excuse me, sir, ma'am.

There's a call for you, Mr. Chandler." She handed Derrick the phone before soundlessly leaving.

Derrick absently continued to rub her legs, and she watched him unobtrusively. She bet he could charm a snake out of its skin without even trying. She half listened to his conversation and realized that he was talking to Cam. She prayed they would not have to go out for the evening—she just didn't have the strength.

"Yes, Cam, everything is fine." He smiled at her. "Thanks, but we're looking forward to an evening alone."

She could have kissed him for refusing Cam's invitation.

"Alesha's had a rough day and I'm tired, too," he explained and then drily laughed. "Yes, Cameron."

He hung up and stared at her. His hands reached out and grabbed hers, pulling her until she was sitting upright. Her legs were still draped over his thighs. Her face was inches away from his. They stared at each other intensely. Whenever he was near, she completely forgot everything, except for the wonderful way he made her feel. She held her breath, waiting and longing for him to kiss her. Just the slightest movement on her part and their lips would touch. However, neither of them moved to initiate it.

"Cam says hello." He traced her cheek with his thumb, setting off little eruptions within her.

"Oh."

"Hmm." His fingers moved to her burgundy lips, taking extreme care to outline every curve. "What do you want to do tonight?"

"Let's stay in."

"And do what?"

Enigmatic eyes stared into her aroused ones. His voice was low and sexy. It touched her in all the right places.

"Let's make some popcorn and watch a good movie," she said.

He smiled. "That sounds like a good start."

"Yes."

He stood, took her hand and pulled her up with him. "But after the movie, I get to decide what we do next."

Her pupils dilated and she leaned toward him. "Deal."

They smiled at each other, both glad the unpleasantness of last night was behind them. He placed a quick kiss on her lips before leading her out into the hallway.

Chapter 11

They sat side by side on a soft black-leather sofa, watching a horror movie. The lights were off and the atmosphere in the room was both eerie and romantic. At a particularly scary part, Alesha screamed and automatically sought out the comfort of Derrick's chest, hiding her face there. He laughed at her, but his arm went around her shoulders as he pulled her closer.

"It's all right."

She felt him smile against her hair. Suddenly realizing the intimacy of their positions, she prepared to move away. His arm, however, tightened around her shoulders, pulling her closer.

"Don't move."

She didn't want to move from his comforting presence. So she did as he indicated and stayed right where she was. Tucking her legs underneath her, she turned her head until her cheek was resting on his warm chest and she continued to watch the movie.

She felt and heard the strong thudding of his heart. That wonderfully woodsy-smelling cologne he wore drifted up to tickle her nose, almost tempting her to unbutton his shirt and bury her face in his muscular chest until she was absorbed by his intoxicating smell.

His hand absently massaged her shoulder before moving to lightly play with her hair. Early in their relationship, she had realized that he liked to do that, just as much as she liked for him to. She inhaled deeply, again assaulting her senses with his scent. Suddenly, even though she was enjoying the film, the last thing she wanted was to finish watching it. Before she gave in to an irrepressible urge to pull his mouth down to hers, she abruptly stood, taking them both by surprise.

"I'm going to get some more tea." She answered his questioning gaze.

He grabbed her hand as he, too, stood. He noted the slight flush to her face and the pulse beating erratically at her neck. He longed to place his lips on that spot. He instinctively knew that she wanted him to do that, too—that and much more.

"No, you don't want any tea." His arms pulled her close.

His lips found and enclosed hers. She didn't even pretend to resist, sighing in pleasure against his mouth. Her hands drifted upward to rest on his chest. She felt herself sinking to the floor and her hands trailed up to his sturdy shoulders as they continued to engage in a thoroughly enjoyable embrace.

Against her will, he removed his lips from hers and firmly responded, "You want this—you want me."

She was unable to respond as his sizzling mouth covered hers again. He had to be the most fabulous kisser in the world, she thought. She felt herself leaving her body. His touch inflamed her soul, making her feel as if she were the most important person in his life. As her arms encircled his neck, she silently prayed that assumption was correct. Her eyes closed against the blazing heat emanating from his gaze.

"Yes, I do want you," she unashamedly admitted. "I want you very much."

They both lay close together on the softly carpeted floor. His lips fused against hers, their tongues engaged in a heated dance of rising passion. Her mouth caressed his. Once again she felt consumed by him and longed to feel only as he could make her feel. They savored the tastes and textures of each other's mouths.

His hands moved down her back to her softly rounded bottom, to the back of her thigh, intimately draping one of her legs over his, pressing her firmly against his solid length, making her fully aware of the hardening bulge in his groin. His body telegraphed a wild need for hers, a need that matched hers for him.

His roving hands moved to unbutton the front of her blouse with expert ease, slipping beneath to explore her breasts. His lips placed tender kisses down her cheek to her neck before his teeth bit into a pebble-hard nipple through the sheer lacy fabric of her bra. She closed her eyes tighter as mounting pleasure built unbearably within her tingling body.

Her fingers flexed on his shoulders before moving under his T-shirt to caress his chest before exploring his muscular back, her nails raking across his taut skin as her hunger for him surged. His hot mouth teased her flesh until she thought she would explode.

She moaned aloud, clinging to him, begging him with her body to make love to her. In response, his mouth blazed a trail of fire up her trembling body to capture her lips once again, plundering her. One of his legs eased intimately between hers and he rolled until he was half lying on top of her, crushing her body into the floor as he ravaged her mouth. She wanted him so much that it physically hurt and it was a heady feeling knowing that he wanted her just as much.

Her body molded against his perfectly. She clung to him, moaning. His caresses grew more ardent, more insistent. His hands slid down to her hips and then moved to the front of her jeans, slipping under the waistband to stroke the smooth flesh he found there.

His mouth bruised hers, but she didn't care. All she wanted was him—always him and only him. She sighed as her naked chest and abdomen moved against his. She longed to feel his naked body imprinting itself on hers. Her hands moved to his firm bottom, pressing closer to his rock-hard length, silently pleading with him to give them both what they so desperately wanted and needed.

She felt him smile slightly at her actions and she didn't care if he knew how much she wanted him. Nothing mattered except the completeness she felt every time his body claimed hers.

Neither of them heard the doorbell ring, or the door open and close, because they were so engrossed with each other. Neither of them saw the man who entered and stood staring down at them in total shock. Neither of them heard his swiftly indrawn breath. Not until he spoke did they realize they were no longer alone.

"Excuse me!"

Simultaneously they turned passion-glazed eyes to stare reluctantly at Robert. He glanced away, but not until he encountered their intimately entwined limbs and his sister's unbuttoned blouse. Her arms were holding the man who had blackmailed her into marriage and his were around her.

It was Derrick who spoke first, the expression on his face

turning from passionate to annoyed, and then to amused. He sat up and faced Alesha's brother. This was going to be interesting.

"Robert, what are you doing here?" He almost laughed at the look of distaste on the other man's face.

Alesha was mortified! She sat up and shakily rebuttoned her blouse, grateful that Derrick was sitting in front of her, shielding her from her brother's gaze. Her head was lowered and she smoothed her hair, which had seconds before been disarrayed by Derrick's fingers. She couldn't bring herself to look at either man. Derrick grasped her hands once she had finished buttoning her blouse, and they both stood to face her brother.

"What's going on here?"

"What does it look like?" Derrick's disdain was evident. "I was about to make love to my wife," he told Robert.

Robert's eyes darkened in fury and he lunged for Derrick, snarling, "Why you son of a..."

Alesha quickly positioned her small frame between them, and exclaimed with her back to Derrick, "Stop it!"

Derrick's hands automatically moved to her waist, encircling it, making Robert aware that she was his wife—a wife whom he could touch anytime he pleased.

Alesha didn't move away, seeking to forestall any further scene between them. Instead, she asked her brother, "Robert, why are you here?"

"To see how you're doing." His eyes narrowed as they darted to Derrick's hands still encircling her waist, his flat palm resting on her stomach possessively.

"As you can see, we were doing fine before we were interrupted." Derrick's hand possessively pulled her back against him.

"Derrick, please." She turned to stare at him. "Let me speak with Robert alone."

"You don't have to ask his permission!"

"Nor does she have to explain anything to you." Derrick smiled at Robert's indignation. "Whatever predicament Alesha finds herself in is not her fault—it's yours."

"Why, you…" Robert began moving toward Derrick again.

"Derrick, Robert, stop it!" Alesha placed a hand on each one's chest, trying to keep them apart.

"Alesha, I need to speak with you—alone," Robert said pointedly, his eyes spitting darts at her husband, who smiled at his expression, infuriating the other man more.

"Derrick, please leave us alone." She turned to look at him imploringly, both of her hands now on his chest.

He looked as if he were about to refuse, but something in her eyes made him relent. She could automatically sense this. It was remarkable how she had learned to read him— when he wanted her to, she amended. She lowered her hands from his chest, knowing he was about to acquiesce to her request.

"I'll be upstairs in *our bedroom.*" Then, for Robert's benefit and his own pleasure, he bent and kissed her on the mouth before leaving.

Without preamble, Robert began, "What on earth are you doing?"

"What do you mean?"

"You're sleeping with him!"

She defiantly shot back, "Of course I am—I'm his wife. What did you expect?"

"I thought he would have some scruples!" Robert didn't bother to lower his voice.

"Oh, Robert, for heaven's sake!" She raked shaky fingers through her mussed hair. "Derrick's running for office. He can't be seen around town with other women when he's married to me. So I have to perform my wifely duties." She resented having to explain her relationship with her husband to him.

"I can't believe what I'm hearing! You're defending him? What happened to my little sister?"

"She grew up."

"How can you allow him to touch you?" Robert refused to comprehend her behavior.

One word quickly sprang to her mind to answer her brother's question—*easily*. It was no hardship experiencing Derrick's touch, just as it wasn't repugnant living with him as his wife and his lover.

"How could I stop him?" She wished he would leave.

"Do you mean he forces himself…"

"No." She shook her head.

"Then what?" He motioned with his hands, begging for understanding.

She closed her eyes and then opened them again to stare at her brother. "Robert, I'm his wife." She prayed he would leave it at that. He didn't.

"So? You're not his possession." He grabbed her shoulders and shook her slightly.

She pulled out of his grasp. "What do you want from me?"

"I want you to come with me. We have to get you out of here." He grabbed her hand.

"No!"

She wrenched her hand from him. His suggestion was repulsive to her. She didn't stop to consider why.

"Why not?"

"Have you forgotten why I married him?"

"It doesn't matter any longer."

"It does matter!" she responded hotly. "I won't have Mom find out what either of us has done. It would kill her."

"Sis, you've got to listen…"

"No, you listen." Her voice was deadly serious, though quiet. "I am not going to leave Derrick."

"Why not?"

She evaded his eyes. "Because I'm not."

"That's not an answer, Alesha." He watched her closely and illumination widened his eyes. "Do you want to stay here? Is that it?"

That was exactly it, but how could she admit that to him? Would he understand that the man she had married to cover up her brother's theft was a man she never wanted to be parted from?

"Robert, I'm not going to discuss my marriage with you."

"Alesha…"

"Robert, I love you." Her voice lost much of its sting. "But I don't want to hear another word from you about this—okay?" At his reluctant nod, she kissed his cheek. "Good. I'll talk to you later."

She turned and walked up the stairs, leaving him staring after her. He wouldn't have believed it had he not witnessed it—she cared for Derrick and, from the scene he had interrupted, Derrick felt something for her, too. He smiled slightly before walking to the front door. Damned if he had expected this turn of events. And he doubted that either of them had.

As she slowly entered the bedroom, she found Derrick sitting on the sofa by the window, papers strewn around him. He looked up.

"How did it go?" He walked over to her.

"All right." She walked away from him to sit at her vanity table.

He frowned. "Just all right?"

"Do you want a blow by blow?" She didn't want to talk about Robert. She needed to think.

"I want to know if I should expect another visit from your brother."

"Don't worry. I don't think Robert will be back without an invitation."

"Good." His response was brief and cool.

He watched her. As usual, when he was around his wife, strange emotions began to surface in him. Why did he have an almost overwhelming urge to simply hold her and tell her everything would be all right?

Without thinking, he reached out and placed a hand lightly on her shoulder. She jumped from the unexpected contact and he immediately removed his fingers, the kind words he had been about to utter vanishing just as suddenly as they had appeared.

"Don't worry. I'm not going to try to finish what we started downstairs."

He turned and walked toward the door, stopping to pick up his papers from the sofa. He was obviously angry. She glanced up and encountered his cool eyes in the mirror.

"Where are you going?"

"To the study to finish my speech for tomorrow night." He turned away. Something made him turn and face her again. "Unless you want me to stay."

She hesitated shortly before responding. What she really wanted was for him to hold her close and make her forget everything except him. However, she couldn't admit that. Or, more to the point, she wouldn't.

"You go ahead. I think I'll turn in." She lowered her eyes so that he wouldn't glimpse the misery behind them.

"Good night, then."

When she raised her eyes again, he was gone. She lowered her aching head into her hand, trying to make sense out of the situation. Her feelings were so jumbled, so mixed-up. If anyone asked her what day it was, she didn't think she would be able to correctly tell them. Just when she had come to some sort of inner peace about her relationship with Derrick, it seemed that life was throwing up obstacle after obstacle to undermine her tenuous hold on happiness.

She slowly stood and walked over to the bed before sitting down heavily on it. She stared at the door through which Derrick had exited moments earlier. She wanted to ask him what she meant to him. Where did he see their marriage going, if anywhere? Was she more to him than just a means to get elected? She wanted to ask all those things, but she couldn't—not until she was ready to impart a few truths of her own. She wanted to bare her soul to him, but she was afraid of being rejected. She knew he desired her, but did his feelings go any deeper than that?

Things had been going so well on their honeymoon, but ever since they had returned, the fragile happiness and peace they had attained had been sorely tested by outside forces, namely Diana and now Robert. Her feelings for Derrick placed her in enough inner turmoil—she didn't need anything or anyone adding to her already confused state.

One monumental certainty pierced through the fog of her mind—she wanted to remain Mrs. Chandler. Derrick wanted her physically, but did he want a life with her forever? The answer to that single question held the key to her future happiness.

Derrick stared blankly at the pages in front of him. His mind continued to stray to Alesha. Her demeanor a short while ago had baffled and angered him. She was so damn frustrating! Didn't she realize how much he wanted her?

"Dammit!" He hit the top of his desk in frustration. Last night it had been Diana and tonight Robert who had caused unnecessary friction between him and his wife. He seriously entertained the thought of whisking her away from everything and everyone. They seemed to get along so much better when they were all alone. Since they had returned to civilization, all they seemed to do was fight, and he hated that.

At that thought, he tried reminding himself that he was using Alesha as a means to an end—that was all. But he knew he was lying. He could no more stop caring about her than he could stop breathing. He had thought of little else for the years they had been separated. Now that they were together again, she had easily and quickly become an essential part of his life.

He looked forward to coming home to her and talking with her. He loved the fresh way she made everything seem to him. Most of all, he delighted in the way she made him feel. When they made love, there was an undeniable blending of hearts and minds. When they touched on purpose or accidentally, something dormant in him sprang to life—instinctively, he knew it was the same way for her. He needed her. She was crucial to his well-being and his happiness.

God, when had he lost control? What was he going to do to get it back? He sighed as he admitted he had never had any control as far as Alesha was concerned. There was no use in lying to himself anymore about that.

He glanced at his watch and his eyes wandered to the papers strewn carelessly on his desk. He hadn't gotten a thing done. All he had accomplished in the past two and a half hours was to think about Alesha. Sighing once again, he stood and rubbed his tired eyes. All he wanted to do was go to bed, lie down next to his wife and feel complete and whole as only she could make him feel.

She heard the bedroom door opening as Derrick came in. She was lying in bed on her back, pretending to be asleep. She heard him stop beside her before going into the bathroom, closing the door behind him. Seconds later, she heard the shower running.

She lay there, wanting to tell him how miserable she was feeling and have him comfort her. She longed to have him lie down beside her and tell her he could no longer envision his life without her, because that was definitely the way she felt about him.

Derrick emerged from the bathroom a few minutes later, switched off the light and slipped into bed. She forced herself to remain still, her back turned toward him. The heat from his body radiated toward hers and she wished for it to enclose her, dispelling the arctic chill that had encased her heart and flesh.

Suddenly, he rolled over until her back touched his chest and stomach. She nearly purred because it felt so good to be close to him, especially when a warm, strong arm encircled her waist and held her soothingly.

"Alesha?" he said, his warm breath sending shivers of desire down her spine. He softly kissed her ear. "Relax. I have no intention of trying to force myself on you."

His statement was unnecessary. They both knew he wouldn't be forcing her. She would give herself to him willingly, as she always had.

"Derrick…" She paused, not knowing what to say, or rather how to articulate what she desperately wanted from him. So she remained silent.

He pulled her closer still. "I know the confrontation with your brother was hard for you. Let me help. Let me hold you."

She couldn't believe her ears. Why was it she never knew what he was going to do next? His sincere, kind words affected her more than she would have thought possible. If only he would go a few steps further and confess his feelings.

She allowed herself to completely relax, and her hand moved slowly to rest on his as he pulled her near. She closed her eyes and he kissed her neck before resting his head by hers on the pillow. Neither made any further attempt to speak, and before she knew it, her eyes began to droop, but not before the fierce cold that had invaded her body was replaced by comforting warmth, safety and security, unlike any she had ever experienced. Soon her troubled thoughts began to dissipate, making way for restful, much-needed sleep in her husband's tender embrace.

Derrick continued to hold her. He felt the even rise and fall of her chest, indicating that she was fast asleep. Her soft form melted perfectly against his. Her fingers were entwined with his as they rested on her stomach.

Thoughts he had squelched earlier resurfaced, and again he wondered why he felt an overwhelming sense of protectiveness toward her. He pulled her nearer. She shifted slightly and then stilled. He inhaled deeply the wonderful fragrance of her hair, and he acknowledged that he truly thought of her as his wife—not just as a tool to get him elected or as an enemy to punish. He cared about her deeply—why else did the thought of her leaving him on the day their arrangement ended suddenly cause an uneasy feeling in the pit of his stomach that felt much like agony?

He shifted slowly so as not to disturb her, removing his arm from her waist to lie on his back, one hand behind his head. He stared at the ceiling. In a few short months, she had insinuated herself into his life so much that he couldn't even remember what it had been like without her or, more importantly, he didn't want to remember what it had been like without her. Before seeing her again, he had thought he was content; yet, he now knew that had been a lie. She had brought happiness and meaning into his life, which was something he admitted he had been sorely lacking for a long,

long time—since he had last been with her. She made him whole. God, she made him happy.

Alesha suddenly turned until she was lying with her head on his chest. Her arm rested across his waist, and one of her legs sprawled lazily across his.

"Derrick," she whispered contentedly before stilling.

He immediately noted how good she felt against him, as if that was where she had always belonged. Here in his arms was where he always wanted her to be. He tenderly stroked her soft hair before moving to massage her shoulder and back. She sighed comfortably and snuggled deeper into his chest. Her arm moved up to rest in the base of his neck before stilling again.

His arms pulled her closer and he smiled self-mockingly. He had been emotionally snared in a trap of his own making—one he didn't at all want to escape from. He just prayed Alesha felt the same way.

The next morning, Alesha stretched languidly in bed. She could not remember when she had experienced such a peaceful sleep. She reached out her hand in Derrick's direction, but found him gone, much to her disappointment.

She glanced at the crystal clock on the nightstand and saw it was a little after nine. He was probably long gone for the office. Rolling onto her back, she lazily pushed strands of tousled hair away from her eyes as wonderful memories of last night engulfed her.

Her husband had held and comforted her all night long. He had given of his strength unselfishly, and had demanded nothing in return from her. She would never forget how wonderful he had been to her.

She gently touched the place on her pillow where his head had lain. A smile appeared across her face. A very tangible soft spot had formed in her heart for Derrick, and there was nothing she could do to keep it from growing. Her mind tried to convince her that she was in grave danger, yet, remarkably, her heart didn't feel that way at all. She felt totally comfortable with where her relationship with Derrick was heading. She wouldn't allow anything or anyone to spoil the happiness she now felt. She laughed aloud. She was happy— Derrick made her happy and, in her heart, she knew he felt the same way about being married to her.

She lounged around in bed a few seconds longer, contemplating their future before donning a flimsy robe over her silky black gown and going downstairs. For once she would allow herself the luxury of having an unhurried breakfast— remarkably, the entire day was hers to do with as she wished. She had no political functions to attend, until tonight, and no speeches to make. She planned to have a long visit with her mother later and just indulge herself by doing absolutely nothing.

The house was quiet, confirming her suspicions that Derrick had already left. As she passed his study door, though, she heard a voice. Her heart leaped in gladness with the realization that he was still home. Without thinking, she opened the door and went in.

"Derrick, I thought you…" She stopped in midsentence as she found him sitting behind his desk, phone poised in one hand.

She was about to exit when he motioned for her to enter. She only had to wait several seconds before he wrapped up his phone conversation and stood. As he walked over to her, he noticed with satisfaction her relaxed fresh appearance and felt good that he had helped contribute to it.

"Good morning." He smiled tenderly at her.

"Good morning." Her response was given a little shyly.

"How are you feeling?" He eyed her closely.

"Much better." She paused before adding, "Thank you, Derrick."

"You're welcome, Alesha." He stared at her as if he couldn't bear to tear his eyes away.

She returned his intense gaze, wanting to say something, but not knowing what. His expressive eyes roamed over her curvaceous body through the thin negligee she wore before returning to engage hypnotically with hers. Every nerve ending in her body tingled—feeling as if he had reached out and physically explored the path that his eyes had traveled. They began to speak without saying a word, and it was very strange, very powerful and completely entrancing.

Come closer, his eyes seemed to say, and she did.

I want to touch you, her eyes responded.

Then, do it, his invited.

Her hand rose slowly, obeying her desire and his unspoken command. She trailed her fingers down his brow to his cheekbone to the side of his mouth before stopping there. Eyes that had followed the progress of her fingertips gazed into his. She moved closer, or did he? Neither really knew nor cared; it was as if they were one, yet separate, longing to be joined.

Kiss me, she spoke aloud or in her mind—she didn't know which.

I am, she heard his unspoken response as clearly as her own ragged breathing.

Her lips parted the instant his captured hers and she both fell and was drawn into his waiting embrace. Her arms were entwined tightly around his neck. His fingers raked through her tresses, pressing her lips closer to the bruising, yet caressing, force of his.

She closed her eyes and moaned in ecstasy as his strong hands roamed down her shoulders to her midback, pressing her closer. She yearned to feel his naked flesh against hers and shamelessly wished her gown and robe and his spotless charcoal-gray suit would magically disappear. She wanted him so much, and at this moment nothing else mattered, except the need they both shared for each other.

His lips devastated hers again and again. She consumed him. He didn't understand how he could want or need anyone as much as he did her. He knew if the world suddenly ended, he would be all right as long she remained right where she was, in his arms.

They both eagerly anticipated the way this passionate embrace would end, and they welcomed it. However, soon they were interrupted by a very loud cough.

It took several seconds before the sound registered in either of their minds. Reluctantly, his lips departed from hers and his eyes turned in the direction of the intrusion.

Alesha was slower to respond, first wondering why Derrick had stopped kissing her. When she opened her passion-clouded eyes and followed the direction of his gaze, she saw Cam standing in the doorway, smiling broadly. She knew the reason for Derrick's withdrawal.

"I'm sorry to interrupt. I thought you were alone, Derrick." Cam continued, smiling brightly, "Where are my manners? Good morning, Alesha."

She wished he hadn't singled her out. Pulling the folds of her flimsy robe tightly together with one hand and smoothing her tangled hair with the other, she forced herself to meet his gaze.

"Hello." Her voice was a soft whisper as she quickly lowered her embarrassed eyes.

"Is it time to leave yet?"

Derrick easily addressed his friend, and she envied his cool composure. She herself was a mass of quivering jelly.

"Just about." Cam continued grinning at them both.

"Would you two excuse me?" Alesha shot Derrick a quick

glance before she nearly ran from the room and up the stairs to the safety of their bedroom.

"Well, well, well." Cam sat on the side of Derrick's desk.

"Don't start, Cameron." Derrick's eyes darted regretfully to Alesha's hastily retreating back.

"Have you told Alesha how you feel?"

"Not that it's any of your business, but no."

"Why not?"

"Cam, our relationship is complicated."

"Made so by the both of you." He treated Derrick to an exaggerated wink before standing. "Derrick, just tell her! From what I saw, she feels the same way about you."

"You think so?" He walked from behind his desk and scratched his chin.

"Oh, yeah, I think so." He patted his shoulder. "Make it work, man, or you'll regret it."

"Let's go." Derrick picked up his briefcase and preceded him out without answering, though his expression was very thoughtful.

Chapter 12

Alone in their bedroom, Alesha sat on the bed, smiling secretively to herself while replaying the last kiss Derrick and she had shared, fantasizing about the different ending both had wanted before Cam had interrupted them. She gingerly touched her lips and jumped when the phone rang. Sighing, she leaned over to pick up the handset.

"Hello."

"Hi, it's Derrick."

She nearly dropped the phone upon hearing his warm, husky voice. Had he somehow known she was thinking about him? Her insides warmed to know he had been thinking of her.

"Derrick."

There was an uncomfortable pause, each waiting for the other to speak. She had so much she wanted to say, yet she didn't know where to begin.

"What do you have planned for the day?" He asked the question just to hear her voice.

"Well, for a change, my schedule is free." She laughed a little nervously. "I'm probably going to visit Mom."

"That's good. She'll be glad to see you. Give her my best."

"I will."

After a few seconds, he added, "I called to remind you about dinner tonight."

"Thanks, I remember." She chewed on her lower lip thoughtfully.

"Could you make sure my tux is back from the cleaners?"

"Of course, I'll be happy to." She smiled, closing her eyes and picturing his handsome face. "Did you finish your speech?" That was her roundabout way of bringing the conversation back to last night.

"No, but I will at the office." He paused. "I'm sorry Cam walked in on us." He came to the real purpose for his call.

She opened her eyes and was suddenly glad he couldn't see her. Was he apologizing for her embarrassment, or because they had been unable to finish what they had started?

"So was I," she said, realizing how her voice sounded. She quickly added, "What I mean is…"

"I know what you meant."

She could hear the smile in his voice and embarrassment kept her from responding. She wished he was with her now so that they could… She shook her head forcefully, forestalling completion of that thought.

"Well, I'll see you tonight around six."

"Derrick?" She stalled, realizing he was about to hang up.

"Yes?" He waited.

"I—I'll see you tonight. Have a good day." She didn't have anything else to say—she simply didn't want to let him go.

"Tonight," he echoed before ending the call.

She slowly replaced the phone in its cradle. Smiling brightly, she entered the bathroom to prepare for her day.

A short while later, Alesha was still smiling when she sat down beside her mom on the sofa. "How have you been?"

"I've been fine, but I want to hear about you and Derrick. How are the two of you doing?" She smiled.

"Wonderfully, though we're both very busy. I was lucky to have today free." Alesha placed an affectionate kiss on her mother's cheek.

"I'm glad you did." Barbara smiled, adding approvingly, "Derrick is a very nice man. I'm glad you found him."

"Yes, so am I." Her admission came out breathless.

"I've enjoyed our talks."

"Your talks?" Alesha frowned.

"Yes, dear. He calls several times a week and stops by at least once a week."

Her mother's words floored her. Did Derrick really keep in such close contact with her? If so, why?

"He does?"

"Of course. Didn't you know?"

"He didn't mention it. I suppose it slipped his mind."

"You're probably right." Her mother nodded in agreement. "I've told him not to try to fit me into his busy schedule, but he doesn't listen."

"That's Derrick for you." Alesha silently pondered her mother's words.

"A mother couldn't ask for a better son-in-law or husband for her only daughter. He's such a good man."

"Yes, he is, Mom." Alesha smiled contemplatively.

"When are you two going to make me a Big Momma?"

"Momma!" A hand flew to her mouth in shock.

"What?" Barbara laughed at her. "You're not getting any younger and neither am I."

"We've only been married a few months."

She winked conspiratorially. "That's all it takes."

"I know, but let us get used to being married first, okay?"

"What's there to get used to?" Barbara persisted. "That's what's wrong with young people these days—you think you have all the time in the world. Believe me, time waits for no one."

"I know that, but—" she paused as an unnerving thought formed in her mind "—you haven't talked to Derrick about this, have you?"

"Of course not, dear. I was saving my pleading for you."

"Good."

Alesha visibly relaxed. She would have been mortified if her mother and husband had been discussing something so intimate.

"Well?"

"Momma, let me enjoy being a newlywed for a while."

Barbara sighed. "Oh, all right. As long as you remember what I said about running out of time."

"I'll remember."

"Good." Barbara beamed. "I can't wait."

Alesha smiled at her mother indulgently, but wisely remained silent as, for the first time, she fantasized about having Derrick's baby. At the thought of her husband, her heart began to flutter erratically.

She had become so accustomed to being his wife in every sense of the word, even before he had slipped the wedding ring on her finger. And now her mother had planted the idea of having his child, a thought that filled her with joy. How would he react? she wondered.

He cared for her. If she had any doubt about that, last night had erased it. The evolution of their marriage had been natural and inevitable. She had wanted him since that first kiss in his office months ago. She had wanted him every day for the past two years, though she had fought like hell against acknowledging that truth. She smiled at her mother. Life was funny and surprising. She only prayed it would give her what she wanted most—Derrick's heart.

That night, Alesha was dressed in a black, figure-hugging, sleeveless slip dress with a slight train at the back. She wore opera-length black satin gloves. A double-strand pearl-and-diamond bracelet rested on her left gloved wrist, and teardrop pearl-and-diamond earrings dangled from her ears. Her hair was swept loosely up with curls escaping, caressing her neck. A few loose tendrils were flung carelessly over her right eye.

She had told Derrick she was wearing her hair as a compromise—wanting to wear it up, but knowing he preferred it loose. He had laughed at her words, though she had known her explanation had pleased him.

Derrick was dressed in a crisp-white dinner jacket and shirt, and black slacks. He walked out of his dressing room attempting to fasten his tie. Alesha laughed at his predicament and brushed his fingers away.

"Here, let me do it." She picked up the material and tied it perfectly.

She raised her eyes and found him staring at her with the strangest expression. Impulsively, he placed a feathery kiss on her lips, but moved away suddenly to inspect her handiwork in the mirror.

"Thanks."

"You're welcome." She smiled slightly, wishing their kiss had not been so brief or so unsatisfying.

"You look exquisite."

She blushed as his piercing eyes swept over her. It was amazing how a mere look from Derrick could suck the air from her lungs.

"Thank you." After studying his appearance, she added, "You look pretty good yourself."

He smiled at her words and unexpectedly asked, "How did your visit go with your mother?"

"Fine." She walked past him to freshen up her lipstick.

"I'm glad." He smiled as he walked over to stand beside her, searching the dresser top for his cuff links.

She picked up a bottle of perfume and lightly sprayed her bare neck. Derrick inhaled the sensuous scent deeply and their eyes met again in the mirror. Her chest rose rapidly and his eyes darted to her neck. She felt breathless, as if his hands were caressing her, silently wishing they were. She lowered the perfume with one hand and picked up a double-strand pearl-and-diamond necklace with the other, her eyes never leaving his in the mirror.

He took the necklace from her fingers and placed it around her neck before fastening it. His fingers lingered unnecessarily long on her soft flesh. There was no denying what they both wanted.

To remove temptation, he turned and walked over to the bed and sat down. He put on his black shoes. She watched him through the mirror, wondering why he hadn't given in to an impulse she knew they both had shared. He raised his head and caught her questioning gaze before she quickly looked away.

"Mom asked about you." She spoke primarily to have something to say.

"That was nice of her." He stood and placed a handkerchief inside the pocket of his dinner jacket.

"She said something that surprised me." She walked over to where he stood, placing her hand on his strong arm while she slipped into her black pumps.

"What was that?" He looked at her curiously as she straightened to face him.

"That you keep in regular contact with her." She watched him closely.

"So?" He wondered where this was leading.

"So, why haven't you ever mentioned it to me?"

His eyebrows arched slightly and he stepped away to grab his keys off the nightstand. "I wasn't aware I had to. I happen to like Barbara and I care about how she's doing. Do you have a problem with that?"

"No, not at all." She was warmed by his words. "I was just surprised you hadn't said anything about it to me."

He stared at her strangely. "We'd better get going." He picked up her faux-mink black stole and helped her into it.

"I need to put the finishing touches on my makeup. Why don't you bring the car around?"

"You look beautiful." He kissed her cheek before opening the door. "But go ahead and finish your war paint and I'll meet you downstairs."

"Okay."

He quickly descended the stairs and opened the front door, finding Diana loitering there. He didn't bother to hide his displeasure. Damn, what now?

"Diana, what are you doing here?"

"May I come in?"

"No. Alesha and I are on our way out."

"I need to speak with you, darling."

She walked past him into the foyer. He reluctantly closed the door and turned to face her.

"First of all, I'm not your darling and, second, I don't have time to waste on you—now or ever."

"Can we go into your study?"

"No."

Alesha's footsteps faltered and stopped at the top of the stairs as Derrick's voice and a female one she recognized as Diana's wafted up to her. What was she doing here?

"What do you want?"

"I want you to take me back."

"Have you lost your mind?" He looked at her as if she had. "I'm married."

"You don't love her," Diana scoffed.

"And I suppose you think I love you?" At her silence he continued, "Diana, why would I want you back and, more importantly, why would you want me? I never loved you—I made no pretense about that."

Her smile faltered. "That's not true."

"Still delusional, I see." He laughed. "You didn't want a husband. You wanted a puppy dog to follow you around while you embellished your career—something I was never going to be. I wasn't ambitious enough for you then, but now that I have a shot at being a U.S. Senator, I look better in your eyes, is that it?"

"I've realized we want the same things, Derrick. I could help you become the best senator and you could help my lobbying firm once you get in office."

He chuckled as her motives were finally revealed. "Is that what this is all about—the powerful, influential people I will meet once I'm in the Senate? People you think can further your career?"

"Our careers, Derrick." Her eyes pleaded with his. "I can help you in ways she never could!"

"I doubt that."

"Derrick." Her red nails dug into his arm. "Don't be a fool!"

"I was once." His eyes narrowed as he removed her hand. "But never again."

"I'll go to the press."

He raised an eyebrow. "With what? A lame exposé of how I married you on the rebound, quickly realized my mistake and happily remedied it, but not before I felt soiled by you?"

These Arms of Mine

At the top of the stairs, Alesha watched and listened to the exchange with keen interest. She learned more as an observer than she ever could have from questioning Derrick about his ex. This woman had nerve and a half! Angela was right—she was a hussy! Having heard enough, she walked down the stairs, ready for battle.

"You know it's sisters like you who give other sisters a bad name."

"Amen!" Derrick shook his head in agreement.

"Is that right?" Diana turned hateful eyes in her direction as Alesha walked over to stand by Derrick.

"Yes, that's right," Alesha said, placing a possessive hand on her husband's arm. "I was threatened by you, but now I see how silly I was."

"Really?" Diana scowled.

"Yes." Alesha laughed. "You're pathetic."

"Listen, you little…"

"I'm Mrs. Derrick Chandler." She slowly enunciated every word and smiled at Derrick when he placed his arm supportively around her waist. "That's something you'll never be again."

"She certainly won't," Derrick vowed.

"I'll be the one by Derrick's side when he takes his place in congress, not you. You had your chance and you blew it. He doesn't want you. How many ways does he have to say that before it sinks in?"

She'd had her fill of this insufferable woman! Despite the way their marriage had begun, she and Derrick were married. He was hers and she had no intention of giving him up, especially not to the likes of this woman!

"Diana, I don't know what story you think you have to sell to the press, but go ahead and sell it to the highest bidder."

"You don't mean that."

"Don't I?" He pulled Alesha closer. "I have what I want and need right here in my arms and there's nothing you can do to take it away."

"Nothing at all," Alesha firmly chimed in.

"If you want to ruin your own career by spreading malicious lies about our brief, unpleasant dalliance, then go ahead. But knowing how ambitious you are, I don't think you will."

"Now that you've embarrassed yourself beyond compare, will you do us the pleasure of leaving our home and never returning?" Alesha smiled brightly.

"Gladly." Diana's eyes shot daggers at them both. "You two deserve each other!"

"See, darling? I think she finally got the message."

To twist the knife further, Alesha turned into his arms and kissed Derrick. They heard heels clicking and a door slamming, and when they pulled apart, she was gone.

"Good riddance!" Derrick vowed. "The audacity of that woman!"

"She is a brassy one." Alesha laughed, wiping lipstick from his mouth with her fingers. "What did you ever see in her?"

He joined her laughter. "I don't know. She caught me at a low point and I foolishly thought she could help me forget."

"Me?"

"Yes. What an idiot I was." He laughed at himself. "She's nothing like you, which, I guess, was her appeal."

She sobered at his admission. "Derrick, I'm sorry."

"You don't have anything to be sorry about."

"Yes, I do." She closed her eyes briefly and came to a decision. "I want to tell you why I pushed you away two years ago. Everything."

"Now?" He brushed a stray strand of hair out of her troubled eyes.

"Yes, it's about time. Don't you think?"

She was tired of keeping secrets from him, of all people. She needed to be completely honest with him. He deserved it.

"It can wait."

"No. I've held this in long enough. You have been so wonderful to me. You deserve the truth, if you still want to hear it." She placed her palms on his chest and waited for his response.

"I do." He covered one of her hands with his.

She took a deep breath and then released it. "First of all, what I said at your country house after the wedding about my feelings for you frightening me was true."

"I felt the same way." His admission made it easier for her to proceed.

"Do you remember when we were dating before and you wanted me to meet Cam?" She focused her attention on a pearl-white button on his shirtfront.

"Of course. We were going to have dinner, but you had to cancel."

"I was there at the restaurant." She tilted her head until her eyes meet his.

"You were?"

"Yes. I was coming out of the ladies' room. You and Cam had your backs to me and I overheard you telling him that you were so happy to be in a relationship with someone who didn't want anything from you. Someone who wasn't carrying around a lot of excess baggage, or who had a mountain of problems she expected you to miraculously fix." She related his words verbatim.

"Alesha, I didn't mean…" Her fingers on his lips silenced him.

"No, it's all right." She removed her fingers from his mouth to rest on his jaw. "I had just learned that morning that Momma had a life-threatening heart condition—one that was going to require surgery and long rehabilitation."

"Oh, God!" He finally had the missing piece of the puzzle. "She seems so healthy."

"She's been doing great since her surgeries."

"Thank God for that."

"Robert and I wanted her to have the best doctors."

"Of course you did."

"I ended up emptying my savings and other bank accounts and selling what good jewelry I had and my car. Robert did the same and got a second job, but it still wasn't enough. Even after insurance and taking out loans, it left us with huge bills, but about six months ago, she had a slight relapse and her doctor wanted her to see a specialist—one who wouldn't consult on her case unless we came up with our share of the money upfront, and that's why Robert took your money."

He paused before asking, "Why didn't you tell me?"

She shrugged. "I was going to the day we met again, but..."

He sighed. "But I said I didn't care."

"Yes."

"I lied. I did and I do care."

"Thank you for saying that."

"I mean it. Barbara is a special lady."

"She's everything to Bobby and me."

"I know. I'll apologize to him."

"You don't have to do that."

"Yes, I do." His eyes grew intense. "Who is Kevin? Obviously, he wasn't your lover as you led me to believe."

"No." She shook her head. "He's the brother of a friend. He came up to see his sister for the weekend, but she was out of town, so I let him sleep on my sofa. He's like a brother to me."

"Why did you let me think something else?"

"Because I had tried everything to get you to accept my decision to end things between us, and you wouldn't do it. I didn't plan for you to see me and Kevin the way you did— me dressed in a robe and him only in shorts, both obviously fresh out of the shower. The opportunity just presented itself and I shamelessly took advantage of it." She paused. "I knew what it looked like, I knew what you thought and I let you believe we were lovers because I knew that would end things between us once and for all. It hurt too much to keep seeing you and speaking to you on the phone—telling you I didn't want a relationship with you when the truth was that was all I did want, but couldn't have at that time."

"Why didn't you come to me once things were somewhat resolved?"

"How could I after the horrible way we parted?" She shrugged helplessly. "I honestly didn't think you would want to see me again and I didn't want to face your contempt."

Her eyes implored him to understand her actions and the reasons behind them. His thumbs lightly stroked her cheeks and he smiled at her tenderly. His mind sorted through dozens of questions that suddenly seemed meaningless. He had just received the answers to the most important questions.

"Oh, Alesha." He sighed her name. "So there never was anyone else?"

"Never." She shook her head. "I was just so overwhelmed, but now my reasons for pushing you away seem so trivial and stupid."

"You always wanted me?" He skipped to the heart of the matter—the only question he needed answered.

"Always," she agreed without hesitation.

Neither of them spoke for a long time. They simply stared

into each other's eyes, silently telegraphing secret messages of regret, sorrow—and hope.

"It's in the past. Let's leave it there and go forward," he finally suggested.

"That sounds good."

His thumb brushed away a tear that escaped from the corner of her eye. He smiled slightly and kissed her—the gentlest, softest kiss she had ever experienced—and it melted her soul and her heart. He was such an enigma to her. She never knew what he was going to do or say, yet he always seemed to do and say the right thing.

"It hurt me more than I thought anything could when you suddenly and completely shut me out of your life." He tenderly fingered her hair. "It infuriated me that you never gave us a fighting chance."

"I couldn't. You sucked up all the oxygen until I didn't have anything left. Bottom line—my mother needed me and I didn't have the time, inclination or strength to be in a relationship with you, no matter how much I wanted to."

"Did you want to?"

"Yes. In the short time we dated, I felt alive as I never had before."

"Your rejection sent me headlong into a disastrous relationship with a woman I should never have given the time of day."

"Your marriage to Diana."

"Legally." He smiled ruefully. "But what I had with her was never a marriage."

"I was so jealous when you told me about her."

"Why?"

She took a deep breath before admitting, "Because she was your wife, a wife you *wanted* to marry."

"We were married, Alesha, but she was never my wife—not like you."

"I'm just a means to an end."

He frowned. "Do you honestly believe that, still?"

"I don't want to."

"You're my wife, Alesha." His hands framed her face. "That's how I think of you."

"And you're my husband." She paused before asking, "Do you want to stay married to me, Derrick?"

"Do you?"

They smiled at each other tenderly, without answering verbally. She suddenly knew she could never live without him—just as she knew she had fallen helplessly, irrevocably in love with him twice. After all the years of soul-searching she had done, that revelation came as naturally and effortlessly to her as breathing did. For a moment, she thought that she had spoken her feelings out loud, because Derrick's expression shifted to one of total gentleness and understanding. Did she imagine it, or was there a reciprocal wonderment in his eyes as if he, too, had come to the same conclusion?

Chapter 13

At the party, both Derrick and Alesha tried to put the unpleasant scene with Diana out of their minds. They were on the dance floor. Her head lay on Derrick's shoulder, eyes closed. One hand rested on his opposite shoulder, while the other was clasped in his warm hand, close to her face as they swayed to the soft music. His head rested against her hair as he held her close.

"Are you okay?" Derrick's question forced Alesha to lift her head.

"Yes, I'm fine." She stared at him adoringly. More than anything, she wanted to feel his lips on hers.

His eyes shifted to her moist lips, reading her mind, and then moved back to her beautiful face. "We can leave if you want to."

"This is important to you—we can stay." Then at his continued look of concern, she added, "Really, I'm fine."

He gave in to temptation then and grazed her lips with his. He allowed himself to lightly caress her mouth for a few seconds, before he pulled away—knowing if he didn't, things would get embarrassing.

She replaced her head on his shoulder, instinctively knowing why he had ended their brief kiss. Disentangling her hand from his, she slid her hand up his shoulder until both her arms encircled his neck. His hands moved from her waist to her lower back, holding her closer still as they continued to dance.

She closed her eyes again, allowing herself to escape. It felt so good to be in his arms. She didn't want to be anywhere else, except where she was, and she knew that neither did he. This was where she was meant to be—forever.

He wished he had her home right now, because he would make passionate love to her—he would make her forget all the pain she had experienced. He was determined to erase the past hurts and dissolve the years they had spent without each other. In his arms, he would make her feel nothing except complete ecstasy.

Unfortunately, the song ended too quickly, and they reluctantly left each other's arms and walked off the dance floor hand in hand, only to find Cam curiously watching them both. As they approached, Derrick's eyes silently warned him not to make any flippant comments.

"Senator Hatcher wants to speak with you, Derrick," Cam informed him as they reached his side.

"Do you want me to come with you?"

Alesha placed her hand on his arm as she stared at him lovingly. The look she gave him almost took his breath away.

"No, I'll be back shortly. Stay here and try to keep Cam out of trouble, will you?" His eyes darted to his friend.

"I'll try." She smiled. He kissed her softly before walking away.

"Where's Mary?" she asked, referring to Cam's date.

"Oh, she's in the ladies room or somewhere." Cam

seemed to have little interest in his date's whereabouts. "Are you enjoying yourself tonight?"

"I am."

"I know these functions can be very boring, but…"

"They're a necessary evil." She completed the sentence for him with a knowing wink.

"I see you've heard that from time to time."

"Once or twice." She smiled.

Cam laughed. "Derrick can be a workhorse when it comes to his career, but he's also very kind and giving. Of course, you know that, don't you?"

"He's a very complex man." She cautiously eyed him over the rim of her glass.

"Not really, not once you understand his motivations. I hope you'll try to."

"Why is that so important to you?"

"He's my friend—my best friend. I want him to be happy, and you make him happy."

"What about Diana?"

He grimaced. "Please! She wouldn't know how to think about someone else if her life depended on it!"

"Have you seen her since she returned to town?"

"No, and God willing I will be spared that unpleasantness."

She laughed. "You don't like her very much, do you?"

"Nope." He shook his head emphatically. "And I never did."

"Why?"

"Because she is, was and always will be a user."

"You're right about that."

He frowned. "What is she trying to pull?"

"Oh, nothing." Alesha shook her head. "She doesn't matter."

"I'm glad to hear you say that."

"Why?"

"Because I know she came back into town to try to cause trouble for you and Derrick."

"She did, but she can't." Alesha smiled. "We won't let her."

"I think Diana has met her match."

She smiled secretively. "I think she knows that now."

"Derrick would have my hide if he knew I was saying this to you." Cam glanced away briefly to make sure his friend was nowhere to be seen.

"But?"

"But I'm going to say it anyway. You're good for him. As I told him this morning, I don't understand why the two of you won't admit your marriage is real."

"You told him that?" Her face registered surprise and gratitude.

"I did."

"What was his response?"

"What's yours?" he quickly countered.

"Well, I..." She was interrupted by Derrick as he joined them, placing a possessive arm around her waist.

"What were you two so engrossed in?" He eyed them both closely.

"Your campaign. What else?" Cam smiled.

Alesha shot him a grateful look. Derrick noted the quick exchange between them and made a mental note to find out what mischief Cam had been up to in his absence.

Hours later when they entered their bedroom, Derrick helped her off with her stole, placing it on a nearby chair. He reached for the light, but Alesha's hand prevented him from flipping the switch on. Her hand traveled up his muscled arm to his shoulder, coming to rest behind his head as she moved closer to him. She pulled his face toward hers as she placed a lingering kiss on his lips.

She kissed him slowly, enjoying every second, every movement of their lips against each other's. His hands caressed her waist as she continued to astonish and delight him with her forwardness. When she slowly withdrew her lips from his, he stared at her expectantly, yet made no move toward her—leaving the outcome in her hands.

Her fingers deftly unfastened his tie before moving to unbutton his shirt, sliding it and the jacket simultaneously from his broad shoulders. As her fingers lightly touched the hair on his chest, he sucked in his breath quickly, as if the contact burned him. She moved closer to his hard body and her hands splayed across his muscled back as her lips captured his once again.

He couldn't believe this was happening. Alesha was initiating intimacy between them. He had longed for this moment for what seemed like forever. He knew tonight was going to be special beyond compare.

"Will you undo my necklace?" Her question was posed softly.

His lips captured hers briefly, promising a much more satisfying union, before he walked behind her. She raised her hair out of the way as his fingers quickly unclasped her necklace. He kissed her neck, and she reached her gloved hand up behind her to caress the side of his face before moving to his nape, holding him closer. Then she turned around in his arms. He unclasped the bracelet on her wrist. Her hand still held his face—she reluctantly released him to remove one glove and then the other, before placing her hands on his chest.

"Unzip my dress."

He smiled at her words, and readily did as she gently commanded, sliding his hands beneath the material at her back, pulling her closer as the dress fell to the floor. Their lips played with each other's, nipping, caressing briefly and moving away, his fingers unclasped her hair, freeing the silky tresses, running his fingers slowly through it.

"You've wanted to do that all night, haven't you?" she asked.

He returned her smile tenderly before admitting, "Yes. Just as I've wanted to do this." His lips attacked hers with such ferocity she felt as if she were being eaten alive. The passionate mating of their lips caused an answering response in their bodies as they pressed closer.

Her hands clutched at his shoulders, arching against his hard, unbending frame. His hands roamed down her bare back to her hips, pressing her tighter against him as he greedily took what she so freely offered. Soon, however, they knew this was not enough—they needed more, much more.

"Derrick, make love to me. I need you. How I want you."

She was going for broke tonight—she was tired of hiding her feelings. One way or another, she would find out what she meant to him and she would tell him what he meant to her.

He bent and scooped her up in his arms. Walking over to the bed, he laid her down on it before following her with his own body. They kissed passionately as her hands trailed down his flat, hard stomach to his belt buckle, urgently undoing it before unzipping his pants. She touched his skin, softly at first and then more fervently. He was on fire and becoming more inflamed with her every caress.

She watched the expressions race across his face at her ardent manipulations. She squeezed him intimately until his hand covered hers, ending her sweet torture. She tried unsuccessfully to elude his grasp and when he refused to release her, she turned questioning eyes to the fiery depths of his.

"Don't you want me to touch you?" She bit his chin softly.

He closed his eyes shortly before opening them again and hissing, "Yes!"

"Then why are you stopping me?" Her lips traced his jawline, her hand escaping from his, continuing her tantalizing exploration.

"Because if you don't stop, I'm going to go insane." His promise was growled as his lips ardently nipped at hers.

"Good." She sighed between caresses. "I don't want you to be in control. I want you to lose yourself in me as I am in you."

His eyes grew dark at her words as his hands slid down her throat to her smooth shoulders. His lips replaced his hands, trailing across her satiny skin, igniting a fire within that she knew would soon consume them both.

"Make me yours, Derrick. Travel with me to that special place in the universe only we two can occupy together."

She didn't need to ask twice. His mouth devastated hers and she participated eagerly in their passionate, all-consuming kisses. When his lips lifted from hers, their now-naked limbs pressed closely together.

He rasped, "I will. Right now."

"I want you so much that it hurts," she groaned without hesitation.

"Alesha!" He nearly exploded as her wandering hand enfolded and caressed him.

"Do you want me?"

"Yes, more than you know."

"Then take me, darling. Make me yours forever." She arched against his hard body.

His fingers caressed her hair, roughly pulling her lips back to his. She was here in his arms, saying things he had longed to hear her say, responding to him unashamedly, feeling free to touch him.

His hands descended her sides to her hips, pressing her closer as he joined his body to hers without further hesitation. They melted together perfectly—proof that they had been made for each other. She shivered uncontrollably against his throbbing body. She had said she wanted no control and she received none. He claimed her body and heart and she willingly gave him everything she had, and received all in return.

His lips left hers and she bit into his strong shoulder, simultaneously raking her nails down his torso. His body continued to scorch hers. They belonged to each other—nothing was held back by either of them. Their bodies made rapturous music, and after several long, passion-filled hours, the unique love song they had created neared its inevitable, unforgettable conclusion.

They soared higher on wings of pure, unselfish love. He moaned hoarsely and she groaned in ecstasy as waves of intense pleasure cascaded through their souls. It was a total union of hearts and souls—this time, they truly did break the barrier of their bodies as they combined themselves into one life force. He loved her, and she loved him totally without reserve. All pretense of anything else was stripped away. They both knew nothing had ever been, or would ever be, so right again.

Much later, she was nearly sleeping, head resting on Derrick's chest. Her fingers were entwined with his. She sighed in contentment—everything was perfect. Finally, she knew she had all she would ever need—right here in Derrick's arms.

He had never felt as close to anyone as he did now. He belonged to her with every fiber of his being, with all that he possessed. God, he adored her. He finally admitted to himself what he had long felt. How could he possibly deny it?

"You know, Cam has told me on more than one occasion that we should try to make our marriage work." His fingers trailed up and down the satiny skin of her back.

"He told me the same thing tonight." She lifted her head to stare at him lovingly.

"What did you tell him?"

"Nothing, you interrupted us." She smiled.

"Do you want our marriage to work?" He held his breath as he waited for her answer—the most important answer he would ever receive in his life.

"Our marriage does work." She kissed his chest before raising her eyes to meet his again. "We work. I'm your wife and you're my husband. There's nothing false about that, or the fact that I love you more than I thought I could ever love anyone." She finally admitted what had been in her heart for a long time.

He smiled at her as tenderly as she had ever seen and let out a breath that she realized he had been holding expectantly. "I love you, too, very much."

"Really?" She kissed his lips lightly.

"Yes. Didn't you know?" He ran fingers through her tousled hair.

"I hoped."

"So did I." He pulled her head down to his to engage in a passionate, loving kiss. "Alesha…" he whispered against her lips.

"Hmm?" She tried to bring his mouth back to hers, but when he resisted, she opened dreamy eyes to stare into the serious depths of his. "What's wrong?"

"I'm sorry." His solemn words startled her.

"For what?" She traced his furrowed brow with her fingers.

"For forcing you into this marriage." He painfully articulated the guilt that had plagued him for months.

"Derrick, you didn't force me—I always had a choice."

"Yes, but I took advantage…" Her fingers on his lips forestalled his words.

"Shh. I'm where I want to be—I don't care how I got here. I only care that I did get here—that we got here together, finally."

"Really?" He searched her eyes.

"Really." She nodded, allowing every ounce of love she felt for him to shine in her eyes, for him to see. "Why didn't you tell me you loved me sooner?"

He smiled sheepishly. "I was waiting for you to say it."

"Oh, yeah." She laughed softly. "Well, I guess I can't blame you for that."

"I love you so much." He made up for lost time. "I have from the first moment I saw you."

"I love you, too. With all my heart."

Loving fingers caressed her face. His mouth captured hers, ending any response she had been about to make. She wiggled on top of him and stretched her soft body out the length of his. Their legs entangled intimately.

After reluctantly releasing her lips, he groaned, "You have sapped all my energy, but I want you again and again."

"Then take me, darling, as many times as you want me. I'm yours."

"Mine?" His hands roamed down her bare back.

"Completely." She smiled. "Forever."

Their mouths fused together, sealing their promise of eternal love with an endless kiss.

A week later, they were at her mother's, enjoying the unseasonably warm weather with an impromptu backyard barbecue.

"Hey, you guys, is it done yet?"

"In a minute." Derrick laughed at his wife. "You sure have been eating a lot lately."

"Love does wonders for my appetite."

"Mine, too." He bobbed his eyes at her.

"Derrick!"

He and Robert laughed before turning back to the grill. In Barbara's honor, they were having a heart-healthy meal consisting of grilled salmon and vegetables.

Barbara glanced toward the two men. "I'm so glad Robert is warming up to Derrick."

Alesha smiled. "So am I."

"He was having trouble letting his little sister go, but now he knows you're in good hands."

"I definitely am."

"You're happy," her mother responded.

"Deliriously." She reached across the table and squeezed her hand. "Can something so wonderful possibly last?"

"It did with your father and me until the day he died."

"That's what I want with Derrick."

"Then that's what you'll have," Barbara promised. "You two are perfect together."

Robert and Derrick laughed as they fought back flames and quickly removed food from the grill.

"I don't think I've ever seen Alesha happier and I have you to thank for that."

Derrick smiled. "I should be thanking you."

"Why?"

"You brought us back together again and I will forever be in your debt. I know what my life was without her and I never want to experience that pain again."

"You love her." Robert nodded in approval.

"With all my heart."

"I'm happy for you both, Derrick."

"Thanks, Robert. That means a lot coming from you."

"Just keep her happy."

"Always."

"Derrick," he slowly began. "I'm sorry I embezzled from your campaign. I'll pay you back."

"No." He shook his head. "Thank you for your apology, but I don't want your money."

Robert frowned. "Why not?"

"Alesha told me why you took it. I'm a part of this family now and I love Barbara, too."

"Thanks." Robert smiled. "Welcome to the family."

Derrick returned his smile. "Thank you."

They were laughing when they carried the food over to the table. Derrick bent down and kissed his wife briefly before sitting down next to Barbara.

"Here you are." Robert placed a platter of grilled corn on the cob next to the salmon.

"Mmm…" Alesha's eyes sparkled. "It smells and looks wonderful!"

Barbara eyed the healthy feast cautiously. "It does look good, but what I wouldn't give for a plate of ribs!"

"When you taste this, you'll forget all about greasy ribs," Derrick promised, kissing her cheek.

"If you say so, dear." She patted his hand.

"Momma, behave yourself," Alesha chided.

"Mom, you know how bossy she is," Robert said sympathetically.

"She's perfect," Derrick said, coming to his wife's defense.

"Thank you, darling." She blew him a kiss. "I love you."

"And I love you."

Barbara smiled approvingly. "Aren't they cute, Robert?"

He chuckled. "Adorable."

"Just you wait—your turn will come." Alesha wagged her finger at him.

"Let's eat." Robert wisely avoided responding to her prediction.

Everyone laughed and all set about filling their plates. Above the laughter and good-natured banter, Derrick and Alesha's eyes met and held. They smiled at each other secretively. There was no need for words. She loved and needed him—how wonderful to know that he felt the same way about her. All her life, she had searched for this and now it was finally hers. She was so glad to know that her mother was right—they were perfect for each other.

Epilogue

It was the middle of November and Derrick and Alesha
would be celebrating their one-year anniversary in two
weeks. She reclined against the soft back of the sofa, remote
in her hand as she again proudly watched her husband giving
his senatorial victory speech. A fire crackled comfortingly
as Derrick sat beside her, his ear and hands pressed to her
huge stomach, anticipating some sign of activity from their
unborn child.

"Sweetheart," he said, leaning against her stomach
"Aren't you tired of watching this?"

"No, and you're not, either."

"I can't believe a year has passed. I'm a senator and you're
about to give birth to our first child." He repositioned his
ear on her stomach.

"I know what you mean." She smiled down at him.

He lifted his head to stare at her adoringly. He looked
just like a kid on Christmas Day. She laughed out loud at
the anxious expression in his eyes.

"What?"

"You look so cute!" Her smile widened at his scowl.

He sat up, hands still placed gingerly on her huge stomach and indignantly replied, "Cute? I am not cute."

"Oh, yes, you are, darling." She laughed, kissing his nose softly. "Did you feel that?" She beamed as the baby kicked.

"Yes, yes, I did."

He moved his fingers around to see if he could capture that amazing evidence of life growing within her. Her hands covered his as both waited, and another and yet another kick came.

"Our son or daughter is certainly active tonight."

"Yes, he or she is." His fingers lightly caressed her swollen stomach. "Are you in any pain?"

"No."

"Do you think we should get going to the hospital?" He sat up and watched her anxiously.

"No, sweetheart. I haven't had a contraction for a while. I think we still have time." She tried unsuccessfully to soothe his frayed nerves.

"I think we should go now—just in case."

"Derrick, I'll know when it's time to go." She stroked his furrowed brow.

"Well, if you're sure…"

"I am." Trying to get his mind off her impending labor, she replied, "Life is so funny."

"In what way?"

"Well, look at us—two people who were sworn enemies a short time ago, who are now totally in love with each other and anticipating the birth of our child."

"I never considered you an enemy." His hands still wandered over her huge stomach.

"But, darling, I considered you mine." She smiled.

"Really?"

She laughed. "Well, maybe for all of a second."

"I am crushed!"

"No, you're not." Her hand caressed his jaw.

"No, I'm not." He moved closer to her. "But I'm not your adversary anymore, am I?" His lips gravitated to within mere inches of hers.

"Of course not. You're my best friend, the love of my life. In fact, I love you more than life itself." She sighed before his lips closed over hers in a warm kiss. "I'm so happy."

"I'm going to make sure you stay that way." He kissed her again, lingering on her lips this time.

"I will as long as I have you." She snuggled contentedly, placing his head in the crook of her neck.

"You have me forever." They were silent for a while before he spoke again. "Sweetheart, do you ever think of returning to nursing?"

"No. Why?" She wondered where that question had come from.

"I just want you to be content, and I know how much your career means to you." He turned his head to stare at her profile intensely.

"*Meant* to me," she quickly corrected. "I have all I want and need right here in this room."

"Are you sure?"

"Definitely, but I love you for asking." She smiled.

"I'd do anything to make you happy."

"You have and you do."

He repositioned his head in her neck, taking love bites out of her soft flesh. "Gimme a kiss."

"My pleasure." She turned her head ever so lightly, bringing her lips into contact with his. Before their kiss could deepen, though, she winced in pain. "Ouch!"

Immediately his head lifted from her shoulder, concern

and apprehension emanating from every aspect of his being. "Another contraction?"

"Yes." She began to pant slightly. "How long has it been since the last one?"

"About fifteen minutes." He nervously glanced at his watch.

They both looked at each other, and she could tell he was quickly beginning to panic. "Derrick, calm down. Women have babies every day."

"Not my wife!" He jumped up and anxiously began pacing to and fro, unable to decide what to do first. "Can you walk? Do I need to carry you?"

Between the pain and panting breaths, she began to laugh hysterically, unable to stop herself. He was so funny!

"Derrick! Derrick, relax, baby," she pleaded through giggles.

He finally decided on a course of action, running to grab her already packed suitcase. Then he picked up both of their coats and his car keys before rushing back to the sofa where she sat doubled over in pain and laughter.

"It's not nice to laugh at your newest senator." He held out his hands to help her to her feet.

"If your constituents could see you now." She kissed his cheek gently as he pulled her upright. "Don't forget to call Momma and Robert."

"I'll call from the car."

He placed her coat around her shoulders before leading her slowly, yet urgently, to the door. She fought against another bout of laughter as she glanced at his tense, terrified expression.

"I love you." She suddenly stopped, smiled and kissed his lips thoroughly and, she hoped, comfortingly.

"I love you, too."

When she once again winced in pain, he bent down to

scoop her up into his strong arms, tossing the suitcase and his coat carelessly onto the floor.

"We'd better get out of here before this baby is born, because there's no way I'm going to deliver him or her." His face and tone were so serious that she couldn't contain another outbreak of hysterical laughter.

"Let's go have our baby," she agreed between chuckles.

"I'm with you." He smiled before nearly running out of the door with his panting, giggling wife.

* * * * *

THE COST OF
HER INNOCENCE

JACQUELINE BAIRD

'I REPEAT, MISS MASON, do you understand the charge brought against you by this court?'

Jane, in a voice choked with fear, finally answered, 'Yes.'

She still could not quite believe she was standing in the dock, accused of being in possession of a Class A drug with intent to sell. She was in her second year of a Business Studies course and worked five evenings a week in a fast food café to help pay her way through college. This whole thing was like a nightmare and she hoped she would wake up at any second....

But it was no nightmare. This was reality, she finally accepted as the curt tone of the judge's voice demanded, 'How do you plead? Guilty or not guilty?'

She gripped the handrail of the dock to steady her trembling body and, lifting her head, cried, 'Not guilty!'

Why would no one believe her? She glanced desperately across at Miss Sims, the lawyer the court had appointed to defend her, but her attention was on the notes in her hand, not Jane.

Dante Cannavaro lounged in his chair while the preliminaries were adhered to. The case was not one he would normally consider, but Henry Bewick, the head of the law firm where Dante had worked as an intern at the beginning of his career, had asked him to assist as a personal favour to him.

At twenty-nine, Dante was now an international lawyer, specialising in commercial litigation. He had not acted in a criminal trial in years, but he had read the case, and as far as he could see it was cut and dried.

A car had sideswiped Miss Mason's. When the police officer attending the accident had asked to see her driving licence the girl had fumbled around in her tote bag and a suspicious-looking package had fallen out, which had proved to be full of drugs. The only passenger in her car had been a rather drunk Timothy Bewick—son of Henry. The girl had denied all knowledge of the drugs. Her defence was that someone else— she'd implied Henry Bewick's son—must have put the drugs in her bag.

Dante had met Timothy Bewick, and it was obvious the boy was besotted by the girl and reluctant to give evidence against her. Dante, having seen a photograph of Miss Mason, could understood why. A tall, black-haired beauty, in a skimpy top and shorts that displayed her generously curved body and long legs to perfection, Miss Mason was enough to tempt any man. A testosterone raging teenager stood no chance. Dante had agreed to take the case.

He raised his head as she adamantly declared herself not guilty. *Liar,* he thought, studying her with his dark assessing eyes. Today she had played down her looks, wearing her hair scraped back into a tight knot at the back of her head, no make-up and a black suit—probably at her lawyer's suggestion.

But in fact Miss Sims had done her client no favours. From Dante's point of view Miss Mason had played right into his hands. The severe tailoring of her suit fitted her firm breasts, narrow waist and round hips perfectly, and made her appear older than her nineteen years—which would help his case when he called Timothy Bewick to the stand. When the jury compared the two it would be obvious who was telling the truth—the young, lovestruck boy.

He stood up and smiled cynically, deliberately holding her gaze. He saw her big eyes widen pleadingly and thought he witnessed a gleam of sensual awareness in their depths. He noted the flick of her tongue across her lush lips and wasn't fooled for a moment—though surprisingly he felt a sudden tug of lust. God, she was good. No wonder young Bewick was crazy about her! Dante remembered all too well how that felt! Yes, he had definitely made the right decision… It would give him great pleasure to take the delectable Miss Mason apart in the dock and he proceeded to do so.

Jane looked at the tall, black-haired man who stood up to face her. He smiled at her and her breath caught in her throat. Her tummy churned and her heart leapt with hope. At last a friendly face! From his perfectly chiselled features to his long, lean, solidly built body he radiated confidence, concern and pure masculine power. *This* man would recognise she was telling the truth. She knew it instinctively.…

How wrong she had been, Jane realised bitterly as the prison gates clanged shut behind her. Numb with fear, she looked up at the forbidding building that would be her home for the next three years—or, if she was lucky, half that time with good behavior, according to Miss Sims, her worse-than-useless lawyer....

'I hate to leave you here, Helen,' Jane said, looking at the older woman with tears in her eyes. 'I don't know how I would have survived without you these past eighteen months.' She hugged the friend who had literally saved her life.

'Thank you for that,' Helen said, kissing her cheek and stepping back with a smile on her face. But her expression grew serious. 'Now, no more tears, Jane. Today you are a free woman. Stick to the arrangements we have made and you will be fine.'

'Are you sure I can't visit, Helen? I will miss seeing you terribly.'

'Yes, I am sure. My daughter lost her life at eighteen, and a lousy lawyer and so-called friends almost ruined yours. Remember what I told you: the world isn't fair, so never dwell on the injustice of the past—that will only consume you with bitterness. Think only of your future. Now, go—and never look back. Clive Hampton, my lawyer, will be waiting for you and you can trust him. Listen to him, and be careful, confident and proud of the successful woman I know you will become....' She gave her a hug. 'Good luck.'

CHAPTER ONE

'GOODNIGHT, MARY,' Beth Lazenby called to the receptionist as she walked out of the offices of Steel and White, the accountancy firm in the centre of London where she was a junior partner. She paused for a moment on the pavement and took a deep breath, glad to be out in the fresh air—or not-so-fresh air she thought ruefully. She enjoyed her work, but just lately, and especially when she spent time at the cottage, she questioned whether she really wanted to spend the rest of her life in the city.

Beth watched the people hurrying past her, their day's work finished. It was rush hour, and when she saw the length of the queue at her usual bus stop she decided to walk to the next one. The exercise would do her good, and apart from Binkie she had nothing to hurry home for. Her friend Helen had died three years ago from cancer—four months after she had been released from prison on parole.

Dismissing the sad memory, Beth looped her bag over one shoulder and walked on. A tall, striking woman, with red hair that gleamed like fire in the evening sun, her slenderly curved body moved sinuously beneath the grey linen dress she wore as she strolled along. But Beth was oblivious to the appreciative glances of every passing male. Men did not figure large in her life. She had a successful career and was proud of what she had achieved. She was content.

Suddenly she saw a man a head taller than most of the crowd walking towards her and she almost stumbled. Her heart started to race and she swiftly averted her gaze from the black-haired man she hated with a vengeance. A man whose dark satanic image was engraved on her mind for all time—the lawyer Cannavaro, the devil himself as far as she was concerned, and he was a mere ten feet away.

She heard Helen's voice in her head. *Be careful, confident and proud of the successful woman I know you will become.*

Beth tilted her chin at a determined angle and carried on walking. At least Helen had lived long enough to see her success, and she would not let her down now. Cannavaro would never recognise her. The naive Jane Mason was gone for ever, and Beth Lazenby was nobody's fool. But the hairs on the back of her neck stood on end as she passed him, and out of the corner of her eye she caught the look he gave her. Did he hesitate? She didn't know and didn't care. She simply kept on walking. But her sense of well-being faded as memories of the past flooded her mind. Her full lips tightened bitterly as she wondered how many more innocent victims the vile Cannavaro had sent to prison in the past eight years.

She recalled the naive teenager she had been, standing in the dock, frightened out of her wits. Cannavaro had smiled at her, and the deep, sympathetic tone of his voice when he'd told her not to be nervous or afraid had given her hope. He'd said he and everyone else present only wanted to discover the real truth of the case.... Stupidly, she had believed him. He had been her knight in shining armour, her saviour. But then Timothy Bewick and his friend James Hudson had both lied on the stand, and by the time she'd realised her mistake it was too late—she'd been found guilty. Her last view of Cannavaro as she'd been led from the court had been of him and her lawyer talking and laughing together as if she didn't exist.

Dante Cannavaro was feeling good. He had just won a deal for his client—a multinational company—for substantially more money than they had expected. Dismissing his waiting driver, he'd decided to walk to his apartment, where the customised Ferrari he had ordered was due to be delivered in an hour. A satisfied smile curved his lips.

Striding along the pavement he found his dark eyes caught by the flaming red hair of a beautiful woman walking towards him and he lingered, the car suddenly forgotten. She was tall—about five-nine, he guessed—and wearing a conservative grey dress that ended an inch or so above her knees. The dress would have looked bland on most females, but on her it looked stunning, and his captivated gaze roamed over her slender but shapely body and long legs in primitive male appreciation.

He paused, his head automatically turning as she passed him. The gentle sway of her hips was enough to give a weaker man a coronary. In Dante's case it was not a hardening of the arteries in the heart that troubled him, but the hardening of a different part, much lower down. It wasn't surprising he had such a reaction to her, he thought. She was beautiful and sexy and he had been celibate for a month, he reasoned. Before reminding himself that he was engaged to Ellen.

As an international lawyer, Dante had offices in London, New York and Rome. He kept an apartment in all three cities, but considered his real home to be the estate in Tuscany where he'd been born, which had been in his family for generations.

Dante's Uncle Aldo—his father's younger brother and head of Cannavaro Associates in Rome—had died last March, and it had been pointed out to him at the funeral that *he* was now the last remaining male Cannavaro. It was time he stopped indulging his preference for international law, concentrated on the long-established family firm and settled down and had a son or two—before the Cannavaro name died out completely.

Dante had assumed he would marry and have children some day, but now, at the age of thirty-seven, he had suddenly been made to face his duty. He wanted children, hopefully a male heir, while he was still fit enough to be an active father. And so he had chosen Ellen, because he had known and respected her in a professional capacity for a couple of years and she ticked all the boxes. She was intelligent, attractive, and she liked children—plus, as a lawyer, she understood the demands of his work. And the sex between them was fine. It was a perfect partnership, and once Dante made a decision he never changed his mind. Other women were off the agenda for good.

But the redhead was a stunner, and it was in the male psyche to *look*…he consoled himself.

An hour later Beth smiled as she walked down the Edwardian-style terraced street. Unlocking the door of her one-bedroom ground-floor apartment, she entered the hall and kicked off her shoes, slipping her feet into a pair of slippers. She grinned as the only male in her life strolled over and rubbed against her ankle.

'Hi, Binkie.' She bent down and picked up the ginger cat and nuzzled his neck. She walked down the hall, past her bedroom, the living room and the bathroom, to the rear of the building, and entered the largest room—the kitchen-diner.

She put Binkie down, switched on the kettle and opened the cupboard, taking out a can of cat food.

'You must be starving,' she said, filling his bowl with the tuna flavour he loved before placing it on the floor. In seconds his head was in it. With a wry smile at the foolishness of talking to her cat, she made a cup of coffee and, taking a sip, crossed to the back door that was set in the side wall of the kitchen. Opening it, she stepped out onto the patio.

The garden was Beth's pride and joy, and the flowers she had planted in a few tubs on the patio were a blaze of colour. Strolling past them, she admired her handiwork with a sense of satisfaction, and then walked on to the lawn that was framed by a four-feet-high brick wall, with a gate opening into the garden of the two-bedroom apartment above her.

On the other side of her garden a high trellis had been fixed to the wall, and was completely covered by scented jasmine intertwined with clematis. She took another sip of coffee and looked around her with pleasure, dismissing the sighting of Cannavaro from her mind. He wasn't worth a second thought. She walked back to the patio and sat down on one of the wooden

chairs that circled the matching table to drink her coffee and admire her handiwork in peace.

But just as she began to relax Beth's neighbour, Tony,
appeared, leaning on the gate. Tony was sturdily built,
with short fair hair and a round, cheeky face and had
just turned twenty-three. Beth felt a lot more than four
years older than him and his flatmate, Mike. The boys
worked at the same City bank, and were a pair of fun-
loving young men without a care in the world.

'Hi, Beth. I've been waiting for you to get home.
Mind if I join you?'

Not waiting for an answer, Tony strolled through
the gate.

'What is it this time? Sugar, milk or are you begging
a meal?' she asked dryly, watching as he straddled a
chair and propped his elbows on the back.

'For once, none of the above.' He grinned. 'But I
wouldn't mind sex, if you're offering,' he declared with
a mock-salacious grin.

Beth couldn't help it. She laughed and shook her
head. 'Not in a million years, Tony Hetherington.'

'I thought not. But you can't blame a guy for trying,'
he said, his blue eyes sparkling with humour. 'But, to
get down to business, are you at home this weekend or
are you going to the cottage again?'

'No, I'll be here for the next two weeks and then I'm
taking three weeks' holiday to go down and do some
much-needed decorating—and with luck get in some
surfing. I'm hoping you'll keep a check on this place,
as usual. You do still have the spare key?'

'Yes, of course. Consider it done. But to get back to
my problem… As you know, Monday was my birth-
day and I had dinner with my parents—boring! So on

Saturday I plan to have a party for all my friends, and *you* are invited! We're a bit short on women, so please say you'll come.'

'Why am I not flattered by the invite?' Beth queried mockingly. 'Making up the numbers is bad enough, but I also remember your last party, at Christmas, when I served most of the food and drink and then ended up chasing the guests out when you and Mike passed out! Not to mention cleaning up afterwards....'

Tony chuckled. 'That was unfortunate. But it was a great party—and it will be different this time, I promise. For a start, it's going to be a barbecue. The guests are invited for four in the afternoon until late, and we'll be outside, so no cleaning up.'

'Ah! I see. So what you really mean is can you use my garden as it is twice the length of yours?'

'Well, there is that, yes—but more importantly Mike is making a list of the food he thinks we need. Personally, I think a few dozen sausages and burgers and a bit of salad would do, but you know what he's like— he thinks he's a great cook. He's talking marinated chicken, special kebabs, fish and stuffed heaven knows what! As for the salads—you name it and he is going make it. You *have* to help me, Beth,' he declared, looking at her with pleading puppy-dog eyes.

'You are *such* an actor,' she said dryly. 'But your boyish charm does not wash with me.'

'I know, but it was worth a go.' He grinned. 'But, honestly, I really do need your help. We had a barbecue last month, when you were away for the weekend, and it was a bit of a disaster,' he confessed sheepishly. 'I knew you wouldn't mind, but unfortunately Mike nearly poisoned half the guests with his stuffed pork loins. We will never hear the end of it from our pals at the bank.'

'Oh, my God, he didn't?' Beth exclaimed with a laugh.

'Oh, yes, he did,' Tony said wryly, getting to his feet. 'Which, when I think about it, is probably why we are short on females this time. What right minded girl is going to risk getting food poisoning again?'

'All right, all right. I'll come and help,' Beth agreed when she could stop laughing. 'On condition the barbecue is set up in *your* garden. I don't want any of my plants burnt—which is quite likely to happen with you two in charge. The guests can use my garden to drink, eat…whatever. But my apartment is strictly out of bounds. Understood?'

'Yes, you gorgeous woman, you. We can keep the beer bins on your patio.' He grinned and walked back though the open gate. 'And thanks!' he called back, before disappearing into his own apartment.

At seven on Saturday evening the sun was shining in a clear blue sky, and a relaxed smile curved Beth's lips as she looked around the garden, which was crowded with casually dressed people. Some were eating, drinking or standing chatting, whilst others were already dancing to the music. A few more guests were upstairs in the boys' apartment, where the hard liquor was being served. Beer and white wine was stacked in big bins full of ice outside Beth's kitchen window. She had taken the precaution of locking her back door, and had the key in the pocket of her jeans.

'Alone, Beth?' A slightly inebriated Tony slid an arm around her waist. 'That will never do. Thanks to you talking Mike out of his flights of fancy over the food, the barbecue is going great and the party is really taking off. Have a drink.'

Smiling, she shook her head. 'You know I never drink.'

'Well, I'm going to get another—catch you later.' Tony's arm fell from her waist and he half turned, then stopped. 'I don't believe it!' he exclaimed, grabbing her waist again. 'My big brother is here! I left a message at his London office, inviting him, but I never expected him to come. He's a lawyer—the intense, intellectual type—and he speaks about six languages and travels all over the world with his work. In fact he's a workaholic. I haven't seen him since last year, but Mum told me he finally got engaged a couple of months ago. I guess the woman with him must be his fiancée.'

'I didn't know you had a brother,' Beth said with a curious glance past Tony. Then she froze.

There in front of her she saw a hard, handsome face with heavy-lidded eyes that seemed to look straight at her, before the man turned to smile down at the woman by his side. Fear gripped Beth for a moment at the sight of the couple Mike had just led into the garden, and he was now indicating where she stood with Tony.

Cannavaro. It could not be! She stared in disbelief at the tall, broad-shouldered man walking towards them and felt a shiver run down her spine.

Beth noted that the thick black hair was longer now, and brushed the white collar of his shirt. Belted chinos clung to his lean hips and followed the long length of his legs. She stiffened as an icy coldness washed over her. There was no mistake—it was him....

She had only ever seen Cannavaro in a dark suit—the

man in black who had haunted her dreams, her night-mares, for years. But he was just as intimidating in casual clothes, if not more so. His relaxed appearance would fool anyone into thinking he was one of the good guys. Not the smooth-talking devious devil Beth knew him to be.

Beth had not set eyes on him since her court appear-ance eight years ago. She had followed Helen's plan and with the help and guidance of Clive Hampton had settled in London, where it was easy to go unnoticed among the teeming millions of people. Or so she had thought until now.

The odds against bumping into Cannavaro even once in London must be huge, but twice in a week they'd be astronomical… Or just sheer bad luck. And she was going to have to deal with the situation coolly and con-fidently. Running away would simply draw attention to herself.

But surely Cannavaro could not be Tony's brother? For starters he was a lot taller, and he looked nothing like him. Tony was fresh-faced, young, fun, and he laughed his way through life. Cannavaro had black hair, olive-toned skin and, though handsome, his face held a hard ruthlessness, an arrogance that she recognised all too well. Secondly, and more importantly, they had different surnames.

'You don't look anything like each other,' she probed cautiously.

'Same mother. Different fathers. I take after my dad. Mum's Italian, and she was a widow with a thirteen-year-old son when Dad met her in Italy. They married almost immediately and he brought her back to England to live. Dante went to school and university in Italy and

England, so we only saw each other on the holidays—
half of which we used to spend at Mum's old home in
Italy. Mum and Dad still go there, but I haven't been
for years. Being stuck in the middle of the countryside
is not my idea of fun, but Dante loves the place. Actually, it belongs to him now, as he inherited his father's
estate and oodles of money along with half of the family law firm.'

It was that simple. They actually were brothers! Beth
was horrified, and her whole body tensed. She was appalled at the thought of being in the hateful man's presence for even a minute, let alone all evening.

She listened with a sinking heart as Tony continued
speaking. 'With a fourteen-year age difference between
us I've always been a bit in awe of him. Dante has it
all—tall, good-looking, fit and incredibly wealthy. He
doesn't need to work so hard or even at all. I keep telling him, but he just ignores me. He's far too cerebral for
my mind, but he is a great guy when you get to know
him, and all the women adore him. I'll introduce you.'

'No,' Beth said abruptly. 'You and your brother must
have a lot to catch up on, and I need to feed Binkie.'

She tried to excuse herself but Tony's hand tightened
on her waist when she tried to move.

'The cat can wait. Do me a favour, Beth, and play
along with me. With a stunner like you on my arm,
for once I will get one over on my big brother. He has
played the field discreetly for years with a string of
beautiful women. To be honest I'm surprised he's decided to get married.... His fiancée looks lovely, but
she's not as nice as you.'

Beth didn't get a chance to refuse....

'Good to see you, Tony,' a deep, dark voice drawled,

and Beth froze in Tony's hold at the hauntingly familiar sound of the man's voice.

'And you, Dante. I'm surprised you could make it.' Tony grinned and shook his brother's hand. 'And this must be the fiancée Mum told me about.' Tony smiled at the woman at his brother's side.

Dante Cannavaro smoothly made the introductions. 'Ellen, this is my younger brother, Tony.'

'Lovely to meet the woman who can tame Dante,' Tony declared with a grin and, dropping his arm from Beth's waist, he introduced her to the other woman.

Beth shook hands with Ellen and almost felt sorry for her as they exchanged the conventional greetings. She looked to be in her early thirties, her hair perfectly styled, her face perfectly made-up, and her casual trousers and top both designer label. She smiled, but there was condescension in the smile as her blue eyes took in Beth's department-store apparel. Some of Beth's sympathy for the woman faded.

'Congratulations on your engagement. I wish you both a very long and happy marriage,' Beth lied through her teeth. Personally, she hoped Cannavaro's life was hell. 'Have you chosen your dress yet?' she asked enthusiastically. She was not in the least interested, but it delayed the moment when she would have to face the man she despised, and gave her time to control her wildly beating heart and the shock of seeing him again.

Cannavaro was the man responsible for sending Beth to prison, and she had nearly died the first week she had been there. A group of women had thought that because she was in prison on a drugs charge she had the contacts to supply them with drugs. When she had told them she was innocent and that she had no knowledge of drugs she had been dragged into the showers and stripped. Her hair had been cut off and she'd been told her throat would be next... Luckily Helen, a middle-aged woman and her cellmate of three days, had walked in and saved her.

It had been Helen who had convinced her to change her name to Beth Lazenby when she was released, and had made it possible for her to do so. Ironically, the women who had cut off her hair had helped too. Beth was naturally a redhead, but as a child she had been teased unmercifully from her first day at school, and as she had grown taller and bigger than most of her class the bullying had gotten worse.

Finally, when she had been fourteen and they had just moved from Bedford to Bristol for her father's work, her mother had suggested that Beth dye her hair dark before she attended a new school and made new friends. Beth had quickly agreed and the bullying had stopped. Her life had been content for a number of years—until she had turned eighteen and had been in her first year at college.

Her parents, on their first holiday without her, had tragically died when the cruise liner they were on had sunk off the coast of Italy. This had been heartbreaking for Jane as the parents she had lost had been her adoptive parents, who had taken her in when she had been just a baby. Jane had no idea who her biological parents were, and had suddenly found herself all alone in the world.

So the day Jane Mason had walked out of jail after serving eighteen months of her sentence she'd been almost unrecognisable. Her hair had returned to its natural red colour and she'd been almost two stone lighter in weight. With Clive's help she had legally changed her name by deed poll to Beth Lazenby.

Helen's plan for Jane to change her name had made perfect sense; it was hard enough for an innocent young woman to make her way in the world without the totally unjustified tag of a prison sentence on her CV.

Beth owed it to the memory of her friend to show no weakness now.

CHAPTER TWO

DANTE CANNAVARO WAS not in a good mood. When he had called at Ellen's apartment earlier, contemplating their reunion after a month apart, he had casually mentioned his brother's barbecue and suggested they call in. Ellen had yet to meet Tony, and Dante was considering asking him to be his best man at their wedding. Ellen had hated both ideas. Barbecues were 'not her style,' and she was adamant that one of Dante's lawyer friends or a business associate would be much more appropriate as best man.

Finally she had agreed to attend—but only if they went immediately, so that they would still have time to have dinner at their favourite restaurant. This was news to Dante, who hadn't even known they *had* a favourite restaurant!

Ellen had carried on in the same vein for the hour it had taken to get here, and Dante had switched off and let her chatter. But when he had glanced across to where Mike had indicated his brother and seen the woman with him he'd immediately switched on again.

Now Dante studied the tall, striking redhead at Tony's side. There was something about her that niggled at him. He had caught the name Beth, but he could not remember having met anyone called Beth before. Yet there was definitely something familiar about her. Then, as the sun's rays caught her hair, turning it to flame, it came to him—she was the stunning woman he had noticed in the street a few days ago.

Dante barely heard the conversation that continued. His dark gaze roamed over her instead. He noticed the swell of her breasts beneath the lemon silk shirt she wore tucked into white jeans that moulded her slim hips and long legs, before his gaze slid back to trace the creamy skin over the high cheekbones of her face, framed by the red hair that was styled to fall sleekly to her shoulders. Finally his look rested on her big green eyes. He was intrigued as to who she was, and what she was to Tony.

'Beth—my brother Dante.'

Tony made the introduction and Beth had no excuse but to finally look at Cannavaro.

Dante offered his hand. 'It is a pleasure to meet you, Beth.' Her eyes were cold, he noted, and the fingers that briefly touched his and swiftly withdrew were smooth and cool. But the heated sensation he felt at her merest touch surprised him—and her, it would seem. He recognised the flash of awareness in her green eyes though she fought to disguise it. Her lashes flickered down and her full lips tightened. He sensed her antagonism. She had not wanted to shake his hand. Only social niceties had demanded the slight contact.

Dante wasn't a conceited man, but her reaction wasn't the one he usually got from females. This woman had never met him but she was determined not to like him, and he had to wonder why.

'Nice to meet you,' Beth said, but she refused to use

his name. Her fingers stung from the brief contact with his and she took a step back, shocked that he could affect her so intensely. His powerful physical presence provoked an instant reaction—a stomach-churning anger that she was barely able to control.

'I'm considering following you, Dante.' Tony reached his arm around Beth again, holding her close. 'And talking Beth into marrying me. What do you think?' he asked outrageously.

Beth's startled gaze flew to Tony. What on earth was he playing at?

'Beth is a lovely girl, I'm sure,' Dante offered with a cynical smile.

He had met a lot of women in his time, and could see the beautiful Beth was probably older than Tony—maybe not so much in years, but, by the guarded look about her, certainly in experience. She could be more interested in Tony's money than she was in the man. His brother worked in the merchant bank his father, Harry, owned and stood to inherit a fortune. The fact that he chose to share an apartment with Mike in suburbia, rather than a luxury apartment he could easily afford in the city centre, didn't mean Beth did not know exactly who Tony was—an extremely good catch for any woman.

Beth's blood ran cold as Dante's hard dark eyes met hers. Now she recognised the cynicism in his smile immediately—but years ago she had not, and it had been her downfall. Her anger and resentment grew at the memory as he continued speaking.

'But you have only just turned twenty-three, Tony. Isn't that a bit young to be contemplating matrimony?' Dante queried. He had seen the anger in Beth's eyes and his conviction that she was only after Tony's money deepened. This woman was smart enough to know that as the older brother he was a possible threat to her plan. 'Marriage is an expensive business—especially for a young man just starting his career. I'm sure Beth would agree.'

His mocking tone did nothing to quell the bitterness bubbling inside Beth. No wonder Tony wanted to get one over on the arrogant swine. Rashly, she decided to help him. 'Oh, I don't know. Money isn't everything.' She shot Cannavaro a defiant glance before looking adoringly up at Tony. 'Is it, darling?'

'You've got that spot-on,' Tony offered, his eyes dancing with amusement as he planted a brief kiss on her lips. 'Isn't she incredible, bro?' he prompted.

'Yes,' Dante agreed curtly, surprised by the swift flare of irritation he felt at seeing them kiss. His dark gaze flicked to Beth and he caught the gleam in her green eyes. It wasn't passion for Tony, he recognised, but a direct challenge aimed at *him*.

There was nothing Dante liked better than a challenge, and there was something about the striking redhead that had aroused his suspicions the minute he had met her. Now he was in danger of arousing another part of him, and worryingly it had nothing to do with his fiancée. He hadn't reacted to a woman so swiftly in a long time. He enjoyed sex, but was never blinded by it, and he chose his partners carefully—as he had Ellen. He was always in total control, as he was in all aspects of his life. Yet every instinct he possessed was telling him his surprising reaction to Beth was not just sexual attraction. It was as though he knew her—but how?

He needed time to think, and changed the subject.

'What about a drink, Tony? This is supposed to be a party. I'll have a soft drink as I'm driving.' And, concentrating on his fiancée, he added, 'A vodka and tonic all right for you, Ellen?'

'I'll get them, Tony,' Beth offered, her heart pounding in panic as she realised that playing along with Tony's game to irritate his brother had been the height of stupidity. She had let her anger overcome her caution and drawn attention to herself—a big mistake. 'You stay with your guests. You must have a lot to talk about with a family wedding coming up.'

Tony kissed her cheek and let her go. 'Thanks, you're a gem. And bring me a beer as well, hmm?'

Beth agreed, and with a huge sense of relief walked across to get a can of beer, then sprinted up the stairs of the boys' apartment and into the kitchen.

She recognised a couple of their friends from the bank, and responding to their chatter helped her to regain her shattered nerves as she mixed the drinks and placed them on a tray. Caution and confidence, she reminded herself. But even so she was in no hurry to go back down to the party.

Just then Mike appeared. 'I need more food! These people eat like horses,' he declared, and she saw a lifeline.

'You're looking stressed, Mike.' And, handing him the tray, she suggested, 'Why don't you add a drink for yourself and take these down to Tony, relax and enjoy the party? I'll take care of the barbecue—no problem.'

'You are an angel.' He grinned and agreed.

Beth doubted Cannavaro and Ellen would deign to eat from the barbecue. Fine dining was more their thing, and she could hopefully avoid them for the rest of the evening.

* * *

Tony had watched Beth depart with an appreciative eye, then turned to catch Dante doing the same. 'So, when are you getting married, bro?' he asked mischievously. 'At your age you don't want to hang around.'

Before Dante could reply Ellen laughed and launched into a long explanation as to how difficult it was to get the right church at the right time and find the right venue for the reception. He saw Tony's eyes glaze over with drink or boredom—more likely the latter—and he knew the feeling.

Dante had presumed that once they were engaged all he'd have to do was pay up and turn up on the wedding day. The endless lists and arrangements Ellen expected him to be interested in and discuss had come as an unpleasant shock to him.

Eventually Ellen ended with a date in September.

'That's fine,' Tony said. 'Don't forget to send me an invite. I'll bring Beth. Hopefully it will encourage her down the same path.'

'Is that wise? The guests will be family and close friends, and though Beth seems nice how long have you known her?' Dante demanded. Somehow the thought of the emerald-eyed beauty as a guest at his wedding was not one he wanted to contemplate.

'Ever since we moved in, eighteen months ago. She's a great girl and a fabulous cook. Her cakes are to die for. I don't know what we'd do without her. Isn't that right?' Tony asked as Mike appeared with the drinks.

'Yes, she is a diamond—especially to you, mate. And as we're standing in *her* garden, and *she* prepared most of the food and has offered to take over the barbecue so I can enjoy myself, I'd say she is indispensable. And she certainly improves the view....'

Dante had wondered why Tony insisted on living out here, and now he knew. Tony was infatuated by the woman. With a few judicious questions Dante soon found out a lot more about Beth Lazenby. She was twenty-seven, and an accountant for a prestigious firm in the centre of London. She owned a cottage by the sea, and lived in the ground-floor apartment—too close to Tony for Dante's comfort. He wasn't sure why, but his gut feeling was telling him there was a lot more to Beth than met the eye.

He glanced across to the barbecue and saw her standing there, handing out plates of food to a group of men gathered around her, none of whom could take their eyes off her. Maybe that was the problem. She was tall, and so stunningly attractive few men would think to look past her surface beauty. She was an unlikely accountant. With her height and looks she could have been a model—she was slender enough. But maybe her high, firm breasts were a little too much for a fashion model, he mused.

'Dante, darling.'

Ellen's voice stopped his musing.

'I feel like dancing.' Grasping his arm, she smiled up at him.

'Not my kind of dancing, but I'll give it a go.'

Ellen was the lovely, intelligent woman whom he had chosen to be his wife, Dante reminded himself, and it was time he stopped worrying about the redhead and concentrated on his fiancée. Ellen had not wanted to attend this barbecue, but she was making an effort for his sake. Dancing with her was the least he could do....

* * *

Julian, the last man standing by the barbecue, was talking about stockbroking, laughing as he described his latest gamble on the markets. Beth listened politely, her mind only partially on what he said. She seemed unable to stop her eyes from straying towards the people dancing on the patio, and the tallest man in particular. For a big man he was a smooth mover—though he wasn't so much dancing as allowing his fiancée to flit adoringly around him. More fool her, Beth thought. In her experience most men were a waste of time. All she wanted to do was call it a night, get into her apartment and check on Binkie. But there was no way she was going to walk through the crowd of gyrating bodies.

Luckily the music stopped and Mike came strolling over, his face flushed and smiling, obviously having enjoyed himself. 'Sorry, Beth. I didn't mean to leave you so long, but with it still being so light I didn't realise the time. Tony has just gone to change the music. You go and enjoy yourself, and I'll pack up here.'

For Beth it already felt like the longest night of her life, and she leapt at the chance to escape. People were moving to replenish their drinks, and her route was almost clear to her back door.

She was nearly there when the music started again— this time slow and moody—and suddenly her way was blocked as Cannavaro stepped in front of her, crowding her. She wanted to step back, but her pride would not let her.

'May I have this dance? Tony is partnering Ellen, and it will give us a chance to get to know each other. We might all be family one day.'

Beth tensed and looked up at him—which was an

unusual event in itself for her. She noticed that his eyes were not black. They were the colour of molasses—dark and golden. She found herself thinking that once she fell into them she would be stuck for ever. Disturbed by the fanciful thought, she caught the gleam of mockery in those same eyes and wanted to refuse his request outright. But she did not dare. He had not recognised her, she was sure, but she had aroused his suspicion by being less than courteous when they had been introduced. She did not want to compound her mistake by showing her dislike again.

She took a deep breath. 'That's not likely to happen. Tony was just teasing,' she managed to say evenly. 'But, yes, if you insist, I will dance with you.'

'Oh, I insist, Beth.' He drawled her name softly and his arm slid around her waist.

He looked at her, his other hand taking hers, and she was not prepared for the tingling sensation that crept over her skin and made her shiver as he held her close to his long body.

A reaction to the cooling night air, she told herself, but somehow her body, with a will of its own, was moving with him, automatically following his movements.

'You are a very lovely lady, Beth. What man wouldn't insist?' he added in that deep, barely accented silken voice she remembered so well and so bitterly.

She forgot her good intentions. 'Are you trying to flirt with me, Mr Cannavaro?' she demanded. 'And you an engaged man,' she prompted, giving him a derisory smile while trying to control her inexplicably racing pulse.

A quizzical expression flickered across his face for a moment, and his incredible eyes seemed to bore into hers as his hand stroked up her spine to hold her closer still. To her shame she felt a fullness in her breasts when they came in contact with his broad chest.

'No, Beth. I was stating the truth. But if I *was* flirting with you I would not have to try very hard,' Dante opined, fully appreciating the feminine sway of her shapely body against his own, testing his control to the limit. 'I felt you tremble when I took you in my arms, and sensed it in the softening of your body against mine. There is an instant sexual attraction between us—unfortunate, but true. Under the circumstances it is obviously not to be acted upon. But I also sense something more. You seem afraid of me—even actively to dislike me—and I have to wonder why. Are you sure we have not met before?'

God, he analysed everything, and talked like a lawyer even as they moved to the music. His muscular thighs brushed against hers, raising her temperature, and it took all her nerve to hold his dark gaze.

'I shivered because it is getting cooler now,' she lied. 'And, no, we have never met before. I didn't even know Tony had a brother. He never mentioned you until you turned up here in the garden.'

Dante stilled and let Beth take a step back, putting space between them. His heavy-lidded eyes were shrewd and penetrating, and swept over her flushed defiant face before moving lower.

'Interesting if true!' He raised a sardonic eyebrow, noting the thrust of her nipples against her shirt.

The lovely Beth was definitely lying about one part of that statement. He had met enough females in his time, and was experienced enough to recognise when a lustful attraction was mutual. But was she lying about not knowing Tony had a brother until tonight? She had not said *half-brother,* and if she was telling the truth surely she would naturally assume his name was Hetherington, the same as Tony's? And yet she had called him Mr Cannavaro—even though his name had not been mentioned when the introductions had been made. He doubted Tony, who was not into formality of any kind, would have called him anything but Dante or bro in the couple of minutes before they had been introduced. So how could she know his surname unless she *had* met him before, or at least heard of him?

The mystery of Beth Lazenby deepened. His legal instincts told him she was hiding something—but what? And in that moment Dante decided to make it his business to discover everything about her. Not for himself, but to protect his brother, of course.

A wave of heat swept through Beth at his intense scrutiny and it took every scrap of willpower she possessed to control her traitorous body. But at least she was saved from having to respond as Tony and Ellen appeared.

'One fiancée returned to you, bro, worn out from dancing with me—or it could be the vodka I gave her. She wants to go home.' Tony grinned, swaying on his feet, and Beth grabbed his arm to steady him. He had definitely had too much to drink.

'Thanks a bunch, Tony,' Dante said dryly, his expression grim as he wrapped his arm around a slightly glassy-eyed Ellen. And with a goodnight and a curt nod to Beth, much to her relief he left.

Beth took the key from her back pocket and, ignoring Tony's drunken request to dance, slipped into her apartment and locked the door behind her. She fell back against it, breathing deeply, fighting to regain her composure.

Binkie appeared and she picked him up in her arms and carried him through into the living room. Her knees weak, with a sigh she sank down onto the sofa, cuddling the cat on her lap, her mind in turmoil as the significance of Cannavaro being Tony's brother sank in.

Everyone had bad days, she reminded herself, but today hers had gone from good straight to diabolical. She glanced around the cosy room that was her sanctuary, her gaze resting on the two photographs in identical silver frames on the mantelpiece. One was of the parents she had adored, and the other of Helen, her dearest friend. All three were dead now, and moisture glazed her eyes.

Clive Hampton, Helen's lawyer, whom Beth now considered a friend and mentor, was the closest thing she had to family. He had been instrumental in getting her a job in the offices of a local accountancy firm, where she had got the opportunity to train in-house as an accountant. After taking the requisite exams over two years she had eventually become qualified.

She spoke to Clive frequently on the telephone, and often visited him at his home in Richmond. She was meeting him tomorrow for Sunday lunch, and had almost forgotten in the trauma of the evening. He was over sixty now, and thinking of retiring soon, and though she talked to him about most things, telling him how she felt about Cannavaro was not one of them. It was much too personal. She had never even told Helen how badly the man had affected her in court, only that he was clever and that her lawyer, Miss Sims, had been

useless against him. No, this latest development she had
to take care of herself.

Her time in prison had taught her how to build a protective shell around her emotions and present a blank
face in front of warders and prisoners alike. Living in a
confined environment and sharing communal showers
had come as a shock, but she had quickly realised that
women came in all shapes and sizes and soon thought
nothing of stripping off in front of anyone. She told
herself she was no better or worse than anyone else,
but all her life she had always felt the odd one out and
that hadn't changed. And with her new identity she was
even more wary of making friends.

Tony and Mike were the only friends she had in London, though she had quite a few in Faith Cove.

Wearily she let her head fall back on the sofa and
closed her eyes. She had never felt as alone as she did
now. Not since that fatal day eight years ago when she
had stood in the dock, trembling with fear. And the
same hateful arrogant man was responsible.... In her
head she wished she had the nerve to tell Dante Cannavaro exactly what she thought of him, but in reality
she knew she could not.

He was a dangerously clever man: she trembled if
he so much as touched her and he already thought they
had met before. She was not going to take the chance of
him remembering where... Not that it would matter if
he did, but she did not need the aggravation in her life.
What she needed to do was make sure she never met
him again, and if that meant moving she would. Tony
had said he hadn't seen his brother since last year, so
with luck she'd have some time to decide.

Binkie stirred and stretched on her lap. Sighing, Beth

got to her feet. 'Come on, Binkie. I can see you want feeding, and then I am going to bed.'

But once she was in bed disturbing thoughts of Dante Cannavaro filled her mind. The first time she had seen him across the courtroom she had felt an instant connection with him. Her stomach had churned and her heart had leapt and naively she had thought he was her savior. But he had betrayed her. Again tonight he'd ignited those same sensations in her, but she told herself that this time it was anger and hatred for the man.

Yet, as she tossed and turned, hot and restless beneath the coverlet, remembering the strength of his arms holding her as they danced, the heat of his long body moving her to the music, she had the growing suspicion that he could be right. Never in her life had she responded to any man the way she did to Cannavaro. She had met plenty of men in the last few years, and quite a lot had asked her for a date, but she could count on one hand the rare occasions she had accepted.

For all the harm Cannavaro had done to her, could her intense awareness of him, the rush of sensations he aroused in her, be purely sexual, as he said, and not just hatred as she believed? She saw in her mind's eye his broodingly handsome face, the compelling dark eyes, and a shiver quivered through her body. How could she know for sure?

The first boy she had kissed had been the slimy liar Timothy Bewick, and when Cannavaro had questioned her at the trial he had implied their kiss had been a lot more. She hadn't recognised the *femme fatale* he had made her out to be, but the jury had believed him.

By the time Beth had got out of prison she'd been determined to allow no man to get close to her. Her friend

Helen had still been in prison, serving a twenty-year sentence for killing her bully of an ex-husband. Helen had spent years living with his violent rages, and it had only been when she had seen his anger directed at their daughter, Vicky, that Helen had found the courage to divorce him. Five years later Vicky had died while staying at her father's holiday villa in Spain. According to her father, Vicky had slipped and cracked her head open. The Spanish authorities had believed him. But Helen had known he'd finally gone too far and she'd snapped, deliberately running him down with her Land Rover outside his London home.

Helen had told Beth her story, and told her to look around at the rest of the women they'd shared the prison with. Most of the women had been there because of a man. A man who'd told them what to do, whether they were thieves, prostitutes, drug mules or anything else. And they'd done it because they'd been deluded enough to believe the man loved them. In Helen's case she had let grief and hatred of her ex take over, and in destroying his life had destroyed her own too. Helen had warned her never to let any man take over *her* life.

Helen's words of wisdom still held true, and they strengthened Beth's resolve to put as much distance between herself and Dante Cannavaro as she possibly could.

In a moment of insight Beth realised that her cottage in the village of Faith Cove was the only place she felt truly herself.

When Beth finally fell into a restless sleep the nightmare she had not suffered from for a long time returned with a vengeance—only the ending wasn't the same. She was in the dock, with a big handsome man in black tormenting her, twisting every word she said. Then he was smiling, his deep voice and dark eyes drawing her in. And then the nightmare turned into an erotic dream of strong arms holding her, firm, sensuous lips kissing her, hands caressing her, thrilling her.

She cried out and woke up, hot and moist between her thighs and with her heart pounding like a drum.

The next day Beth drove to Richmond for Sunday lunch with Clive, and discussed with him what she had been thinking of doing since the last time she had stayed at the cottage. With Clive's full approval Beth made the decision to leave London.

She was going to move to Faith Cove and refurbish the cottage Helen had gifted to her in her will. Ironically, Helen's brute of a husband, never thinking his wife would have the nerve to divorce him, had put the cottage in Helen's name to avoid tax when he had bought the house fifteen years earlier. When she *had* divorced him there had been nothing he could do about her keeping it.

Now Beth had plans for the cottage. Although 'cottage' was actually a misnomer, as the place was really a large house with six bedrooms, often rented out to families. First she would convert the roof space of the multi-car garage at the rear of the property into a three-roomed apartment. That way she could carry on renting out the house as a holiday let while living permanently either in the apartment or the house when it was vacant. Beth was sure she could make a comfortable living out of it, and she could continue as an accountant for private clients. Maybe she could even convert part of the garage into a surfers' shop later, which would give her even more independence and ensure she could stay away from the man who haunted her dreams.

Dante Cannavaro, with a face like thunder, walked into his office on Monday morning, sat down at his desk and contacted the security firm he used when a delicate investigation was needed for a client.

Minutes later he lounged back in his black leather chair, his mind not on work but fixated on a tall redhead. He had put the wheels in motion to find out exactly who Beth Lazenby was, and if there was anything suspicious about her he would deal with her appropriately.

Miss Lazenby had already messed up his weekend and a hell of a lot more—including his plans for the future. He had taken Ellen back to her apartment on Saturday night, but had not joined her in bed because she had obviously drunk too much. Ellen had taken offence, blaming Dante for taking her to Tony's party in the first place, and not taking her out to dinner. She had accused Dante of being arrogant and uncaring and of eyeing up another woman in her presence—namely Beth. She had claimed that he did not love her and had used a lot of words he had never thought she knew. The argument had culminated in Ellen calling the wedding off and throwing her ring at him as he had exited her apartment.

Dante had returned home in a foul mood, and had then spent a restless night with the image of a flame-haired woman plaguing his mind and his body. He'd had to remind himself that he had gotten over the urge to bed every desirable woman he met years ago. Yet he was still convinced that he knew Beth.... But how and from where he had no idea—and that was his problem.

Dante was as frustrated as hell, thanks to the red-headed witch, and he was damn sure he was not going to let her mess up Tony's life. He glanced at his watch. He had a flight booked to New York at noon, and he expected to be there for a few weeks at least. He called his driver to pick him up and got to his feet, a ruthless gleam in his dark eyes.

When he returned to England, whatever the outcome of his enquiries, he would take great pleasure in dealing with Beth Lazenby personally. There was no way she was marrying Tony! Just the thought of being faced with Beth as his brother's wife at every family gathering for the rest of his life was enough to make him shudder.

About to get in the car, he stopped and took his cell phone from his pocket and called Tony, realising his younger brother was impulsive enough to marry the woman without a second thought. Proof or not, it was his brotherly duty to warn Tony of his suspicions for his own good

'Dante—to what do I owe this honor?' Tony answered. 'You rarely call me—and never during working hours.'

'I want to let you know Ellen and I have split up. The wedding is cancelled and I am going to America for a while.'

'Sorry, but I can't say I'm surprised. In fact I told Beth I was amazed you'd got engaged in the first place. Why settle for one when you can take your pick, bro?'

Dante heard his chuckle and grimaced. 'Yes, well, I've learned my lesson. But knowing how impulsive you can be, I thought I should warn you in case you make the same mistake.'

'Warn me? That sounds ominous.'

'Not ominous, just cautious… I've met Beth's type before—a beautiful woman who probably knows your father owns a bank and is as interested in money as she is in you.' Dante heard Tony laugh out loud and gritted his teeth. His brother never took anything seriously.

'Ah, Dante, you really are too serious to be believed. As for Beth—I really couldn't care less if she knows Dad owns a bank or not. You've met her. She is absolutely gorgeous! Do you honestly think I, or any other red-blooded male who was lucky enough to have Beth in his bed, would give a damn about the money? You must really be getting old, Dante, but don't worry—I won't do anything you wouldn't do…. *Ciao.*' And, still laughing, he clicked off.

Dante slipped his phone back into his pocket, feeling a complete idiot. Tony's parting shot *did* worry him, and as he got into the car, his lips twisting wryly, he acknowledged that his brother's assessment of the male of the species where Beth Lazenby was concerned was probably correct.

CHAPTER THREE

It was a blazing-hot day, and Beth's carefully straightened hair was already beginning to wave in the heat as she searched the kitchen one more time.

'Got you!' she cried triumphantly and, cradling Binkie in her arms, she carried him into the hall and closed the kitchen door with her hip. Finally she was ready to go. Her luggage was loaded into the boot of her car, and had been for hours, but Binkie was not. It was a five-hour drive to Devon, and she had planned on leaving at one. It was now three, but with luck she would easily make it before dark.

She eyed the cat carrier standing open in the hall. Binkie hated travelling, which was why she had spent ages trying to coax him out from under the kitchen units, after having chased him around the garden and the apartment. Now all she had to do was put him in the carrier and they could go.

Beth had given in her notice at work on Monday and, with the three weeks' holiday she had yet to take, did not need to return to the office. She had spoken to Tony last night, but had not mentioned she was leaving permanently. She intended to do that when she came back to clear her apartment. Tony had promised to keep an eye on the place, and had also told her his brother's engagement was off. Dante had gone to work in America for a while, conveniently escaping the flak from their mother over the cancelled wedding. She had already bought a hat!

Tony's news had been music to Beth's ears, and she'd realised she had probably worried unnecessarily. But she was pleased that Dante's appearance in her life again had focused her mind and forced her to make a decision. Now, sun, sea and a new chapter in her life beckoned, Beth thought happily, bending down to lower Binkie into the carrier—which was easier said than done. He had leapt out of it twice already.

'Stop wriggling, you useless ball of fur,' she told him, and was just about to draw one hand free to shut the carrier when there was a ring at the front door—peremptory and sharp.

Ignoring it, Beth leant over, using her body to block Binkie's escape, and swiftly closed the lid.

'All right, all right—I'm coming!' she yelled as the bell rang again and kept on ringing.

She got to her feet and, leaving the carrier on the floor, walked to the door. Probably some salesman, she thought. But whoever it was she would get rid of them quickly. She opened the door.

The social smile froze on her lips and she simply stared at the man standing before her. A dark, unsmiling figure in a charcoal pinstriped suit, jacket unfastened, the white shirt beneath open at the neck and startlingly brilliant against his tanned throat. Her stomach clenched and she stiffened, straightening her shoulders. It was the man she hated with a passion but had dreamed of far too often in the past two weeks for her peace of mind. Cannavaro...

Dante had received the report on Beth Lazenby a week ago in New York, and what he had read had confirmed his suspicions about her. He had arrived back in London this morning, and after a shower and a change had leapt in his car and driven here. Now he was on her doorstep. His features hardened as slowly he took in every detail of the way she looked: her hair was dishevelled, her face clear of make-up—and as for what she was wearing...

If he'd had the slightest doubt of the investigator's findings that Jane Mason and Beth Lazenby were one and the same, it vanished as he noted the snug fit of denim shorts that showed off her long legs and the skimpy white top that revealed a tantalising cleavage and stopped six inches short of the toned flesh of a slender waist and abdomen. She was slimmer than before, but still had curves in all the right places, and she was more striking than ever.

He felt a surge of lust and saw again in his mind's eye the image of that girl in the picture, wearing almost the same outfit as this woman wore now, but with one dramatic difference. The girl in the picture had had long black hair—as had the girl who'd stood in the dock and been found guilty of being a drug dealer.

He had been right to be suspicious of the redheaded beauty who had captivated his brother. She had latched on to a younger boy when she was a teenager, and been prepared to use his infatuation for her to ruin him and save her own neck when she had been caught in her reckless drug dealing. It would seem that she had ensnared his younger brother in much the same way. She obviously had not changed—only in the colour of her hair, which couldn't be real. The thing that surprised him was that he had not recognised who she was sooner.

'Hello, Beth. Or should I say Jane?' he queried sardonically.

'My legal name is Beth Lazenby,' Beth stated bluntly.

The air between them was crackling with tension.

'Maybe now. But it wasn't when you were in the dock at nineteen.'

'You've finally recognised me. Bully for you,' she snapped sarcastically, seeing no point in denying it. So he had remembered where he had seen her before? Her temper rose at the audacity of the man, confronting her on her own doorstep.

'Not exactly. But the investigator I hired to check on you refreshed my memory.'

Beth's temper very nearly exploded at that revelation, and only by a terrific effort of will did she control the anger simmering inside her—along with other emotions she refused to recognise. She reminded herself she was no longer a gullible teenager but a confident woman, and she flatly refused to let Cannavaro intimidate her again.

'Shame you wasted your money. I'm going on holiday now, and have already spent ages chasing the cat—which has made me late. You need to leave.' And she caught the door handle with the intention of slamming the door in his face.

'Not so fast.' He put his foot in the door. 'I want to talk to you.'

'Well, tough. Because I have absolutely nothing to say to you.' She turned, hanging on to her temper by a thread, and went to retrieve the cat in order to go.

But, remembering the time and pain Cannavaro had already cost her, she decided she had nothing left to lose, and spun back to find him towering over her.

She looked up at him, her green eyes spitting fury. 'Except to say you have some nerve investigating me. Call yourself a lawyer? You are without doubt the most arrogant, devious, manipulative, lying bastard it has ever been my misfortune to meet. Got it? Now, go.'

His face was like carved granite and his eyes hard as he watched her mouth spew out the angry words. Suddenly he moved and a long arm shot around her. His large hand splayed across her back whilst the other grasped the back of her head and jerked her body towards him. He dipped his head, his mouth crashing down on hers, relentlessly prising her lips apart with the powerful thrust of his tongue. Shocked and furious, she tried to pull away, but his hands clamped her in position. Her head was so close to his she could not drag it from beneath his all-consuming mouth. The steel band of his arm was holding her pressed hard against his long body. She tried to struggle, but he was too strong—and shamefully, instead of feeling revulsion, she was floundering in the wave of heady sensation flowing through her body.

Frantically she tried to lift her hands and shove him away, but she was held so tightly against the hard wall of his chest that all she could do was claw at his broad shoulders as he wreaked sensual havoc with his penetrating kiss. Still she tried to resist, but he explored her mouth, hotly igniting a flame of arousal deep inside that scorched through her defences—and suddenly she wasn't clawing, but clinging to him.

His fingers wound into her hair, pulling it back to

tilt her head to one side, his mouth trailing the line of her neck to suck on the frantically leaping pulse there.

This could not be! She hated the man. She began to struggle so wildly that their bodies swayed and crashed against the wall, his long, hard length pinning her there. She was aware of his hot, male scent and the strength of his muscular and highly aroused body against her own in a shockingly intimate way she had never experienced before.

He lifted his head, her breath catching as she saw his face. He was staring at her with dark, mesmerising eyes as his hand moved from her head to the neckline of her top, his long fingers slipping beneath the fabric to graze a swelling nipple. Involuntarily her body arched, and she bit back the moan that rose in her throat.

Her voice seemed to have deserted her, and her heart was thudding so hard she thought it might burst. Her passionate hatred of him had been overtaken by passionate desire.

'You can't help yourself. You want me,' he said in a deep, thickened voice.

'No, I hate you,' she said hoarsely.

He gave her one long look, his face suddenly wearing a cold remoteness that was frightening in itself. He straightened up and pulled her closer against him, his hand circling her throat to tip her head back. 'Hate away. But think yourself lucky I only kissed you. If any man had said what you did to me he would be on the floor now. I will not tolerate anyone defaming my character—and certainly not a conniving ex-con like you. Understand?'

Shaken, and battling to control her overloaded senses, she heard his words and they were better than a cold shower. How typical of the arrogant devil. Beth shook her head in disgust.

'Now we will have that talk.' His hands dropped from her and he took a step back—and stumbled over the cat carrier. He swore, and Binkie shot out beneath his feet. Dante struggled to avoid the cat, lost the battle, and fell to the floor.

Beth laughed—if a bit hysterically. Perfect karma, she thought. The stunned look on his handsome face was priceless.

'How the mighty are fallen,' she quipped, and bent down to grab Binkie, ignoring the furious mountain of a man leaping to his feet. 'There, there, Binkie,' Beth said as she walked into the living room, cuddling the cat over her chest and shoulder to comfort him—and to disguise her tight nipples. 'I know the nasty man kicked you, but he's going now.'

Dante straightened up, not quite sure what had just happened. He'd been kissing her like a savage beast gone wild one minute, the next on the floor in a heap! He could still taste her on his tongue, and Beth—Jane—whoever she was—had for the first time in his life left him knocked out sensually and physically.

'I did not kick the cat,' Dante declared, following her into the room. His pride was seriously dented and he raked a distracted hand though his hair. What *was* it about this witch of a woman that turned him into a primitive, clumsy oaf? He had never tripped over his feet since he was a child. He looked at her, with a great lump of red fur the same colour as her hair clamped to her chest, her slender fingers stroking the cat's head, then moving to scratch the animal under the chin.

She raised her eyes and looked at him. 'You kicked

over his carrier with him inside, which is the same thing—isn't it, Binkie?'

Dante could not believe she had actually asked the damned cat. Maybe he had fallen into a different dimension. Maybe she really was a witch and the cat was her familiar, he thought, as two identical pairs of green eyes stared accusingly at him. The cat bared its teeth and he was sure he heard it hiss in agreement with his mistress.

He shook his head to clear his brain. The woman was driving him crazy. What hope would his impressionable young brother have with her? None—and his express purpose for being here was to get her out of Tony's life.

'I am not going anywhere—and neither are you until we talk,' he commanded between clenched teeth. To emphasise the fact he shrugged off his jacket, crossed to one of the sofas flanking the fireplace and dropped it on the arm before he sat down.

Beth was a realist. She had to be. She saw the cold determination in his hard face. The wild, passionate interlude in the hall had been exactly what he had said—a punishment for daring to impugn his good character. Which was a joke, because as far as *she* was concerned he didn't have one.

'I'll give you five minutes,' she stated, her lips twitching as she sat down on the opposite sofa. She kissed the cat and put him down beside her. 'Go on, Binkie. You can have another roam around the kitchen before we leave.' She watched him jump off the sofa.

'Do you always talk to your cat?'

She turned her cool gaze on Dante, trying to ignore the lingering warmth in the rest of her body that wasn't being helped by the sight of him in a tailored white shirt and pleated trousers that fitted snugly over his muscular thighs. 'Not always, but he is one of the few honest males I have met, and he is a great judge of character.' She glanced down at Binkie, who had walked straight across to Cannavaro with his back arched, fur bristling as though he was about to attack. 'He certainly recognises *your* type,' she said dryly.

'That cat does not like me.' Dante stated the obvious, eyeing the hunchbacked animal with equal dislike. He was amazed to see that at the sound of his mistress's voice the cat turned and looked at Beth, then crossed to rub slowly up against her bare legs before walking out of the door.

She shrugged her shoulders 'Binkie is a tomcat and you are a strange male invading his territory. His natural instinct is to protect it.'

'Not that strange. I have known you a long time, Jane.' He deliberately used her old name, determined to get down to business.

Beth let her eyes rest on him for a moment. He was sitting on her sofa, making himself at home, with his long legs stretched out in casual ease, his black hair falling over his brow. He seemed so supremely sure of himself. To her shame, Beth felt her body responding to his potent masculine appeal and anger resurfaced— almost as much with herself as him.

'If you think by calling me Jane you can intimidate me, forget it,' she said bluntly. 'I am no longer an innocent teenager you can browbeat in the dock.'

A black brow arched sardonically. 'Innocent! I seem to recall it was the jury's unanimous opinion that you were one hundred percent guilty.'

'You mean the opinion *you* talked them into believing?'

'What's that supposed to mean?' His brow lifted again. There was no sign of conscience on his face.

Beth shook her head dismissively. What was the point in arguing with him? She had lost eighteen months of her life because of Cannavaro and she wasn't wasting any more. Rising to her feet, she deliberately let her gaze roam over his darkly attractive face, broad shoulders and the glimpse of black body hair revealed by the open-necked shirt before moving it lower over his long body....

He was a supreme physical specimen of masculinity, with the ability to arouse any woman, and her own innate honesty forced her to admit she was no exception. He had been right about the attraction between them. Even now, angry as she was, she could feel the sexual tension shimmering. But it didn't make him any less of a lying toad in her eyes.

'My name is Beth. You are in my home uninvited, supposedly because you want to talk, but so far I have heard nothing that I have not heard before. So get on with it. No thanks to you, I *do* have a life to get on with.' She deliberately glanced down at her wristwatch and back up to him, her green eyes clashing with his. 'You have two minutes, then I am leaving.'

'You are very confident for an ex-con. But will you be so confident when I tell Tony of your past, I wonder?' he drawled, lounging back against the soft cushions, obviously not about to move. 'I recognised the type of woman you are the first time I saw you in the dock. You would do anything—even try to destroy a young boy who's infatuated by you—to save your own skin. Now you have Tony equally infatuated with you and wanting to marry you, for no other reason than just because you can or—more likely—you want him for his wealth.'

That made Beth smile. 'Not very flattering to your brother, are you? But feel free to tell him. I don't mind, I don't think Tony would either. A lot of young men his age consider it really cool to have a girlfriend who has done time in jail.'

His dark eyes watched her penetratingly and she knew she had got to him.

'You could be right. But, believe me, I do not make idle threats. You will move out of this apartment and leave Tony alone—no contact of any kind—or I will tell your employer exactly who you are: a convicted drug dealer who has spent eighteen months in prison. I'm sure that's something you probably missed off your CV. Steel and White is a highly respectable firm and will take a dim view of the omission. You will be out of a job—your carefully crafted reputation ruined.'

Beth listened to him with rising anger, realising he must have had her investigated immediately after the barbecue—otherwise he would know she had given in her notice to Steel and White on Monday. She did not know much about men, but she wasn't a fool. The way Cannavaro had treated her earlier in the hall had surprised and aroused her, but there was no disguising the fact that he had been equally aroused—and she seriously doubted he was doing this just for his brother!

This man had destroyed her once and he was trying to do so again. But he wasn't quite as clever as he thought. Prison life had taught her to control her body and her temper rigorously, but she could not resist goading the sanctimonious jerk.

'That could happen, I suppose,' she agreed, without

batting an eyelash. 'But I am a good accountant, and there are plenty of other jobs. Or I could set up my own business. You obviously haven't thought this through, because short of following me around for the rest of my life there is nothing much you can do to me. According to you, I committed a crime—but I have served my time and am now a reformed character. So I changed my name by deed poll? That is perfectly legal. And for over six years now I have led a perfectly honest life. Can you say the same? I doubt it,' she said derisively. 'As for your threats—they don't bother me. Thanks to you I grew a thick skin in prison, and I don't have to do a damn thing you say. But, if it helps, I have no intention of marrying your brother—or any other man for that matter. Now, your two minutes are up. Time to go.'

He rose to his feet. She thought for a moment she had won, and turned towards the door, but a large hand clamped around her upper arm and spun her back to face him.

'Not so fast,' Dante declared, uncomfortably aware that the words of her spirited response was true. His investigator's report had confirmed she had led a blameless life since her release from prison, but it did not make her any less guilty of the crime in his eyes. However, it did make him think again about what he was about to say. He studied her from beneath narrowed lids, noting the slight flush that stained her cheeks and the glitter of anger in her huge green eyes as she glared up at him. He was struck by her bravery in trying to defy him—but not enough to change his mind and let her go. And it had absolutely nothing to do with the growing ache in his groin!

'This conversation is not over yet, Beth. I didn't get

around to mentioning your good friend Clive Hampton—the lawyer of your old cell mate, I believe.'

Beth stilled. 'Clive?' she murmured, and despite her brave words she suddenly felt wary.

'He is a fine lawyer, known for his charity work and nearing retirement. There are rumours he will receive a decoration in the New Year's Honours list.' His eyes watched her. 'Such a shame if his reputation is destroyed by his friendship with you. Maybe he could even be disbarred by the Law Lords.'

'No…' she breathed. 'You can't do that. Clive is the most caring, honest man I know. He has never broken a law in his life, I'm sure.'

'He doesn't have to break a law. But his close relationship with you could be perceived as *bending* the law. He collected you from prison, found you a place to live and recommended you to a business acquaintance of his to get you a position with an accountancy firm without revealing your change of name. Then there is Helen Jackson, your cellmate, whose divorce he arranged and whom he later defended unsuccessfully on a murder charge. It was rumoured that Helen was more than just a client to Clive, and with a beautiful woman like you to spice up the story the tabloids will have a field day.'

'I am not news, and Helen is dead. Why would they bother to resurrect old history?' She asked the question but already knew the answer. She saw it in the glint of triumph in his night-black eyes.

'I have connections with the media. I can make sure they do.' He shrugged, as though destroying a man's reputation was nothing to him.

For a moment Beth was speechless and simply stared at him. 'You would actually ruin Clive Hampton, a man respected by all who know him, simply because you think I am a criminal low-life after your brother and his money?'

'I don't have to think. I *know* you are an ex-con, and I *know* you used your considerable charms to get young Bewick under your spell. Now you are doing the same with Tony. He is infatuated by you. As for the money... I can't be certain. But I do know Helen left you a house and a nice chunk of money. Maybe your talent for ensnaring men extends to females too.' He shrugged his shoulders 'Not my business. But Tony is. I stopped you once and I will again.'

He was so wrong that Beth couldn't help but smile. 'You make me sound like the Wicked Witch of the West,' she quipped.

Dante's lips quirked at the corners, but he said nothing. She was too close to what he had been thinking earlier.

Beth wasn't surprised at his lack of response; the man had no sense of humour—although she thought she'd caught the hint of a smile just now. Anyway, what did it matter? Beth had very few options left open to her—if any.

She could tell him the truth about how she had been set up by Timothy Bewick and his partner in crime, James Hudson, and how the pair of them had lied at her trial. But what was the point? She had protested her innocence years ago and the jury had found her guilty. Cannavaro had made up his mind about her and nothing she said was going to change it now.

'Okay, you win,' Beth conceded. She needed to get away fast, because she was far too aware of him and was watching his lips for a hint of that smile she thought she'd seen… 'Originally I was just going on holiday to Devon, but now I will definitely stay there.'

Beth had often dreamed of living at the coast one day, and after discussing it with Clive it had been an easy decision to make. In the past two weeks plans for the garage conversion had been prepared and submitted to the council, and a contractor had been hired for the refurbishment of the house, but she saw no reason to enlighten Cannavaro. It would feed his monumental ego to let him think she had given in to his demands and he had won.

'I will have to come back for a few days to empty the apartment and retrieve the key Tony keeps for me. Then you and Tony will never see me again. Satisfied?' she demanded caustically.

'No…I would not say that,' Dante drawled softly.

'But you've got what you wanted,' Beth said, confused. Then she saw the way he was looking at her, his eyes roaming over her body with lazy masculine appraisal before moving to her face. His hand on her arm tightened and for a moment she couldn't move, couldn't break away from the eyes holding hers, blatantly showing his sexual desire. Suddenly she was afraid—not of him, but of herself, as the same heated desire held her in thrall and she could no longer ignore the way her body reacted to him.

'Not quite everything… You are an experienced, sophisticated woman and Clive Hampton risked his reputation for the privilege of having you in his bed.'

'That is disgusting. Clive—' Beth cut in, the heat between them instantly turning to anger.

'Don't bother denying it. You still see him and spend the occasional weekend at his home in Richmond. Who knows how many other men enjoy the pleasure of your body?'

Beth stared at him in furious disbelief. 'That is the most despicable, vile lie I have ever heard. I have never slept with Clive. He is a truly honorable man…and you really are a first-class bastard, aren't you?'

Even Dante could see Beth's outrage was genuine and that she was telling the truth—but then he had never really thought Clive was her lover. He had used Clive as a ploy to get his own way, and he felt slightly ashamed, because as well as the anger he also saw the hurt in her emerald eyes.

'Maybe I have been a bit harsh to you, but I am not interested in your other lovers—only Tony.'

Surprised he had actually admitted to being harsh, Beth looked up at him. 'Tony isn't my lover. He is a friend. I do have some,' she said dryly.

'I don't doubt it.' He lifted a finger to stroke her cheek and Beth sucked in a breath, her pulse going haywire. 'You are a lovely woman and even if I believed you and your story that you will stay in Devon, you've said yourself I can't follow you around for the rest of your life. What is to stop you calling Tony? He is my kid brother and, much as I love him, he is far too young to marry but impulsive enough to do just that. I can't take that chance. Which is why I want him to have complete freedom from you.'

At his mention of freedom Beth fought down the urge to scream. *What about my freedom?* The freedom he had taken away so ruthlessly once. She had no doubt that given the chance he would do so again.

As though sensing her frustration he let go of her and stepped back, running a distracted hand through his hair. 'It gives me no pleasure to fight with you, Beth. I know you have succeeded in turning your life around, but you are who you are. Try to see it from my point of view. If you had a young brother who wanted to marry a girl who was a convicted drug dealer, would you be happy about it?' he asked.

Put like that, Beth could see he had a point. 'No, I don't suppose so,' she said. Except in her case she was innocent of any crime.

'You must understand I simply want to protect Tony.' He flopped down on the sofa and glanced up at her. 'And that means getting you out of his life,' he said, a wry smile twisting his lips. 'I flew in from America this morning and have been travelling for hours. Maybe if you made me a coffee it would help me think clearly and hopefully between us we can find a mutual agreeable solution to our problem.'

For a man who did not want to appear harsh, he had an odd way of showing it, Beth thought, but did not say it. 'Fine, I'll make you a coffee. I could use one myself anyway.'

Relieved to escape from his overwhelming presence, she walked out of the room and into the kitchen, taking a few deep breaths to calm her still-racing pulse. Automatically she filled the coffee machine, her head in a whirl. What other kind of solution had he in mind? she wondered. Banishing her to Outer Mongolia, maybe?

She ought to pick up Binkie, walk straight out of the door and go on her way without ever speaking to Cannavaro again. If she only had herself to consider she would. But the thought of Clive stopped her. It was unthinkable that his reputation could be ruined because of her....

Finally Beth decided that all she could do was tell the truth, calmly and succinctly. Maybe Cannavaro would finally listen to her and accept that he had no need to worry about his brother. She would explain again about her friendship with Tony and the non-existent affair, and that she really was moving out anyway. In fact he could check with Steel and White that she had already handed in her notice. Surely that would convince him to believe her, and leave her alone?

Filling two cups with coffee, she placed them on a tray and carried it through to the living room. There was no sign of her guest. Then she heard the sound of curtains being drawn and realised where he was. She exited the room in a rush, to enter the bedroom next door. The curtains were half open and Cannavaro was standing in the bay window.

'What are you doing in here?' Beth demanded. She loved her bedroom and it felt far too intimate, seeing him standing there, all virile male, legs slightly apart, looking out of the window. She had never had a man in her bedroom before, and the picture he presented was very seductive.

It was large room with a high ceiling, and Beth had decorated it in mint green and ivory. The bed was centred on one wall, and on another were wardrobes and her dressing table. Next to the window was her pride and joy: an antique ladies' bureau.

'I am not familiar with this area or the parking.' He turned to look at her. 'So I thought I'd check my car. I only took delivery of it three weeks ago, and I have been abroad for two of them. I wanted to make sure it was okay.' He smiled ruefully. 'I have to confess my secret pleasure is cars. I can't resist buying them and changing them. At the moment I have a dozen, from vintage to the latest model. Ten at home in Italy and two here now.'

He gave her another smile and Beth was surprised that he actually seemed quite human when he was talking about his cars, and not the devil she had thought him.

'I would never have put you down as a petrolhead,' she said. 'You should meet the man who takes care of my car. He is a real fanatic.'

'Your car being the distinctive white one parked outside, I presume?'

'Yes…' Beth was very proud of her car, and had even given it a name. Given what Dante had just told her, his desire to check on his car sounded feasible.

'Very nice…'

He glanced out of the window and then back to her. 'Ah, you have the coffee.' Walking over, he took a cup from the tray and strode back to the window. 'The paintwork on your vehicle is highly original. Come and explain what it represents.'

Beth put the tray down on the dressing table and crossed to the window. Her eyes widened in appreciation at the sleek black Ferrari parked by the side of the road behind her modest Volkswagen, and she could understand perfectly why he was worried about his car. But standing so close to him like this was not a good idea, and she was suddenly very conscious of the close proximity of his body to hers. The quicker she told him about her car, the quicker she would get him out of her bedroom and her apartment. Which was what she wanted, wasn't it?

'The turquoise swirls along the side are meant to

represent the waves of the sea, and if you look really closely you can see the outline of a mermaid and the name "Jess" spelt out by the spray on the crest of a wave. A young man who used to be a graffiti artist with a penchant for stealing cars is now an apprentice mechanic at the local garage. He offered to personalise my car and we chose the design between us.'

'Is his name Jess?' Dante asked, frowning down at her.

'Good heavens, no. Jess was my best friend for a long time, but she's gone now.' As a child Beth had created an imaginary friend called Jess, and such had been her loneliness and desperation in prison she had remembered her again. Suddenly it hit her: how sad for a grown woman to remember such childish things. She sighed. It would seem she would never be truly free of her past.

Dante put the coffee cup down on the windowsill and stepped closer. 'I'm sorry if I have revived sad memories for you, Beth. Contrary to what you think, I do not want to cause you any harm. I simply want you out of Tony's life. He is far too young to be thinking of marriage.'

She looked up into his dark eyes. They were no longer hard and cruel, but gleaming with a warmth that seemed genuine. But she had been fooled by him before, she remembered, and thought again of her decision to explain her situation to him fully.

'From what I know of Tony he is perfectly able to look after himself—though he and Mike do tend to borrow milk, sugar, food…you name it. But, hey, what are friends for?' She shrugged. 'And you are totally wrong. Tony has no desire to marry me or any woman.

He has said so often enough. The only reason he made that comment about wanting to be my fiancé was to get one over on you.'

She looked squarely at him.

'Apparently you are a noted connoisseur of women, and Tony thought that with me on his arm his status would increase a hundred percent in your eyes. It was a joke. He was teasing you because he thinks you are far too serious. In a rash moment I decided to go along with him. Misguidedly, as it has turned out, or you would not be here,' she said wryly. 'And I certainly do not want to marry Tony or any man. I value my independence far too much to risk losing it again. As for money—I have enough of my own, and I really am moving out of here. If you don't believe me you can call Steel and White. They will tell you I resigned five days ago.'

'That won't be necessary, Beth. I believe you. Tony has always been a bit of a joker. You are a beautiful woman. Any man would want you in his bed—I know I would. Two consenting adults…there is nothing wrong with that…but Tony is not like you and I. He is still idealistic enough to equate sex with love. But I realise I may have overdone the protective older brother bit and been a little hard on you.'

Stunned that he believed what she'd said, and even more stunned by his comment that he wanted her and classed her in the 'consenting adults' department, Beth lifted her eyes to his. What she saw in the glittering depths of his eyes made her drag in a trembling breath before continuing. 'That must be a first. You never believed a word I said before.'

'It is not solely a woman's prerogative to change her mind.' He gave her a twisted smile. 'Since meeting you again I've realised I may have misjudged you. I admire the fact you have managed to turn your life around. You are an incredible woman,' he said, and, dipping his head, he brushed her lips with his.

CHAPTER FOUR

BETH STARED AT HIM, her tongue involuntarily tracing her lips, absorbing the taste of him. Heated colour stained her cheeks as she struggled to make sense of her reaction. His kiss had made her forget he was her enemy, the man who had ruined her life.

'You really do believe me?' she murmured.

'I said so. But that does not solve my problem.'

'Problem?' Beth licked her tingling lips; she was losing the plot, she thought. She had told him the truth and he had believed her.

'Don't look at me like that, Beth,' Dante said huskily, having followed the path of her pink tongue as it caressed her lip. 'Just listen to me. There is no need for you to leave your job unless you really want to. I will never say anything to anyone about your name-change or Clive. But I won't be satisfied until you have moved out of this apartment and away from Tony. With that in mind I will find you another apartment. You will not lose out in the monetary sense at all, I can assure you.'

Still struggling to control the trembling his kiss had evoked, it took a long moment for Beth to let the import of his words sink into her fuddled mind. Then she recalled exactly what he had said, and just how clever he was with words, and realised he didn't really believe her at all. Nothing had changed....

As for his offer of an apartment and the mention of money—with his reputation, and given that he'd said he wanted her and had kissed her—she had to wonder if he expected her to come with the apartment too....

Beth glanced up at him, big and strong—all raw sexuality—and wondered whether she would be that averse to the idea if he *did* mean it. If she was brutally honest, she had to admit that she probably wouldn't be. She was still hot from his kiss, and looking at him simply increased the heat... But she was not cut out to be any man's mistress. She had suffered more than most for her freedom, and she was never giving it up again for anyone.

She could not help thinking that Dante Cannavaro had haunted her dreams for long enough. But he thought her guilty of just about every sin in the book, and maybe at twenty-seven it was finally time she tasted those sins. And who better to do it with than the man before her? Exorcise him from her head, her life, for good...?

At least it would show him that she wasn't the *femme fatale* he had accused her of being, with a string of lovers in her wake. It might even do him some good—show him he wasn't infallible—and maybe he would not be so quick to judge others, she reasoned. Though, being honest, she knew it wasn't just reason driving her. She wanted him in a physical way she had never felt for any man in her life.

'That's an idea,' she said slowly, her mind made up. She never flirted with men, but there was always a first time for everything. She half closed her eyes to shut out the disturbing darkness of his handsome face, then, drawing in a shaky breath, deliberately glanced up at him through the thick veil of her lashes and ran the tip of her tongue over her lips. 'I will certainly consider it.' She saw his eyes glitter with triumph before darkening with a different emotion that brought an answering response in hers.

'Good,' he growled as his hand snaked round her waist, his long fingers splaying across the naked band of skin. She shivered at his touch. 'I knew you would see sense, Beth.' And as he spoke the last word he pulled her gently against his long body and brought his mouth down on hers again.

This wasn't sense, Beth thought, and panicked for a second. But with the lazy heat of the summer afternoon filling the shadowed confines of her bedroom her pulse quickened and her body turned hot and sensitive beneath her clothes. Willingly her lips parted to the slow penetration of his tongue, stroking and exciting all her senses. She ignored the voice in her head that tried to warn her that this was wrong on so many levels. Her slender body melted against him, the long, passionate, drugging kiss driving every sane thought from her head.

Her eyes were tightly shut, and she was conscious of the swelling fullness of her breasts against his broad chest and the damp moistness between her thighs. She was floating blindly on a sea of erotic sensations she had never knew existed before. Involuntarily her hands grasped his arms. She could feel his body heat through the fine silk of his shirt as her fingers traced the contours of muscular biceps and moved up to curve over his broad shoulders. She had felt an instant affinity with Dante the very first time she had seen him and had never understood why, but now she did—with every atom of her being.

When he pulled his head back she was clinging to him, her hands tight against his neck, her face uplifted. Her emerald eyes slowly opened and her soft lips parted, swollen with passion.

'*Dio*! You are beautiful,' he groaned, one hand lifting to sweep a few strands of her hair from her brow. Long fingers stroked the delicate arch of one eyebrow and the curve of her cheek before finally moving to the outline of her lush lips. 'So beautiful,' he repeated, his head lowering.

His kiss and the almost feverish movements of his hand on her back, her hips, and down her thighs to her bare legs, sent a white-hot flame of passion through her, consuming them both. Her lips clung hungrily to his, her hands stealing up his neck until they buried themselves in his black hair, twining among the thick strands.

Without removing his lips from hers he lifted her and carried her to the bed. Lowering her onto it, he slid down beside her. She felt the pressure of his great body against her, his kiss burning her lips as though he could not bring himself to stop.

'Wait…' Beth murmured against his mouth, her heart thudding like a jackhammer. The sensations he was arousing were so overwhelming she was having second thoughts—but not for long. Her body seemed to have a will of its own and she was aching for more.

'Why wait?' Dante said hoarsely, lifting his head to stare down at her. 'I've wanted you from the moment I saw you and I believe you feel the same.' His eyes burned black. 'Tell me it is so.'

She saw the dark stain of desire in his face and knew it was reflected in her own as he shrugged off his shirt. She felt her throat tighten, and knew she could not deny him—didn't want to. 'Oh, yes…' she said breathlessly, totally enthralled by the sight of his broad muscular chest, the golden skin and the light tracing of black curling body hair. Eagerly, like a child, she reached out to touch him, her fingers stroking over his chest in a caress.

He reared back. 'In a moment you can touch me everywhere,' he said huskily, and reached for her.

With the deftness of long experience he removed her clothes, and the rest of his, and leant over her.

She had never seen a totally naked man in the flesh before, and Dante was magnificent—from his broad shoulders down over his flat stomach. Her eyes widened at his powerful erection; it was vaguely frightening, but fascinating, and she was totally mesmerised by the beauty of his big golden body. Beth didn't have time to be embarrassed by her own nudity or the aroused male scent of him. The hard-packed muscular length of him was a potent aphrodisiac and excitement exploded inside her. *So this is what sex is about,* she thought, and then stopped thinking altogether.

His lips and hands were all over her, touching her, kissing her throat and her shoulders. His fingers caressed her and the incredible sensations searing through her obliterated everything except this moment. His mouth found her breasts, and the hot, seductive suckling and nipping went on and on until she was mindless, her hand grasping the back of his head to hold him there.

He moved to kiss her mouth again and their tongues duelled in the thrust and parry of passion. She reached around his broad back, her slender fingers stroking over his satin-smooth skin, her fingertips tracing the length of his spine before trailing over the hard curve of his buttocks. She trembled as he leant back and stared down at her with molten black eyes, his strong hands shaping her breasts, the indentation of her waist and her hips, before parting her legs.

'You *are* a redhead,' he said huskily, his palm cupping her feminine mound.

She gasped as his long fingers delved into the hot, wet warmth, a finger pressing on the nub of feminine nerves, and she shuddered uncontrollably.

'You like that,' Dante growled, his eyes burning into hers, and he bent his head to lick the tip of one breast while his fingers continued their skilful torment.

She could not speak, she could barely breathe as a sensual storm spread like wildfire to the core of her. She reached out to him, her hand roaming over his massive chest, her nails grazing a hard male nipple, and felt him shudder. Her hand slid lower to his rock-hard erection, touching and exploring him intimately. She wanted him with a passion and a hunger she had never felt before in her life.

His breath caught audibly in the back of his throat. 'Beth…' he growled, and grasped her wrist to pin her hand to the bed. 'You are sure you want this?' He lowered his dark head and kissed her breasts and her mouth again, whispering her name between kisses while his fingers renewed their torment at the very centre of her femininity, driving her into a vortex of sensual pleasure she had never even imagined existed.

'Yes,' Beth whimpered, as her body bucked and writhed beneath him. The incredible seductiveness of his mouth and his hands and the heat of his powerful body, sweat-slicked and taut against her flesh, was driving her insane. Frantically she ran her hands over his shoulders, her nails digging into his broad back, lost to everything but Dante.

He eased back her thighs and rose over her. He was there, where she ached with need for him, probing gently, then thrusting harder, and suddenly her body tensed, torn by a sharp pain.

He stopped, staring down at her with shock widening his smouldering black eyes. 'No!' he growled, his face taut with passion.

Instinctively she locked her long legs around his waist and with a low groan he moved again slightly, slowly stretching her to accept him. Miraculously the pain was gone, replaced with unimaginable pleasure as he gradually thrust deeper and deeper.

His heart thudded against her as she felt the exquisite tension tighten and grow, until she thought she could not bear it any more, and finally she fell shuddering into a kaleidoscopic world of a myriad sensations and ultimate satisfaction, taking him with her.

Eyes closed, Beth was conscious of every muscle, sinew and nerve of her body in a new way—a wonderful, awesome way that there were no words invented to explain. Euphoric and completely at one with Dante, she relished his heavy naked body over hers, his head resting on her shoulder, the rasping sound of his breath and the thundering beat of his heart against hers gradually slowing.

When he moved to roll onto his back Beth opened her eyes to see him lean up on one elbow and look down at her. Her lips parted in a wide smile, her green eyes shining like emeralds in her flushed face.

'Beth—Jane—whatever your name is, you are an exquisitely desirable woman and one hell of a surprise,' he said, but did not smile back.

Beth's smile faded a little as she stared at his hard, handsome face, not sure if he meant that as a compliment. He was frowning, and she saw the glint of anger in his night-black eyes. Why was he angry?

'Dante?' She said his name questioningly.

'Finally you say my name. It comes a little late after what we have just done, don't you think?'

Beth heard the hint of mockery in his tone and was chilled by it—but then what had she expected? Avowals of love? Never in a million years. With her euphoria fading fast, she came back to reality. At the barbecue he had told her they had a mutual sexual attraction but that it could not be acted upon.

Now he was no longer engaged and that was no longer the case. It was sex—just sex. Something he engaged in on a regular basis with a variety of women. The fact it was new to Beth meant nothing. It was still just sex. The reason she was here now was to get him out of her head once and for all. Not the best idea she had ever had, but she had proved a point.

'You know what they say—better late than never,' she forced herself to say lightly. 'And after this I don't think I'll have to say your name much more.' With her body still throbbing, she put on the act of her life. 'Your problem is solved. Now you know you were wrong about me. I have never had sex with Tony or any man.' Rolling away from him, she slid her legs over the side of the bed and stood up. She glanced down at him to add, 'And after this I probably never will again—once was enough.'

Unconscious of her naked state, she gathered up her clothes and put them back on without looking at Dante again.

The silence between them was interrupted by the doorbell ringing.

'Don't answer,' Dante commanded.

Beth ignored him and, slipping her feet into her sandals, ran her hands through her hair to sweep it back behind her ears as she walked out of the bedroom. It would probably be a salesman, she thought. But she found that she was wrong. Before she got to the front door she heard a key turn in the lock and Tony walked in.

'Beth—I thought you would be long gone by now. I saw your car outside and wondered what had happened to you.'

'I got delayed by Binkie,' she replied, and conveniently the cat chose that moment to stroll into the hall and wrap himself around her ankles. 'Then I had an unexpected—'

But her weak explanation was cut off by another voice.

'Tony—nice to see you. I wondered when you'd be back.'

Beth tensed and glanced back, to see Dante leaning casually against the doorjamb of the bedroom wearing his trousers with his shirt half buttoned and his black hair curling damply on his broad brow. She cringed with embarrassment.

'Dante!' Tony frowned. 'What are you doing here?'

'I called to see you to show you my new Ferrari and knocked on the wrong front door. Beth answered and we had a coffee and a chat.' He nodded towards the bedroom. 'I was just looking through the front window to check my car was still there.'

Beth was surprised at his glib answer, but also relieved.

'Oh, yes!' Tony drawled. 'I saw the car. It's in my usual parking spot.' His blue eyes flicked suspiciously between Beth and Dante, and finally settled on Beth. 'Is he right, Beth? I thought you were leaving at one? It's five o'clock now. That is a heck of a lot of cups of coffee.'

Bending down, Beth picked up Binkie and hugged him to her chest, her mind spinning. The truth was always the best option—or some of it, she decided. 'I was supposed to be leaving at one, but it was after three before I managed to get Binkie in his carrier for the third time. The doorbell rang and I forgot to fasten it before I answered the door. Dante came in, tripped over the carrier, and Binkie shot out again—causing Dante to stumble and fall flat on the floor. It was quite a crash. He is a big man.'

She saw Tony smile.

'You fell over her cat?'

'Yes,' Dante said dryly, not in the least amused.

'Now, *that* I would have liked to have seen.' Tony chuckled. 'I'm surprised Beth didn't kick you out there and then for harming Binkie. She loves that cat.'

'Tony! Poor Dante was really winded,' Beth chipped in. 'Though I did consider it.' It gave her some satisfaction to see Dante discomfited for a change.

'Well, it's not surprising he was winded. He *is* a lot older than you and I, Beth.'

Beth saw the sparkle of devilment in Tony's eyes

and smiled at his quip about his brother's age. It was either that or cry—and Cannavaro had caused enough tears in her life already. She wasn't about to shed a single one more.

'True...' she said, holding the smile. 'But I have been delayed long enough. If I want to get there by dark you two will have to go now. I'm going to put Binkie into his carrier and we can finally leave.'

'Okay,' Tony agreed, then added, 'I can see you are in a hurry, and I can only apologise for my brother delaying you.' He grinned at her. 'Shall I still check on your apartment until you get back?'

'Yes, of course.' Beth couldn't help smiling. Tony was an incorrigible but very likable young man—the exact opposite of his hard-faced, cynically arrogant brother... She realised she was going to miss Tony and Mike. Their happy-go-lucky attitude to life had been a tonic for her. But it was for the best that she was leaving.

'You heard, bro. Beth wants us out—and in case you've forgotten I'll see you later at the parents' anniversary party.' He turned towards the door, and then turned back. 'Oh, by the way, Dante—don't forget your shoes. The barefoot look really doesn't suit you....' he said, and walked out.

'So once was enough, hmm?' Dante drawled as the front door shut.

Still holding the cat, Beth stared at Dante as though she had never seen him before. 'More than enough,' she intoned icily.

'If you had told me I was your first I would have been more careful.'

'You've got to be joking. You never believe a word I say—though you pretend to when it suits you.'

'Maybe. But I'm curious, Beth. Why did you hang on to your virginity for so long? No, don't bother answering. I know...' he said without pause. 'You told me Tony was just teasing when he said he wanted you to be his fiancée, but I think it was you that was doing the teasing. That is how you operate. You get pleasure from leading young men on and denying them what they want until they're crazy about you and will do anything you say. First Timothy Bewick and now Tony. There have probably been many more,' he declared cynically.

He could not have said anything more likely to enrage Beth and, putting Binkie down, she moved towards him, her anger so livid her cheeks were scarlet with it. She registered the arrogant stance of his big body, his hands tucked easily into the pockets of his trousers. He appeared every inch the sophisticated lawyer, with his confident summing-up of the situation, and it was not surprising the jury in her case had believed every word he said.

Even half dressed he exuded an aura of power, conviction and a sheer masculine magnetism that was almost impossible to ignore. It was inherent in his every move, every gesture, but this time Beth was immune to his lethal appeal. She fought down the urge to rant and rave at him and instead stopped a few inches in front of him, deliberately raising her gaze to his hard face, her green eyes contemptuous.

'No. But if that is what you want to think to salve your conscience, be my guest. We both know that at my trial, when you painted me as some *femme fatale* who slept with young men to control them, the real liar was you.' She dropped each word slowly and precisely into the tense silence. 'You try living with that, as I have for the last eight years. You might actually discover a conscience, though I doubt it. Your sort never does.' Disgust was evident in her tone. 'As for Tony—you saw for yourself we are just good friends. But then I doubt a man like you *has* any friends.'

Dante shrugged and, taking his hand from the pocket of his pants, ran one long finger down her burning cheek to tilt her chin up and study her flushed and furious face.

'You are overwrought, and in a way I don't blame you. I am much older, more experienced than the boys you usually play with, and you got more than you bargained for. But you were with me all the way, so don't try to pretend otherwise. You are only fooling yourself. I have never known a more eager lover. And I did not lie in court. As a lawyer I simply implied—there is a difference.'

Beth shook her head, unable to deny what he said, and stepped away from him. 'Yes, you are right, of course. The difference in my case was freedom or a three-year sentence,' she said caustically. 'Now, if that is all, for about the tenth time of asking, will you get out of here? I never want to see you again.'

'The feeling is mutual. You can rest assured I will never be back.'

'At last a mutually acceptable solution. We have a deal. We will stay far away from each other—a continent would be good,' she sniped, and walked into the kitchen, battling to contain the pain and anger he had revived in her.

She hated him, and she must never forget it again. She had heard it said that love and hate were different sides of the same coin, but she could not let herself think that way—could not let herself think of the pleasure his body had given her. It was just sex, she told herself again, and her overreaction was probably because she had waited so long to experience it.

Dante resisted the urge to follow Beth. Finding his shoes, he put them on and returned to the living room to retrieve his jacket. He had done what he'd set out to do. Beth was moving out, Tony would be free of her influence and that was what Dante had wanted... So why did he feel like the lowest of the low? Probably because Beth had hit a nerve with her crack about his performance in court. She had done him no favours with her crack about his performance in bed, either....

Oddly, he felt guilty on both counts...and it was not an emotion he was familiar with. But then he was not a man prone to emotions of any sort. It would pass.

Dante got in his car and drove away without a backward glance. Beth was a stunning woman, but not for him. She was not wife material, and she was far too dangerous to his peace of mind to be his mistress.

Although in a way he could not help admiring her. She had managed to change her life very successfully and perfectly legally, he thought as he skilfully manoeuvred the car through the rush-hour traffic. Jane—or Beth—or whatever her real name was had grown into one beautiful, intelligent, feisty woman whom he suspected could hold her own with either man or woman. She had certainly given as good as she'd got from *him*.

He was still smarting from her *once was enough* comment—not that he believed her. Beth was the most naturally sensual woman he had ever met, and had reacted to his lightest touch and caress. She had instinctively known how to return the pleasure too. She had been fire and light in his arms, eager to take everything he could give her, and he could still feel the sting of her nails on his back. He couldn't remember ever having lost control with a lover the way he had with Beth, and the scent and feel of her luscious body beneath him had blown his mind. His body stirred again now at the thought of her.

Suddenly another thought hit him like a thunderbolt. He had forgotten protection. How could he have been so careless?

And in the next second Dante Cannavaro did the unthinkable—for him—and compounded his carelessness by rear-ending the pickup truck in front of him, having not noticed the traffic had stopped for a red light.

He reversed out from under the flatbed of the truck—to the further detriment of his Ferrari—and pulled up to exchange details with the driver of the pickup. Dante loved his cars, and he had never so much as dented one in his life until he'd met Beth Lazenby. Maybe she was a witch and had put a hex on him, he thought, stifling a groan as he surveyed the battered bonnet of his new Ferrari.

He debated going back to tell Beth about his mistake in forgetting to use protection, then, coming to his senses, thought better of it. Given the type of woman he knew Beth to be, he was pretty sure that if his mistake resulted in a pregnancy she would contact him with dollar signs in her eyes.

CHAPTER FIVE

BETH OPENED HER EYES to see the early-morning rays of
the sun flooding the bedroom and stretched lazily. She
looked across at the large windows that folded back to
open almost the whole room to the balcony and the sea
beyond and sighed contentedly. She loved this house,
she thought, a soft smile curling her lips as she glanced
around the master bedroom.

The cream-and-blue flower-sprigged wallpaper with
matching curtains and bedlinen were a little faded now,
as the master suite with bathroom and dressing room
had been refurbished to Helen's taste when she had been
released from prison. Beth never wanted to change it
as the room reminded her of her friend and gave her a
feeling of serenity. It was her safe haven from the rest
of the world.

A builder and decorator had completed the refurbishment of the rest of the house last week. The other
three bedrooms on this floor had en-suite bathrooms
now, plus the two bedrooms on the top floor. The house
had never looked better, and the rental potential had increased significantly. Beth was quite happy with what
she had achieved.

Sliding her legs over the side of the bed, she stood

up and walked into the dressing room, collecting briefs and an exotically printed slip dress, and then entered the bathroom.

Yesterday she had received notice that her plans to convert the roof space of the garage into a two-bedroomed apartment had been passed. The builder was due to start in three weeks' time.

With a sense of satisfaction she stepped into the shower and turned on the water. She had slept without dreaming of Dante Cannavaro or thinking of him the minute she woke up for a couple of weeks now, and her plan to exorcise him from her mind by having sex with him seemed to be working.

She had definitely made the right decision. She loved her new life—the freedom to work when she wanted to or walk out of the door and breathe the fresh sea air or take a swim and go surfing if the mood struck her. She had even acquired a slight tan, and for the first time in ages no longer felt she had to be careful or fearful of the past coming back to haunt her. She was her own woman, mistress of her own destiny, and Cannavaro had been shoved back into the box he had occupied for the last few years and was not worth thinking about.

She slipped on her briefs and dress and ran a brush through the tangled mass of her hair. Down here she never bothered with a hairdryer or the electric straightening tongs that had been a part of her daily routine in London in order to present a sleek, professional image. Much as she had liked her old job, Beth had not really enjoyed living in London. But she had fulfilled Helen's wish and become a success. Now she was out of the rat race and hoping to be equally as successful in her new venture.

She had certainly made a good start, she thought happily. She already had a few bookings for next year, by which time the garage apartment would certainly be ready. She would have to work two days a week in the house when it was rented out, but that was no problem—and much preferable to working all week in an office.

An hour later, having fed Binkie and with a cup of tea and two slices of French toast in her tummy, Beth was ready to face the day. Janet was coming over at two with her daughter, and they were driving into town to shop before returning to the house for dinner.

Janet's father had been employed on a part-time basis here for years, as gardener and caretaker, and Beth had met Janet the first time she'd visited. Now she considered her a friend. Janet had married young and had a four-year-old daughter called Annie. Tragically, her soldier husband had been killed in Afghanistan last year, and after his death Janet was back living with her parents. Sometimes Janet and Annie stayed with Beth for a night or two, and it suited them both.

Carrying her second cup of tea and her sunglasses, Beth opened the front door onto the long terrace that ran the length of the cottage, with steps down to the garden path and the road, with the beach and sea beyond. She sat down on one of the eight captain's chairs and looked out over the bay. The sea was as calm as a millpond.

Blinded by the glare of the sun on the water for a moment, she blinked and put on her sunglasses—then blinked again as the roar of a car split the silence.

A big black Bentley...

She watched as the luxury car stopped in front of her gate and with a sinking heart recognised the driver as he opened the door and got out. Her heart sank further at the sight of Dante Cannavaro, standing surveying the bay.

His black hair gleamed like polished jet in the sunlight. Aviator sunglasses hid his eyes, but nothing could detract from the golden chiselled perfection of his features. His great body was clad in a black polo shirt open at the neck, and hip-hugging black jeans that clung to his muscular thighs and long legs like a second skin. He was strikingly attractive. Simply looking at the man was enough to make most women go weak at the knees.

Beth was glad she was sitting down, because her plan to rid him from her mind—which only earlier she had thought was working—had obviously not worked after all. Why, oh, why, she wondered despairingly, after twenty-seven years of hardly being aware of the sexual side of her nature, had she only got to *see* Dante Cannavaro for her pulse to race and her temperature to soar?

Filled with self-loathing at her reaction, she lifted her cup and took a drink of tea, trying to ignore him. She did not know what had brought him here and she was not going to ask. He certainly wasn't a typical daytripper. As a super-rich, sophisticated international lawyer, a luxury resort somewhere exotic was surely more his style.

Looking around, Dante was surprised by the beauty of the cove—and more so by the house. He had pictured some quaint old cottage as he had driven over the headland and down the cliff road to the harbour. He had called at the local pub to ask directions to the cottage of Miss Lazenby, and had been treated to a glowing tribute to Beth by the landlord. He had also been informed that the cottage was the best holiday rental for miles around, and a great little earner for Beth, and then told how to find the place. Dante had driven to almost the opposite end of the bay, as per instructions, and had been surprised.

The 'cottage' was a large white-rendered double-fronted house, with a wide terrace that ran the width of the building. Another balcony ran the length of the first floor, and in the roof was a third, complete with a flagpole and a telescope fixed to the glass guardrail. All the windows were virtually walls of glass that opened onto the respective terraces. It was in a magnificent position, looking straight out to sea, and set in about an acre of garden with a stone wall surrounding it. The road that ran between the house and the beach came to a dead end a few hundred yards farther on at the foot of the cliffs in a small car park.

Turning, Dante shook his head in amazement. Somehow he could not see the elegant redhead, the professional big-city accountant, settling down in a place that looked as if time had forgotten it. But then he had trouble seeing Beth as anything but naked beneath him, and knowing the mistake he had made was driving him crazy.

As for Faith Cove—if it had more than a thousand residents he'd be surprised.

Carved in the stone column of the house's entrance gate was 'The Sail Loft' and, appropriately, a sailing dinghy was parked on the hard standing to one side of the house. A rack for surfboards with two in evidence stood beside it. On the other side was a long drive that led to a large garage at the rear of the property. The doors were open and her very distinctive Volkswagen was visible.

He was impressed. The land alone, situated as it was with spectacular views of the bay, had to be worth a good deal of money, Dante realised, never mind the house.

He tensed as he caught sight of Beth, sitting on the terrace, and surprisingly felt a moment of doubt. Ironically, he had arranged his schedule to have the month of September free to get married. Instead he had spent the first few days catching up on estate business and then supposedly relaxing. His housekeeper, Sophie, had made relaxing difficult, though. She was another woman who had already 'bought the hat' for the wedding that never was, and she'd spent most of her time giving him dire warnings that if he didn't marry soon he would be lucky to see his children grow up. It was hard to argue with a woman who had changed his nappy as a child, and finally he had given up and gone to Rome where he'd accepted a new case. He'd had a couple of dinner dates with an old flame, determined to get on with his life, but it hadn't helped....

Far from forgetting Beth Lazenby, as he'd intended, he had found she'd occupied his thoughts for the last eight weeks to the point of distracting him from his work—not something that had ever happened to him before. Women had their place in his life—usually his bed. But never in his head...

He had reread the investigator's report on Beth and realised that Jane Mason had lost her parents only twelve months before her trial. He was surprised that her lawyer, Miss Sims, had not brought that fact up in court. Any good defence lawyer would have used the death of her parents as part of a character profile—troubled young lady who had lost her parents recently....

But then Miss Sims had not been a good lawyer. She had barely challenged anything he had said, and had stopped him on the way out to congratulate him, he recalled. Suddenly Dante found himself making excuses for Beth. Had he been too harsh with her? Alone in the world, she might easily have gone off the rails with grief... Not that it mattered. The evidence had been solid and the jury had found her guilty, he reminded himself. But he was a man always supremely confident in his decisions and he never second-guessed himself. The fact that Beth was making him do just that shocked him rigid. It had to stop.

Finally, yesterday morning, after a frustrating weekend, he had rationalised that there was nothing to be gained by waiting with the sword of Damocles hanging over his head. He needed to make sure Beth was definitely not pregnant before he got involved with another woman. His legal team could take care of work. His presence wasn't essential until a client meeting on Wednesday.

His decision made, he'd taken a flight to London. He'd called Tony, pretty sure he would know where Beth was, but had got no reply. Then he'd called at her old apartment on the off-chance that she had lied about everything and was still living there. Only to be faced by a young man who said he had no idea where the last tenant had gone.

Finally he'd caught up with Tony late afternoon and discovered Beth had been gone for weeks and had set up in business for herself. But as her loyal friend Tony had refused to give Dante her phone number or her address at Beth's specific request.

After checking the investigator's report again he had found the address of her cottage and set off at the crack of dawn to drive here, confront her, and dismiss doubt and the woman from his life once and for all and get back to normal.

At least that was what he'd told himself. But now, as he looked at her exquisite profile and the contrast of her red hair against the ever-so-slightly sun-kissed skin of her bare shoulders, a basic, more earthy desire began to heat his blood.

Beth heard the click of the gate and glanced down to see Dante stalk up the path and leap up the steps to come and stand towering over her. He became a big black shadow against the sun and memories of the past came rushing back. Involuntarily she shivered. Whether it was because of the old dreams or the sex or both, she wasn't sure. All she was sure of was that his physical presence disturbed her far too much for her peace of mind.

'Good morning, Beth. Lovely place you have here—though a little hard to find. I've been driving since six and could join you in a cup of coffee,' he declared, glancing at the cup in her hand as he sank down onto another captain's chair.

'It's not coffee, it's tea. And if you go back the way you came there is a small café next to the shop on the harbour. Try there,' Beth suggested bluntly. Dante Cannavaro had said he would leave her alone. He had some nerve, turning up here.

'Oh, come on, Beth. That's not very hospitable after

all we have been to each other....' he drawled, and removed his sunglasses.

She saw humour in his dark eyes, and more as he let his gaze roam over her, lingering on the swell of her breasts beneath the cotton of her dress with undisguised male lust.

'No way,' she snapped, feeling uncomfortably warm. 'You agreed we would never meet again. I've kept my side of the deal, so what's your excuse for turning up here and breaking it?' she demanded.

'Extenuating circumstances—and strictly speaking you're wrong. I never actually agreed to stay out of your life, only never to reveal...' He paused, then continued, 'My inside knowledge of you.'

Beth felt her eyes widen and the colour rise in her face at his choice of words, as she was sure he had meant it to. Without thought, she swung her hand in a swift arc to slap his face, but he caught her wrist.

'Now, Beth, that is no way to greet an old friend,' he drawled in a deadly low tone, and lowered her arm down to her thigh.

She tugged her wrist free but had more sense than to try to hit him again.

'I had a pretty tough job finding you again.'

'You shouldn't have bothered. You are not welcome here,' Beth said bluntly. Leaning forward, before she could stop him, he flicked off her sunglasses and his dark eyes clashed with her angry green.

'That's better, Beth. I want to see your reaction when I tell you the reason I am here.'

Beth went very still, her face expressionless, when really she was so mad she wanted to throttle him. But she realised his being here and his last comment sounded like a threat. She looked out to sea for a long moment to regain her composure and reviewed every one of her past encounters with him in her mind. She came to a conclusion. She slowly turned her head to glance up at his harsh, handsome features through the fine curtain of her lashes.

'There is nothing that you can do or say to me that is worse than you have done already,' she said with deliberate softness.

Amazingly, dark colour washed up his face and he drew back, his mouth twisting. 'I sincerely hope not,' he said cryptically, a frown creasing his broad brow.

Beth had the odd notion he was not only embarrassed, but worried.

'But get me a coffee and I will tell you.'

His tone was hard and demanding again, and it set Beth's teeth on edge. For a moment there she had begun to think that Dante was almost human. Big mistake... and not one she intended to repeat.

'No,' she said defiantly. 'I remember what happened the last time you demanded coffee....' She glanced up and caught the gleam of desire in his dark eyes that the memory of their last meeting had evoked and felt an answering surge of heat spread through her body. Stupid thing to say.... She lowered her eyes to try to gather her wits. But focusing on the open neck of his polo shirt was not helping her....

'I did not invite you here, but obviously your investigator informed you I own this place,' she said in a voice that was not quite steady. She ploughed on regardless. 'I do not want you here. I have absolutely no interest in a single word you say. Is that clear enough for you?'

'Yes, but it might be difficult,' Dante said, looking down at Beth.

He felt a strange tightening in his chest as he did so. It was incredible how young, how innocent she looked, with her hair washed and left to dry in surprisingly silken waves. She wore no make-up, and was wearing a simple, brightly patterned summer dress that skimmed over her breasts and slender body. He noticed she wasn't wearing a bra and stiffened, remembering the full firmness of her breasts and the erotic taste of her nipples in his mouth. He also remembered that thanks to him she was not physically innocent anymore—and, of course, the real reason he was here.

His mouth tightened grimly. He was angry for letting her obvious attributes get to him and, straightening up, dismissed the wayward thoughts from his mind, determined to get this over with quickly.

'Look at me, Beth,' he demanded, and watched her raise her head, her expression guarded. 'This is a serious matter. Are you on the pill?'

'No, of course not,' she said without thinking.

'In that case we might have a problem. It may have escaped your attention, but I did not use protection when we had sex. You could be pregnant, and if you are I need to make suitable arrangements.'

'What?' Beth cried, appalled, as the true reason for Dante being here registered in her mind. It had never occurred to her that she might get pregnant—how stupid was that? Would she never learn? Was she sentenced to go through life being made a fool of by this man? she wondered. 'You didn't use…?' Of course he hadn't. She hadn't noticed, but he had just said so, and she suddenly had a hysterical desire to laugh.

'No. It was my fault and I take full responsibility. I am prepared to take care of everything, all the monetary aspects, should the worst circumstance arise.'

'You are unbelievable! You sound like a lawyer even when you drop a bombshell like that on me!' Beth exclaimed, thinking the only thing that would be arising was her stomach if his suspicion was true. Because no way would she take a penny from Dante Cannavaro under *any* circumstance.

'What can I say? I am what I am?' He shrugged negligently.

Ignoring him, Beth swiftly thought back over the eight weeks she had been here and realised she had been so busy planning and working she hadn't noticed she had missed her period. Suddenly Dante's fear was a very real possibility. Her recent aversion to coffee, which Janet had remarked on when Beth had switched to drinking tea, now held a different connotation. But she hadn't been sick—well, not physically. Though she *had* felt nauseous and had blamed it on the pervasive smell of the decorator's paint that had filled the house for weeks.

The little colour she had leached from her face. The very idea filled her with horror; not the thought of a baby—she would love to have a child of her own, someone to love unconditionally—but with Dante Cannavaro as its father! To be connected to him for years by a child didn't bear thinking about....

Then another even more disturbing thought occurred to Beth. What exactly was he offering to pay for—take care of?

She looked at him with dislike. 'By "monetary aspects" do you mean you will pay for an abortion if I am pregnant?' she asked.

'Is that what you want?' he prompted, his hard face expressionless.

'No, never,' she said instinctively.

'Good, because if that *was* what you wanted I would have done everything in my power to convince you otherwise. So, are you pregnant or not?'

She turned her head to stare out to sea again, suddenly very afraid. Dante was a powerful, clever man, and very persuasive—as she knew to her cost. If she *was* pregnant, and if she had a healthy baby and he decided to claim custody, where would that leave her? She was probably worrying unnecessarily, but Dante was a lawyer, and she had no doubt he was ruthless enough to use her past history against her in court. What chance would she have of keeping the baby herself?

Beth looked back at Dante and considered lying. She had loved her adoptive parents, and had no idea who her biological parents were. All she knew was that as a baby she had been left in a sports bag in the emergency department of a hospital. Her mother had never been found. With her own lack of a true identity she knew instinctively that there was no way she could refuse her own child the right to know its father.

'I don't know. It's too early to tell,' she said calmly. It wasn't really a lie, there could be other reasons why she was late, but offhand she could not think of one.

'Don't be ridiculous.'

He rose to his full intimidating height and Beth swallowed hard.

'You are an intelligent, adult woman—you must know if you have missed menstruating.'

'I am not the ridiculous one here,' she shot back. 'I have some excuse, but for a man of your age and experience to forget protection is ridiculous.'

'Point taken.' Dante grimaced. 'But you still have not answered my question. Have you missed your period?'

'Maybe. I don't know. I'm not regular anyway,' Beth said, and immediately wished she had told an outright lie. But she had been so shocked at the thought of pregnancy, and Dante had been so blunt, she had not had time to think things through properly and had simply reacted.

'I don't have patience and I am a busy man. I need to know now, so I can rearrange my schedule if I have to without too much inconvenience. I have a meeting in Rome at midday tomorrow as it is. When I arrived in London yesterday I expected to find you there—not miles away in the middle of nowhere. You said there was a café? Come, I need a coffee.' He reached out a hand. 'And if there is a pharmacy we can get a pregnancy test at the same time and settle the matter now.'

Beth's mouth fell open. 'Are you crazy? I could never buy a pregnancy test in the chemist here. Everyone knows me and it would be around the village in a flash.'

'So we will go to the nearest town.'

Beth tried to argue with him. What man in his right mind went looking for a woman after what had been basically a one-night stand and demanded a pregnancy test? The nearest town was a forty-minute drive away, and she was going there this afternoon with her friend Janet and her daughter anyway. She would get one then.

But he was not prepared to wait. Nothing she said would deter him, and ten minutes later she was sitting in his car.

Silently seething in the passenger seat, Beth watched as he walked around the bonnet and slid into the driving seat. She caught the male scent of his aftershave as he closed the door, saw his chiselled profile, the slight darkening of his firm jawline and the sensuous mouth. Hastily she dropped her gaze, but the denim pulled tight across his thigh so close to hers was no help. Everything about him was so masculine... Her heart skipped a beat and it was hard to breathe. He affected her senses in every way, and yet he was the last man on earth she should be attracted to.

'Nice car. What happened to your Ferrari? Tired of it already?' Beth asked snidely. Anything to take her mind off the sheer physicality of the man and her own troubled thoughts.

'*You* happened,' Dante shot back.

'What do you mean, I happened?' Beth queried.

He turned in his seat to look at her, a rueful smile twisting his lips. 'After I left your apartment I was driving back to my place when it suddenly struck me what I had done—or, more precisely, *not* done. It was just as big a shock to me then as it was to you today, and for the first time in my life I ran into the back of a truck at a red light and buckled the front of my car.'

'You hit a truck?' Beth exclaimed, her green eyes sparkling with amusement. 'With your new Ferrari?' She knew that Dante loved his cars, and it gave her great pleasure to realise he was just as likely as the next man to crash his car.

'It is back in the factory in Italy being repaired—which is why I am driving the Bentley. I was in America until ten days ago, and I meant to pick it up when I got back to Italy. I never got time.'

'You seem to have plenty of time to come here,' she said flatly.

'Yes—but only because I made a mistake with you. I do not like indecision of any kind and I am not prepared to wait any longer. It is essential that I know if you are pregnant. If you are I will need to make some readjustments to my life and so will you. We are in this together, Beth, whether we like it or not.'

Dante had ended on a serious note, and Beth looked away as he started the engine and they moved off.

He was right, she thought fatalistically. Better to find out now. Though in her heart of hearts she had a growing conviction that she was. If the pregnancy was confirmed she was going to have to deal with Dante Cannavaro…and, given her past experience with the man, the thought did not fill her with confidence….

CHAPTER SIX

TWO HOURS LATER a very subdued Beth got out of the car in front of her house, still mortified by the way Dante had behaved at the chemist. He'd had no shame, demanding to know from the female assistant which was the most reliable pregnancy test while Beth had stood embarrassed by his side, wishing the ground would open and swallow her up—or preferably Dante…

Now, after so long in his company, her nerves were stretched to breaking point and the thought of what lay ahead added to her stress levels. Her happy mood on waking up was long gone….

'Let's go inside and get this over with,' Dante commanded and, clasping her hand in his, he led her up and into her own house.

'Wait a minute.' Beth stopped in the large hall and tugged her hand free from his, her palm tingling. She looked frostily up at him. 'I am quite capable of taking care of this myself. In fact I would prefer to.'

'No way. This is my responsibility and I want to know.'

'Are you stupid or what?' Beth demanded in exasperation. 'I am giving you a Get Out of Jail Free card.

You can walk away—forget you ever met me. Most men would leap at the chance.'

'I am not most men, and I can't do that. I remember all too well that we had sex, and if a baby is the result then it is mine as much as yours. Though the thought of being a father, wondering if I will be a good one, *is* worrying.'

Inexplicably Beth's heart squeezed at the hint of vulnerability in the dark gaze he turned on her.

She had not seen Dante look anything but arrogantly sure of himself, and it was a shock to see his big body tense. She realised this was probably even more of a shock for him than for her. Dante Cannavaro was not the type of man who ever made a mistake in his business or personal life and he did not tolerate other people's mistakes. He believed his judgement was infallible, and now he had made a possibly life-changing mistake.... No wonder he looked shaken....

'Take this.' He pressed the pregnancy kit into her hand and glanced around. 'Tell me where the kitchen is and I'll make myself a coffee while you do the test.'

They were standing in the wide hall, which had two doors opening off on either side to the reception rooms. The main focus was a central staircase that divided halfway up and curved into a galleried landing on the first floor.

Beth indicated with one hand to the right of the staircase. 'Down there is the kitchen.'

To her astonishment he wrapped an arm around her shoulders and gave her a hug, dropped a light kiss on her lips. 'Don't worry—it will work out fine either way. I will make sure it does,' he declared, and turned to walk away.

Stunned, Beth looked down at the box in her hand and up again. She wanted to throw it at Dante's back as he strolled off to the kitchen. He was so confident everything would be fine…while she was the opposite—a nervous wreck. But she knew she was only delaying the inevitable and began to ascend the stairs. Her lips were tingling from his kiss, her head was spinning with the enormity of what she was about to do, and her feelings on the result were ambivalent…

Twenty minutes later Beth walked downstairs and entered the kitchen, her face a blank mask. She dropped the test on the table, where Dante sat, and without a word stalked out and down the hall to her sitting room. With a sigh she sank down on the sofa and let her head fall back against the soft cushions.

Binkie padded over to rub against her ankles and Beth's lips quirked at the corners in a brief smile. 'Soon, Binkie, it will no longer be just you and I. There will be a baby as well.' Somehow saying the words out loud finally brought it home to her that she *was* pregnant.

'Amazing. You can tell your damn cat you are pregnant, but I get the test thrown at me.'

Beth glanced up to find Dante bristling with anger, staring down at her. Her own temper rose at the injustice of it all. 'I love my cat, whereas *you* I could not give a damn about. And whichever way you get the news delivered the answer is the same—and it is *your* fault. If you hadn't tracked me down to tell me I might be pregnant I wouldn't have realised for ages, and when I did I definitely would *not* have told you,' she spat, her pent-up emotions finally boiling over. 'It seems to be your goal in life to try to destroy mine. First you are instrumental in sending me to prison, then you try to chase me out of my apartment with your threats and finally you seduce me. A hat-trick is the term in football, I believe. But as I am pregnant it seems you have scored an own goal.'

Beth spoke derisively, but inside she was falling apart. This morning she had got out of bed, happily looking forward to the day ahead. Then Dante had turned her life upside down yet again.

Dante, like most Italian males, was mad about football, and his lips twitched at her last comment. She was sitting down, her arms folded across her middle—which pushed her perfect breasts upwards. Not that they needed any help. His blood heated at the thought.

Damn it, how could one redheaded woman have such an instant effect on his libido? This was serious.

'Look on me as the villain if you must,' he said curtly. 'But it does not alter the fact that you are expecting a baby, and as the father I intend to be fully involved with my child, with or without you...understand?'

Beth looked up at Dante, towering over her, and let her eyes trace the hard bones of his tanned face, the cool, determined eyes, the powerful jaw and tight mouth.

'Yes.' She understood all right. It was what she had feared when he had dropped the bombshell on her a few hours ago. But this time she was ready for him. It was amazing how knowing she was having a baby gave her strength, and she determined to fight him anyway she could. 'That is easy for you to say, but have you really thought this through, Dante?'

Beth deliberately drawled his name, looking up at him through the veil of her long lashes.

'After all, you are an extremely powerful and extremely wealthy man, according to Tony. What will your friends think when they discover the mother of your child is a convicted drug dealer *you* sent to prison? You threatened me with the press. I can do the same.' She saw his dark brows shoot up in surprise. 'Not so nice, is it, when a threat goes against you?' she opined. 'When you demanded I kept out of Tony's life you labelled me as some kind of *femme fatale*. So maybe I decided *you* were a better bet and deliberately allowed you to seduce me in the hope of getting pregnant and getting your money. Can you live with that?'

Dante felt a muscle begin to beat in his temple. It was anger, but it was something else as well. Her spirited attempt to defy him and the sultry look from her green eyes shouldn't have anywhere near the sensual impact it did. The cynic in him *had* had the fleeting thought that Beth might have got pregnant deliberately for money, but he had quickly dismissed the notion as he'd recalled every moment in her bed: the silken caress of her hands against his flesh, the taste and the scent of her. He hadn't been able to get enough of her. And it was making him want to repeat the experience with an urgency that was growing painful.

With that in mind, he lowered his long length on the sofa and slid his arm along the back of the sofa behind her. He noted her flinch. 'An interesting scenario, Beth, but I don't believe you would reveal to the world your criminal past to thwart me, knowing your child would eventually suffer from the knowledge. As for money— it is not something that bothers me. Right now I want to get acquainted with our baby.'

He was right, damn him, and Beth's breath caught

in her throat at *our baby*—and at the gleam she saw in his dark eyes as they moved down her body.

'May I?'

He placed his hand on her still-flat stomach and for a long moment a strange quivering trance held them both as the enormity of what they had created finally sank in.

Dante raised his head, his dark eyes meeting hers, and she was vaguely aware that his other hand was resting on her shoulder. His long fingers stroked her midriff, tenderly edging higher, and suddenly a trance of a different nature shimmered between them.

His arm tightened around her shoulders. His mouth brushed gently across her lips. His hand moved to cup her breast. Beth caught her breath and his mouth covered hers, his tongue stroking along the curve of her lips to seek entry. Her eyes fluttered closed as he kissed her long and deeply, with a seductive tenderness she had never felt before.

Dante raised his head and Beth stared dazedly into his molten eyes as his long fingers circled her neck to trail down her throat, their touch caressing and arousing. Then with a groan his sensuous mouth found hers again, to kiss her with a deepening passion, and his tactile fingers reached the swift rise and fall of her breasts to pluck at one tight nipple. Her lips parted on a low moan as his mouth caught its partner to lick and suckle, and a shaft of sensual pleasure shot through her slender body. Her mind demanded she tell him to stop, but her body was brought vibrantly alive by his touch.

He raised his head and she saw the passionate intent in his dark eyes as she heard his voice. 'You want this, Beth?'

The question and the sound of his deep, husky voice

broke the trance she was in and made Beth realise what she was inviting. 'No!' she cried, and scrambled along the sofa, fighting to catch her breath and still her frantically racing heart. Suddenly she realised the straps of her dress were halfway down her arms, baring her breasts to his avid gaze. How or when it had happened she had no idea....

She could not look at him. She was mortified at how easily she had succumbed to his skilful caress. She pulled the straps of her dress back over her shoulders. The fabric hurt her sensitized breasts, but nowhere near as much as she hurt inside.

Finally she glanced sideways at Dante. He had straightened up, his head resting on the back of the sofa, and she could see the pulse beating in his strong throat, the rise and fall of his muscular chest and the unmistakable bulge in his jeans....

Swallowing hard, she looked away. Knowing she was not the only one suffering was some consolation, and she hoped it hurt. She could not believe she had almost made the same mistake again....

Was she destined to be fatally attracted to this man for the rest of her life? Had his fiancée, Ellen, felt the same? The thought came out of nowhere and made Beth feel worse. Their engagement had been broken the weekend of the barbecue, she knew. But they could be back together by now. They *had* to love each other if they had been arranging the wedding.

A large hand cupped her chin and turned her head, so she was forced to look up at Dante. 'Given your initial response, I don't believe "once was enough" after all,' he drawled, a hint of humour in the dark eyes that held hers. 'I know you, Beth, and I was right. You are a tease, but you also have a natural talent for sex. It is only your stubborn determination to hold a grudge against me that is stopping you. But I can wait.' And he grinned.

It was the grin that got her. She knocked his hand away and leapt off the sofa to stare down at him for a change. 'And you would know because you are such an expert. Tell me, what is Ellen going to say when she discovers you've made me pregnant? Weren't you two supposed to be getting married this month? Or maybe you are not my baby's father? Have you thought of that? I could have had another man since you.' Mentally she kicked herself for not thinking of that sooner.

'No, you haven't. You are as transparent as glass in some respects, and the idea of another man has only just occurred to you—too late to be believed, I'm afraid.' There was no humour in his eyes now, she noted, as he added, 'As for Ellen—she is none of your concern or mine any more. We broke up and the wedding was cancelled, remember?'

'So just like that you dismiss the woman who loved you?' Beth said, dropping the 'other man' plan as pointless. Even if he believed her a DNA test would prove otherwise, and Dante was nothing if not thorough.

'Grow up, Beth. Love had nothing to do with my relationship with Ellen. I decided it was time I got married and Ellen and I are in the same profession, with the same background. She seemed the perfect candidate. We were compatible. I wanted a child, an heir, and she said she wanted the same—until she got emotional and told me I didn't love her enough, threw the engagement ring back at me. I realised she wanted a lot more than I was able to give.'

'How can you be so calculating? I'm not surprised she broke off the engagement!'

'Easily. And I've just realised that now you are pregnant my problem is solved. I have no need to look further. I want this child, and I will pay you whatever you want, whatever it takes, for you to have a healthy baby.'

At his mention of money again Beth's eyes widened in horror as she realised what he really meant. Dante was lounging there, his face enigmatic, as he casually offered to *buy* her baby—which underscored exactly how little he thought of her as a prospective mother.

'I am sure we can come to an acceptable arrangement between us that we can both live with comfortably,' he continued coolly.

'I very much doubt that. And as I can only be eight weeks pregnant it is far too early even for a ruthless devil like you to suggest *buying* my baby,' she said, eyeing him with bitter contempt.

Dante leapt to his feet and his hand shot out. Long, tanned fingers closed round her wrist and he folded her arm around her back to hold her close to his taut body. 'I never suggested buying the baby. Only you and your twisted mind could think such a thing,' he snarled.

For a moment Beth could not move, could not speak. All she could do was feel... The warmth of his breath against her face, the surge of heated emotions battling inside her... Angrily, she was aware that not many minutes ago she had almost succumbed to his lethal sex appeal. If anyone had a twisted mind it was Dante, she thought, recognising the disgust in his tone and finding her voice.

'That is what it sounded like to me—and there is nothing wrong with my mind,' she said bluntly. 'Plain common sense tells me it is far too soon to be discussing arrangements for the baby.'

'Not for me,' he said between his teeth. 'I intend to get this settled now. And you should know that I always get what I want in the end.'

Beth refused to be afraid. 'Yes, I know better than most that with your implications and lies you will stoop to anything to achieve your own ends. If you had taken more care of your own relationship instead of interfering in your brother's life we wouldn't be in this mess,' she told him scathingly.

His face darkened and he held her tighter still to his long body. 'What is done is done—and don't you *ever* think of or refer to our baby as a *mess*.' He threaded his other hand in her hair and tipped her head back, staring down into her defiant face with black searching eyes. 'I know you for what you are, Beth—a beautiful woman with a less-than-salubrious past. Not the sort of woman I would have chosen as the mother of my child, I admit, but you are, and I accept that—and I accept that you have succeeded in living down your mistakes. It is time you accept me as the father, stop flinging insults and start thinking of what is best for our unborn child. I have told you I will provide you with everything—a home where you can live in the lap of luxury and devote all your time to looking after our baby. That is how it is going to be. Understand?'

His head dropped and as though compelled he brought his mouth down on hers, his hand sweeping up her back to splay across her bare shoulder blade with a pressure that flattened her against him.

The long, demanding kiss inflamed Beth's senses, and though she fought to resist her eyes closed involuntarily and she gave in to the persuasive power of his sensuous mouth. When he pulled his head back her arms were wrapped around his waist and her soft lips were parted. Realising what she had done yet again, she dropped her arms, her hands curling into fists at her sides, and stared up at him, trying to read the look in his narrowed gaze. She caught a gleam of desire and some other emotion that she did not recognise.

'Why did you kiss me?' Beth broke the taut silence between them, trying to appear nonchalant while battling the force of feelings his kiss had aroused.

'Because I can't keep my hands off you,' Dante responded—and it was the truth. When he should be comforting Beth, reassuring her, all he could think of was stripping her naked and thrusting into her sleek, hot body as fast and deep as he could…. 'Or maybe to get you to listen,' he added, trying to ignore the throbbing in his groin.

Surprised by his admission that he could not keep his hands off her, and still held against his hard-muscled frame, Beth was intensely aware of Dante in a basic carnal way. The strength of his erection was very evident, she realised, which made her hot and angry with herself almost as much as she was with him.

'I did listen.' She desperately latched on to his last words and added what she hoped were some stinging ones of her own. 'You said you will take care of everything. Does that include marrying me, I wonder?' she asked with a sarcastic tilt of a delicate eyebrow. 'I notice a proposal was not on your list.'

'Yes, of course I am going to marry you.' His hands dropped from her, his dark eyes quizzical. 'I thought I had made that obvious? I told you I would provide everything—money, a house that we can live comfortably in…'

'No! Never in a million years!' Beth exclaimed, horrified by his response. Her sarcasm had backfired spectacularly.

She moved away, shaking her head, and sat carefully down on the one armchair in the room, determined to take control of the situation.

'I only mentioned marriage to make you see sense and face facts. For a cool, staid lawyer you have been acting like a man possessed from the moment you arrived here, and I've let you drag me along with you. But the reality is I am not even nine weeks pregnant, and anything can happen in the first twelve weeks. I don't need this conversation now. I need to get used to the idea of a baby and relax and rest by myself. Get in touch with me in a few weeks' time, if you must, and we can discuss the situation then. If that inconveniences you, then tough. But I am definitely not marrying you. This is *my* body, *my* baby, and that is how it is going to be.' And it was Beth's turn to add, 'Understand…?'

Dante ran his hand distractedly though his hair. He didn't like hearing it, but she could be right. He had told himself he needed to know she was *not* pregnant so he could move on. But dashing down here to confront Beth and drive her to a pharmacy was completely out of character. It was important to Dante that he stayed focused on his work and in control of his private life without compromising the first for the second. His father had taught him that at a young age, and he had rigidly adhered to that philosophy. He was not going to change now.

But neither was he going to allow Beth 'weeks' on

her own. Going by her past behavior, and what he knew now, she wasn't wealthy by his standards, but she *had* inherited a healthy amount of money along with this house. She could disappear anytime she liked, and he wasn't taking that chance.

'I understand your reasoning, and that you want some time to accept the fact you are about to become a mother.' He frowned, noting the slight violet shadows beneath the wide eyes she raised to his. The wary expression in the green depths made him grimace. 'I have to be in Rome tomorrow and I want you to come with me. I will ensure you see the best doctor there is, and you can stay at my place in the country. The house is fully staffed and you will be well looked after. You can rest there.'

After which she was going to marry him whether she liked it or not. A civil ceremony could be arranged in two or three weeks....

'No, thank you. I have my own doctor and I prefer my own home.'

Dante noted the determined tilt of her chin and his lips twisted. He wasn't surprised she had refused. In spite of her shady past she was still incredibly naive in some ways. It was obvious the thought of getting pregnant had never crossed her mind until he had mentioned it, and it must have come as a hell of a shock to her when she discovered she was. He had no intention of leaving until he had got her to agree to marry him, but he could wait a while.

'I can see you have a nice house here, but it is rather isolated for a woman alone.'

'I am not alone. I have friends, and I am perfectly

capable of making my own arrangements without any help from you,' Beth said bluntly.

Dante was standing two feet away, his dark eyes holding hers, his deep voice sounding concerned, but she did not trust him. From the first moment she had seen Dante in court she had felt an instant affinity with him and had believed it was hope, but now she was beginning to believe it could be something much more dangerous to her in the long run.

'What arrangements?' Dante demanded, his sensuous lips thinned into an uncompromising hardness and his voice no longer gentle.

Slowly Beth stood up. Dante was not and never could be her friend. He had his own agenda and had actually said that one of his reasons for marrying Ellen had been to get an heir. Beth being pregnant had solved that problem for him.

'Obviously seeing my doctor is first on the agenda. He will book me into the local hospital, which has an excellent reputation.' She stepped towards him. 'Now we have got that settled you can leave. See yourself out.' She paused, waiting for him to move.

Without a word Dante stood aside to let her past. Beth could have her space but it would be a few minutes—certainly not weeks. He was absolutely determined she would marry him, and he knew he did not have time to waste. He was proud of the Cannavaro name and over two hundred years of family history. There was no way a child of his was being born illegitimate.

CHAPTER SEVEN

BETH WALKED PAST DANTE and headed for the kitchen. She was suddenly ravenous. She checked the fridge and withdrew a carton of eggs, two slices of ham, a chunk of cheese and the makings of a salad from the vegetable box. She placed them on the kitchen bench along with some herbs, and then took out the omelette pan and placed it on the hob.

'Can I help?'

She had not heard Dante walk in, and glanced over her shoulder to find him right behind her. 'No. You have done more than enough already,' she said dryly. 'And I thought I told you to leave?'

'I have not eaten since I left London this morning. I suppose I could stop at the local pub for lunch. Bill seems a hospitable guy, and he obviously likes you. He told me where to find you. He'd probably appreciate being the first to know you are pregnant.'

'No. I don't want anyone to know—not until the pregnancy is confirmed by a doctor.' Beth was clinging to straws, she knew. 'Take a seat.' She nodded her head towards the kitchen table. 'I suppose I can feed you before you go. Cheese and ham omelette with salad is all I've got.' She was babbling again, but Dante was too big and too close, and he made her very generously sized kitchen feel like a rabbit hutch.

'Thanks.'

To her relief he moved to pull out a chair and sit down at the table.

Beth placed the salad bowl on the table, along with condiments and cutlery. Then she broke six eggs into a bowl, and in a matter of minutes had heated the oil in the pan and cooked the omelettes. Placing one on each plate, she crossed to the table and put them down, pulling out a chair to sit opposite Dante.

'Enjoy,' she said automatically and, picking up a knife and fork, cut into the fluffy omelette and ate in silence.

'That was delicious,' Dante said, and she looked up to see he had cleaned his plate. 'You really can cook.' A genuine smile indented the lines around his mouth, and there was a gleam of surprise in the dark eyes that met hers.

'Don't sound so surprised! My mother taught me and she was a brilliant cook.' Beth's eyes softened as she remembered. 'Mum made the most gorgeous cakes—probably the reason I was a bit plump as a child.' With food in her stomach and the shock of her situation fading a little, she smiled wryly. 'But after she died the weight began to fall off.'

Dante's breath caught at her gentle smile. 'I am sorry you lost your parents so young, Beth,' he said compassionately. 'I didn't realise your parents had died only a year before your trial. I understand how grief can make people behave irrationally….'

'Oh, please stop. I don't need false sympathy from *you*,' Beth mocked, her shoulders tensing, her green eyes blazing at him. 'And don't insult my intelligence. I was innocent and I was stitched up by Bewick and his friend—and you made sure of it. Tell me, how many more innocent people have you sent to jail? Have you any idea?'

Dante prided himself on his integrity and his honour and was deeply insulted, but he was not about to argue with Beth when she was carrying his child. Instead he stated the facts. 'None. You were found guilty by the jury, not me. As a lawyer, I did what I was hired to do—make the case to the best of my ability on the evidence presented by the police and witnesses, not just you. There was nothing personal about it and any other decent lawyer would have got the same result on the evidence. It was also my last criminal case. International commercial litigation is my specialty.'

Beth's eyes widened incredulously on his darkly brooding face. 'I was your last criminal case? That *really* makes me feel a whole lot better,' she said in a voice dripping with sarcasm. 'You said it without a trace of irony and you sound so plausible—but then that *is* your forte.'

'You will think what you want.' For an instant an expression she did not recognise flashed in the depths of his dark eyes and was gone. 'In my experience women usually do.'

Beth shoved back her chair and stood up. 'You are such a chauvinist,' she said, and picked the plates up from the table.

'Well, I don't wash dishes,' he quipped.

She almost smiled as she carried them to the sink, put in the plug and turned on the tap. Idly, she swirled the water around with her hand, then turned off the tap and added some liquid soap, mulling over in her head what Dante had told her.

Maybe he had a point when he said it was nothing personal. He probably spent most of his life in a court-room and must have had hundreds if not thousands of cases. He could not possibly remember all the people involved.

Beth grimaced. He had not remembered her at the barbecue and probably never would have done if not for Tony's joke about marrying her, which had made Dante suspect she was after his brother and his money. She, on the other hand, had recognised Dante the first time she'd seen him again in the street as the man who had haunted her dreams for years. So what did that say about *her*?

Strangely, it put things into perspective for Beth. The day she had left prison Helen had told her not to look back, never to let bitterness affect her new life… But at her trial Beth had fixated on Dante and blamed him personally for the result. She had hated him for years. Now she realised that, given the evidence against her, she would have got the same result with another lawyer. Not that it made any difference. Dante was still the su-premely confident, arrogant man he had always been.

She rinsed off the plates and the pan and stood them on the drainer, then turned around at the sound of his voice. He had his cell phone to his ear and was talking in rapid-fire Italian, his other hand gesturing wildly. He looked and sounded so animated and so very foreign to her, and she felt an odd twinge in her heart.

He lifted his head, a smile still curving his lips. 'Work,' he said, and slipped the phone in his jeans pocket.

Beth caught her breath. She was tempted to smile back, and that frightened her. He was a handsome, charismatic man when it suited him, but she had seen the dark side of him—the clever, domineering and unbelievable bossy character—and she needed to get rid of him....

'You know, Dante, I have hated you for years and now I realise it was a wasted emotion,' she said, schooling her features into a blank mask. 'You will never change and you are always right—which does not bode very well for the future of my baby. An autocratic father is the last thing a child needs. And I really think you should go now.'

'I agree. But I want you to come with me. I don't like the idea of leaving you on your own here.'

'I won't be on my own. I told you Janet and Annie are coming to stay and we are going out for the rest of the day.' She flashed him a smile that did not reach her eyes. 'Have a safe journey.'

Beth turned back to the sink and pulled out the plug, watched the water drain away.

She heard the scrape of a chair on the floor. Good, he was going.... Hopefully by the time she saw Dante again—if she saw him again—she would have a plan to deal with him. Maybe a monthly visit...something like that. Firmly settled in her new life, with people around her she trusted, the thought of having a baby was not so scary after all. In fact she was thrilled, and loved the baby already. Working from her own home was the perfect solution for a single mother. No nursery, no childcare and a great environment to bring up her child.

Beth picked up a teatowel and dried her hands and turned around to make sure Dante had left—only to see him standing in front of the table, his steely gaze focused on her.

'I thought you'd gone.' Her eyes clashed with his and a sliver of fear trickled down her spine. He still exuded an aura of firmly controlled masculine power, and yet she sensed something had shifted. She felt the heightened tension in the air, saw the hard resolution in his dark eyes, and resisted the urge to moisturise her suddenly dry lips.

'I don't take orders, but when I give them I expect them to be obeyed—something you will have to learn when we are married.'

'Married?' she parroted dumbly.

'Yes, married.'

Beth was shocked rigid for a moment. To want to marry her after all that had been said between them—he must be crazy....

Stony-faced, she squared her shoulders and bravely held his gaze. 'Let me make this very clear. I am not marrying you. I'd have to be out of my mind to marry a man who thinks I am a criminal or a *femme fatale* who preys on young men. And my opinion of you is as bad—if not worse. I don't *like* who and what you are, let alone love you.'

'I am not that keen on you as a wife,' he said dryly. 'But there is a baby to consider. As long as we are civil to each other and concentrate all our energy on giving the child the nurturing and love it deserves I don't see a problem. We are sexually compatible, and in my experience lust is preferable to love—if love even exists, which I doubt.'

Beth felt the colour rise in her cheeks as images of her tussle on the sofa with him filled her mind—and the full-blown sex that had got her into this position in the first place....

'That is the most cold-blooded argument for getting married I have ever heard, and typical of you,' she declared scathingly.

'No, it is eminently sensible. I want my child born legitimately and brought up in Italy, as I was, on the family estate. But I travel abroad a lot, and spend quite a bit of my time in London, so I don't mind if you keep this house and stay here when I'm in the city. So long as you devote all your time to our child.'

His arrogant attitude infuriated Beth. 'No. Marrying you is out of the question. It is never going to happen.'

'As I see it there are only two options. We get married or I take you to court for sole custody of the child— which will be a long, drawn-out process that could go on for years, and you know I will win eventually. You choose.'

Beth felt as if all the air had left her body and she stared at him in horror. He meant it. She recognised the cold, implacable determination in his voice.

'That is no choice at all!' she exclaimed and, taking a steadying breath, she tilted up her chin, just as determined as Dante. 'My mother—whoever she was—abandoned me as a baby in a hospital emergency department. Much as I loved my adoptive parents, I would never give up custody of my child. But I certainly would not fight you in court after the last time. I'm not that stupid. I know what a devious devil you can be and I have little faith in your sort of justice. As for marrying you? Spending the rest of my life with *you* does not bear thinking about.'

Dante had not realised she was adopted. The investigator had not gone that far back. But in her last comment his fertile mind saw a way to get what he wanted...

'Then don't think about the rest of your life. Nothing lasts for ever,' he stated with a cynical arch of a black brow. 'And though I am not in favour of divorce, under the circumstances I am prepared to make allowances. If by the time the child is three—old enough to really know its parents—you find married life intolerable, I will give you an amicable divorce with shared custody of the child. In fact I will draw up a prenuptial agreement stating as much.'

Beth's eyes widened a fraction. Her first thought had been to dismiss marriage out of hand, but now Dante had surprised and shocked her. Had he said it deliberately? she wondered, and studied him for a moment. His expression was watchful but not malicious, she decided. A wry smile played around her lips. He was so insensitive, so self-centred, that he did not recognise the irony in offering her a divorce after three years. Her prison sentence had been three years....

'A marriage with a get-out clause you mean?' she said, and amazingly she found herself considering it. She had done one prison sentence because of him, and got out after eighteen months. Who was to say she could not get out of the marriage sentence sooner? While loving her child she could be the wife from hell. Making Dante's life a misery would be sweet revenge for all he had put her through....

He continued to look at her with that unwavering dark gaze. 'Yes, exactly as I stated.'

Beth wanted the best for her child, and though she hated to admit it Dante's offer was probably the best she was going to get. She would not have to stay in Italy all the time, as he had said. He spent quite a lot of time travelling all over the place with his work. Dante might be the biological father of her baby, but she couldn't see him being a hands-on father. In fact she might not see much of him at all, she realised. She glanced around the kitchen, her brain ticking over.

'Do I have any choice?' she questioned cynically.

'You know the alternative. Is that what you want?'

'No, definitely not,' Beth said. She could see no other way out.…

Dante caught her shoulders and stared grimly down at her.

'Then make up your mind. What is it to be? Yes or no?'

'Then yes, I suppose,' she said fatalistically. 'But I want an iron-clad pre—'

A voice cut her off.

'Hey, Beth—that is some car outside. Do you know whose it is?' Janet asked as she walked into the kitchen with Annie. She stopped dead, her gaze settling on Dante, still holding Beth.

'No,' Beth said quickly. 'Yes, I mean. This is…'

She stopped as Dante dropped a swift kiss on her lips, let go of her and moved to Janet.

'Allow me to introduce myself. I'm Dante, a very close friend of Beth's, hoping soon to be much more. You must be Janet,' Dante said smoothly, and Beth stared open-mouthed with shock as he smiled and took her friend's hand. 'Beth has told me so much about you. It is a pleasure to finally meet you and your adorable little girl, Annie.'

'Oh…oh, hello,' Janet stuttered. Overawed by his formidable presence she turned huge blue eyes on Beth.

'You dark horse, Beth. I didn't know you had a boy-friend.'

'We met years ago and renewed our relationship earlier this year, but Beth likes to keep me hidden,' Dante declared outrageously. 'While I want her to come to Italy for a holiday to show her my world and persuade her to marry me.'

Beth could not believe the glib devil, and watched as he bestowed a megawatt smile on Janet the like of which she had never seen before.

'Ah, a Latin lover—I should have guessed.' Janet turned to her, and much to Beth's chagrin she blushed. 'Beth, I can't believe you never once mentioned this gorgeous man. I can't say I blame you. If he was mine I'd keep him to myself as well.' She grinned and glanced admiringly back up at Dante.

Beth silently groaned. Janet was a great friend, but hopelessly outspoken. 'You don't understand...' she began.

'What's to understand? A holiday in Italy sounds great to me—and the man hopes to marry you! Accept quickly, before he changes his mind.'

'I can't just take off to Italy. I can't leave Binkie, and the builders are going to start on the conversion soon.'

'Don't worry. I'll take care of Binkie. And as for the conversion—you can have at least two weeks holiday before it starts.'

Somehow, ten minutes later, Beth found herself standing by the Bentley with Dante, her future more or less decided.

He kissed her—for Janet's benefit, she guessed—then told her he would call her the next day to confirm arrangements. He already had her house phone number, and he gave her his card with a list of numbers where she could contact him. She supposed she should be grateful he did not whisk her away there and then. At least she had a couple of days to think of an alternative.

By the time Beth went to bed that night she was exhausted, but her head was filled with the events of the day and she could not sleep. Janet had asked her umpteen questions but Beth hadn't had the heart to tell her that she was pregnant. In fact she was having a hard time accepting it herself. As for Dante saying he was hoping to persuade her to marry him—she didn't know why he bothered prevaricating.... He had left her no choice *but* to marry him.

Beth called Clive the next day and told him she was going on holiday to Italy for two weeks. She hadn't the nerve to tell him the truth, and was still hoping it would all miraculously go away. She told him she would ring him when she got back, but he said he was going away himself on a three-month lecture tour around the universities in Australia, and somehow Beth felt more alone than ever.

It was two o'clock on Friday afternoon when Beth stepped off the plane in Rome. She was met by a uniformed gentleman who whisked her through Customs, telling her that her baggage would be taken care of, and ushered her into a VIP lounge, informing her that Signor Cannavaro was to meet her there.

Beth had never flown first-class before—in fact she had only ever flown four times. Nervously she smoothed the oatmeal cashmere dress she wore down over her hips and looked around. There were a few business types, but no sign of Dante. With a bit of luck he might have changed his mind and she could go back to England straight away, instead of in two weeks' time as Dante had agreed.

Dante's meeting had run on for longer than he'd expected, and the traffic to the airport was horrendous. He stopped at the open door of the lounge at the sight of Beth, walking down the room. She was wearing a long-sleeved sweater dress that followed every seductive line of her body to end above her knees, and high-heeled shoes accentuated her fabulous legs. She looked sensational, and a vivid image of those legs wrapped around his waist, his body buried to the hilt in hers, filled his mind.

He took a deep, steadying breath to control his raging libido and moved forward, noticing that every other man in the place was watching her. For a moment he saw red....

Beth was beginning to wonder if Dante really had changed his mind. There was still no sign of him and she looked again at her wristwatch.

'Beth, *cara*.'

She heard his voice and turned to see him walking towards her. Butterflies took up a war dance in her stomach and her breath caught in her throat. He was wearing a charcoal suit, white shirt and striped tie, and for such a big, powerfully built man he moved with the lithe ease of an athlete. He looked fabulous—but he also looked furious, she realised.

His hands caught her shoulders and a firm male mouth descended on her parted lips. She lifted a hand to press against the hard wall of his chest, but for some reason her fingers spread out over the soft silk of his shirt.

It was Dante who ended the kiss. 'I'm sorry I'm late, but did you *have* to parade up and down the lounge?'

'Parade?' Beth queried, her green gaze flicking up over the hard planes of his handsome face, his smooth tanned skin and square jaw. She saw masculine strength and, surprisingly, bewilderment in his extraordinary dark eyes.

Dante shook his head. 'I can't believe I said that. You are an impossible woman, Beth.' Taking her arm, he added, 'Come on—let's get out of here.' And he marched her out of the airport so fast she almost had to run to keep up with him.

Five minutes later a chauffeur held open the passenger door of a sleek black limousine, and Dante told her to get in quickly.

Beth sat in the back, as far away from Dante as she could get. It was warmer in Italy than she had expected, and the cashmere dress had not been a good choice, so she was grateful for the air conditioning. She glanced across at him and the resentment she had bottled up since the last time she saw him got the better of her. 'You gave me only days to prepare to come here for a holiday I don't want, and now you race me out of the airport like a marathon man. What's the rush?'

'You have a doctor's appointment and we are going to be late.'

'What doctor's appointment?' Beth demanded, glaring at him.

'The one I have made for you. Don't worry—he is the top man in Rome.'

'Wait a minute. I thought you said I was staying at

your home in the country? In any case I can't step off a plane and go straight to a doctor.'

A frown lined his broad brow. 'Why not? The sooner you see a doctor the better. I want confirmation that the baby is fine before I take you to the countryside.'

'Yes, I see your point,' Beth said—and she did. He wanted to make absolutely certain she was pregnant before he married her. Well, that was fine by her. She didn't want to marry him any more than he wanted to marry her. They were only doing it for the baby.

It was obviously a private clinic, and Dr Pascal was a lovely man who spoke English, much to Beth's relief. He asked them both a few questions, and the only awkward moment came when he asked Beth if she knew of any hereditary illnesses in her family. For a moment she was lost for words.

'My fiancée was adopted at birth,' Dante answered for her, and reached for her hand, squeezing it reassuringly. 'So she can't answer that.'

'Never mind. I have enough information.' He called a nurse in and asked her to take Beth to the examination room, and told Dante to wait in his office.

When Beth finally followed the doctor back into the office Dante leapt to his feet. 'Is everything all right, Doctor?' he demanded, not even glancing at her.

For some reason—maybe because it had finally sunk in that the baby was real—she felt hurt that he had not spoken to *her*.

The doctor smiled. 'Everything is perfect, Signor Cannavaro—the baby is fine. You are a lucky man.' He turned admiring eyes on Beth and then back to Dante. 'Your fiancée is an extremely fit and healthy young woman about nine weeks pregnant. I have made an appointment for a scan in two weeks' time.'

Dante showed no emotion as he thanked the doctor in Italian. They spoke for a few moments longer and then they left.

Beth slid back into the limousine and stared out of the window as it manoeuvred through the Rome traffic, oblivious to the city's great landmarks, lost in her own thoughts. In the days since Dante had burst back into her life and she'd discovered she was pregnant she had not been absolutely certain that it was real, but now there was no doubt. A child deserved to be born with love, not this way, she thought sadly.

'So there is no going back,' Dante stated. 'If you give me your passport I can complete the arrangements for a civil marriage in Rome in two weeks. Under the circumstances we will not inform friends or family until after the fact.'

Beth's spine straightened, her eyes widening in shock. There was not a hint of softness or real emotion in Dante's hard gaze. 'Surely we do not need to rush into marriage? It makes more sense to wait until the child is born.'

'Maybe with any other woman, but I am not taking a chance with you. You are a flight risk. You have already changed your identity once, you have no family, no employer, no real ties of any kind, and you are not exactly penniless. You could disappear at any time, and I can't spare the time to track you down again.'

'You—you...'

Beth spluttered furiously. 'What is to stop me taking off *after* we are married? Or do you intend to keep me a prisoner for the next three years?'

'Nothing so dramatic,' Dante drawled in a mocking undertone. 'Once we are married I would not have to waste *my* time looking for you. You'd be a missing wife and the forces of law would do it for me.'

Beth sucked in air. She wanted to kill him, but she couldn't even trust herself to speak.

'We will marry in two weeks, as I said, and I will fly back with you to London on Sunday and introduce you to my mother as my wife. Then we will return to your cottage in time for the builders' arrival on Monday…agreed?'

'Agreed,' Beth murmured, her face expressionless. She opened her bag, withdrew her passport and handed it to Dante. Her fingers brushed his and she flinched. For the first time since Helen had died Beth felt like crying. Hormones, she told herself, and took a deep breath.

'Are you all right?' Dante queried, dark brown eyes narrowing on her face. 'You look tired.'

'Yes. You heard the doctor—I'm fine. But it is good of you to be concerned.' If he noticed the sarcasm in her voice she didn't care. All she cared for was the baby.

The rest of the journey was conducted in almost complete silence. Beth was simmering with resentment at the position Dante had put her in, which was not helped by the self-satisfied look on his handsome face….

'Beth, wake up—we have arrived.'

Her eyes fluttered open and she realised she was held in the protective curve of Dante's arm, her head on his chest. Then she shot up and smoothed the skirt of her dress over her thighs, mortified that she had fallen asleep on him, and—worse—that she had enjoyed the comforting feeling.

CHAPTER EIGHT

BETH STEPPED OUT of the car and glanced around. It was dark, but she had a brief glimpse of the façade of the house, and large double doors standing open, sending a broad beam of light into the night as Dante took her arm and led her inside.

Dante introduced her to Sophie, his housekeeper, and her husband, Carlo, and three more staff whose names she didn't register as he walked her across the marble floor to a grand staircase.

'I'll show you to your room.' He glanced at his wristwatch. 'You have forty-five minutes to settle in. Sophie insists on serving dinner no later than nine, and as she has worked here since before I was born I don't dare argue with her.'

'That's good of you,' Beth said with a surprised smile, and her smile broadened when Dante ushered her into her room. It was unmistakably feminine, all white and pastel pink, with painted antique furniture, and definitely not the master bedroom—which was a huge relief to her.

'Thank you. This is a lovely room.'

'Don't thank me, thank Sophie. It was her choice.

I told her a female friend was staying for a couple of weeks and obviously she is trying to impress you.'

'I will,' Beth murmured as he left.

Carlo arrived with her luggage and a maid, who showed her the dressing room and bathroom.

Fifteen minutes later, feeling refreshed and slightly more relaxed, Beth stepped out of the shower and wrapped a soft white towel around her before walking into the dressing room. The staff were gone and her luggage was unpacked, and she quickly found the drawer that contained her lingerie, withdrawing matching white lace briefs and bra and slipping them on.

Sitting at the dressing table, she brushed her hair and applied moisturiser to her face. With a flick of mascara to her long lashes and a touch of tinted gloss to her lips she was ready.

After exactly forty-five minutes Beth descended the staircase to the hall, wearing a knee-length wraparound green jersey silk dress that tied in a bow at the side, and black kitten-heeled shoes.

Reaching the bottom of the stairs, she looked around the huge reception hall. She tried the first of two doors on the left and was relieved to see it was the dining room. She walked in and paused.

Standing by a marble fireplace, a glass in his hand, was Dante.

'Drinking already!' she blurted, insanely disturbed by the sight of Dante in a black lounge suit. His stunning physical presence was almost overwhelming, and suddenly she was no longer relaxed but tense.

'I could say you are enough to drive any man to drink in that dress,' he responded, his dark eyes roaming appreciatively over her as he crossed to where she stood and took her arm. 'You look beautiful.'

'Thank you,' she murmured. The warmth of his strong hand on her arm was sending her pulse haywire. She was just about holding herself together, but if he didn't let go of her soon she was liable to melt in a puddle at his feet—or strangle him. Dante infuriated her and fascinated her in equal measure. He was like a force of nature—magnificent but sometimes deadly....

Minutes later, with Dante seated at the top of a long dining table and Beth to his right, Sophie appeared with the first course. Carlo followed with the wine and offered to fill her glass.

Beth said water would be fine for her.

Dante's dark brows rose, but as realisation hit him an approving smile curved his firm lips. 'Which would you prefer, Beth? Sparkling or still?'

'Still water, please.' Shaking out her napkin, she put it on her lap.

Sophie served the meal—a plate of delicious antipasta, followed by a tasty mushroom risotto and then perfectly seasoned sea bass.

Dante drank wine and kept her glass topped up with water, and made easy, informative conversation. Beth learned his was a working estate, which included a vineyard, and he regaled her with stories of his childhood—how as a six-year-old he had tried to tread grapes in a bucket to make his own wine, much to his father's amusement, and other episodes that despite herself made her chuckle.

She mentioned the painting hanging above the fireplace and he told her it was of his father, who had died at the age of fifty-two in a car accident. The paintings in the hall and on the stairway were of his ancestors. Somehow the family portraits brought home to Beth just what she had let herself in for over the next three years....

Beth's appetite had disappeared by dessert—mainly because she was beginning to warm to this relaxed, witty Dante in his home environment and could not relax herself. She found her eyes straying to his mouth, found herself swallowing hard as he unselfconsciously licked his lips.

When he suggested they have coffee in the main salon she pushed back her seat and stood up. 'If you don't mind I'll give the coffee a miss.' She deliberately patted her stomach. 'I'm tired after all the travelling, the doctor and everything. I'd like to go to bed.'

His dark eyes narrowed on her. 'Okay, I'll see you to your room.'

Ascending the stairs with Dante's oddly protective hand on her back, she asked herself how the cool, successful Beth of three months ago could have been dumb enough to get herself in this position. She turned at the door to her room and glanced at Dante, to say goodnight. But the hand at her back slid around her waist, and with his free hand he opened the bedroom door and backed her inside.

'Goodnight, Dante,' she said firmly, and put her hands on his chest to ward him off.

He caught her hands on his shirtfront in one of his much larger ones. 'Surely our relationship warrants a goodnight kiss—?'

'That's not necessary,' she cut in. His dark eyes met hers and she saw the gleam of desire in their black depths. She could not move.

'It is necessary for me,' he said huskily before his mouth captured hers.

It all happened so fast. One minute she was outside her room, saying goodnight, and the next she was inside, held against Dante's long body, her hands flailing ineffectually at him. But with humiliating speed her resistance faded under the seductive persuasion of his lips. Her hands were no longer hitting him but clasping his broad shoulders, and a soft moan escaped her as his mouth drew her deeper into the kiss.

Dante raised his head, his glittering gaze skimming over her. His eyes lingered on the curve of her breasts revealed by the wrap-over neckline of her dress, and he slipped light fingers beneath the white lace bra to stroke and shape a burgeoning peak. 'I like your lingerie, Beth, but I prefer you naked,' he said throatily, and took her lush mouth with his again.

She linked her hands behind his neck as his tongue twined with hers, stoking the heat of arousal simmering inside her. Beth was aware only of Dante, of the heady taste of him, the pleasure of his touch driving every conscious thought from her mind.

So it was all the more shocking when suddenly his hands gripped her waist and he physically lifted her to hold her at arm's length.

Limbs weak, she swayed towards him—but his grip tightened and her eyes widened, finally focusing on his harshly handsome face. She saw leashed passion in the dark eyes, but she also saw a determination in the hard line of his mouth that told her the ardent lover was gone and in his place was the autocratic Dante.

'I want you, Beth, and I could have you now. Your body tells me that every time I touch you.... If it is any consolation it is exactly the same for me. The physical chemistry between us is dynamite,' he said bluntly. 'But we need to get a few things straight.'

Battling to control her wayward senses, Beth was mortified—and suddenly becoming aware the bodice of her dress was gaping wider to reveal her bra simply made it worse. Though knowing this fire in the blood, this instant attraction, was the same for him was some consolation. Speechless, she stared at him.

'To make this marriage work we need some ground rules. The first one being obvious. We will have a normal relationship; I am not cut out to be celibate and neither are you.'

Beth tried to adjust the top of her dress.

'No, not tonight,' he said with a hint of self-mockery. 'I can wait until we are married. The doctor told me you are a healthy woman, and that sex won't harm you or the baby.'

'You actually asked the doctor?' Beth finally found her voice.

'Of course. I intend to take good care of you and the child. Which brings me to my second point.' Surprisingly, he let go of her waist and adjusted her dress by tightening the bow at her waist. 'You are far too distracting,' he said with a wry twist of his lips. 'We have to put on a united front in front of friends and family, with all that entails. No flinching away from me would be a good start—especially in public, as I expect you to play the part of my wife to the full. I have also arranged a personal account for you at my bank.'

'That is not necessary.'

'Yes, it is, Beth. No argument. Tomorrow we are going to Milan to purchase a ring and a suitable wardrobe for you. I attend quite a few social functions, and once we are married naturally you will accompany me. I have to return to Rome tomorrow, but I will try to get back next weekend. If not I will be back to collect you the following Friday for your hospital appointment. The civil ceremony will be on Saturday. In the meantime you can rest and relax as you originally suggested. Is everything clear?'

'Yes.' Beth agreed. She was slowly becoming resigned to the fact that her life was going to be inextricably linked to Dante's for years to come. 'Now may I go to bed? I really am tired.'

'Of course. Anything else can wait until tomorrow.' Dante's lips brushed hers. 'Sleep well.' And with a sardonic arch of a black brow he added, 'If you can,' and left.

Beth stood where he had left her and to her shame realised Dante was right. She was too weak to resist her sexy soon-to-be husband. Maybe she shouldn't even try, a little devil on her shoulder whispered. One of her mother's favourite sayings had been, 'You've made your bed and you have to lie in it.' Well, Dante had certainly made hers by getting her pregnant, so why not enjoy the experience while it lasted? How difficult could it be to play the part of Signora Cannavaro as he'd suggested—or more precisely ordered?

Her parents had brought her up well. As an accountant she had wined and dined wealthy clients, mixed with the best and the worst. Sophisticated society didn't faze her at all. And with Dante's track record where women were concerned she had no illusions. He would probably tire of her within months, if not weeks....

But she would still have her child to love and care

for, and that was all that mattered to her. She doubted she would look at another man even when the three years were up.

The sunlight streaming through the window made Beth blink sleepily, and the strong smell of fresh coffee made her eyes fly open and her face pale. She sat up to see Sophie by the bed, a tray in her hands.

'Just leave it on the bedside table, Sophie,' she said weakly. 'I need the bathroom and a shower first.'

'Ah, I understand,' Sophie said, a broad smile lighting her plump face. 'What would you like for breakfast?' she asked.

'Tea and toast will be fine,' Beth said.

She waited till Sophie had left and then slid out of bed, picked up the coffee and headed for the bathroom to tip it down the toilet. Fifteen minutes later, showered and dried, she opened a wardrobe and eyed the contents. What did one wear to shop in Milan, Italy's capital of fashion? she wondered. Her choice of clothes was limited. She had packed a few casual clothes and not much else except for the dress she had worn last night, plus another dress, and one smart suit. After perspiring in the cashmere yesterday, and with the blazing sun this morning in mind, she opted for the linen dress.

Dante was waiting impatiently at the foot of the stairs when Beth came down. He took one look and knew he was in big trouble. She was beautiful and elegant and she took his breath away. He recognised the pale grey dress she wore immediately, and it had the same effect on him now as it had the first time he had seen her wearing it in that London street. But now it was worse. Now he knew what he was missing....

Her glorious red hair fell in natural waves to brush her shoulders. Her make-up was restrained—a touch of eyeshadow, long thick lashes accentuated by mascara, lips glistening with a rose gloss—and her flawless skin positively glowed.

Why the hell hadn't he taken her to bed last night when he'd had the chance? Instead he had set out the rules for their marriage and said no sex until after the wedding. He must have been out of his mind.

Reaching up, he took her arm before she got to the last step.

'Good, you are ready. But what did you do to Sophie? She is dancing around the kitchen with a broad grin on her face, making tea and toast.'

'Good morning to you, too,' Beth said dryly. 'And I didn't do anything to Sophie. She asked me what I wanted for breakfast and I told her. So if you don't mind I'd like to go and eat it before we leave.'

Dante saw Carlo approaching and pressed a swift kiss on her open mouth. 'Fine, *cara*, but make it quick. I'll go and check the helicopter.'

Of *course* Dante would pilot his own helicopter. He always had to be in control, she thought as he strapped her into the seat beside him.

'I though cars were your secret addiction, not helicopters?'

He shot her a slanting smile. 'They are. But anything with an engine floats my boat. Actually, I have a speedboat and a yacht down at my villa in Portofino.'

Beth grinned and shook her head. 'Why doesn't that surprise me?'

The helicopter landed on the top of a tall building, and Beth looked around at the sprawling city below with a growing sense of panic.

Dante urged her into the building. Beth tensed when she saw the elevator. The next minute she was inside, with him standing next to her like a jailer as he pressed the button for the ground floor and the metal doors slid shut. The elevator began to descend, and so did Beth's stomach. She clenched her teeth, every muscle in her body locking in panic, and stared straight ahead.

Dante glanced down at Beth and saw the frozen expression on her face, the tension in her body. 'Are you all right?' he asked, curving an arm around her rigid shoulders.

'Fine. I'm just a bit claustrophobic in elevators— have been ever since I got out of prison. I think it's a light thing. I have no problem with glass ones on the outside of buildings.'

'Why didn't you say so? Most women I know would be shouting it from the treetops, but you barely tell me anything.' It was true, Dante thought, frustrated by her reticence, not only today but since the moment he had met her again.

'What would be the point? You rarely believe anything I say.'

Her eyes were fixed on the control panel and Beth didn't see Dante wince. When the light flashed for the ground floor she was out of his protective arm and through the doors before they were fully open, and she didn't stop until she was on the street.

She took a few deep, steadying breaths. At least she

had not been sick this time, she thought with some relief as Dante once again looped an arm around her waist.

'How are you feeling?' he asked, and tilted her chin up with the tip of his fingers, his dark eyes studying her face.

'Fine. I told you—it's not a problem,' she said, shaking her head to dislodge his fingers from her chin. 'Now, let's go shopping. That's why we're here, isn't it? I need the distraction of some retail therapy.'

'Okay. First the jewellers and the ring,' Dante said as they started walking. 'As it will be a civil ceremony a wedding gown is not necessary, but if you want one...'

'No way,' Beth cut in, shooting him a sidelong glance. 'Sackcloth would do me, but I'll settle for anything you like,' she said dryly.

If only that were true, Dante thought, and a fantasy of Beth naked and bound to his bed flitted through his mind.

Five minutes later they were seated in an exclusive jewellers with an assortment of platinum wedding rings on display in front of them. 'Choose which one you like,' Dante commanded.

'No, you choose,' Beth shot back. 'After all, this is your idea.'

And in two minutes Dante had done just that. To her amazement he'd picked a pair of matching wedding rings and the jeweller had sized them. Dante paid, left his Rome address for them to be delivered to and they left.

'I don't know who was more surprised, the jeweller or me, when you picked those rings,' Beth said as Dante took her hand and they continued walking. 'I didn't see you as the sort of man to wear a wedding ring.'

'Somehow I don't think you see me at all,' Dante said enigmatically, and ushered her into a designer boutique.

While Beth stared around in awe at the elegant interior Dante had a long conversation with two very attentive female assistants.

'Beth?' He came back to where she stood, like patience on a monument. 'These two ladies will take care of you, and you can show me the results.' He lowered his lean, long-limbed body down on a plush sofa and smiled up at her. 'Go on, Beth—we don't have all day.'

'Yes, oh, master,' she mocked. She saw another assistant appear and offer Dante coffee. By the way she fussed over him a lot more was on offer, Beth thought snidely, and turned away. She wondered how many other women he had brought here. He seemed to be well known.

What followed was a revelation to Beth. She paraded before Dante in casual outfits and then suits, day dresses and finally evening dresses. All the time Dante lounged on the sofa, with a smile on his handsome face and a wicked gleam in his dark eyes, making personal comments on the fit and style, thoroughly enjoying himself at her expense. Beth was getting more incensed by the minute.

Finally, wearing a slim-fitting silver evening dress the assistant had virtually poured her into, which clung to her hips and bottom like a second skin, she'd had enough.

'Now, *that* I like. We'll take it,' Dante said, sitting up straighter as she walked towards him.

She slowly turned around and heard his intake of breath at the rear view. Glancing back at him over her shoulder, she saw the stunned look on his face, and a provocative smile curved her lips.

'Are you sure?' she said, and, turning, she sashayed over to him and sat down on his lap. She curled an arm around his broad shoulders and lifted a finger to trace the outline of his firm lips. 'Do you really think this is me?' she asked throatily.

Dante was speechless. Beth approaching him with a smile and touching him was a first. Forgetting where he was, he wrapped his arms around her as she nuzzled his ear, the soft warmth of her breath making him hot.

'Enough is enough,' she hissed vehemently. 'Remember the reason I am here. This dress is a waste of money—I will never get it on in a couple of weeks.'

He turned her head and covered her mouth with his in a fierce kiss.

The kiss caught Beth by surprise. All she could feel was the heat of desire, the pressure of his hand on her bare back and the hardening of his body against her buttocks. When he broke the kiss she was breathless.

'You're right, of course, Beth,' Dante said and, grasping her by the waist, took her with him as he stood up, lowering her down his long body. 'And I was also right. You are a natural-born tease.'

Beth's provocative action was a salutary reminder to him of what she was really like. He had been in danger of forgetting in the shock of her pregnancy. 'Go and get dressed. I'll settle things here. Shopping is over. We are leaving.'

He let her go and walked across to the desk to settle the bill. After a few words with the assistant, he made a phone call to his driver. A few minutes later Beth reappeared. There was no denying she was incredibly lovely, with a perfect figure, he thought clinically, but so were plenty of other women who were *not* ex-cons. He was only marrying her because she was pregnant.

He took her arm and led her outside—and stopped.

Glancing up, Beth tracked where he was looking—at his watch—and when he lifted his eyes to hers they were hard.

'It is only twelve-thirty. We could be home in an hour,' he opined, 'or if you prefer we can lunch here. I do have to be in Rome by this evening, so we will have to be quick.'

'Your home is fine by me,' Beth said, because deep inside she knew it was never going to be *her* home.

'Good. I have had the helicopter moved to a ground-level helipad and a car is picking us up in a minute.'

In other words he had already arranged to leave, making his offer of lunch about as genuine as their marriage was going to be.

It was the longest conversation they were to have on the journey back. The car ride was short, the helicopter was standing in a field, and once on board no conversation was necessary anyway.

It did not get much better when they got back to the house.

Belatedly Beth remembered to thank him for the clothes. Dante simply shrugged and led her into his study, where he presented her with a prenuptial agreement.

'Sit here and read it. I have had it translated from Italian to English. Make a note of anything you want to query. I'll go and tell Sophie to prepare your lunch.'

Beth sat at the desk and started to read. The document was only four pages and quite succinct. Yes, it was there in black-and-white. After three years she could have a divorce and joint custody of their child, and the amount of money he was prepared to give her was enormous. Her first thought was to refuse the money, but common sense prevailed. She might not want his money, but she could think of a lot of people who needed it. She could give it to charity. Dante could certainly afford it.

When Dante came back she told him it was fine, and he took the document and left.

Beth replaced the phone on the bedside table and sighed.

It was odd that she had no trouble talking to Dante on the phone. Since their trip to Milan and his swift return to Rome he had called her most mornings. At first the conversations had been brief, with him just asking how she was, but gradually they had lengthened. He had not come back last weekend, citing pressure of work— much to Sophie's disgust and Beth's relief.

Sophie had shown her around the house and gardens, Carlo the rest of the estate, and Beth had done a lot of exploring on her own. Dante had asked her what she thought of the place, and she'd told him the house and grounds were beautiful. They had discussed all sorts of things, and Beth had found herself enjoying his calls. But now Dante was coming back and she was a bundle of nerves.

CHAPTER NINE

GLANCING AROUND THE feminine bedroom Beth had grown accustomed to, she wondered if she would ever sleep there again. Dismissing the disturbing thought, she slid off the bed and quickly showered and dressed in one of her new purchases—a midnight-blue trouser suit teamed with a heavy white silk blouse. Her own clothes were already in a suitcase, along with a couple of new additions courtesy of Dante. After adding her toiletries she was ready.

A leisurely breakfast in the kitchen with Sophie had become a habit she had acquired quickly rather than endure the formality of eating on her own in the breakfast room. Today they were interrupted by Carlo, entering to inform them that the helicopter had landed.

Beth walked into the hall and glanced around, her eyes lingering on the family oil paintings that adorned the walls. One day would a painting of her child as an adult hang here? she wondered. Not that she would see it. Once her child was three she would probably never be back here again....

Dante walked in through the door. Her eyes locked with his and then slid away as he crossed the wide expanse of marble floor. Her heart thudded.

'You're looking more lovely than ever, Beth.'

His deep voice played across her nerve-endings.

'How do you feel?'

He cupped her chin in his hand and tilted her head up to his. The familiar male scent of him filled her nostrils. This close he appeared to tower over her, all broad-shouldered and vibrantly male. Shockingly, she had a vivid mental image of his great golden naked body over hers, enclosing her, possessing her. She pressed her trembling thighs together. No way was she telling him how she really felt.

'Fine,' she managed to say, and his mouth descended on hers briefly.

'Sorry I could not be here to show you around. I have missed you,' he said in a deep, husky voice, his dark eyes unreadable as he held her gaze.

Something stirred deep inside Beth and she realised that against all reason she had missed Dante. She opened her mouth to say so, but Sophie burst in with a string of Italian aimed at him that saved her from making a huge mistake. He had obviously only said he missed her for Sophie's benefit.

Five minutes later Beth sat in the helicopter with Dante at the controls. He turned towards her and handed her headphones so they could communicate. Not that she wanted to. The enormity of the day ahead was finally hitting her.

Within an hour they had landed in Rome and were being whisked away from the helicopter in a chauffeured limousine to the hospital. The building looked impressively modern, Beth thought as she entered the luxurious reception area with Dante at her side.

The ultrasound was embarrassing with Dante hovering over her, but as the nurse pointed out the outline of their baby on the screen for an awesome moment they simply stared, then looked at each other and grinned in amazed delight.

Back in the car, Beth looked in wonder at the photo of her child—until she realised the car had stopped.

'My lawyer is expecting us.'

Dante took her arm and helped her out of the car into the offices of his lawyer. In twenty minutes the prenuptial agreement was signed and they were back in the car.

Beth glanced at Dante, a foot away from her in the back seat. He had taken out his smartphone and she presumed he was working. He was certainly efficient, she thought. The speed with which they had seen his lawyer had surprised her. But it should not have done, she realised. Of course he'd wanted absolute proof of the baby before he deigned to give his name to the woman he thought her to be. Thinking about it, she was surprised he had not demanded a DNA test. He didn't trust her any more than she trusted him.

The car drove out of the city and finally through iron gates and up a wide drive, to stop in front of the entrance to a magnificent old building surrounded by perfectly manicured lawns and colourful gardens.

'Is your apartment here?' Beth asked, turning to Dante, sure he was the type to have a super deluxe apartment in the city centre.

'No, I have an apartment on the top floor of the Cannavaro building. But it is more like an extension of my office than a home. I thought you would prefer a hotel so I booked a suite here for two nights.'

Beth was even more amazed, and slightly intimidated as she looked around the elegant sitting room. She glanced at Dante as he handed the porter some money and then turned to walk towards her, and she had the oddest notion that the distinctive, self-assured Dante was not as calm as he appeared.

'You should be comfortable here, Beth. There is an excellent spa and beauty salon, a boutique—everything you could want. And as it is unlucky for the bride to see the groom the night before the wedding, and we need all the luck we can get,' he said dryly. 'I'll leave you to rest and relax. Enjoy the facilities—buy whatever you like. I'll call you tonight to make sure you have everything you need and be back at three tomorrow afternoon to pick you up. The ceremony is at four. Now, order some lunch. I'll see you later.'

Beth watched him walk out through the door, leaving her alone at last. Why did she feel deserted? She dismissed the disturbing thought and prowled around the suite, discovering a bathroom and another room that contained a huge widescreen TV. But there was only one bedroom. Big and beautifully proportioned, with two arched windows and the biggest bed she had ever seen set between them. There was a walk-in closet, and the en-suite bathroom had a double shower, his and hers vanity basins, and a bath wide and deep enough to accommodate two people even as big as Dante.

Ordering a light lunch, she sat down to enjoy the meal. After she had finished eating she thought she would make the most of what was on offer and ordered a spa treatment for eleven the next morning. Then she unpacked and lay down on the bed to rest, the photo of her baby in her hand. This miraculous baby was why she was here, and she would marry the devil himself to keep her child. Her only problem was that she no longer thought of Dante as a devil…. The nightmares of a man in black no longer haunted her. Instead, erotic and sometimes stupidly romantic dreams of a happy-ever-after with Dante had taken their place, and that was what worried her most.

After a stroll around the hotel and gardens she returned to the suite to have a delicious dinner and a surprisingly good night's sleep.

The following afternoon, having been waxed and polished, with her hair styled and her make-up applied to perfection, Beth finally put on the winter-white suit and matching camisole Dante had bought for her in Milan. She slipped her feet into high-heeled shoes, courtesy of the hotel boutique, and walked into the sitting room just as Dante appeared.

'You are ready—good. Let's go and get this over with.'

Beth simply nodded, because the sight of him had taken her breath away. He looked tall and effortlessly elegant in a silver-grey designer suit with a tie shaded in grey, a white silk shirt and the glint of platinum cufflinks. His black hair was brushed back from his brow, his handsome face stern. Lethally attractive, Dante exuded sophistication and innate masculine power—and very soon he would be her husband. The reality terrified her, but if she was brutally honest it also thrilled her, and she had trouble tearing her gaze away.

Half an hour later, intensely conscious of Dante at her side, Beth glanced around the wood-panelled room in the town hall. In her childhood dreams, before real life had caught up with her, she had pictured her wedding as a fairy-tale affair—nothing like this. The suit she wore with its silver trim was as close to bridal as she was ever going to get.

Beth glanced at the celebrant. The man conducted the service in Italian and English, but the ceremony had to be one of the briefest on record.

'You may kiss the bride.'

The words jolted her out of her musings.

She looked up into Dante's eyes as his arms wrapped around her and his lips touched hers, firm and warm and tender. Her hands went to his chest and she felt the beat of his heart beneath her palm as his tongue slipped between her parted lips and found hers. Involuntarily she responded, her body softening against him.

The celebrant cleared his throat and said something to Dante, and his arms tightened around her before reluctantly easing her away.

A camera flashed and Beth blinked.

'Smile, please,' Dante instructed, tucking her arm through his. 'This one is for the baby,' he said, placing a gentle hand on her stomach. 'Every child wants to see a picture of their happy parents on their wedding day—even when the marriage no longer exists.'

'So that is the reason you insisted on buying this suit?' she said, surprised by his forward-thinking.

'Even an autocratic lawyer can have flashes of inspiration sometimes,' he said drolly, and then tugged her arm through his and led her out of the building and into the waiting car.

Back at the hotel, she could not look at him as they ascended the stairs to the first-floor suite. Her panic was mounting with every step as the enormity of what she had done filled her mind. She was married and pregnant and in a few minutes she would be alone with Dante. Her stomach knotted with nerves.

When they reached the suite, Beth's mouth fell open in shock. The elegant suite had been transformed into something incredibly romantic, with dozens of red roses in vases, others in exquisite arrangements, and candles scattered all around. Champagne stood on ice on a silver stand, and next to it was a table exquisitely set for two, with a single red rose in a silver flute as a centrepiece.

'I can't believe this,' Beth said, and Dante reached for her, his hands clasping her waist, drawing her nearer. She felt her body flush with warmth and her pulse quicken.

'Would you believe I'm a romantic at heart? I believe every bride deserves a bridal suite on her wedding night.' He grinned.

Seeing Beth in the hospital had caused a seismic shift in Dante's thinking. For years he had considered her beneath contempt as a drug dealer and the type of immoral woman who would play on her beauty to entrap men for her personal benefit. But when he had seen the scan of their child inside her an emotion he had never experienced before had overwhelmed him. From that moment on he had looked at her in a new way—a different way.

He had sat in the car pretending to work, his mind spinning, and realised she would feel trapped in his apartment, twelve floors up in an elevator. Hurriedly he had booked the hotel. Later he hadn't been able to get out of the suite quickly enough. He'd wanted her so fiercely, but as the mother of his child and his soon-to-be-bride she'd deserved much better than a quick coupling the night before her wedding. He had stopped at

Reception as he left and given strict instructions that she was to be given anything she wanted, and he'd ordered the transformation of the suite for the following afternoon.

Beth looked at Dante, stunned he had bothered. His hand lifted to curl a strand of hair behind her ear, the other slipping behind her to press in the small of her back and hold her close. The brush of his hard male body against her stomach sent heat from low in her pelvis pounding through her veins. Her eyes lifted to the chiselled lips, the sensual mouth. It was impossible to ignore the way her body reacted to his.

But Beth tried. 'No, I wouldn't believe it,' she said, in a last-ditch attempt to deny the fatal attraction Dante held for her.

Her gaze lifted to his dark long-lashed eyes and she felt herself drowning in the glittering depths. She had thought she hated Dante for so many years, but now she wanted him with a hunger and a need for physical contact that she could not control. She raised her hands to his chest....

'I guessed as much,' he murmured, and the teasing brush of his mouth was on hers, making her lips tingle and part. 'But at least give me credit for trying, and allow me to try to prove you wrong.' He chuckled softly and tilted her head to one side. His tongue touched the silken skin below her ear, then trailed kisses down her slender throat.

Beth dragged in a ragged breath and Dante lifted his head, a long finger running along her tremulous lower lip. Dizzy with longing, she instinctively pressed her body closer and felt the jut of his erection against her belly. It was shockingly intimate and incredibly arousing to think she could do this to him, and it made her forget about the past—only the moment and Dante existed.

'Trust me, Beth, today is a new beginning for us, and I want to make it right for you.'

And she did trust him.... Meeting his lips with her own, she signaled her total capitulation.

His mouth explored her with gentle expertise, his tongue curling with hers, teasing, tasting, and she was lost in the wonder of his kiss.

Dante raised his head and had to battle to resist his basic instinct to take her where they stood. He cupped her head in his hands and looked down into her sparkling emerald eyes. The pupils were dilated to black pearls of passion and he stifled a groan.

'Not here, Beth.'

Swinging her up in his arms, he carried her into the bedroom and lowered her gently onto the bed. He had never believed her *once was enough* comment—although ironically it was that one time when he had made her pregnant. But Dante had never suspected Beth was a virgin, and could not help feeling that if he had known he could have done better. Now she was his wife, the mother of his child, and he was determined to give her the wedding night she deserved and would remember with pleasure.

Beth glanced at yet more candles, then stared in awe as Dante stripped off his clothes, his great body gleaming golden in the candlelight. The fine black hair across his chest arrowed down over his washboard stomach to curl at the junction of his thighs, and his powerful erection sent a primordial feminine thrill quivering through her slender frame.

Then he was leaning over her, her clothes were being peeled from her body, and she lay without shame, naked before him, mesmerised by the burning gleam in his eyes as they raked her from head to toe.

'You are exquisite, *mia moglia*,' he rasped, and kissed her forehead, her nose, briefly her lips, and moved lower to her breasts and the soft curve of her stomach, where he lingered, murmuring in Italian.

He raised his head and the intensity in his magnificent dark eyes made her heart squeeze. All her doubts and fears for the future faded away, and she linked her hand around his neck, hungry for his kiss.

Finally his mouth found hers, and she responded intuitively to the searching passion of a kiss that left her breathless and wanting more. Her hands unfurled from his neck to clasp his broad shoulders, while his hands traced slowly and gently over her breasts and stomach, brushing the soft curls as he reached the apex of her thighs. With every silken touch of his fingers Beth's hunger for him grew. Moisture and heat pooled low in her body, which was pulsing with need. His long fingers flicked around her inner thighs, so close to where she ached. His hands swept back up her body, firmer now, cupping her breasts, his thumbs stroking the rosy peaks.

'Slightly larger, I think,' he said huskily, his glittering gaze on her breasts.

His head lowered and his mouth closed over a pouting nipple. She moaned low in her throat. His tongue rolled the rigid tip and his teeth nipped and tugged. The pleasure was almost pain before he licked the throbbing peak and excitement threatened to explode inside her.

Her fingers pressed into his muscular shoulders, nails digging into his flesh. When she could stand no more her hand fisted in his hair to pull his head back, and with a husky groan his mouth closed over hers with the powerful, possessive passion that she hungered for....

His hands, big and strong, caressed her skin and his mouth followed—kissing, tasting, discovering pleasure points she'd never known she had. But Dante knew...

Oh, how he knew...

Beth writhed beneath him, aroused to fever-pitch by his prolonged sensual exploration. His mouth returned to hers, playful, teasing and passionate, while his long fingers continued their delicate exploration of every secret place with an erotic skill that drove her wild....

She was burning up. Her slender hands stroked him and found the thick, hard length of his erection. She knew he was as desperate as she was. With a guttural growl he tore her hand from his body and his mouth found hers again, devouring her. His hands lifted her, and his great body was tense as steel as finally he was where Beth madly, desperately wanted him. He began to probe gently—too gently—and she locked her legs high around his back, her body arching as with supreme control he probed a little deeper, stretching her...

He withdrew.

'Dante!' she cried, desperate for all of him. 'Please!'

With a husky groan and a thrust of his hips he answered her. his hard length filling and holding her. He drew a taut nipple into his mouth and raised his hips and thrust again. Then he paused and suckled its twin, and a starburst of feelings blinded her to everything but Dante. He moved in a fluid, ever increasing rhythm, harder and faster, pulsing inside her until she convulsed around him in a blaze of heat and light, like a star going nova, and she heard his cry of triumph as he followed her, his life force spilling inside her.

'I'm too heavy for you,' Dante rasped some time later, and with a gentle kiss on her love-swollen lips he rolled onto his back and slipped a hand beneath her waist, easing her into the curve of his shoulder.

Beth rested a slender arm across his broad chest. She had thought the first time Dante had made love to her had been incredible, but tonight had surpassed that. She had never felt so complete, so languorous, so perfectly at peace in body and mind in her life.

'How do you feel, Beth? I didn't hurt you, did I?' He stroked the hair back from her brow.

She raised herself up on one elbow and looked down at Dante. His hair was all over the place, his incredible eyes serious, and she let her hand stroke over his chest, her fingers playing with his chest hair. 'No, you didn't hurt me. Though I have to admit...' She paused teasingly, and surprisingly felt his body tense. 'You were right. Once was not enough.'

'Why, you little tease.' He grinned and pulled her head down to his to press his lips against her mouth.

In minutes they were making love again.

Dante took his time to explore her and to show her various ways to please him that surprised and excited both her and Dante! Their senses were on a knife's edge, and when he finally surged up into her with a few pounding thrusts they climaxed together.

Beth lay across Dante's body in the aftermath, totally sated. She had been on top during their lovemaking—something she had never envisaged before—and as her head rested on his chest she found herself too languorous to move. Instead she listened to the heavy pounding of his heart gradually steady.

'Beth?'

Dante said her name and she glanced up at him.

'Sorry to disturb you.' His strong hands clasped her by the waist and he lifted her as if she was as light as a feather and sat up, placing her flat on her back on the bed. 'These damn candles are a fire risk. I can smell burning.'

'So much for romantic gestures,' Beth said, and burst out laughing.

Dante slid out of bed and snuffed out the candles. Beth watched him as he walked to the bathroom. Big and lithe and stunning from the rear, with long legs and firm, tight buttocks—not something she had ever really noticed in a man before, but now she found every inch of Dante fascinating.

They slipped on the robes the hotel had provided and Dante ordered room service. They shared an intimate dinner, and then went back to bed.

The next morning they took a flight to London and Beth fell asleep on the plane....

'Not too bad, hmm...?' Dante said, with a guiding hand on Beth's back as they walked out of his mother's home in Kensington. 'My mother adores you. And when we finally tell her you are pregnant—if she hasn't already guessed—she will worship at your feet. As for Harry— he made his feelings very clear.'

Beth chuckled. 'Yes, he did.' She had been dreading meeting Dante's mother, Teresa—a lovely petite woman, with black hair and brown eyes—and her husband, Harry, but they were a delightful couple and had made her feel completely at ease. Harry was an older version of Tony, and Beth had not been able to help saying so—which had led to her admitting she had lived in the apartment beneath Tony until a few months ago. Dante had added smoothly that that was where Beth and he had met—at Tony's barbecue.

'So *you* are the angel girl who supplied my Tony and Mike with food and all kinds of help!' Teresa had exclaimed, and from then on everything had been plain sailing.

Lunch had been a happy affair, and an eye-opener for Beth as Teresa had regaled her with stories of Dante as a child—much to his embarrassment.

Beth turned now as Teresa and Harry followed them out to say goodbye, with hugs all round and promises to return soon. They were finally about to leave when there was a screech of tyres and Tony arrived.

With a 'Hi, Mum—Dad,' he stopped in front of Beth. 'I don't believe it, Beth! You actually married Dante. What on earth possessed you when you could have had me?' Grinning broadly, he gave her a big hug and a kiss on the cheek. Beth laughed.

'Yes, she did marry me—so you can take your hands off her,' Dante said with a smile that verged on triumphant as he slipped a proprietorial arm around her waist.

'You're a lucky devil, bro, and I'm not surprised you whisked Beth away and married her. I noticed you couldn't take your eyes off her at the barbecue….' Tony said. 'Mind you, I'm not sure you deserve her—'

'That's enough, Tony,' Dante cut in, and the tone of his voice brooked no argument.

'Okay…congratulations. You do make a striking couple. So, where are you going for the honeymoon?'

'Somewhere hot—the Caribbean or the Indian Ocean, as it will be December before I can free up any time. Beth can decide.'

'*I* can decide?' A honeymoon had never entered Beth's head.

'Yes—why not?' Dante gave her a sexy smile. 'I have been all over the place. You can have fun choosing somewhere you would really like to go.'

'Is that wise, Dante?' Tony queried. 'Knowing Beth, it will be a surfers' beach in Hawaii—hardly your scene!' he quipped, then added, 'Trust me, I still shudder at the thought of when she tried to teach Mike and I how to surf.' He grimaced. 'But wherever you go you'd better take good care of her, or you will have me to deal with.'

'I intend to—and thanks.'

'Thank you for that, Tony,' Beth said with a grin. Tony was such a joker, and he enjoyed winding people up, but he was a truly lovable young man.

'Now we really must get going,' Dante commanded, and with final goodbyes all round Beth slid into the passenger seat of the Bentley and they left.

Dante concentrated on negotiating the city traffic, with a frown on his face that had little to do with his driving and everything to do with Beth. Seeing the easy interaction between Beth and his brother, and after spending time with her and getting to know her intimately, he could tell there had never been anything sexual about their relationship. Tony was an irrepressible flirt, like most twenty-three-year-old males, but Beth just laughed and ignored it. And Tony's ready acceptance of their marriage confirmed he had never been serious about her....

Which made Dante question his own actions—not something he was prone to do—in threatening Beth with dire consequences unless she left Tony alone. He now knew a lot of what Beth had told him was the truth, but did it change anything? Her past was inescapable, and he would still have felt duty-bound to tell Tony why she was unsuitable as a wife, conveniently ignoring the fact that *he* had married her.

He cast a sidelong glance at Beth; she looked so relaxed, so beautiful, and she was carrying his child. Yesterday had been their wedding day and last night he had enjoyed the best sex of his life. He only had to look at Beth to want her, and he knew she felt the same. The past was the past and there was no point in dwelling on old mistakes, he told himself.

'You really do like Tony?' he prompted.

'Yes, I do. He is so easygoing, happy and carefree,' she said with a wistful smile. 'It must be nice to be so uncomplicated. What you see with Tony and Mike is what you get, and they make me laugh. I can't remember when I felt young like that—if ever.'

Dante heard the hint of sadness in her tone and could have kicked himself for reminding her of the past; the present and their baby was all that should concern him. 'No wonder they are a carefree pair, with you helping them out all the time.'

'I told you—we're good friends. Though sometimes I think I was more like a house mother to the pair of them.'

Dante shook his head. 'You are far too soft for your own good, Beth.'

* * *

Where Dante was concerned Beth knew she was…. This morning she had awakened in his arms and they had made love again. Bedazzled in the aftermath, she had told him he was a perfect lover. But Dante's response—'I always aim to please, *cara*!'—had struck a discordant note in Beth's mind. Just how many women *had* he pleased? she'd wondered, and it had brought her back to reality.

Dante didn't make love—love never entered his vocabulary. He was a sophisticated man of the world and he must have had sex with dozens of women. The only reason Beth was in his bed was because she was pregnant with his child. She must never think it was anything more than a convenient marriage for the good of her child and herself.

But it was hard when a smiling, tactile Dante was so irresistible as they'd shared breakfast in their hotel suite. He had fed her food from his plate and planted kisses on her mouth between bites. He only had to look at her and she wanted him, and she had to keep reminding herself it wasn't going to last….

She cast Dante a sidelong glance. His focus was on the narrow, twisting country road, but nothing could detract from the sculptured perfection of his profile and her heart skipped a beat.

As if sensing her scrutiny, he slanted a knowing smile her way.

'Not long now.'

Her tummy flipped.

'It's a shame I can only stay one more night. When I get back next weekend we need to discuss more permanent living arrangements.'

Later Beth would wonder if she'd had a premonition that night, when she'd decided to share the main guest bedroom with Dante instead of her own room, the master suite.

CHAPTER TEN

THE LAST DAY of September, and for the past week England had been basking in an Indian summer. The temperature was balmy as Beth walked out of the sea, a smile on her face.

The marriage deal she had struck with Dante that had filled her with such trepidation was turning out to be nothing like what she had feared. The two nights they had shared had been a revelation; he was an incredible lover and generous in every way. Walking up the beach still smiling, Beth realised she actually felt the happiest she had in years.

'On a day like today it makes you glad to be alive,' Beth said, and stopped and grinned down at Janet, who was showing Annie how to build a sandcastle. 'I really enjoyed my swim.' She reached for a towel from her beach bag on the sand and saw her phone flashing. She picked it up and read the text. 'Dante's in a meeting that looks like it's running late. But he will be back here tomorrow evening.' She dropped the phone back in her bag. 'I'll reply later. The waves are rising and I'm going to get my surfboard....'

'No, you won't. A swim is okay, but surfing is definitely out in your condition. And from the black clouds on the horizon it's not going to matter anyway,' Janet said, and rose to her feet. Looking past Beth, she exclaimed, 'Will you look at that? Oh, my God!'

Beth turned to see what Janet meant, and to her horror at the end of the beach she saw a child with a pink plastic ring around her waist, being swept from the shallows by the fast-rising tide.

Beth didn't stop to think—she ran.... A man dashed into the sea and then stopped. Frantic, he yelled that he could not swim, and without hesitation Beth dived into the waves.

What followed was the stuff of nightmares. She managed to reach the child and grab hold of her, but when she tried to turn back the rip tide caught her and they were both swept farther out.

Battling to stay afloat, Beth felt another large wave crash over her, then another, and another. However hard she fought, she could not beat the current, and was being dragged farther out towards the rocky headland. A massive wave submerged them, and for a heart-stopping moment Beth was convinced the end had come. With that came the thought she would never see Dante again....

Suddenly she could breathe again, and with the terrified child's arms locked tightly around her neck Beth twisted to protect her as they were flung against the rocks. She felt a stabbing pain in her back. But the pain in her heart was worse than any gash from the rocks as she realised that against all rhyme and reason she loved Dante.

Clutching the child with the last of her strength, she managed to scramble up onto the rocks. A backward glance told her the tide was coming in fast, and she could not swim back to the shore with the child.

She sat down on a flat rock before her legs gave way completely, cuddling the sobbing child to her chest and breathing great gulps of air into her oxygen-starved lungs in between murmuring words of comfort to the little girl—whose name, she discovered, was Trixie. She had no idea how long she sat there, soothing the child and anxiously watching the water rise. Then she saw the coastguard rescue boat ploughing through the waves and heard someone shouting her name. She rose to her feet, handed Trixie into the outstretched arms of a man in the boat, and almost collapsed with relief—the child was safe.

The rest was a bit of a blur.

She remembered being hauled into the boat, having a blanket wrapped around her and Trixie placed in her arms again. At the harbour an ambulance waited, and Janet had brought her clothes and her bag from the beach. The ambulance crew were insisting on taking them to the hospital.

Later Beth sat in the hospital, with the blanket still around her, waiting to see the doctor. She took her phone out of her bag and read the text Dante had sent her earlier. She texted back that she was fine and that she would see him tomorrow night. She thought of ending with *love*, and didn't quite dare. But Beth knew she loved him without a shadow of a doubt—though she would have preferred to realise it without half drowning in the process.

Perhaps she always had loved Dante? Maybe there *was* such a thing as love at first sight? she mused. All along there had been that deep underlining attraction that had begun in the courtroom when she was only nineteen and too innocent to recognise it, and after the trial it had been easier to hate him. Now she was married to him and carrying his child, and though he didn't love her he wanted her physically. With a child between them she could hope he would grow to love her. The three-year time limit was a minimum, not a maximum....

A young couple with tears in their eyes came up to her and thanked her over and over again for saving their little girl Trixie.

Beth smiled as they walked away, but there was more—much, much more than she had ever expected—until finally she fell into an exhausted sleep.

'Mrs Cannavaro...' Beth opened her eyes and saw a woman in a blue uniform, standing by her bed. She glanced around. The room was white and she was completely disorientated for a moment. Then, as the events of yesterday came flooding back, she closed her eyes again.

'Mrs Cannavaro.'

The nurse repeated her name, and reluctantly she opened her eyes.

'Good news. Your husband will be here soon, and a cup of tea and food is on its way. I need to check your vitals, and then you can have a wash and get dressed,' she told her with a broad smile. 'Dr James will be here to see you soon, and after that you can be discharged. And don't worry—you are very fit and an extremely brave young woman...you will be fine in no time at all.'

The nurse was so unrelentingly cheerful, while avoiding the elephant in the room, that it made Beth want to scream. But she didn't. Stoically, she said, 'Thank you.' And then asked, 'How is Trixie today?'

'Oh, the little girl is fine—thanks to you. She went home with her parents last night.'

'Good,' Beth said, and suffered the nurse's ministrations in silence, reliving the tragic events of yesterday that had put her here. In her mind she blamed herself, though she knew she could never have done anything different. Trixie was safe and that was all that mattered.

But now she was no longer quite so certain.

At nine last night a doctor had told her that the pain that had suddenly doubled her over as she was leaving was the start of a miscarriage. Probably brought on by the tremendous amount of physical energy it had taken to save the little girl. The bruising and the gash on her back had not helped, and it had cost the life of her own baby. By eleven it had all been over, and for the first time since Helen died Beth had broken down and cried until she had no tears left.

Now she felt nothing at all—just totally numb inside.

She nodded and said yes and thank you to the nurse's endless chatter, until finally she was washed and her hair was combed. Wearing the clothes Janet had handed her yesterday, she sat on the edge of the bed and drank a cup of tea. The food was of no interest to her.

Dr James arrived and after checking her over, his eyes full of compassion, he told her how sorry he was and made an appointment for her to see him on Monday to confirm everything was clear. He told her that she was a healthy young woman and he was sure she would have no trouble getting pregnant again when she wanted to, not to worry. It had been an extraordinary set of circumstances that had caused the miscarriage, and it was extremely unlikely to happen again.

Beth smiled and said thank you again, and sat down

on the bed as he turned to leave. She heard the door close behind him. Suddenly the numbness that had protected her bruised mind and body faded away and her shoulders slumped. Her spirit was broken. She could never regret saving Trixie, but it had cost her a soul-destroying price. But then that seemed to be the story of her life, she thought, looking back over the past few years that had led her to this point.

She heard the ring of her cell phone and automatically reached into her bag and answered. It was Janet. She had called at the cottage and the builder was there but Beth wasn't. Janet wanted to know why she was not at home. In a few terse sentences Beth told her, and listened to her compassionate response. She asked if there was anything she could do to help. Beth said nothing except to tell the builders to take the day off. She wanted to be alone for a while, and Dante would be arriving later. She rang off.

Beth did not want to see anyone or talk to anyone. She wanted to close her eyes and forget the last twenty hours had ever happened. But it wasn't to be. She heard the door open again and looked up to see Dante enter the room. His handsome face looked drawn, black stubble shadowed his jaw, and his mouth was a firm straight line. His eyes blazed with some powerful emotion.

Beth saw a chink of light in the darkness of her soul and rose to her feet. She loved him so much. Maybe he would recognise her pain and take it away, fold her in his arms and comfort her. But Dante made no move towards her. He simply stared.

'Beth, how do you feel?'

How many times had he asked her that? she wondered. It seemed to be his favourite question. The chink of light was extinguished. Deep down she had always known it was the baby he was concerned about, not her. And it slowly dawned on her that the emotion she saw in his dark eyes was anger. Why had she expected anything more? He had married her for the baby—nothing else. She had actually fooled herself into thinking that it might have been something more this week and she'd been happy. But not now. The baby was gone and there was no longer any reason for Dante to be here.

The blood turned to ice in her veins; the numbness returning.

'Fine. Can we leave now?'

The fear and the fury Dante had felt since he'd heard the news at midnight eased a little. Beth looked pale and so beautiful, so tragic. He wished he had been here for her. He wanted to take her in his arms…

'I need to get home to feed Binkie.'

'Forget the damn cat!' Dante exclaimed, his fear and anger boiling over. 'I have spoken to the doctor. You have just lost the baby and you are battered and bruised with a slashed back. What on earth possessed you to dive into the sea? You could have died!'

'I am not having this conversation now. If you don't want to drive me home, I'll get a cab.' Beth picked up her bag, refusing to look at him, intent on leaving.

Dante ran a hand though his hair. He had no right to be angry with Beth; she was his wife and she had lost their baby. He had promised to take care of them both and he had spectacularly failed. Worse, he could not control or explain the emotions churning inside him….

He grabbed Beth's arm as she tried to walk past him and spun her into his arms. 'I'm sorry. I didn't mean to upset you.'

Held close against his strong body, Beth felt nothing. It was too little, too late. 'You didn't.' She lifted expressionless eyes to his. 'I have been sitting here thinking of everything that has happened since I first met you and you are right—I am guilty as charged. I did lose your baby.'

'*Dio!* No—I never meant it like that.'

Beth saw the shock in his eyes and didn't care. 'Maybe not, but it is true. What happened yesterday proves the old adage that no good deed goes unpunished, and today I realised it was the story of my life. I offered two boys I thought were friends a lift and ended up in prison. I saved a little girl and lost my own child. I've finally learned it is best not to get involved with anyone. Now, can we leave? I want to get home.'

Dante looked at her pale blank face. The doctor had told him her injuries were not serious—a few scrapes and bruises and a gash that had needed eight stitches. As for the miscarriage—there was to be a minor procedure on Monday and in a week she should be fine. But after losing the baby she might be a little depressed for a while, and he must be patient with her. Dante knew he should not have lost control and shouted at her.

'Yes, of course,' he said softly, and took the bag from her hand. Taking her arm, he left the hospital.

He glanced across at Beth as he drove through the country roads. Her head was back, her eyes closed. Maybe that was best. Dante was not an emotional man, and though he was gutted at the loss of the baby he could not find the words to express how he felt.

Back at the cottage, as soon as Beth walked in the door Binkie was there. Bending, she picked him up in her arms, stroking and murmuring to him as she headed for the kitchen. She put Binkie down and methodically prepared his bowl of chicken. Then she made a pot of coffee—perhaps to prove her baby really was gone.

Dante followed her into the kitchen. 'It is no good ignoring me, Beth. We need to talk about this.'

Beth turned expressionless eyes on him. 'Not now. I am going to have a coffee and then shower and change,' she said in a cool voice.

'I'll join you.'

'For coffee.'

Filling two mugs from the pot, she handed him one. Her emotions were in deep freeze, and she was immune to the brush of Dante's fingers against hers.

She walked back though the house and out onto the terrace. She sat down on one of the captain's chairs, took a sip of coffee and stared out across the sea. The morning sun shimmered on the calm green water and the waves lapped against the fine sand. Her gaze strayed to the headland. As if to mock her, the tide was out and the rocks were barely fifteen feet from the water's edge.

Beth heard a footstep on the terrace but did not turn her head. She took another drink of coffee.

Dante took the chair beside her, his eyes fixed on her delicate profile. 'I honestly didn't mean to upset you any more than you already are, Beth. I know how hard it must be for you. As for me—I have never felt so awful in my life as when I got the call from the hospital and heard what had happened to you. I really wanted our baby. Never doubt that.'

Beth turned her head, her green eyes resting on Dante. She didn't doubt it for a second. She knew he'd wanted the baby. It was her he had never really wanted and had got stuck with.

'It was never meant to be,' she said flatly. 'The baby was conceived for all the wrong reasons. I was stupid, and you wanted me out of your brother's life. If that wasn't bad enough you and I agreed this child was going to be the product of a broken home before it was even born. I don't know what I was thinking of... I must have been out of my mind. But not any more. I've had enough. I love it here. I relocated here to get out of the rat race and this time I am staying.'

'Having got that off your chest, aren't you forgetting something?' Dante prompted. 'You are my wife, and I have some say in your future.'

'Not for much longer. The reason for our marriage is gone. I want nothing from you so we can get divorced straight away. You're a lawyer—I'm sure you can arrange it.' Beth rose to her feet before adding, 'I'm going for a bath.'

Dante watched her walk back inside but didn't follow her. Instead he looked out over the bay, his eyes narrowed as he considered his options. One thing was certain: he was not ready to let Beth go....

The more he got to know her the more he questioned his original assessment of her. She was an amazing woman... He couldn't think of a single female he had ever met who would have leapt into the sea after that child. Most would not risk getting their hair wet, let alone risk their own life, but Beth had.

His angry outburst when he'd first seen her hadn't been because she had lost the baby but because he had feared for her life....

Rising to his feet, he strolled back into the house.

* * *

With the dressing on her back in mind, Beth had had
a bath in about nine inches of water. Stepping out, she
took a towel and carefully dried her aching body. She
found an old blue tracksuit in one of the drawers. It had
loose pants, so would not press against the cut on her
back. Then, barefoot, she walked into the bedroom, slid
open the glass door to the balcony and stepped outside.
She sank down on a lounger, safe in her haven, and
closed her eyes.

'Beth?'

Reluctantly she opened her eyes at the sound of her
name, and saw Dante walking out of her bedroom on
to the balcony, carrying a tray.

She sat up abruptly. 'What are you doing here? This
is my room.'

'Looking for you. I was under the impression the
room you and I shared last Sunday was the master bedroom, but I see I was wrong. This is much larger,' he
said, his dark eyes resting on her.

Beth didn't need reminding of that day. 'If you've
brought me food you can take it away. I'm not hungry
and I want to be alone.'

He put the tray down across her knees. 'What you
want and what you need are entirely different,' he said
and, pulling up a lounger, sat down.

'Now, eat. I am going to sit here until you do.'

Beth looked at the plate of open sandwiches—ham,
cheese, egg, tomatoes, salami and prawns, plus a token
couple of lettuce leaves. 'You must have raided the
fridge for this lot.'

'I did—to tempt your tastebuds. In the last twenty-
four hours you have been tested to the limit physically

and emotionally with the loss of the baby. You need to build up your strength again.'

She picked up an egg sandwich and realised she had not eaten since lunch yesterday. She took a bite and found she could finish it. 'There's no need for you to stay. I *am* eating.'

She glanced up into the black brooding intensity of Dante's dark eyes without a flicker of emotion in her own.

'I am staying. Not just to see you eat, but for as long as it takes to make sure you are fully recovered.'

Spoken like the despot he was, Beth thought. But it didn't bother her. She was immune to him now. And from what she knew of Dante he was not cut out for the quiet life of Faith Cove. He'd be bored out of his mind in a couple of days and would go back to his high-flying life. She'd never see him again.

'Please yourself. You usually do. As long as you understand you are not sharing my room.' He didn't argue and she wasn't surprised. With no sex available, why would he?

By Monday morning, when he insisted on going to the hospital with her, Beth was not quite so sure he would leave. He was a good house guest. He cooked—though not very well—he made his bed in his own room, and he had clothes delivered and his laundry collected by a concierge service. Yes, he had a tendency to wrap an arm around her or drop a kiss on her brow, but it had no effect on her.

Over dinner on Tuesday night Beth had a rude awakening.

Dante was not the most patient of men, and being

blanked by Beth for four days was getting to him. When he touched her she was like a block of ice. If he told her to eat, she did. If he suggested a walk, she agreed. To-night he had cooked spaghetti, one of the few dishes he could make well, and she had sat down like an obedient child. He'd had enough. He wanted the feisty Beth back.

Dante watched her full lips part as she forked food into her mouth and felt the familiar tug of desire. She wore no make-up, her glorious hair was swept severely back from her face—she looked beautiful, but remote.

'My mother called me today and she sends you her love. She hopes to see us soon. As she missed our wedding, she wants to arrange a post-wedding party for family and friends. I agreed. I think a party will do you good. I have to be in New York next week, probably for three or four weeks, so I suggested mid-November.'

Beth couldn't believe her ears. 'A party? No way! We are getting a divorce, remember?'

'I recall you mentioned divorce, but you were ill so I said nothing.'

The way Dante was looking at her suddenly made Beth feel threatened. He was big and golden, and the dark glitter in his eyes, the slightly predatory curl of his mouth, contained a message she did not want to recognize. She knew she had to tread carefully.

'But I thought you'd agreed when you didn't say anything against it?'

'We had just got back from the hospital. I did not want to upset you and I certainly wasn't going to argue with you. You *did* read the prenuptial agreement?'

'Yes, of course.' Beth didn't get the connection.

'Then you must know you have not fulfilled your part of the deal.'

'What do you mean?' From just *feeling* threatened Beth knew she was being threatened, and she received an answer that astounded her.

'It states quite clearly that three years after the birth of our first child I will agree to give you a divorce if you so desire. As sadly we don't have a child yet, I don't have to give you anything—certainly not a divorce unless I want to, and right now I don't want to.'

'Are you telling me I have to get pregnant again?' Beth exclaimed.

'Hell, no. I am not that much of an ogre. Though it is something we could consider in the future.'

Beth stood up, her green eyes flashing. 'You and I don't have a future together. We never did. I'm going to bed.'

Dante had seen the angry sparkle in her eyes and knew he was getting through to her. 'I'll walk you to your room.'

Where had she heard that before?

Beth remembered and felt a slight flutter in her tummy—which wasn't helped by Dante's strong arm curving around her waist. The numbness that had protected her was fading fast, but she didn't want to be aware of him again, and said, 'You are hurting my back.' She spun out of his arm and out through the door.

Dante was going to follow her, but hesitated. She had suffered a traumatic shock with the miscarriage. He could wait until tomorrow. Because he had sensed when he held her the ice had broken. He was winning her over. He simply had to persevere a little longer.

Beth undressed and got into bed, but she couldn't sleep. She heard Dante walk upstairs and the door of his room open and close. She heaved a sigh of relief

tinged with regret for what might have been if she had
not lost her baby....

By the time Beth crawled into bed on Thursday night
she could no longer pretend she was immune to Dante.
On Wednesday she had tried to avoid him by working
in her study. But as the study looked out over the back
garden she had caught sight of Dante, stripped to the
waist, helping the builders. She had not been able to tear
her gaze away from him, and suddenly the unseasonably warm weather had felt even hotter. And this morning when he'd slipped his arm around her waist she had
trembled. She had blamed it on the cut on her back.

'Back still sore, Beth? I thought the stitches dissolved in seven days,' Dante had drawled mockingly.
He'd known perfectly well she was faking it, and exactly how he affected her....

This evening had been the final straw. He had insisted on taking her to the pub for a meal, saying she
needed to get out. She had watched him, looking devastatingly attractive in blue jeans and a grey sweater,
laughing and talking with easy charm with the other
customers, thinking of how patient he was being with
her when she had expected him to be long gone. She
knew she was in big trouble. She loved him and it terrified her.

Beth had told herself so often that she hated him, but
her heart told her something else. He said he didn't want
a divorce and would like another child. If she actually
was the type of woman he thought she was it would be
easy to stay married to him—handsome, rich and good
at sex. She stirred restlessly in the bed. But she wasn't
that type of woman.

She loved him, and staying married to him would

destroy her. He was convinced she was guilty of a heinous crime and that would never change. He wanted her and he felt affection for her—he'd proved that by staying and caring for her this week—but there could never be any equality in their relationship. She would always be the guilty party, inferior in his mind and not really to be trusted, and she could not live with that. Without trust there was nothing. She had fought long and hard to be a successful woman in her own right and she was not prepared to be an appendage to Dante's life.

When Beth finally fell asleep her decision was made.

CHAPTER ELEVEN

BETH OPENED HER EYES and glanced sleepily at her alarm clock. Nine o'clock. She blinked and studied the clock again. She must have slept through the seven o'clock alarm.

She stretched luxuriously beneath the covers and then pushed them back so she could get up. When the door opened and Dante walked in her first instinct was to dive back under the covers, but that would be childish, so she settled for sitting up and pulling her nightshirt down her legs.

'Good morning, Beth. Did you sleep well?'

'Yes, thank you. Did you?'

Their eyes met briefly. 'Not as well as I would have done with you,' he said.

He was wearing black jeans and a sweater and he was smiling down at her. Suddenly she was filled with the most intense sensual message, and though outwardly motionless she quivered inside.

'I was about to get up,' she said hastily.

'So I see.' He sat down on the side of the bed and wrapped his hand around her wrist. 'But I need to talk to you first. The manager of my New York office called me when we got back last night in something of a panic.

I have to be at an emergency meeting there tomorrow. It's all going to be a bit of a rush. Our flight is booked for five this afternoon from Heathrow, so we will have to leave soon.'

'We?' Beth interjected. 'Why? This has nothing to do with me.'

Suddenly he lifted her wrist and wrapped his arm around her to draw her close. His mouth covered hers, his tongue stroking and delving into the sensitive interior. All her logic of last night was forgotten as she was swept up to the dizzy heights of passion by his kiss.

'*That* is why,' Dante rasped, looking into her eyes. 'I want you with me.'

Beth was almost convinced by the taste of him on her lips and the tight knot of desire in her stomach—until he added, 'I spoke to the builder when he arrived this morning and you don't have to be here. If he needs to get in the house he can get the keys from Janet or her father. And Janet has agreed to take the cat for the three or four weeks we will be away. All you need to do is pack a few things.'

Beth was stunned. From dizzy heights back to earth in one moment. Dante really had thought of everything—except asking her first. She'd been right. She was just an appendage to his life.

Withdrawing her hand from his shoulder, she eased away from him. 'Just one query.' She raised a delicate eyebrow. 'Do you want me with you for sex, or because you are madly in love with me?' she asked, putting him on the spot. She noted the hint of colour that accentuated his high cheekbones and saw the answer in his eyes.

'I want you with me because you're my wife.'

Clever sidestep, worthy of a good lawyer, Beth thought, and was amazed at how quickly passion could fade. Sliding her legs over to the opposite side of the bed, she stood up and turned to look at him. He was the most handsome man she had ever seen, and she loved him so much. But a one-sided love was a recipe for disaster, and she had had enough of those in her life already.

'I want to stay here and get a divorce. So I guess we will have to agree to differ,' she said with a nonchalance she didn't feel.

Dante rose to his feet, seething with anger and frustration. If he had said he loved her they would be in that bed now, but he refused to be manipulated by any woman. He had spent a week waiting on her when he should have been working—something he had never done for any other woman. In fact he didn't know what the hell he was waiting for, wasting his time. He glanced furiously around. Beth could stay in this place she loved so much. He didn't need her in his life, compromising his work. She could have her damned divorce.

'No. You can have a divorce—and a word of advice. I know your cellmate died in your arms in this room. It's time you got the place decorated instead of hanging on to your less-than-salubrious past like a safety blanket, or you will never move on in life.'

And with that parting shot he stormed out.

Beth watched him go. His last unemotional parting comment had cut deep but proved what she'd known all along. How could she still love him? She was glad he was gone. It was what she wanted, she told herself. So why did she feel like crying? She glanced around the room, seeing it through Dante's eyes. The décor was faded. She ran her hand along the bureau, remembering the first time she had made love with Dante in this room—because for her it *had* always been love. Dante was right. It was time she moved on instead of clinging to the past. Just not with him....

December, and Dante was back in London, seated next to Martin Thomas, an acquaintance from his university days, at the Law Society's annual dinner. He was regretting that he had come, but he regretted a lot lately. Especially walking out on Beth. Why hadn't he just told her he loved her? If the last two months without her had taught him anything it was that he couldn't live without her—and if that wasn't love he didn't know what was.

'You know old Bewick, don't you, Dante?' Martin asked. Not waiting for a response, he continued, 'You have to feel sorry for him. He doted on that son of his— Timothy. It must have come as one hell of a shock to him to hear he was arrested for drug smuggling.'

'What? His son? Are you sure?' Dante asked, frowning.

'No doubt about it. Baby Face Bewick is one of the biggest suppliers of drugs in the country. The drug squad had his operation under surveillance for a year, and now they've arrested him and his sidekick, Hudson, and recovered drugs worth over two million. The two of them were refused bail and are in jail awaiting trial. I'm prosecuting the case and it is watertight— plus Hudson is singing like a canary. Bewick started dealing drugs while at public school, apparently. Hudson helped him and they continued at university. Actually they were nearly caught in the first term, but they fitted up some teenage girl—Jane someone—and got away with it. Hudson probably wishes he hadn't now. Juvenile detention would have been much easier than where he is going.'

Dante had heard enough. Abruptly he got to his feet and walked out.

The next morning he called a friend at Scotland Yard and confirmed that Jane Mason was the girl who had been set up and given three years in jail. She was probably in line for some hefty compensation....

Twelve days to Christmas, and after a day shopping with Janet and Annie Beth waved them off and unpacked her purchases—gifts, decorations, food, stuff for the apartment that was now finished. Beth was feeling good.

Later that night, after spending ages looping a new string of one hundred Christmas lights around the tree, she decided the baubles could wait till tomorrow. Beth took a shower, then curled up on the sofa wearing an oversized T-shirt and a white fleece robe. Binkie curled against her leg, purring like a train. A log fire burned in the open grate, and she reached to stroke Binkie's back just as the doorbell rang—and rang again. She glanced at the mantel clock—eight-thirty.

Who could it be? she wondered. Probably church carol singers, she thought as she walked down the hall and opened the door. She pulled her robe tighter around her as a blast of cold air hit her and looked up with a welcoming smile—before her mouth fell open. Not carol singers. Dante... Her heart lurched in her breast.

Dante saw Beth in the doorway, covered in a long white robe and smiling, her green eyes sparkling bright and clear. The hall light behind her picked up the sheen of her red hair and formed a halo around her head. She looked like an angel, and the guilt and despair he felt almost overwhelmed him.

'What are you doing here?' Beth asked when she had recovered her breath.

'I need to see you. It's important, Beth. Please invite me in. This won't take long.'

She didn't want to invite him in, but it was freezing cold. 'All right.' She stood back and waved him inside, closing the door behind him, then turned to see him watching her.

In the light she was shocked by how gaunt he looked. His high cheekbones were sharper, his mouth a grim line, his eyes were deeper in their sockets, and she saw pain in the dark depths. But for her he was still the most beautiful man she had ever seen—and she had thought she was getting over him....

'Come and sit down.' She walked into the room where the fire burnt brightly. 'Let me take your coat.' He was wearing a heavy black overcoat, and after slipping it off he handed it to her. 'Would you like a hot drink?' His cream sweater hung loosely on his tall frame, the denim jeans were not such a close fit, and she wondered what had happened to him. He looked ill.

He straightened his shoulders. 'No, thank you.' Binkie leapt off the sofa and padded over to rub against Dante's leg. 'Hi, Binkie,' he said, and the glimmer of a smile twisted his stern mouth.

Traitorous cat, Beth thought. But in the week when Dante had stayed with her he had made friends with Binkie.

She folded his coat and laid it over the back of an armchair. Now she was over the shock of seeing him the disturbingly familiar scent of his aftershave, his hair, his skin was reaching her, reminding her of intimate moments she had fought hard to forget. Her breasts swelled. A quiver of sensation flowed through her body.

Beth tensed and walked past him to curl up on the sofa again. 'Why are you here?' she asked. She had never heard from him since he had walked out, and had been expecting divorce papers. 'To deliver the divorce papers personally?' she queried. She could think of no other reason.

'No. Timothy Bewick.'

Beth sat up straight at that, and looked Dante squarely in the eyes. 'This is my home, and I will not have that name mentioned in it,' she said firmly. 'I'd like you to leave.'

'I will. But first I want to apologise—though I know no apology can begin to excuse what I did to you. That is why I am here.' He looked uncomfortable and uncertain, and Beth was intrigued. 'If you will just hear me out, Beth, and then you will probably throw me out—which is no more than I deserve.'

'What are you apologising for?' Beth was totally mystified.

Dante straightened his shoulders, bracing himself to continue. 'Last night I found out that Baby Face Bewick, as he is now known, is one of the biggest suppliers of drugs in this country and is currently in jail with Hudson, awaiting trial. Hudson has admitted they once set up a girl—you—Jane Mason—to take the fall for them as teenagers.'

Beth shrugged. 'So? I've always known I'm innocent, and it doesn't matter now. Life has moved on.'

'It matters to me,' Dante said in a driven tone, his

glittering dark eyes raw with pain and regret. 'I can barely live with myself, knowing what I did to you. I put you in prison—stole eighteen months of your life. When I think what you must have suffered it tears me up inside. Your claustrophobia—and worse, I'm sure— is all down to me. I can't believe I was so arrogant, so blind as to fall for the lies.'

'Don't beat yourself up about it. Nobody's infalli- ble—not even you. As you said yourself, any decent lawyer would have got the same result.' Now he knew the truth Beth felt vindicated, and pleased in a way, but seeing the cool, arrogant Dante humbled was not as sat- isfying as she'd used to imagine it would be.

'How can you be so calm, Beth? I ruined your life,' he said vehemently.

'Because I have lived with the knowledge for years and there is no point in letting bitterness take over. That way you only destroy yourself.'

'*Dio*, Beth.' He moved and sat down beside her. 'When I think of how I behaved when I met you again… I threatened you, said hateful things. I am sorry from the bottom of my heart, though I know no apology can ever make up for the way I treated you. But I had to come and see you—tell you. Beth, you deserve that much and so much more. The irony of it is I was regret- ting going to that dinner—I was regretting not telling you I love you—and then I heard about Bewick.'

He grabbed her hands in his and squeezed them so hard she winced, but he seemed not to notice. Beth was reeling in shock from his 'I love you'. Her heart was racing, and suddenly she was aware of the warmth of his breath on her face as he studied her with incred- ible intensity.

'I understand why you said you hated me, Beth, and I don't blame you. I hate myself. I'm amazed you could even bear to speak to me.' The raw emotion in his tone was unmistakable. 'I'd give everything I own—my life—to give you back the time that was stolen from you.'

His grip tightened on her hands as he gazed at her with those incredible dark eyes, and all of a sudden it was as if the world was standing still…waiting. Beth was intensely aware of the slow pulse of her blood flowing though her veins, every breath she drew, and the silence lengthened. She had the oddest notion that Dante was afraid.

'I don't expect you to forgive me. And I know I have no right to ask this—not after what I have done. But I love you so much. If you could find it in your heart to give me another chance… I'm not asking you to love me, Beth, just to let me back in your life—let me try to make amends. Please.'

Beth's heart overflowed. Dante sounded so vulnerable, and the 'please' brought moisture to her eyes. He had said he loved her not once, but twice, and she wanted to believe him. So she did, and it felt as if all her Christmases had come at once.

'Yes,' she said, expecting to be swept into his arms

Instead Dante lifted her hand and kissed her palm almost reverently. 'Thank you, *cara*.' His mouth brushed hers gently. 'I know I don't deserve you, but I do love you, and I swear I will spend the rest of my life making it up to you,' Dante murmured, his tongue seeking entry to her mouth.

Warmed by his words, she opened to him. Her heartbeat quickened and she wrapped her arms around him and put her heart and soul into the kiss.

He eased her robe off her shoulders and she slipped her arms free to wrap them around his neck. She felt his hands skim down to her thighs, felt the slide of her T-shirt up to her hips and lifted herself to help him slip it over her head. She watched as he stood up and stripped off his clothes, and there, with the log fire burning and the fairy lights glittering, they lay on the long sofa kissing, caressing lovingly.

She trembled at the heated stroke of his hands over her shoulders, her breasts, down to her stomach and thighs, his long fingers running gently over her silken skin as if worshipping her body. Beth encouraged him with muted sighs, her delicate hands sliding down his great torso to settle on his taut buttocks.

They made love slowly, and Dante tasted and touched—as did Beth.

Finally their senses were at breaking point and their bodies joined in frantic need, pulsing, plunging, senses on fire as the climax hit and release shuddered through them both.

Beth lay breathless, her body quivering, and Dante tucked her up against him and stroked her hair.

'I can't believe this has happened. I came here tonight in the pit of despair, not really expecting you to let me in. You have such a generous heart. You are beautiful inside and out. I will spend the rest of my life and beyond loving you.'

Beth looked up into his incredible eyes. Love was plain to see in the gleaming depths. 'And I love you. I think I always did. I saw you in court and thought you were my knight in shining armour—my saviour. It has taken a long time, but now I *know* you are.'

He swept her up in his arms and carried her up to the bedroom they had last shared, where they made sweet love all over again.

Dante loved her in every way, Beth thought happily, and yawned widely. Cuddled against his big body, she slept.

Dante watched her sleeping and could not believe his luck. She had forgiven him and taken him back—this beautiful, brave, wonderful woman he would love till the day he died and beyond. He pressed a gentle kiss on her cheek. Then he realised he had made the same mistake again and forgotten protection. He considered waking Beth, but decided against it. She would find out soon enough.

He folded her closer in his arms and fell asleep.

Eleven months later a huge party was held at the Cannavaro estate, for all the family and friends of Dante and Beth, to celebrate their wedding—admittedly a little late—and also the christening of Francesco Cannavaro, their new son and heir. Much to his grandmother's delight—and Sophie's—they finally got to wear their wedding hats.

* * * * *

MILLS & BOON

Desire

Indulge in secrets and scandal, intense drama and plenty of sizzling hot action with powerful and passionate heroes who have it all: wealth, status, good looks… everything but the right woman.

LET'S TALK
Romance

For exclusive extracts, competitions
and special offers, find us online:

 facebook.com/millsandboon

 @MillsandBoon

 @MillsandBoonUK

Get in touch on 01413 063232

MILLS & BOON

THE HEART OF ROMANCE

A ROMANCE FOR EVERY READER

ODERN

Prepare to be swept off your feet by sophisticated, sexy and seductive heroes, in some of the world's most glamourous and romantic locations, where power and passion collide.

TORICAL

Escape with historical heroes from time gone by. Whether your passion is for wicked Regency Rakes, muscled Vikings or rugged Highlanders, awaken the romance of the past.

EDICAL

Set your pulse racing with dedicated, delectable doctors in the high-pressure world of medicine, where emotions run high and passion, comfort and love are the best medicine.

ue Love

Celebrate true love with tender stories of heartfelt romance, from the rush of falling in love to the joy a new baby can bring, and a focus on the emotional heart of a relationship.

Desire

Indulge in secrets and scandal, intense drama and plenty of sizzling hot action with powerful and passionate heroes who have it all: wealth, status, good looks…everything but the right woman.

EROES

Experience all the excitement of a gripping thriller, with an intense romance at its heart. Resourceful, true-to-life women and strong, fearless men face danger and desire - a killer combination!

To see which titles are coming soon, please visit

millsandboon.co.uk/nextmonth